BEFORE THE BELLE

The Chronicle of Hot Stuff - the First Eighth Air Force Heavy Bomber to Complete Twenty Five Combat Missions during WW II

CASSIUS MULLEN
WITH
BETTY BYRON

Copyright © 2015 Cassius Mullen, Betty Byron
All rights reserved
First Edition

PAGE PUBLISHING, INC.
New York, NY

First originally published by Page Publishing, Inc. 2015

This narrative is based on historical facts that occurred during World War II. The main characters, places, dates, and events are real. To give the narrative a human touch, the dialogue was added by the authors.

ISBN 978-1-68213-621-8 (pbk)
ISBN 978-1-68213-622-5 (digital)

Printed in the United States of America

Preface

This historical narrative provides the reader with compelling facts concerning the first heavy bomber in the United States Eighth Air Force during WW II to successfully complete twenty-five combat missions. In this effort, we attempt to combine a human quality with factual details during the unfolding of actual historical events. The magic number of twenty-five combat missions was a benchmark established by the Army Air Force for bomber crews in order to be rotated back to the United States where the plane and its crew would tour the country to promote the sale of war bonds. The crew would visit defense plants, participate in parades, and in general, lift the morale of the American people. Any time an American aircraft came under hostile fire over enemy territory it was considered a combat mission. This included attacks by enemy aircraft and/or hostile anti-aircraft fire.

For decades, this honor had been bestowed upon a Boeing B-17 named Memphis Belle, assigned to the 324th Bomb Squadron, 91st Bombardment Group. This aircraft and its crew were dramatized in the 1990 motion picture of the same name. Research has shown Memphis Belle as perhaps one of the first B-17s to achieve the magic number of twenty-five combat missions; however, it was not the first heavy bomber in the Eighth Air Force. Memphis Belle flew its twenty-fifth combat mission over Lorient, France on May 17, 1943. On June 8, 1943, Memphis Belle was then flown back to the United States where the B-17, and its crew received accolades.

This honor should have been conferred upon a Consolidated B-24 named Hot Stuff, assigned to the 330th Bomb Squadron, 93rd Bombardment Group. To substantiate our premise, we have documented each of Hot Stuff's combat missions from the first through the thirty-first. Upon examination of Hot Stuff's certified bombardier's log, the B-24 achieved its twenty-fifth combat mission on February 7, 1943, over Naples, Italy, while flying missions out of North Africa. At this time Memphis Belle had nine combat missions. After completing two more combat missions out of North Africa, Hot Stuff returned to England and participated in four more combat missions with the thirty-first mission being flown on March 31, 1943, over Rotterdam, Netherlands.

Our research shows in actuality Hot Stuff had been selected by the Eighth Air Force as the first heavy bomber and crew to be rotated back to the States after accomplishing twenty-five combat missions. In fact, when the selection was made, Hot Stuff and its crew had completed thirty-one missions. In addition, Hot Stuff was honored to be chosen by Lt. General Frank Andrews, commander of all American Forces in the European Theater of Operations, to fly him and his staff to Washington, DC. It was a secret mission to be flown out of Bovington, England, bound for the United States by way of Iceland. However, because of the size of Andrews's entourage, five of Hot Stuff's original crew were left behind in England.

Prior to General Andrews assuming command of all American Forces in Europe in January 1943, he had been commander of two other theaters: the Caribbean Defense Command and US Forces in the Middle East. After arriving in Washington, he was to receive his fourth star and assume command of all Allied Forces in the European Theater of Operations. However, it was not to be. Andrews and the high-value passengers on Hot Stuff, including four of the five members of the original crew were lost in a tragic accident in a frigid mountainous area of Iceland on May 3, 1943. It was at this time the accomplishments of Hot Stuff and its crew along with Andrews were doomed to be unheralded in the annals of World War II.

Our narrative has been inspired and enriched by the research and personal experiences of the following:

First, it was Jim Lux who brought the journey of Hot Stuff to our attention. It began when he first heard about Hot Stuff from his friend and golfing buddy, Bob (Jake) Jacobson. Jake was the bombardier and last living member of the crew. We first learned of Hot Stuff when Jim volunteered to speak at a monthly West Point Society luncheon in Austin, Texas. One of the authors is a West Point graduate who engages speakers for the monthly gatherings, and he contacted Jim for more information. Shortly before the luncheon, Jim presented material on the research he had gathered over a five-year period. It was at that time he offered to provide the necessary background material for us to write this historical narrative. To him, we are most grateful.

Second is Bill Gros, a former B-24 radio operator on Eager Beaver and friend of Hot Stuff's crew. It was his firsthand knowledge of the 93rd Bombardment Group and its exploits that have given us an in-depth and personal sense of what it was like to be a B-24 crewman during combat. He has over the years felt and still feels today that history should be corrected by giving Hot Stuff and its crew their true place in World War II history.

And last but not least is Fred Bothwell, a fellow West Point graduate whose father was an army air force officer during World War II. Fred provided background material on Grenier Army Airfield in New Hampshire where a B-24D was delivered to an untested ten-man crew who christened the aircraft Hot Stuff and brought it to life. We thank Fred for providing insightful suggestions and recommendations to our narrative.

It has been a privilege for us to chronicle this historical narrative to set the record straight and honor Hot Stuff, its heroic crew, and General Frank Andrews.

CHAPTER 1

May 3, 1943
Off the Coast of Iceland

The Consolidated B-24 Liberator had been in the air for over seven hours. It had taken off at 0922 from Royal Air Force Bovington Aerodrome in southeast England on a secret mission. Initially bound for Prestwick in northern Scotland, the plane was scheduled to be refueled there for continuing the flight to Gander, Newfoundland. While in flight, it was decided that landing at Prestwick would be an unnecessary waste of time.

As the aircraft didn't have sufficient fuel to fly to Gander, Newfoundland, it was to top off in Iceland before proceeding to the United States. The weather forecast for Iceland was grim. The meteorologist in northern Scotland was not happy with the report. It was obvious to him the weather was not fit for flying.

After another half hour, the pilot banked the bomber west and north along the coast of Iceland's Reykjanes Peninsula at about sixty feet above the sea. The Liberator's radio operator was unable to establish contact with several stations in Iceland. With the extremely low ceiling, it was now apparent to the pilot a landing at Reykjavik was questionable. The runways there were short and were surrounded by built-up areas. He didn't want to endanger the local populace. The RAF Kaldedarnes aerodrome was briefly spotted though the clouds, and the heavy bomber circled the field and dropped flares to signal their intention to land. The British didn't see the flares but heard the Liberator as it circled the field and sent up green flares signaling it was clear to land. However, the Liberator was back in the clouds in driving rain and snow and never saw the signal.

Meeks Field, a new American airfield in Keflavik, was less than thirty miles away, so the pilot turned west flying along the coast at about sixty feet above the water and within sight of land. They reached the west end of the Reykjanes Peninsula and turned north. Reykjanes bout du monde, a large granite rock protruding out of the water suddenly appeared directly in front of the B-24. The pilot and copilot strained at the controls to pull the nose of the Liberator up and turn away from the jagged rock formation. The bomber was close to stall speed as it nosed up and banked sharply to the right. The left wing just cleared the top of the jagged rock. They were in the clouds once again and quickly dropped in altitude to forty feet above the water. Flying below the cloud cover, the pilot circled the aircraft, attempting to get a visual sighting of Meeks. The airfield had become obscured in the heavy fog and driving rain and snow. After considering his options, the pilot decided to turn back, retrace their original flight path, and attempt a landing at Kaldedarnes. Visibility began to improve, and they were flying at an altitude of 850 feet, just below the clouds following the coastline. As the Liberator turned north just west of Grindavik, they abruptly ran into heavy cloud cover. Before the pilot had time to turn east toward the sea, the clouds parted to reveal an ominous dark mountain directly ahead.

"Jesus Christ! Pull up! Pull up!" the pilot shouted as he advanced the throttles. He and his copilot strained as they pulled back on the controls. The four 1,200 horsepower Pratt & Whitney engines screamed as the propellers bit into the heavy cloud-shrouded air. All contact with the aircraft was lost at 1530 hours.

Sixty Six Years Later

The stars and stripes billowed and snapped in the hot Texas winds at Lost Creek Country Club golf course in Austin. A clear blue sky promised yet another dry summer day in the Lone Star State.

Jim Lux and Robert (Jake) Jacobson stood on the eighteenth tee. Each man removed his brimmed golf cap, took the small terry-cloth towel from his golf bag, and wiped the sweat from his brow. Jake gazed up at the relentless sun. "This may be the hottest day of the summer so far. It's got to be over a hundred degrees out here."

Jim nodded. "I can't wait to get to the nineteenth hole for some liquid refreshment and a little lunch." Jim pulled a seven iron out of his bag, teed up the ball, and took a couple of practice swings. He was thinking, *It's a short par three over water, and I always swing harder than I should when I have to go over water.*

The only sound on the course was the whip of the club as it met the ball.

"Wow! Nice shot, Jim. It's Birdie time!"

After thirty years, James Lux had retired from IBM marketing and product development. Interested in World War II aviation history, he learned members of the Central Texas (CENTEX) Wing of the Confederate Air Force, now the Commemorative Air Force, were about to finish restoration of a Lockheed P-38 Lightning, his favorite World War II airplane. This persuaded him to join the organization.

Lillian Ayars, the CENTEX Wing leader had just completed negotiations with the City of San Marcos on a long-term lease on a dilapidated World War II hangar. Unfortunately, there was only two hundred dollars in the bank to begin the building's restoration and finish work on the P-38. The bank was a cigar box Lil carried with her to monthly Wing meetings. The Wing finance officer, Leon Thomas checked how much money was in the "bank" so he could give a report during the meetings. It was obvious the Wing was in financial distress.

Jim suggested organizing an air show to raise money. The Wing had lost money on previous air shows; however, Lil believed it still was a great idea. She thought inviting veterans of World War II as honored guests at a dinner dance would attract more interest. The combined air show and dinner dance would be called a Gathering of Memories.

Jim and Lil worked together organizing the air show and the dinner dance. The first Gathering of Memories (GOM) air show was so successful a real bank account was required to hold all the money. Revenue from that air show and six follow-on air shows paid for restoration of the hangar, the P-38 as well as a Bell P-39 Airacobra, and made the CENTEX Wing financially stable.

Highlights of the shows included vintage airplanes simulating the great battles of World War II. The intention was to honor those who built, flew, and maintained the aircraft during the war. Each year, the shows became more spectacular featuring pyrotechnics and military reenactors with WWII vintage materiel. A simulated air raid was added to the dinner dance held in the renovated hangar. It featured a siren warning of an impending air raid, search lights, the sound of bombers approaching, and fighter planes taxiing to meet the incoming bombers.

The military reenactors fired weapons into the air as explosions lit up the sky. The orchestra dressed in vintage army uniforms continued playing "big band" music during the air raid. The sound of the bombers eventually faded away, and the siren sounded the all clear and the dinner dance continued. Jacobson would later attend several GOM air shows as an honored guest.

BEFORE THE BELLE

Jim often talked about airplanes and the air shows with Jake while playing golf. Jacobson was a quiet, humble man and seldom talked about World War II. He did mention with obvious pride that he had been a bombardier during World War II where he had completed thirty-one combat missions in a B-24 Liberator over Europe. He had also completed an additional fourteen combat missions over Japan in B-29s. His last mission was on August 14, 1945, the day the Japanese surrendered. The United States didn't recognize the surrender until August 15.

During their golf games, the two often discussed various aircraft flown by the Allies and Axis powers around the world and how they impacted the outcome of the conflict. However, this day was to be prophetic for both Jim and Jake.

After missing the putt, not unusual for Jim, and Jake making par, the two headed for the clubhouse to cool off and have lunch. As they sat in the dining room, the two talked about their golf game and ordered salads and beer. At ninety-one years, Jake shot an admirable eighty-nine as did Jim.

After their lunches arrived, Jim forked a mouthful of salad before he opened the discussion on his take regarding a movie he had recently seen on TV. It was about the crew of the Boeing B-17 Flying Fortress bomber named Memphis Belle.

"Jake, your completing thirty-one missions was quite an accomplishment considering the heavy losses the Eighth Air Force sustained. I'll bet that crew of the Memphis Belle lost a lot of buddies before their last mission."

"I was there, and I can tell you I personally lost a lot of friends," Jake lamented, his eyes staring out the window onto the fairway.

Jim broke the protracted silence. "The crew of the Memphis Belle was among the fortunate to survive. I understand the losses the Eighth Air Force took exceeded those the marines sustained in all the island hopping in the Pacific by several thousand. Sixty B-17s were lost on one Schweinfurt raid alone—that's over six hundred men, the size of an infantry battalion."

Jake looked Jim in the eye as he gestured with his fork. "I'll give you the Memphis Belle was probably the first B-17 to successfully complete twenty-five bombing missions. And the men who manned her received deserved accolades when they returned home to parades and war bond drives. However, they were *not* close to being one of the first crews in the Eighth Air Force to actually complete twenty-five bombing missions."

Stunned, Jim swallowed his cold brew and set his glass down. "Really? I never knew this. I've been studying about World War II aviation for years. You've got to be kidding."

"No, I'm not. Ever heard of the 93rd Bombardment Group or a B-24 named Hot Stuff?"

Jim thought for a moment. "I've heard of the 93rd Bomb Group but not Hot Stuff."

"I never told you details about what I did when I was with the 93rd?" Jake revealed.

"You're right, you never did. All I recall you telling me was you were a bombardier in Europe and completed thirty-one missions."

"I was a member of a ten-man B-24 crew that came together at Barksdale Army Airfield, Louisiana in May 1942. We served together on Hot Stuff from August 1942 to May 1943. We had completed twenty-five missions when the crew of Memphis Belle had only nine under its belt. In fact, we completed thirty-one missions more than a month and a half before Memphis Belle reached twenty-five."

"If this is so, why hasn't Hot Stuff been recognized historically?"

"Because when the aircraft was returning to the United States for its well-earned recognition, it crashed into a mountain on Iceland. Tragically, all but one onboard were killed."

"Obviously, you were the lone survivor?" Jim asked.

BEFORE THE BELLE

"Hell, no," Jake exclaimed. "I was bumped along with four other crewmembers at the last minute. Seems a general by the name of Andrews and members of his staff wanted a ride back to Washington. Instead of waiting for another aircraft, the General, being a pilot himself, decided to take the copilot's seat on Hot Stuff. His staff had to ride on cushions on sheets of plywood placed over the bomb bay doors for hours—not very comfortable. It was our tail gunner Eisel that survived. Understand he was pinned in the badly damaged tail section for over a day before he was rescued."

From this moment on, Jim became transfixed with the history of Hot Stuff and wanted to set the record straight. "Tell me about your experiences while a bombardier on that B-24."

Jake took a sip of his beer. "Jim, it's a long story. Are you up to it?"

"I sure as hell am. I want to know everything you can remember. This is a part of history that needs to be told. I'm going to do all I can to make it happen."

Jake rubbed his chin and stared out at the fairway. "Let's see. I guess our crew first came together in May of '42…"

Shortly after Jake's revelation, Jim began searching the Internet for information on the 93rd Bombardment Group. The following five years, Jim researched every scrap of information he could find related to the B-24D named Hot Stuff. He traveled extensively around the United States and finally to the crash site near the fishing village of Grindavik, Iceland. From his findings, he constructed the triumphant history of Hot Stuff and her crew from its inception in the late spring of 1942 until the tragic end in May 1943. Jim established a fund with the help of the 93rd Bombardment Group Association for a monument to be erected at the crash site in memory of the aircraft and those who lost their lives there.

During this time, Jim rarely saw Jacobson who had given up golf due to age and failing health. When it came time for Jim to get back to Jake with what he had uncovered, his dear friend suddenly passed away at the age of ninety-three, the last surviving crewmember of Hot Stuff.

Now Lux travels widely through the United States speaking to various audiences on Hot Stuff, including the United States Military Academy at West Point, New York; the United States Air Force Academy in Colorado Springs, Colorado; the Smithsonian National Air and Space Museum in Washington, DC; and the National Museum of the Air Force in Dayton, Ohio.

Jim begins his presentation with the words "let me take you back to the beginning…"

CHAPTER 2

The Crew

During June and July of 1942, the 93rd Bombardment Group of the United States Army Air Force, commanded by Colonel Edward (Ted) Timberlake, operated out of Page Field near Ft. Myers, Florida. There, the newly assembled B-24 crews formed into four bomber squadrons and practiced high-level bombing missions over the Gulf of Mexico. This encompassed developing the skills necessary for the pilots, navigators, and bombardiers to work together as a team to be able to accurately locate and place ordnance on designated targets. The crews' gunners honed their proficiency by firing their .50 caliber machineguns at towed aerial targets.

Due to a shortage of aircraft, the thirty-six crews of the 93rd BG had to share six older model B-24Cs and a few later model B-24Ds. Needless to say, these "training" aircraft would suffer a high degree of wear and tear resulting from extensive usage. The turnaround rate impacted the time allotted for proper ground maintenance.

In addition to training for high-level bombing, the 93rd BG was given the mission to conduct antisubmarine patrols over the Gulf of Mexico. This was necessitated by a change in tactics by the Allies to use bombers to counter the German U-boat submarine wolf packs that had inflicted a high toll on Allied shipping in the Atlantic.

With America's entry into the war, the U-boats audaciously began attacking convoys in the Gulf of Mexico as well. USAAF and Navy staffs deemed the long range B-24s to be aptly suited for this mission. As a result the 93rd's bomber crews received additional training in submarine identification and low-level bombing techniques. Such was the case with pilot Lt. Robert (Shine) Shannon, a Washington, Iowa, native, and his crew.

After one year at Washington Junior College, Shine attended Iowa State University. As far back as he could remember, he aspired to be a pilot. In 1940, he enrolled in a civilian pilot training course at the Washington, Iowa, airport where he earned a civilian pilot's license. With hope of becoming a military pilot of one of the heavy bombers, he enlisted in the United States Army where he received air training in California. In early 1942, he completed training and received his wings along with a commission as a lieutenant in the Army Air Corps. After a few months as a fighter pilot, his request to become a bomber pilot was approved. In mid-1942, because of his being an accomplished pilot with leadership ability, he was selected to be lead pilot of a B-24 Liberator in the 93rd Bombardment Group. Now stationed at Page Field near Ft. Myers, his squadron, the 330th was assigned the mission of convoy escort off the Gulf Coast of Florida.

It was late July 1942 as Shannon piloted the older B-24C on an oval course over the convoy several thousand feet below. His thoughts were on his days as a P-40 fighter pilot. He remembered how anxious he was at being selected to be transitioned to a bomber pilot and what kind of crew would be assigned to his aircraft. It was May 1942 at Barksdale Field near Shreveport, Louisiana, where his crew was first assembled. After a few months training with his crew, Shine thought how fortunate he was to have his fears set aside when he found his crewmen to be highly competent and compatible.

Now as an aircraft commander and pilot of a heavy bomber, he was responsible for the Liberator, the largest bomber in the American inventory at that time. The B-24 was powered by four Pratt & Whitney 1,200 horsepower engines. Cruising speed was 225 miles per hour and maximum speed was 303 miles per hour at twenty-five thousand feet. Its flying ceiling was thirty-two thousand feet. The maximum payload of the Liberator was eight thousand pounds. With a five thousand pound payload, its range was 2,300 miles. Without a payload, the maximum range was 3,500 miles. The wingspan was 110 feet, and the length of the fuselage was sixty-six feet. The height of the B-24 was eighteen feet at the vertical fin. The wing area was 1,048 square feet. The aircraft was armed with ten .50 caliber machine guns: three in the nose, two in the upper turret, two in the tail turret, two at the waist, and one in the belly.

B-17 pilots often joked about the B-24 being a "flying boxcar." Shannon knew better and smiled; the B-24's newer design outclassed the B-17 in range, payload, and speed.

As command pilot, he had learned as much as possible about each of the crewmember's functions: knowing how to navigate by the stars, how to drop bombs, fill the fuel tanks, send messages by Morse code, hit a target with the onboard .50 caliber machine guns, and how to operate the turrets.

Shannon had learned the B-24 was definitely a man's aircraft. It demanded super strength, always requiring considerable muscle. Heavy on the controls, the aircraft exhausted both pilot and copilot during missions. Although the high-winged aircraft was relatively agile at medium altitudes, it was harder to control at high altitudes when heavily loaded.

He looked to his right at his copilot, Lt. John Lentz. Lentz was a tall 190-pound muscular man who hailed from Chicago. His size and strength were assets, which proved valuable in helping control the Liberator at low altitudes and speeds, particularly when taking off and landing. Besides assisting Shannon in flying the aircraft, Lentz was the Liberator's assistant plane commander and engineering and fire control officer.

His bombardier, Lt. Robert (Jake) Jacobson, whose home town was Cedars, Mississippi, sat below and forward of the flight deck facing out the Plexiglas nose, his bombsight mounted in front of him. On either side of his seat levers and panels of dials and switches fed data to and from the secret Norden bombsight. The bombsight allowed the B-24's deadly payload to be released at the right time required to hit the target. It used an analog computer having a system of gyros, motors, gears, mirrors, levels, and a telescope. As the bomber approached the target area, the bombardier would provide the computer with air speed, wind speed and direction, altitude, and angle of drift. The bombsight would then calculate the trajectory of the bombs. The bombardier would assume control of the aircraft from the pilot while over the target area for proper release of bombs.

Jacobson graduated from bombardier school near the top of his class. During practice bombing runs, the crew was amazed at Jake's ability to put the "pickle in the barrel" from any altitude.

Lt. James (Jimmie) Gott, the Liberator's navigator, a native of Berea, Kentucky, was situated at a small desk below and forward of the flight deck behind the bombardier. Gott took a lot of teasing from his "Yankee" crewmembers because of his thick southern drawl. Nevertheless, Jimmie took it all in good stride and didn't let it interfere with his ability to always accurately position their bomber. This was because he had learned his skills well in navigator school: coding, mathematics, maps and charts, aircraft and naval recognition, aerophysics, altitude equipment operation, and gunner. His additional duties were assistant bombardier, oxygen equipment officer, and first-aid specialist.

The aircraft's radio operator, Technical Sergeant Kenneth (Ken) Jeffers sat behind the copilot at a small tabletop three feet below the flight deck facing the right side of the aircraft. On his left was the radio with the Morse code key on the right. Jeffers claimed to hail from Oriskany, New York. No crewmember had ever heard of it and joked that there was no such place. Jeffers's principal job was to service, maintain, and operate all radio communications equipment. This included tuning units, frequency meters, the radio compass, emergency flare supplies, the telegraph key, the radio transmitter, and navigational aids. His secondary duties consisted of being able to man the various gunner positions, act as assistant aircraft engineer, and be able to administer first aid.

The flight engineer and top turret gunner, Staff Sergeant Grant Rondeau, sat behind the pilot three feet below the flight deck. Rondeau, a native of Racine, Wisconsin, proved his worth time and again as he kept the B-24's four engines running smoothly on every mission. His aerial gunnery matched his flight engineer proficiency. As flight engineer, he was the leader of the crew's enlisted men and was proficient in aircraft maintenance. He monitored engine and generator performance while in flight. His additional duties were assistant radio operator and first-aid specialist. Prior to takeoff, he was responsible for inspecting the aircraft internally and externally.

The two waist gunners, Staff Sergeants Paul McQueen and George Farley hailed from New York. They were located at rectangular openings in the fuselage to the rear of the bomb bay. Both proved proficient in their abilities to handle the .50 caliber Browning machineguns. McQueen was also an assistant radio operator. From the large open side windows they, more than other crewmembers, were able to more easily identify aerial and ground targets.

The tail turret gunner, Staff Sergeant George Eisel, a Columbus, Ohio, native, sat within a turret between the aircraft's twin tails. He proved to be the best .50 caliber gunner on the aircraft and possibly in the squadron. Because of his "position of the past," he was Shannon's primary eyes for many miles to the rear of the plane.

Staff Sergeant Joe Craighead, from Bedford, Virginia, had the unenviable job of tunnel or belly gunner. He knelt in a position located between and below the waist gunners with a view to the rear underside of the fuselage. He never complained and was anxious to get into action.

All gunners were trained to assume the position of another should the need occur. In addition to operating the .50 machine guns, they were adept at the care and maintenance of the weapons.

Flying at only several thousand feet over the Gulf of Mexico, high-altitude flying gear and use of oxygen masks weren't necessary. The crew of Shannon's B-24 was comfortable in shirt sleeves and leather bomber jackets. The cooler air at that altitude was refreshing after the heavy humidity and heat of the Ft. Myers area.

"Boring. Boring. Boring. Back and forth. Back and forth over that goddamned convoy. Weeks of this shit is driving me nuts," waist gunner, McQueen groused before he took the last two pieces of his Black Jack chewing gum and stuffed them in his mouth. He opened his thermos and sighed. "No! Can ya' goddamn believe it? I'm out of Joe now." He nudged his fellow waist gunner, "George, you got any coffee left?"

Farley put down his binoculars, passed McQueen his thermos, and shouted over the rushing air and relentless drone of the Liberator's four engines. "After seven hours, that crap they call coffee will be hardly lukewarm, but help yourself." Farley picked up his binoculars and resumed his search of the waters around the convoy below.

Through the heavy humid summer haze that hung over the blue waters of the gulf, Farley peered out the open waist gunner's window at the American convoy below. It was made up of over five dozen tankers and freighters escorted by eight destroyers. The ships carried the vital fuel, munitions, aircraft, and ground combat vehicles essential for Great Britain's survival against the German onslaught. The ships in the fleet originated in various ports on the gulf and had assembled off the Florida panhandle. The convoy now approached Key West. There it made an inviting target for German U-boats lurking in the warm blue-green waters. In the preceding months, a number of Allied ships had been sunk in the gulf by the Unterseebotten of the German Kriegsmarine.

Shannon's Liberator had been flying at only a couple of thousand feet in order to facilitate the crew's observation of the seas below. "Hey, Lieutenant, can we listen to some music?" McQueen asked over the intercom. He was thinking about his date with the cute little USO brunette later after chow. Besides being a real corker, she was a ducky shincracker. He really looked forward to dancing with the great-looking dame.

Shannon nodded his head. "Okay." He then spoke to the radio operator, "Jeffers, see if you can pick up some nice music, but not too loud."

The radio operator smiled and responded, "Can do, Lieutenant." He immediately began searching for a station that played all of the latest hits. Soon the soft strands of "I'll Be Seeing You" wafted throughout the aircraft's intercom.

Moments later, the B-24's intercom crackled with the excited voice of the right waist gunner. "Lieutenant Shannon, Lieutenant Shannon, I see something."

During the time Shannon and his crew had been flying together, they had become a cohesive smooth-running team. Besides having practiced high-level bombing of stationary targets and self-protection with the onboard machineguns, they had become adept at low-level attack approaches to engage submarines. Although two aircraft in the 93rd BG had been credited with sinking enemy submersibles, Shannon's crew had never even so much as spotted a German U-boat. Now maybe they had a chance to apply the antisubmarine warfare skills they had honed.

"Okay, McQueen, where is it?"

"It's at about five o'clock," the staff sergeant replied.

Five pairs of binoculars began panning the Gulf of Mexico off the right side of the Liberator. It was the copilot, Lentz, who confirmed what McQueen had reported. "Shine, McQueen's right. There's a wake trailing something. It's not constant, but it could be a periscope going up and down." He looked at Shine and smiled. "Maybe it's a lone wolf looking to pounce on our convoy."

"If so, it looks like we're finally going to get into this war, Boys," Shannon spoke into the intercom as he banked the B-24 to the right. "Now, just like we had practiced, we'll approach the target from stern to bow. If our luck holds out, maybe we'll be able to take the bastard by surprise."

Flying well off to the stern of the suspected submarine's location, Shannon again banked the aircraft in a 180-degree arc, decreased its speed, and descended to just over two hundred feet above the surface. Shine, an excellent former P-40 fighter pilot who was transitioned to fly B-24s was relatively short and small in stature. Lentz was tall and lean, and Shannon welcomed his added strength in helping maintain stability of the lumbering B-24 while flying low at slow speeds.

As the pair of pilots aligned the Liberator with the axis of the elusive submerged target, Jacobson raised his binoculars and peered out through the aircraft's glass nose. In the distance, he could just make out a faint shadow beneath the surface. He laid down the binoculars and began focusing his bomb sight on the target. "Shine, I've got the son of a bitch."

"It's all yours," Shine responded as Jacobson took control of the Liberator with the bombsight from his position in the nose.

The B-24 carried a load of eight three-hundred-pound depth charges in the bomb bay. The plane had carried the antisubmarine munitions for weeks unused. Now was their chance to make good work of them.

The B-24 was well known for its instability at low speeds. It was all the more so when the hot, less dense air of the gulf provided less lift. Jacobson struggled to keep the aircraft steady with the bomb sight controls but managed to align the shuttering B-24 toward the elusive target in the distance.

"Let's make it good," Shannon shouted into the intercom. "We'll only have this one chance before that Nazi dives out of sight."

The tension grew as the B-24 continued to shake and bounce violently in the low cross winds. All eyes focused on the wake made by the perceived U-boat's periscope. The intercom crackled with voices of disappointment as the wake disappeared beneath the waves. The sound of the approaching bomber had been detected by the U-boat and the underwater craft's shadow began to fade as it dove for safety.

Sweat poured into Jacobson's eyes as he strained to hold the Liberator's flight path along the line of attack. He estimated where the bow of the submarine would be for the correct release point. Using his bomb site and a bit of "Kentucky windage," he estimated the point to release the depth charges so that the deadly ordnance would sink and detonate at a point of convergence with the U-boat.

"Eisel, get this on film," Shannon spoke over the intercom. The tail gunner quickly reached for the small eight-millimeter motion picture camera and wound the spring-driven mechanism.

Jacobson's left leather glove-covered hand reached for the switch that opened the bomb bay doors. Next, from the electric selector panel, he selected a pair of depth charges that he intended to release over the target. It was only a matter of seconds now. In spite of the jostling of the B-24, Jake was able to look through the bombsight and adjust the focus with his right hand. His left hand fondled the bomb release switch. Was his calculation correct for release? A film of perspiration formed over his upper lip as he released the two depth charges. "Bombs away! Take that, you bastard." This was the first time Shannon's crew was to deliver deadly ordnance in anger.

From his position in the aircraft's tail, Eisel aimed the lens at the two disturbances in the water to the rear of the B-24 where the depth charges had splashed down. He activated the camera. Suddenly two huge geysers erupted from the sea. Eisel had captured the action for posterity.

Shannon spoke over the intercom as he took control of the aircraft from his bombardier. "Let's see if we got the son of a bitch."

Shine and Lentz pulled up on the ailerons and increased engine speed. The Liberator began to slowly gain altitude and bank right. After flying a small racetrack-shaped oval, Shannon flew the B-24 over the target area. All eyes strained to see if an oil slick emerged from the depths. Nothing. Even after two more passes, there was no sign that they had destroyed their target.

"Sorry, Shine," Jacobson lamented over the intercom. "I was so sure I put the depth charges right down that bastard's throat."

"Don't worry, Jake, there will be other days for us," Shannon said. "Time to get back on station. Everyone back to lookout." He then spoke to Gott, the navigator. "Jimmie, give the latitude and longitude of our sighting to Jeffers and have him radio it to HQ."

"What should I say?" Jeffers asked.

Shannon sighed, "Send 'suspected sub sighted and possibly sunk' along with the location and time-date group." A voice in the back of his mind whispered, *We all believe we saw something, but maybe it's because our imaginations are overactive.*

Jeffers was known as a poor speller. Gott wrote out the entire message and handed it to the radio operator for transmission to HQ.

While the message was being sent, the Liberator climbed to station altitude and continued flying convoy escort for two more hours.

At the end of their patrol, Shannon's B-24 was relieved by another aircraft of the 330th squadron. Shine's crewmembers waved to the relieving bomber as he pointed the Liberator toward Page Field.

BEFORE THE BELLE

The field was located three miles south of Ft. Myers, Florida. At the beginning of World War II, it was appropriated by the United States Army Air Force for antisubmarine patrol and B-24 training.

After Shannon's plane landed and the crew debarked, the aircraft was serviced and prepared for another mission with a different crew. This early in the war, there was a shortage of aircraft and this necessitated several crews using the same B-24 to fly training and antisubmarine patrol missions. This also added to the wear and tear on the aircraft.

It was following the post mission debriefing when Shannon and his crew learned the 93rd BG was to depart the Ft. Myers area and fly to Grenier Field, New Hampshire. There they were to receive factory-fresh B-24Ds delivered by ferry crews. However, due to the lack of ample airlift capability, a number of the flight crews had to travel by train. By luck of the draw, Shine and his crew were selected to fly north.

The next few days were spent in preparation for the move. This included inventorying and packing equipment for shipment along with numerous briefings for the various crewmembers and ground support elements. All air combat crews were issued new flight gear and the group's ground support elements received new equipment that would be compatible with the new B-24Ds.

McQueen tried on his new issue sheep-lined leather jacket, pants, boots, and gloves, which were to be worn when flying at high altitudes. Sweat poured down his brow. "Can you believe it? It's hotter than hell here in Florida, and the army wants to make sure I'm warm enough. Typical, situation normal, all screwed up."

Farley shook his head. "Paul, stop your goddamned bellyaching. You're going to really appreciate this gear when we're flying at twenty-five thousand feet over Europe. I've heard at that altitude, we have to keep the gloves on at all times because the bare skin would freeze to metal, particularly the .50s." Farley looked at the electrical cord connectors dangling from the leather exposure suit. He read a label attached to one of the cords. "Seems like if we really get cold, we can plug ourselves into the electrical outlets in the plane for additional warmth."

Eisel tried on a flak helmet. He noticed it was a modified version of that issued to ground troops. It had metal attachments that covered the ears. "Hope I can get this piss bucket over my headset." He stuck his fingers between his ears and the helmet flaps.

Before the 93rd was to depart for Grenier, they learned some three-star general by the name of Frank M. Andrews was going to inspect the troops in ranks. Lieutenant General Andrews, as commander of all-American forces in the Caribbean Theater, was responsible for establishing an effective multiservice air patrol, which proved to be effective in reducing the German U-boat threat against Allied shipping in the Gulf of Mexico and the Caribbean. The 93rd had contributed to that effort.

The enlisted men were ordered to wear fresh khaki uniforms with white leggings. In preparation for the inspection, the men had to bleach their olive drab issue leggings.

On the day of the inspection, the squadrons stood in four lines. The soldiers had been instructed to respond to any questions asked by the inspecting general in the shortest manner possible—hopefully with a "Yes, sir," "No, sir," "No excuse, sir."

The hot humid Florida air quickly prompted profuse sweating among the airmen standing in the late morning sun. The fresh khaki uniforms were soon soaked with perspiration.

As General Andrews, accompanied by Col. Timberlake, inspected the 328th squadron, he came upon a soldier who was not wearing leggings. "Sergeant, where are your leggings?" he asked.

The airmen responded, "Some son of a bitch stole them, sir!"

Col. Timberlake cringed at the airman's answer. General Andrews momentarily stood stunned at the soldier's response then laughed, "He was a son of a bitch, wasn't he?" After his comment, he continued his inspection. Those in ranks who overheard the comments laughed out loud.

At the conclusion of the inspection, General Andrews addressed the men and congratulated them on their minimizing the German submarine threat in the Gulf of Mexico and the Caribbean. He emphasized that since they began conducting antisubmarine patrols, convoy losses dropped dramatically, thereby keeping the survival life line to Great Britain open.

Following dismissal, the crews went to their respective officer and enlisted mess halls.

As Hot Stuff's enlisted men walked toward the mess hall, McQueen quipped, "Who was that fat-head in the 328th who mouthed off to the general?"

Jeffers replied, "He's Bill Gros, a friend of mine I met at radio school."

"He sure has balls to talk to a general like that and get away with it," the waist gunner commented. "With my luck, I'd be busted and swabbing latrines for a month."

They all laughed and fell in line to the door of the mess hall.

Following chow, Shannon, Lentz, Jacobson, and Gott walked over to the group headquarters for briefings on their pending flight north. There was no air-conditioning in the briefing room. They sat on hard metal folding chairs, sweating profusely through their khaki uniforms. The pilots, navigators, and bombardiers in attendance were fortunate enough to be selected to fly to New Hampshire with their crews; others were to make their way north by train.

This being the day before they were to takeoff, the bomber group's operations officer stood on a low stage and uncovered a large map of the east coast of the United States. Colored strings were tacked to the map, and the staff officer used a long wooden pointer to designate the flight paths that the group was to follow up the coast. The planes were to fly in serials by squadron. It was planned that the air echelon of the group would depart on August 5 for Grenier Field and was to arrive late on the same day. A weather specialist presented the forecast for the entire journey. Following a brief question and answer period, the officers were dismissed. At last they were on their first leg of a journey that would carry them to war.

The 93rd BG ground echelon was to travel by troop train to New York. The newly issued ground support equipment already loaded on flat cars was to accompany them. At the New York harbor port of embarkation, the troops were to board the Queen Elizabeth along with their equipment and were to sail for England on August 31.

Along with the 93rd BG's ground echelon, the ship was to carry nearly eighteen thousand troops and war materiel. Included in this number were ground echelons of other air groups as well as American and Canadian army elements. This was to be the Queen Elizabeth's second voyage as a troop ship. Since it was the largest and fastest vessel afloat at the time, it was determined that U-boats would have little chance to intercept it and would quickly and safely sail a zigzag four and a half days across the Atlantic. One factor that aided in the ship's successful voyages was it was equipped with the latest in radar. The 93rd BG's ground echelon personnel and equipment were to arrive at their new airfield in England and set up operations well before the group's aircraft were to land.

CHAPTER 3

Hot Stuff Is Born

After arriving at the year-old Grenier Army Airfield, Shannon learned the entire airbase had been constructed within six months. Construction had begun during the heavy snows of a New England winter in January 1941 and was completed by June of that year. By the summer of 1941, the airbase, with its three concrete runways and ninety-four buildings, had become fully operational.

"Our new B-24s are inbound!" a bomber group staff officer shouted through the door to the Grenier officer's mess. It was the morning of August 8. Shine finished his breakfast coffee and looked at his watch. "Earlier than expected. Must be they had a good tail wind." He stood, grabbed his "crushed" service cap, and tapped his copilot on the shoulder. "Come on, John, let's get onto the flightline and get a firsthand look at our new Liberator."

The two pilots walked out to the edge of the concrete runway at Grenier Field. They joined their crew and other pilots and crews of the 330th Bomber Squadron who were waiting for their new Liberators to be delivered. The planes were being flown by ferry pilots out of San Diego, California, where the Consolidated aircraft plant was located.

The sun shone bright, and there were no clouds in the New Hampshire sky. However, the wind was blustery as was normal for August. Lentz gazed out over the runway. "Looks to be some strong cross winds across the strip."

Shannon nodded. "It may make for a shitty landing for the guys bringing in the planes."

Lentz chuckled. "Hope these new Liberators come with training manuals. Heard there are a bunch of improvements over the older models we've been flying."

"Don't know. Hope these ferry pilots can give us some overview on what the differences are."

Another quarter of an hour passed before the heavy sound of approaching aircraft drew all eyes to the sky. As the line of B-24Ds approached the airfield, the deep drone of the engines caused the ground to shake. Thirty-six of the new Liberators flew over the field before they formed into a line for landing.

"Wow, John, what a beautiful sight," said Shine as he put his hand on his copilot's shoulder.

They watched as one by one, the new aircraft touched down and rolled past the onlookers. Shannon pulled a piece of paper from his trouser pocket, which contained the tail number of his assigned Liberator. It was the nineteenth B-24D to touch down that had the correct identification: 41-23728. He and the crew watched as the aircraft was directed by ground crewmen to park on the concrete apron.

As the engines shut down, the two pilots and crew walked over to their new bomber. The ferry pilot exited the aircraft and stood by the glass nose of the new B-24D. He removed his khaki cap, took a handkerchief from his pocket, and wiped the perspiration off his forehead. The bare head revealed a balding pate with a close-cut red fringe. Shannon was surprised to see the slim, medium-height ferry pilot was a naval officer. He and Lentz shook hands with Lieutenant

Junior Grade Harry Byron. "I had no idea the navy was involved in ferrying planes across the country," Shannon said.

"As you can imagine," Byron responded, "we're short-handed everywhere. Every so often, they take me off flight instructor duty to ferry planes where they're needed. Seems like they're building them faster than we can get pilots to ferry them. As of now, I'm qualified to fly just about everything in the inventory." They found out Harry was from Louisville, Kentucky, and had a commercial pilot's license. He had volunteered to serve right after Pearl Harbor.

A female voice spoke up. "Harry, you're not the only one who's qualified to fly most all of our military aircraft." The voice was a soft Southern accent accompanied by a beautiful smile through freshly applied lipstick. The woman wore a khaki jumpsuit and leather flying jacket emblazoned with a *WAFS* patch.

"Oh, excuse my gross oversight," Byron said as he introduced his copilot, Florene Watson. The crew stared and grew silent as she removed her leather flying cap and let her hair fall onto her shoulders. They found out the five-foot-six woman was from Odessa, Texas, and like Byron, had been a commercial pilot. She was one of the few women aviators who had a ground school instructor rating. Having volunteered her services to the war effort, Watson was a member of the newly formed Women Auxiliary Ferry Squadron (WAFS) that would later be integrated into the Women Airforce Service Pilots (WASP).

McQueen whispered to Farley, "If she was my pilot, I'd fly with her to hell and back and enjoy it."

"Thanks for bringing us the plane," Shannon said. "We're itching to get to England and into the fight."

"I can understand how you feel," Byron said. "What model B-24 have you been flying?"

"We've trained on the C model."

"Well then, come on. Let's take a look at your new D model."

McQueen extended his arm and touched the olive-drab and gray fuselage. The side of the aircraft wore the national insignia authorized shortly after Pearl Harbor: a blue roundel enclosing a white star. "A brand-new Liberator totally without a scratch on her. Son of a bitch, this is Hot Stuff."

The navigator, Gott, overheard McQueen's remarks and smiled. "Hot Stuff! That's what we ought to call her. What do ya say, Shine?"

Shannon looked at the smiling faces of the crew. "Why not?" He turned to face the waist gunner. "McQueen, since it's your idea, make it happen." He gazed at the crew for a moment. "Watch your language around the lady."

McQueen casually saluted, "Yes, sir!"

While the lecherous enlisted crewmembers followed Watson into the aircraft, Byron led the officers into the forward area of the bomber. The first thing that captured Lentz's senses was the scent of the interior. The B-24 they had flown in Florida reeked of oil, fuel, and sweat. "Smells like a new car in here. Reminds me of my dad's '39 Buick just after he bought it new."

Byron asked Shannon and Lentz to sit in the pilot's seats while Jacobson and Gott went to their respective bombardier and navigator positions. As on the C model, the pilot's seats were fully adjustable. For the next half hour in the spacious cockpit, Byron discussed subtle changes in the B-24D's controls.

"How does she handle?" Shannon asked.

"Like a dream," Byron said, "but like the C model, it can be difficult when flying just above stall speed or in rough weather. As you know from your experience on the older model, it's heavy on the controls and on long missions can really tire the best of pilots."

During the orientation of the pilots, Byron handed Shannon and Lentz new issues of the *Pilot Training Manual for the Liberator, B-24*. The two pilots looked at each other. "Looks like we have some cramming to do before we fly this beast," Lentz remarked.

Another half hour passed and Byron said, "You should be in good shape to fly this baby." He scratched his day-old red beard and said, "I'd like to clean up and get some shuteye." The naval officer yawned. He was worn out after the long flight from a stopover at Glen View Naval Air Station northwest of Chicago. "We're flying out of here at 2000 hours." Before exiting the aircraft, he grabbed his canvas flight bag.

At that moment, Florene had finished taking the remainder of the crew through the new B-24 and left them speechless with admiration. She walked up to the other three pilots carrying a leather overnight bag. "I agree with Harry. Where can we clean up and catch a nap?"

Shine motioned toward a group of cream-colored two-story wood barracks set back from the large base headquarters building some two hundred yards off the taxi apron. "This way to the visiting officer quarters."

The four pilots approached a line of lap-board structures along a paved road. An entrance door, windows, and a fire escape defined the ends of each VOQ. The first two VOQs were specifically designated for female officers. Military policemen stood guard at the entrances.

"It's not the Ritz, but it's a decent place to bunk down," Shannon said. "There should be some empty rooms inside. Just pick one."

"I've slept in worse," Florene said. "Right now the way I feel, I'd take a pup tent." She opened the door of the two-story structure and glanced down the narrow hallway that ran the length of the year-old building. She noticed the wood walls that made up small rooms were painted the same color as the exterior and a common bath was located at one end of the structure. When she entered the building, the sound of her flying boots echoed off the bare concrete floor with every step. She opened one room door at a time and found the third room on the right unoccupied. After dropping her bag on the floor, she heard Lentz shout, "Florene, see you at the O Club for drinks at 1700. You can't miss it, just ask the MP."

Watson leaned out the doorway of her room. "See you then." She turned and closed the door. The small room was sparsely furnished with a steel folding bed, a small desk, a chair, and a dresser with a wall-mounted mirror. Since there was no insulation, the air in the room was heavy with the heat of August. A clean towel and bar of soap had been laid out by an orderly. Florene opened the window and "crashed" onto the bed, asleep within minutes.

As they approached a VOQ several buildings down, Shannon asked Byron if it was okay for Florene and him to have a drink so soon before flying. "Not a problem," the naval officer said. "We're going to catch a hop out of here. Someone else'll do the flying." He yawned again. "See you at the O Club."

Nothing disturbed the sleep of the two ferry pilots, not even the aircraft landing and taking off only a couple of football field lengths away. It was the gentle knocking on the room doors by enlisted orderlies that roused them six hours later in time to prepare for dinner.

The one-story building that housed the officers' club was constructed similarly to the barracks. The sparse cream-colored interior was devoid of any partitions. On the concrete floor sat small tables with a makeshift bar along one wall. A radio played hit tunes softly in the background as the four pilots walked up to the plywood sheet that served as the bar. A sergeant stood behind the barrier. "Sirs, ma'am, what'll you have?"

Florene ordered a long-neck beer, Harry a scotch on the rocks, and Shine and John each had a beer on tap. Shannon paid the tab, and the four of them sat at a table about the size of a small kitchen dinette. The room was already half filled with other officers. The harsh lighting from the bulbs hanging from the exposed ceiling cast deep shadows in the corners of the area.

Lentz took a sip of his beer. "Where are you two heading now?"

Watson leaned back in the hard steel folding chair and took a swig from her bottle. "I'm getting a hop as far as Love Field on the C-47 that's taking Harry back to San Diego. I have to fly another B-24 fresh from the Ft. Worth plant to God knows where. Then back to flight instruction at Love Field."

"I've got flight training in San Diego myself," Byron said. "After that, more ferrying, but won't know for sure until I get back."

"Florene, how did you qualify to become a member of the WAFS at such a young age?" Lentz asked. "I'd guess you couldn't be much over twenty."

Florene nodded and pointed the beer bottle at Lentz. "You're right, John. I've been flying since my father bought a plane for us kids back when I was a preteen. He saw war brewing and wanted his older children to be able to contribute once America entered the war. By the time Pearl Harbor happened, I had more than enough flying hours to qualify for military wings."

Lentz looked around the room. "I see that there are a couple of other WAFS here besides you. How many are there?"

"Only twenty-eight of us now, but the number is growing," Watson said. "Even I was surprised at how many women from all walks of life had been piloting planes for years. And it seems a lot of them volunteered for whatever flying jobs were available to help the war effort. More and more women are qualifying to fly all types of military aircraft. Bet we could have over a thousand women in the WAFS before long."

Harry sipped his scotch and asked Lentz if he had played football before the war. "You're a pretty big fellow."

John shook his head. "Hell no. Never played sports much. I worked in a rail yard loading cargo onto freight cars to pay for college. All our family members are big and my lifting all that heavy stuff sort of built me up."

Shannon gestured toward Lentz with his beer glass. "John sure makes it a lot easier handling that big bird in rough weather."

Harry nodded. "Yeah, I can believe it. It took Florene and me all we had with our feet pressed on the pedals and pulling on the ailerons to land here in that crosswind."

Just then, Gott and Jacobson walked up to the table, drinks in hand. "Mind if we join you?" Gott asked.

"Pull up a chair," Shannon said. He gestured toward Byron. "You know, Harry here is from Louisville."

Gott smiled and spoke in a deep drawl. "I'm from Berea. Went to college at Eastern Kentucky."

"I've never heard of your home town," Byron said. "Where is it?"

"It's a small town way southeast of Louisville," Gott said. "Since you're from the big city and all, I figure that's why you never heard of it."

After dinner, the officers shook hands with the ferry pilots on the aircraft parking apron. "Have a safe flight," Shine said.

Byron put his hand on Shannon's shoulder. "You take care out there in the real war. Good luck to you and your crew." They both exchanged casual salutes. Byron and Watson turned their backs on Shannon and his fellow officers and walked to the waiting C-47. Shannon recognized the aircraft as the military version of the civilian Douglas DC-3 airliner nicknamed "Skytrain."

At 2000 hours, Shannon and the officers in his crew watched as the aircraft carrying Byron and Watson along with other ferry pilots lifted off the runway and headed west into the clear star-studded night.

CHAPTER 4

Going "Over There"

Shannon's crew along with the entire 93rd BG spent the next two weeks flying the new Liberators over the forested areas of New Hampshire and Vermont. While in the air, they were able to work out small problems with the new aircraft, practice flying in formation for high-level bombing, and instrument flying. The whole group was itching to fly to England and get into the real war.

During the training period, the radio operators were issued radio-compass equipment that had to be installed on the new B-24Ds before any new Liberators could attempt long-range flights over water or fly through poor visibility. The group's radiomen were assembled in an empty hangar where they spent a half day receiving instruction on how to install the equipment.

Following the class, Jeffers carried the wiring kit to his assigned B-24. He teamed up with another radioman and spent the next day connecting the radio-compass gear to the installed radio equipment, the antenna, and the pilot's instrumentation. After installation, he was concerned whether it would function properly once they were airborne.

Hot Stuff's gunners picked up new Browning .50 caliber machine guns still packed in Cosmoline, a gooey heavy-grade petroleum used as a protective coating for firearms and metal. They spent the next day cleaning the sixty-one-pound weapons and test firing them at a range on a remote area of the air base. The gunners knew the .50s were inaccurate beyond one thousand yards and were trained not to fire until they estimated their targets were within range. Otherwise, they would be wasting precious ammunition. With the help of the ground crew, they installed the machine guns on mounts at their designated positions on the B-24. They were ready to be test fired in the air.

McQueen's hand caressed his .50's receiver. "Think I'll name her Annie Oakley. That dame was a real dead-eye dick." As he wrapped the freshly cleaned weapon with a canvas cover, he murmured, "That's what I want to be."

"Get bent," Farley announced. "I'm naming mine Doc Holliday."

"Why would you do that?"

"Annie only shot at targets. Doc killed bad guys, just like I want to do."

One morning after only a few days of training with their new B-24 at Grenier, Shannon's crew walked out to the flight line. On each side of the forward section of the aircraft, they saw the name "Hot Stuff" emblazoned along with a nude woman riding a bomb. The painting had appeared overnight and was a surprise to most of the crew.

Shannon, his arms akimbo, asked, "McQueen, who did the great artwork?"

"Well," the waist gunner said with a sly grin, "I found an artist in the squadron maintenance section, and for a couple of cartons of smokes, he said he'd do the job. The guys and me took up a collection and what you see is the result. Hope you like it, sir."

"I think it's great!" Lentz said as he slapped the command pilot on the back. "What do you think, Shine?"

Shannon stared at the painting on the side of the aircraft for several seconds. He looked around at the rest of the crew and saw nothing by smiling faces. "It's just the ticket! We'll call her Hot Stuff from now on out!"

"Besides that, we talked the artist into painting names on our .50s," McQueen announced.

Flying in formation for high-level bombing was tricky and called for absolute precision and discipline on the part of the pilots. After taking off, each nine plane squadron rendezvoused at a pre-determined location at high altitude and then formed up into its planned part of the group formation. This required the squadron to form into flights of three aircraft each, one forward and two aft at slightly different altitudes. The other three squadrons similarly formed up and joined the aircraft already airborne to create a layered high-level bombing formation of thirty-six Liberators. The main purposes of the formation were to allow for interlocking fire from onboard machineguns for maximum protection against enemy fighters and to mass the effect of bombs on designated targets. This massed formation was nerve wracking due to the possibility that a slight miscalculation could cause a mid-air collision. This was all the more tenuous with trying to maintain the formation while changing direction.

While flying in formation, the air crews practiced intra-squadron and group radio communications with the purpose of increasing radio proficiency and discipline including use of call signs, codes, and changing frequency channels. The intra-unit communications did not exceed thirty miles and was designed for tactical operations; long-range transmissions using Morse code were used for communicating with distant stations. The radio compass and ranging were to be used for direction finding and location of distant points that transmitted homing beacons.

After a week and a half of training, McQueen was noticeably more agitated than usual. "I'm gonna be an old fart by the time we actually get into the war. When the hell do we get Hot Stuff into the real fight with the bastards?"

Lentz looked down at the five-foot-eight waist gunner. "I promise you when we get into the real war, the Nazis will give us all the fight we're looking for and then some. And I heard the scuttlebutt from headquarters the shitty weather is finally clearing up for us to fly to Gander, Newfoundland. It looks like we'll be taking off the day after tomorrow. So tell the rest of the crew to start packing their gear. We're one step closer to the war in Europe."

On August 25, the crews received briefings for their nine-hundred-mile flight to Gander. The aircraft were to fly in squadron formation just as was rehearsed and were to depart early the next morning.

The next day, after a four-hour flight, the 93rd Bombardment Group successfully landed all thirty-six aircraft at a weather-beaten godforsaken Royal Air Force aerodrome. After Hot Stuff parked on the cracked concrete apron, the crew was glad to be back on solid footing.

McQueen jumped down onto the Newfoundland soil and gazed around at his surroundings. He pulled out a pack of Chesterfields from his leather flying jacket and lit up. "Well, looks like we've set down somewhere between a shit hole and hell." Although it was late August, the weather was chilly, and clouds of steam mixed with cigarette smoke left his mouth as he spoke.

At Gander, the group had to again impatiently wait for favorable weather before crossing the North Atlantic to Scotland some 1,800 miles to the east. The restless crews of the 93rd had to sit out a long dreary week for the weather to break before their thirty-six olive drab aircraft would be winging their way east. The dreary Newfoundland sky complemented the barren and rocky terrain, and there wasn't anything for the crews to do but wait.

A makeshift movie theater in one of the hangars provided the bored crews with some entertainment. During each movie showing, the light beam from the projector illuminated clouds of cigarette smoke floating throughout the interior. Only a few movies were on hand to be shown.

During the fourth showing of John Wayne in the movie *Stagecoach*, Eisel groused as he inhaled his tobacco smoke. "If I see this goddamned movie one more time, I'll know all the lines by heart."

Between bites of a Baby Ruth candy bar, McQueen shouted, "Let's see *Sergeant York* again."

His remark was greeted by loud guffaws and boos from the audience.

"I'd rather see *Yankee Doodle Dandy* again," Jeffers yelled.

The lights came on, and a master sergeant from morale and recreation walked in front of the audience and motioned for silence. Under his arm, he carried three canned movie reels. After the crews settled down, he proudly announced they had just traded *Yankee Doodle Dandy* for another movie.

The crowd erupted into cheers and laughter. "What is it?" a voice shouted from the throng.

The morale NCO proudly announced the new movie was *Wuthering Heights* staring Lawrence Olivier.

"What the hell is *Wuthering Heights*?" came a loud voice from the rear of the audience.

"It's a movie based on one of the classic English novels of all time," the morale NCO proudly announced.

Over four hundred voices roared disapproval. Several of the men threw their caps and swore at the hapless NCO.

A few days later, as Hot Stuff's sergeants walked back to their Quonset hut, McQueen remarked, "You know, that *Wuthering Heights* place kind of grows on you after a couple of days." He looked around at the dismal surroundings. "That English moor looks a lot like this hole. Hope when we get to England there'll be more to see and do."

Finally on September 4, it was determined the weather had become satisfactory for the long flight to Scotland. The group began taking off from the RAF aerodrome at midnight. The ridges surrounding Gander posed a danger to the aircraft in daylight, and taking off in darkness made it all the more perilous. The pilots were directed to make a forty-five-degree turn one minute after becoming airborne. By virtue of their design, the Liberators were slow to gain altitude, and each pair of pilots struggled to lift their aircraft off the runway and avoid crashing into the surrounding hills. The squadrons took off in thirty-minute intervals and flew in the rehearsed nine-plane formation. At the proper time, all machine gunners practiced firing their weapons as the possibility of encounters with enemy aircraft would become highly probable the closer they drew to Great Britain.

This was to be the first time bombers were to fly across the North Atlantic in formation. They were to maintain radio silence to keep broadcasts from being intercepted by surfaced U-boats, German submarine supply vessels and German radio stations on the French coast. These points were known to send false radio direction signals to confuse pilots. Prior to this, several B-17s had broken radio silence and a number were pinpointed by German radio direction finders. Several aircraft were lured by the German radio stations and were lost. Furthermore, the B-17s had flown singly and, as a result, were highly vulnerable to attack by enemy fighters, whereas the B-24s of the 93rd Group flying in squadron formation of nine aircraft maximized protection from attack.

BEFORE THE BELLE

The last plane in the group to take off from Gander had to cope with a weather front that had moved in. Fortunately, the pilots were able to successfully negotiate the hills surrounding Gander and get aloft.

The group was to land at Prestwick, in northern Scotland, some 1,800 miles distant before continuing on to their final destination at Alconbury, England. The plan was for the entire group to land in daylight. The thirty-six aircraft flew across the North Atlantic at an altitude of ten thousand feet. At that altitude, the crews found their Liberators half iced up, and vision was impaired. They were glad to be wearing the heavy sheep-lined leather flying suits; however, because of the lower altitude, they didn't require oxygen masks.

The long flight to Scotland was going to be boring for those not engaged in flying and navigating Hot Stuff. Anticipating this, McQueen, Eisel, Craighead, and Farley set up a poker game on a small sheet of plywood. Jeffers couldn't participate because he had to stay on the radio during the entire flight. Rondeau likewise kept busy monitoring the engines. Before they left Gander, they loaded up on all sorts of sweets and cartons of cigarettes they bought at the small post exchange. With his gloved hand, McQueen pulled out a candy bar from his bag of goodies, unwrapped it with his teeth, and took a bite. He turned to his fellow waist gunner. "Hey, George, my goddamned Hershey bar is frozen solid. Almost broke a tooth on an almond."

Sitting cross-legged on the floor, Farley looked at the king-high flush in his gloved hand. "Stop stuffing your face, will you, Paul? What have you got?"

McQueen broke off a sizable piece of the chocolate bar and put it in his mouth to defrost. Through the mouthful, he mumbled and showed his hand, "I've got three deuces."

Farley just threw his cards down.

Eisel, the best poker player of the crew slapped his cards onto the plywood. "Goddamn, beats me."

Craighead shook his head. "You son of a bitch, Paul, you're the luckiest poker player I've ever known. You won the goddamned pot again." He threw his cards at McQueen. "Your deal!"

McQueen's glove-covered hand swept his winnings into a small pile in front of him. "This pot of cash is going to be my ticket to a hot night in Paris."

The tail gunner guffawed, "Fat chance, Paul. You'll be lucky to see Paris from twenty thousand feet."

"We'll get a night in Paris, you'll see. Why did I join the AAF anyway? It wasn't to look at your ugly mugs day in and day out."

"Okay, we get the point," Eisel said as he handed the remaining deck of cards to McQueen, "and your Hershey bar is running down your chin."

The two leading squadrons, including the 330th, flew the entire 1,800 miles in formation and successfully landed at Prestwick some ten and a half hours after takeoff from Gander. Colonel Timberlake and key members of his staff were spread among those two squadrons. After landing, Timberlake and his operations officer stood in Prestwick aerodrome's control tower and began to take a tally of the arriving Liberators. It was there they found the follow-on two squadrons had run into bad weather. The crews had to fly on instruments and several of the aircraft had encountered problems with their equipment. Timberlake was worried that they would overfly Scotland and land in enemy territory or crash into the sea.

He breathed a sigh of relief when it was reported to him that seventeen of the follow-on squadrons' eighteen Liberators landed at either Prestwick or alternate landing fields. Concerned, Timberlake stood in the control tower for an hour more in hopes that the missing aircraft would be reported as having landed safely. But it was not to be. It had been in contact with the other planes in the squadron and refused to alter course; the aircraft never showed. It was lost without a trace and became the first casualty of the 93rd BG. It was believed the aircraft was lured over the sea by a fake radio direction signal and crashed.

After notification of the loss of one of their own, the group chaplain held services within an unoccupied hangar on September 6. Shannon and his crew felt they were fortunate to have made the perilous transoceanic trip without incident. Some of Hot Stuff's crew had known those who were lost. It made them feel the seriousness of the pending danger that awaited them—the fickleness of the weather and a determined enemy.

After a few days of rest and aircraft maintenance, the 93rd lifted off for Alconbury. The former RAF airbase located near the southeastern tip of England awaited them. The main runway of the 150-acre aerodrome was an asphalt-covered concrete strip that had been lengthened to six thousand feet to accommodate the American B-24s. The base also had two ancillary runways of four thousand four hundred feet each. All runways were 150 feet wide. The base had two hangars and numerous outbuildings for officers' quarters and operations.

There the 93rd's air elements were united with the ground support crews that had traveled the dangerous sea route on the Queen Elizabeth. The group had officially become a part of the fledgling United States Eighth Air Force.

Initially, while at Alconbury, the enlisted aircrews found themselves housed in tents. "What a shit hole," McQueen groused as he dropped his duffle bag on the wet dirt floor of the tent. "Just when you think things couldn't get worse, the AAF proved me wrong again. Those bastards must be out to kill me." He jammed a Lucky Strike between his lips and lit up as he looked around the expanse of the tent. "We even have to sleep on the damned ground." McQueen turned to look at the tail gunner. "George, when did we sign up for the goddamned infantry?"

"Get used to it for now, Paul," Rondeau countered. "Scuttlebutt has it we're going to get something called Nissen huts, sort of like Quonset huts."

"I heard we're going to get paid in British Pound Sterling, whatever that is," Craighead added. "Understand it's going to be confusing making change."

McQueen looked through the mist at the drab gray buildings across the airstrip where the officers were housed. The antiquated RAF quarters appeared to be somewhat dryer than the tents. "Bet they have beds and sheets."

During the next three weeks at Alconbury, the group practiced high-level live bombing raids in a designated area known as the Wash, an isolated bay off England's east coast. Shannon, Lentz, Gott, and Jacobson sharpened their respective skills to accurately drop the deadly ordnance on floating targets while flying singly and in close formation while at the same time Jeffers honed his radio proficiency. When *Hot Stuff* flew alone, the gunners practiced firing with live ammunition at sea gulls.

Typical of the autumn weather in southeastern England, fog, frigid winds, and mud plagued operations. As the days turned into weeks, the pilots and crews became more agitated as they had not anticipated the bleak weather conditions would keep them grounded and inactive. To most of the crews, the waiting was more unsettling than having to face the perils of combat.

There were no laundry facilities at Alconbury for the crews. Women in surrounding villages volunteered to do their part for the war effort by taking in laundry. The 93rd BG headquarters in conjunction with the British Government provided names and addresses of British citizens who wanted to do their part. As a form of payment, crewmembers were issued British ration coupons for services rendered rather than Pound Sterling. The coupons were more valuable to the local citizens than currency as they were to be used for hard-to-get-items such as fresh meats. In addition to the coupons, the crewmen were issued necessities such as bars of soap to present to their hosts in payment for services rendered.

The flap of Hot Stuff's enlisted tent opened. Staff sergeant Bill Gros, the radio operator on Eager Beaver in the 328th Squadron and friend of Jeffers since attending radio operator school poked his head in. "Ken, I'm going into town. Want to come with me?"

"Oh, Bill. Good to see you. Come on in." Jeffers was sitting on a damp blanket writing a letter. "Gimme a minute to finish up."

"Sure, I'll wait," Gros said. "I know a pub where we can some decent hot grub, and on the way, there we can get our clothes cleaned at the same time."

Jeffers signed the letter and stuffed it in an envelope. He left the flap unsealed for inspection by military censors. By necessity, all mail back to the home front was censored in case it dropped into enemy hands.

As Hot Stuff's radio operator stood, Gros asked, "How about taking your laundry along? Don't forget to bring some coupons for payment. I'd like you to meet this nice Brit couple. The Walkers are middle-aged and have three children, all in the service."

"Sounds good to me," Jeffers said as he grabbed his uniform blouse and cap along with a bag full of his dirty laundry. "Let's go!"

Gros smiled and gestured toward the tent flap. "Let's move it. The truck leaves for town in a few minutes."

After a slow half-hour ride, the truck carrying the American airmen stopped at the edge of the nearby village of Huntington. The town was typical of those located throughout the English countryside. The village itself consisted of quaint narrow and winding streets, fine old houses, stately ancient churches, a town hall in a market square and two inns.

Ten minutes after jumping off the two and a half–ton truck, Gros and Jeffers stood in front of the weather-worn dark green door to a small two-story vine-covered brick cottage at the end of a quiet Huntington street. Gros knocked and a short, thin balding man greeted them. He smiled and gestured for the two airmen to enter. Once inside, Gros introduced Jeffers to Mr. and Mrs. Walker.

The middle-aged housewife took the laundry bags from the two Yanks. "Would you boys care for a cup of tea and scones?"

"Why yes, Mrs. Walker, that's very kind of you," Gros said. He and Jeffers, like other airmen leaving the base, were cautioned to be on their best behavior and particularly to watch their language when talking to the locals.

During the conversation around the small kitchen table, Jeffers learned more about the couple's three adult children. Their son was serving as a tank driver in the British Eighth Army in North Africa. One daughter was doing ground duty in the British Women's Auxiliary Air Force where she packed parachutes and the other was a driver and mechanic in the army.

Mr. Walker, a World War I veteran, was the stationmaster at the Huntington village railway station a few miles distant. Gros joked about Mr. Walker being henpecked with so many women in the family and spent long days at his job just to get some peace and quiet.

After tea, the two radiomen presented the couple with several valuable ration coupons for fresh meats and coffee. Mrs. Walker looked at the coupons. "Oh, my dears, this is too much."

"Keep it all," Gros said as he wrapped his hands around the woman's outstretched palm. "We'll be back in a day or so to pick up the laundry."

"Oh, almost forgot." Jeffers reached into his pocket and pulled out two bars of Ivory soap and two packs of Lucky Strike cigarettes and handed them to Mr. Walker.

A few minutes later, the two American airmen found themselves in a crowded pub aptly named "The Empty Tankard." They made their way through the heavy cigarette smoke to the bar. There they smoked, drank warm ale, and indulged in conversation with the locals. Often they were teased by the locals that the Yanks were *overpaid, oversexed, and over* here! All was taken in good humor.

After a hot meal of fish and chips at the pub, the one staple that was not rationed in war-torn England, Jeffers looked at his watch. "Bill, we don't want to miss our ride back to the base."

Both men downed the last of their ale, tossed several shillings onto the bar, and made their way to the door.

CHAPTER 5

Merry Olde England

The next morning, a cigarette drooped from Lentz's lips as he threw another dart at the circular cork board. "Shine, I think we've found ourselves in the land of never-ending miserable weather. I just want us to do what we're getting paid to do."

The officers' mess was crowded with bored, grumbling pilots, bombardiers, navigators, and staff officers. The heavy haze of cigarette smoke permeated the confines of the old RAF officers' club.

Shannon poured himself yet another cup of coffee and lit a Lucky Strike. "I agree. This waiting around is driving me nuts." He looked at the officers gathered at the bar. "I can see why there's so much goddamned liquor consumed around here."

"I know another real reason," Lentz said. "I talked to some of the B-17 guys, and to hear their stories, I can understand why the heavy drinking. Bet we'll be like that after a couple of missions ourselves." He stared out the small grimy window into the cloud-shrouded sky. "That is if we ever fly again."

"We can only watch so many movies and throw so many darts," Shine said as he reached for his leather jacket and crushed service cap. "Come on, let's get some fresh air." He tossed his cigarette into a butt can as he walked out into the dreary fog-shrouded Alconbury afternoon followed by his copilot.

Lentz lamented, "As our English friends refer to as utter madness, I'm going completely 'buggers' myself. I can't wait to get some combat missions under my belt."

Hunched over with hands in pockets the two pilots silently meandered out onto the soggy field where the Liberators were parked. Without a word, the pair approached Hot Stuff. Before Lentz climbed aboard, he crushed his cigarette into the muddy grass. Because of gasoline fumes, the crews were ordered not to smoke on their aircraft.

English rain dripped from the visors of their caps as they took their seats in the flight deck.

Lentz inhaled. "Hot Stuff still smells new. Think we're ready for our first mission, Shine?"

"I guess we won't know for sure until we're tested."

"I overheard McQueen and Eisel grumbling," Lentz said. "It seems Eisel was getting fed up with McQueen."

"What's the problem?" Shannon asked.

Lentz chucked. "McQueen filched a movie from back at Gander. I overheard him talking to Eisel."

"What did he say?"

"He asked McQueen why did he bring that goddamned movie from Gander?"

"What movie?" Shine asked.

"It was *Wuthering Heights*."

"Why in the hell would McQueen steal a movie we've all seen over and over again?"

"It seems he could identify with the hero, Heathcliff. According to McQueen, the guy was real smart, but nobody loved him except that rich dame. Then she ups and runs off with another guy, but in the end, she tells this Heathcliff guy she never forgot him. Then she dies."

"Well," Shine said, "that sums up the story, doesn't it?"

Lentz chuckled. "McQueen said that it reminded him of his own love life."

Shine laughed out loud. "Is this what we've come to? We're all starting to feel sorry for a man who never was, in a book none of us has ever read?"

Lentz removed his service cap and beat the beads of water off of it. "Jesus, we've got to get out of here before we all go crazy. Why couldn't we have gotten passes to London?"

Shine leaned back in his seat. "Probably because the bigwigs want us to be available on short notice to conduct missions. This shitty weather has kept us from putting pressure on the Nazis, giving them time to strengthen their defenses."

Just then a voice shouted from the rear of the aircraft. "I've been looking all over for you guys," Jacobson shouted. "The weather is breaking, and we'll be getting orders for our first mission. The entire group will marry up with B-17s tomorrow."

It was three weeks into October 1942 before Hot Stuff would finally takeoff on her first combat mission.

During this three-week period, British workmen erected Nissen huts to house the enlisted crews of the 93rd. The buildings were similar to the Quonset huts they had lived in while in Gander—round prefabricated metal walls, wood floors, electricity, and coal-fired stoves along with metal cots and wall lockers.

Hot Stuff's sergeants spent three luxurious days in their new quarters before they received notice of their first mission.

"Wouldn't you know it?" McQueen grumbled as he lay back on his cot, hands behind his head. "No sooner do we get settled in something I would consider halfway civilized and some guy in HQ decides we're too comfortable."

"Aw, poor Paul," Farley said as he looked around at his crewmates. "Like he's the only one who has to put up with the crap from the higher-ups."

"Personally, I'm more than ready to get on with this war," Eisel said. "Shut up and let's get some sleep. They'll be rousting us out of here before dawn."

CHAPTER 6

October 21, 1942
First Combat
Mission: Lorient

On the morning of October 21, the bright ceiling lights of the room housing Hot Stuff's officers exploded into Lentz's dream. "Goddamn, I feel like I just closed my eyes." He glanced at his watch. It was 0400.

"Time to rise and shine. Gentlemen," the squadron duty NCO shouted through the open door. "It's your time to make history."

All four of Hot Stuff's officers groaned at they rolled out of their bunks. "It took me hours to get to sleep, and now this bastard rudely interrupted my beauty nap," Jacobson bemoaned.

"Has the crew been awakened?" Shine inquired of the duty NCO.

The enlisted man replied, "Yes, sir. They're being rousted out right now."

The shrill of a whistle and the glaring overhead lights of the Nissen hut welcomed Hot Stuff's enlisted personnel to the predawn of their first combat mission.

After shaving and donning their uniforms, the crew shuffled over to the mess hall. There they loaded their mess trays with pancakes, scrambled eggs, sausage, toast, and coffee—one of the few meals considered edible by the crew.

Eisel watched McQueen stuff his face with his hearty breakfast. "Coffee and toast is all I can handle this morning," the tail gunner said.

"What's the matter, George, ain't ya hungry?" the waist gunner asked.

"You're not the one bouncing around back there in the tail section, Paul. I know lot of tail gunners can only take hour after hour of that before they get queasy and throw up. A lot of them quit. I, by the grace of God, have been able to handle it. Just got to watch what goes into my belly. Besides, Shannon flies like the fighter pilot that he is, quick, jerky moves. I can always tell when Lentz has the controls, nice and smooth flying."

"Great! Can I have your pancakes?" McQueen said as he reached over Eisel's tray and forked up pancakes and a pair of sausages.

"When you're ready to puke, I hope George can move fast enough to get out of range," Eisel commented as he lit up a Lucky Strike.

An indignant McQueen grabbed a cigarette from the tail gunner's half empty pack and retorted, "That only happened once. And that was because the milk I drank was bad that morning."

"Funny, it didn't bother me, until your puke made me sick," Farley said. "I sure as hell didn't like cleaning up your mess after that mission over the gulf. Let's see if we can keep Hot Stuff clean and smelling good."

After breakfast, the crews went to the morning mission briefings. The large Nissen hut was crammed with pilots, navigators, and bombardiers sitting in the front rows with radiomen, flight engineers, and gunners in the remaining rows of metal folding chairs. It was at this briefing the crews first learned of the target. Mission information was purposely withheld until the last minute for security reasons.

Major Keith Compton, the group's operations officer, stepped in front of a large canvas-covered map next to an expansive screen. The low buzz of excited conversations filled the confines of the building. The officer called the assembled crews to attention. Immediately, all conversations ceased as the attendees stood at attention and faced the front of the building.

Col. Timberlake, the group commander strode hurriedly from the rear of the building to the stage and stepped onto the low platform. "At ease! Take your seats!"

He waited while the more than three hundred men sat, all eyes glued on their commander. "Finally, today we're going to make our mark on history," Timberlake said as he whipped the canvas from the gigantic map board. It revealed most of the British Isles and the western coast of France. Red tape denoted the flight path from Alconbury to Lorient, France, with two way points where the bomber formations would change direction. His long wooden pointer indicated where they would drop their lethal ordnance. "Our target for today's mission is the German sub pens at Lorient." A slight buzz emanated from the crews. "Hold it down!" the commander ordered. After a few seconds, he continued with his briefing.

"As you already know from your experience, conducting anti-submarine patrols over the Gulf of Mexico, the German U-boats have been forming into "wolf packs" and have been extracting a heavy toll on Allied shipping. Today, our mission is to neutralize one of the havens for the U-boats."

At that moment, the lights dimmed, and an aerial photograph of the target area was projected on the screen next to the map board. Timberlake pointed to the large rectangular shapes at the water's edge. "These are the pens we're going after. British commandos had unsuccessfully raided the area, suffering high losses. Now it's our turn." Another photograph was projected. It showed the massive concrete structure with entranceways for the enemy submarines. "The Lorient steel-reinforced concrete roofs are twelve to fourteen feet thick. Five hundred-pound bombs have no effect on these pens. Therefore we'll be attacking them with 1,600-pound armor-piercing naval bombs. We believe they're the only bombs capable of shattering the pens."

After a few pep talk remarks, Timberlake turned the briefing over to Major Compton. The staff officer then told the crews what type of flak to expect, the fighters they may encounter, the weather, detailed target information, the takeoff time, and estimated time of arrival at the target. At the end of the briefing, the crewmen were called to attention and Timberlake left the building.

After being dismissed from the briefing, the crewmen returned to their barracks to prepare personal gear for the mission. When they were to fly at high altitudes, the men wore the electrically heated flight suits they were issued at Page Field. In addition, each crewmember wore an oxygen mask. Every crewmember had his own personal flight bag, which included extra wool socks and underwear. Just before boarding the aircraft, the parts of the flight suits—jacket, pants, boots, and gloves were hooked together. Once airborne, the crewmen could plug their cumbersome high-altitude gear into an outlet on the plane for additional heat. At the high altitude, bare skin could not touch any metal components without the skin sticking, much like a child touching his tongue to a metal flag pole in the middle of winter. The gloves had to be worn until the aircraft reached lower altitudes.

Each crew took along K rations or C rations that froze at high altitudes and could only be eaten when the plane dropped low enough to thaw them out. D rations, thick, rectangular chocolate bricks were the only edible food at higher altitudes; they were so hard they could only be gnawed on and not broken off like a Hershey bar. Every crewmember had a bag with a parachute and harness, flak helmet, life preserver, goggles, throat microphone, oxygen mask, and a .45 semiautomatic pistol. Should the plane be shot down, the bag included an escape kit which contained a silk scarf imprinted with a map of the surrounding area and money corresponding to the country they were flying over. Before their first mission, each crewman had a photo taken of himself in a civilian shirt, tie, and coat so members of the French resistance could forge documents for the downed airmen.

After the crewmen's gear was assembled, the next stop was the armorer's tent. There they drew their weapons, namely the plane's machine guns. They were advised not to wear their side arms on missions. The reason being should they have to bail out over enemy territory, it was deemed safer not to be wielding a weapon when surrounded by armed enemy combatants. Out of the 1,800 men in the group, each crewman in the air had four men on the ground to support him. Ground echelon personnel maintained and repaired the B-24s, uploaded bombs, and .50 caliber machinegun ammunition. The gunners cleaned and maintained aircraft weaponry. Thirty-six–round machinegun ammunition drums were placed on both sides of the gunners' positions in the aircraft to facilitate rapid loading while engaging enemy aircraft.

As Shannon and his crew rode a two-and-a-half-ton truck toward Hot Stuff, ground crewmen were loading the last of four huge 1,600-pound bombs. The truck slid to a stop on the muddy ground alongside the B-24 and the crew dismounted. The four gunners who rode in the rear portion of the Liberator waddled in their high-altitude suits carrying their parachutes and flight bags. Since the forward portion of Hot Stuff's fuselage was warmer than the rear at high altitudes, the pilots, navigator, bombardier, radio operator, and flight engineer were sufficiently comfortable in their leather flight jackets and high altitude trousers and boots.

All the crewmembers wore their life preservers and parachute harnesses. Once inside the aircraft, they attached their chutes to the harnesses.

"I hope they find a better way of feeding ammo into our guns," Eisel remarked. "Those damned thirty-six-round drums don't hold enough. I sure as hell don't want to be caught reloading while one of those Nazi bastards is shooting at me."

Overhearing this, Shannon interjected his thoughts. "Eisel, never doubt good old American know-how. Someone'll figure out a way to belt feed our guns just like on our fighters."

Once aboard, Shine and Lentz adjusted their seats as they used their parachutes as cushions. A moment later, they received the signal to start engines. One by one, the four Pratt & Whitney 1,200 HP engines roared to life. Each belched black smoke that reeked with the odor of undetonated high-octane gasoline until it warmed up.

Before takeoff, Eisel sat on the floor of the aircraft just aft of the waist gunner positions. He was trained not to enter the tail turret until the B-24 was airborne and to exit it before landing. The reason was the whip and acceleration at the rear of the Liberator could cause his head to pitch onto the gun sight when the main wheels impacted. Before approaching the target at high altitude, he would close the turret doors behind his back to protect himself from the arctic blast once the bomb bay doors were opened.

A radio message from the airbase tower directed each plane to line up for takeoff. A flare was fired into the air and the first B-24D of the 93rd BG began to slowly increase its speed down the runway and lift off the asphalt surface.

The Liberators took off in thirty-second intervals. When Shannon's turn came, he pushed the throttles forward, released the brakes, and *Hot Stuff* began to roll down the runway. As the Liberator reached takeoff speed, Lentz helped Shannon pull back on the controls and the nose of the heavily loaded plane edged upward followed by the wheels under the wings lifting off the ground. After clearing the trees at the end of the runway, Shannon ordered, "Wheels up."

Lentz engaged the switch that folded the tricycle landing gear into the wings and fuselage; at that moment the two pilots felt less drag on the controls.

As Hot Stuff gained altitude off the coast of England and slipped into formation, Shine spoke over the intercom, "Test your guns." Each gunner, Eisel, McQueen, Rondeau, Jacobson, Craighead, and Farley would fire five or six rounds into space and report back their weapons were operational.

As Hot Stuff climbed through twelve thousand feet, Shannon spoke over the intercom, "It's time to go to oxygen," Each crewman then donned his oxygen mask and reported back to the command pilot oxygen was flowing.

The formation had flown at an altitude of twenty-thousand feet for over an hour and a half in a southwesterly direction when it reached the first way point and changed to a southerly course. The purpose was to skirt around the coast of France to avoid detection by German radar.

"I'm on fire. I'm on fire," McQueen shouted over the intercom.

"Jimmie, go back there and find out what's wrong," Shannon ordered.

The navigator unplugged his headset and clumsily scrambled through the "tunnel" under the flight deck. He carefully navigated the nine-inch catwalk across the bomb bay to the waist gunner's position. Farley had already sprayed the arm of McQueen's flight suit with a fire extinguisher. Gott reached down and unplugged the electrical cord from the waist gunner's leather gear. "Must be a short in the suit," he said. He looked at McQueen. "Are you all right?"

"Think my arm's burnt," the waist gunner replied.

Gott and Farley removed McQueen's jacket and saw the left sleeve of the wool shirt underneath was blackened. The navigator removed his leather gloves and rolled up the sleeve, revealing a red blistered forearm. "Farley, get the first-aid kit."

After a few minutes, McQueen's lower arm was coated with a gel compound and wrapped with gauze. "How's that feel?" Gott asked.

"Thanks, that feels a lot better already."

"Good." Gott said as he slipped his leather gloves over his cold fingers. "Farley, help me get McQueen's jacket back on. It's too damned cold to be exposed for long."

"Okay, but dammit don't plug it in," McQueen said as he inhaled the stench of burnt leather and skin.

Gott patted McQueen on the shoulder and scrambled back to the navigator position. After connecting his headset, he reported to Shannon what had happened.

"I've heard of this happening before," Shine said. "We need to make a report out on this when we get back."

Less than another hour later, the formation reached its second way point and headed in an easterly direction toward Lorient. The bombers were to descend for a low-level bombing run. They were just minutes away from the target and the lead bombardier reported that the entire coastline was socked in. It was determined the entire mission was to be scrubbed and the aircraft were to return to base.

"Shit. So much for our first combat mission," Lentz said. "Thought we'd see some action."

Shannon spoke over the intercom as he banked the aircraft, "I know you're all disappointed as I am, but I can assure you there will be other days and other missions where we'll be tested."

Hot Stuff and two other B-24s formed the rear echelon of the large formation as it turned away from the French Coast and out over the Atlantic.

"Uh-oh," Eisel blurted over the intercom. "There's about a dozen enemy fighters coming up our rear and fast!" The tail gunner stared at the profiles of the incoming single-engine aircraft. After having studied the silhouettes of Luftwaffe fighters in gunnery school, he identified the enemy planes as Messerschmitt Me 109s, a main fighter in the German inventory. The single-seat plane was armed with two thirteen-millimeter machine guns and a deadly twenty-millimeter cannon. He felt fear clutching his chest since in gunnery school the targets never shot back. Eisel knew he was going to be tested for the first time.

"Where are they?" Shannon shouted.

"They're at about five o'clock high. They're Me 109s," the tail gunner reported.

"Gunners, stay alert!" Shannon ordered.

A half minute passed, and the enemy planes dove for the rear elements of the bomber formation, their guns blazing. The German pilots concentrated on attacking the vulnerable tail sections of the Liberators.

Rondeau swiveled the upper turret and began firing at the first of the approaching German fighters. McQueen traversed his .50 machine gun to his right and squeezed the trigger. The limited number of rounds in the ammunition drums were quickly expended and the two gunners hastily reached for full drums.

Eisel patiently waited and at the right moment squeezed the triggers of the twin .50s. The large caliber rounds smashed into the fighter bearing down on Hot Stuff's tail. Black smoke streamed from the Me 109's engine as the fighter skimmed within feet of the B-24's fuselage.

A second enemy fighter attacked from the starboard side while McQueen was bent over picking up a fresh ammunition drum. Rounds from the Me 109 pierced the fuselage where the waist gunner's head had been only a split second earlier. Bits of aluminum sheet metal glanced off McQueen's helmet.

"Jesus Christ, that was close," the waist gunner shouted. He adjusted his helmet and with shaking hands, attached the ammunition drum to his .50 machine gun and pulled back on the receiver chambering a round. Just as McQueen completed reloading another German fighter headed straight for the starboard side of Hot Stuff.

He took aim and unloaded all thirty-six rounds from the drum at the enemy aircraft. Several of the tracers could be seen piercing the attacking aircraft's wings. As the German fighter flew over Hot Stuff, Farley opened fire at the tail of the Me 109 with his machine gun, his rounds ripping into the enemy's tail section. Rondeau had just reloaded his twin .50s and swiveled the upper turret to add to Farley's deadly fire. He expended all the ammunition in his drums at the wounded Nazi fighter as it retreated back to the coast.

Shannon and Lentz watched as the Liberators at the rear of the formation formed an umbrella of deadly .50 machine gun fire around them. The entire fight was over in minutes as the enemy planes peeled off toward the French Coast.

"What was it you were saying about 'thought we'd see some action?'" Shannon said as he looked at Lentz's wide eyes.

The copilot cleared his throat. "Should have kept my big mouth shut."

"Anyone hurt?" Shannon spoke into the intercom.

All crewmen reported they were "okay."

"Well, that was interesting," McQueen muttered. "I almost crapped in my pants." He tapped the steel headgear his was wearing. "This helmet saved my life."

Farley looked over his shoulder at the holes in the fuselage near McQueen's head. "One thing's for sure, I'm never going on a mission without a helmet."

The 93rd BG had no procedures for landing with a live bomb load. The bombs had to be released before the planes could land. Shannon spoke into the intercom, "Jake, we've been ordered to drop our load into the Wash before we land."

"Okay, boss," Jacobson said. "It's a shame to waste these scarce 1,600 pounders in our practice area."

"Like General Sherman once said, 'War is hell,' Jake," Shannon quipped. "So let's get ourselves back to Alconbury in one piece so we can get back into this war."

Three hours later, as Hot Stuff approached Alconbury, it flew into thick clouds and heavy rain. As Shannon banked the B-24 to align with the runway, he quipped, "There it is, boys, home sweet home."

Upon debarking, Hot Stuff's crewmen, still in high-altitude gear, awkwardly climbed aboard a waiting two-and-a-half-ton truck. After a short ride, they jumped out and trudged through mud toward the debriefing room. Many of them lit up, smoke dissipating in the rain.

At the end of their debriefing, the crews were informed they would receive credit for completing their first combat mission; a gift from the Luftwaffe. A combat mission had been defined as any time aircraft came under hostile fire over enemy territory.

The gunners were told to remain in the room. It was at this time they were informed of the operational improvement on their Browning .50s. The unwieldy process of changing the thirty-six-round drums during air engagements was to be replaced with automatic belt feeding systems. Instead of the paltry thirty-six-round drums, each .50 was to be fitted with plywood ammunition boxes that continuously fed six hundred rounds of the deadly ordnance. The modifications were to be installed before their next mission.

"Well, I'll be goddamned," Eisel remarked. "I just talked to Shannon about those damned thirty-six-round drums. He said someone'll come up with a way to belt feed our .50s. He must have a direct line to the higher-uppers."

"Maybe we should take all our gripes to him," Farley said. "It's looking like just talking to him seems to make things happen."

CHAPTER 7

Land's End

The rain-sodden, wooden door of the Nissen hut flew open caught by a capricious gust of wind. Bill Gros, Jeffers' friend from radio operator school stuck his head in. "Ken, I got a pass to go into town. Want to join me?"

Hot Stuff's radioman looked up as he hastily threw personal items in a small duffle bag. "Sorry, Bill, can't go. The whole squadron's to fly to some place called St. Eval in this crappy weather. It's a hurry-up mission. Don't know exactly why."

"Well then, when you get back we'll get together," Gros said. "Good luck." He shook Jeffers's hand.

A half hour later, Hot Stuff was "wheels up" and, after reaching flight altitude, formed up with the rest of the 330th.

"Any idea why we're flying to St. Eval?" Jacobson asked Shannon. "Must be some sort of hush-hush operation."

"We'll find out when we get there, Jake."

Overhearing the officers' conversation, McQueen moaned as he looked out into the clouds. "Just what I wanted to hear, a flight into the goddamned unknown through this shitty weather."

The Liberator bounced and shuttered as it flew in formation through the hostile climate.

"You look kinda green, Paul," Farley said. "If you're going to toss your cookies, aim away from me."

Just then, McQueen lost his breakfast all over Farley's boots. "Jesus Christ, Paul, couldn't you have stuck your head out the window? It stinks to high heaven in here."

McQueen, his face pale white, spoke in a weak voice, "Sorry, George, guess I shouldn't have eaten a second helping of SOS. It tasted so good at the time." He wiped the sweat off his forehead as he muttered, "Not so good now."

An hour and a quarter later, the 330th landed at St. Eval, an RAF base on the most southwestern tip of England. The aerodrome was strategically located for the express purpose of conducting anti-submarine and anti-shipping patrols. It also was a base of operations for aerial reconnaissance and meteorological flights, convoy patrols, and air-sea rescue. From the air St. Eval, with its three extended asphalt-covered concrete runways and outlying buildings appeared similar to Alconbury.

While the planes were being serviced, the crews were fed, and afterward assembled in the briefing room. There the 330th's squadron commander, Major Kenneth Cool, stepped up onto the low stage and revealed a large map. Pipe in hand, he pointed to several red ribbons streaming from south to southwest away from St. Eval across the Bay of Biscay off the west coast of France.

"Men, the reason we couldn't divulge why we were ordered to fly here on short notice is we'll be providing air cover to protect Allied convoys sailing through the Bay of Biscay. This is a classified mission that will be supporting the coming Allied invasion of North Africa. That means no one is to speak of it off base. Is that understood?"

Heads nodded as the room erupted with excited chatter. "Hold it down," Cool ordered.

When quiet fell across the assembled crews, Cool continued, "Our job here is to protect the invasion convoys, and by that, I mean sink or at least scare the hell out of enemy subs and shipping that could pose a threat. As you already know, there are a number of sub pens along the French coast and the German U-boats assemble in wolf packs in the Bay of Biscay. They are a deadly threat.

"Most of you recall our conducting antisubmarine patrols over the Gulf of Mexico last summer. You'll be doing the same thing operating out of St. Eval. By flying out of southwestern England, we can easily extend our range over the convoys to the Straits of Gibraltar. That's the reason we displaced from Alconbury.

"We'll be flying singly, and we can expect to encounter long-range Luftwaffe interceptors." He gestured with his pipe stem. "You gunners can expect to earn your pay this mission. Also, keep in mind our guys and the Brits on those ships are depending on us. We cannot fail them!"

At this point, Cool jammed the pipe between his teeth and nodded to the squadron operations officer to proceed with his detailed briefing.

On October 28, Hot Stuff and several other Liberators of the 330th were to be sent out singly on antisubmarine patrol over Biscay Bay. Allied command had realized a marked reduction in shipping losses since the implementation of air patrols over regions of the Atlantic known to be crawling with U-boat activity. The B-24s, with their long range capability were deemed ideally suited for the job. Until the RAF had sufficient planes to take over the mission, the AAF was called upon to fill-in and the 330th squadron in particular was given the mission.

The Liberators from the 330th were selected on a rotational basis to conduct antisubmarine patrols over Biscay Bay around the clock in such a manner as not to impair the strapped bombing capability of the 93rd for other missions. Those B-24s of the 330th that were not on patrol were made available to augment the other three squadrons on bombing missions. None of the aircraft on antisubmarine patrol were to be given credit for combat missions unless they were actually engaged with the enemy over hostile territory. Hot Stuff was one aircraft of the squadron that earned the distinction on four different occasions, the first being on October 28.

CHAPTER 8

October 28, 1942
Second Combat Mission:
AntisubmarinePatrol

Early on the morning of October 28, 1942, three of the 330th's B-24s, Hot Stuff among them, loaded with depth bombs, took off to fly antisubmarine patrol within their assigned zones over Allied convoys.

After eight hours into the wearisome mission, Hot Stuff's crew endured several changes in weather ranging from calm and clear to dark and stormy. Shannon banked the Liberator to gain a better view of the Allied convoy through breaking clouds. He saw an unfamiliar vessel steaming several miles from of the line of Allied ships bound for North Africa. He nosed Hot Stuff down to take a better look at the unknown ship. He was surprised when the ship's antiaircraft guns began firing at his Liberator.

Shine spoke into his radio, "You guys better watch out or we'll come down and fight it out."

On closer examination, the former fighter pilot identified the unknown vessel as a British battleship. "Jesus Christ, it's one of

BEFORE THE BELLE

ours." Immediately, Shannon realized discretion was the better part of valor. With the help of Lentz, Shine pulled back on the controls and high-tailed Hot Stuff out of there.

As the B-24 attained cruising altitude, a voice shouted over the intercom, "Two Me 210s just broke out of the clouds." Farley swiveled his .50 in the direction of his sighting. He recognized the twin-engine heavy fighters from silhouettes he had memorized in gunnery school. The Messerschmitt-built plane was manned by two: pilot and gunner. It was armed with two twenty millimeter cannons and two thirteen millimeter machine guns. A deadly force to reckon with.

"Where are they?" Shannon asked.

"They're at eight o'clock."

As the Luftwaffe aircraft approached Hot Stuff's portside, Rondeau rotated the upper turret to the left. "I see them!" The flight engineer noted the enemy fighters flew somewhat slower than the Me 109s they had previously encountered making them easier to engage.

Eisel rotated the tail turret to his right in the direction of the enemy fighters bearing down on them. As enemy bullets pierced Hot Stuff's aluminum fuselage the three gunners opened fire surprising the attacking aircraft.

This early in the war, German pilots often mistook B-24s for British Lancaster bombers, which were armed with only smaller caliber .30 machine guns, which had shorter range and less hitting power. A much easier target for the Luftwaffe.

This time, the Nazi pilots were surprised as the heavier longer range .50 bullets from the Liberator ripped into the fuselages of the German aircraft.

"God, my .50 loves the automatic belt feeding," Farley extolled. "I can fire at those sons of bitches all day."

"Paul, they're coming over to your side," Rondeau shouted as he rotated the upper turret. He could see the tracers from his twin .50s penetrating the wings of the enemy fighters.

As the pair of Me 210s passed over the Liberator, McQueen fired his .50 at their tails. "Take that, you bastards."

The two German heavy fighters dove and turned to attack the soft underbelly of the Liberator. Lentz looked to his right. "Craighead, they're coming up on you."

"I see them." The belly gunner rotated his .50 at the approaching targets. He squeezed the trigger, and the heavy machine gun spewed it lethal fire right into the cockpit of the leading enemy fighter. The plane suddenly veered off toward the French coast.

The second ME 210's thirteen millimeter machine guns peppered the lower fuselage of the Liberator and turned to make another pass at the Hot Stuff's tail.

"You're mine, asshole," Eisel muttered into the intercom. He waited until the attacking aircraft was in his crosshairs and squeezed the triggers. "Welcome to hell, you son of a bitch."

One of the Daimler-Benz engines on the German fighter caught fire. The enemy pilot had enough and bolted for the French coast.

Shannon spoke into the intercom, "Good shooting, guys. Anyone hurt?"

Miraculously, every crewmember responded they were "okay."

Farley's shaking hands released their iron grip on the machine gun, and he gazed around Hot Stuff's interior. Light streamed in through the multiple holes in the fuselage. He patted the aluminum side. "You're one hellava flying machine, girl."

Hot Stuff's arduous day on patrol ended, as another B-24 from the 330th flew alongside and "wagged" it wings. Shannon spoke into the intercom, "We've been relieved. We're headed back to base."

The following day, Shannon was saddened to hear a good friend of his, Bill Williams, had crashed in heavy clouds on the southern coast of England after returning from a patrol mission. There was only one survivor. Shine realized hazardous weather could be as deadly as the enemy.

CHAPTER 9

October 31, 1942
Third Combat Mission:
Antisubmarine Patrol

On October 31, Hot Stuff was again assigned the mission to fly patrol over a convoy. This time, it was now off the coast of Portugal.

They had been on station for five hours when the belly gunner shouted over the intercom. "Hey, Lieutenant, I think I see an enemy fighter."

Shannon scanned the gray ocean around the B-24. "I don't see it. Where is it, Craighead?"

The belly gunner clearly identified the aircraft by its configuration. "It just came out of a cloud. It's a Ju 88 right below us." He remembered from gunnery school the Junkers multipurpose twin-engine heavy fighter had a crew of four and the aircraft was armed with six 7.92-millimeter machine guns.

The ex-fighter pilot banked the Liberator slightly to the left. He looked down at the slow-moving Luftwaffe heavy fighter in the low clouds. Shine smiled. "Jake and Rondeau, get ready with your .50s. We're going to have some fun."

Lentz looked at the command pilot. "What the hell are you thinking?"

Shannon's gloved finger pointed down as he looked out the side window. "We're going to get that bastard. We can't let it close on the convoy. "He felt the old fighter pilot excitement begin to course through his veins.

When Shine shoved the controls forward, Hot Stuff began a steep descent. Lentz grabbed his controls and watched as the altimeter reading dropped and the air speed increased alarmingly.

Rondeau gripped his twin .50s as he was pressed forward in the upper turret. Craighead was right. The enemy plane was a Ju 88; its only defense against the diving B-24 was a pair of 7.92-millimeter aft machine guns. The Luftwaffe fighter's other armament pointed forward and down and were useless against Hot Stuff's attack from above.

The Liberator's waist gunners clung to the fuselage as the plane dove toward the enemy fighter, their unattended .50s swinging freely within the confines of the interior.

"What the hell's going on?" Farley shouted.

"I think Shannon wants to knockout a Jerry," McQueen bemoaned as he clung to the metal framework.

"Let's hope we can pull out of this dive before we kiss the waves," Craighead screamed as he slid forward on his belly toward the bomb rack.

Just then, Rondeau pressed the triggers of his twin .50s, and Jake followed suit with his nose machinegun. Flashes from the German heavy fighter's rear gunner could be seen as the enemy aircraft returned fire. Several of the enemy's rounds pierced Hot Stuff's Plexiglas nose.

"Give the son of a bitch the whole nine yards," Eisel voiced over the intercom as he hung on to the tail turret's twin .50s.

The tracers from Rondeau's twin .50s bracketed the enemy aircraft. "I think I hit the bastard," the flight engineer shouted from the top turret. "He's turning away."

Although the Ju 88 fired back, it appeared the Luftwaffe pilot realized he was in trouble. He pointed the nose of his fighter east and fled for the safety of the Iberian Peninsula.

As the enemy aircraft began to fade in the distance, Shannon shouted, "Pull up!"

Hot Stuff was shaking violently as it plummeted toward the sea, its speed steadily increasing every second. "This thing isn't built to go this fast," Lentz lamented as his gloved hands in a death grip pulled back on the controls.

Both pilots struggled as the plane screamed and shuddered. Hot Stuff was slow to respond at first. Then eventually the Liberator's descent began to slow. When the aircraft finally leveled off, Lentz looked at the altimeter; it read two hundred feet.

"Jesus, Shine, I could almost have used my .50 as a paddle," Jacobson chided as he braced himself against the nose glass.

"I think I feel the sea spray on my face," McQueen panted.

"Christ's sake that was close," Farley exclaimed as he looked at his fellow waist gunner, "and that's not sea water running down your ugly mug; it's sweat."

As Shannon took the Liberator back up to patrol altitude, Lentz exhaled and remarked, "You know, Shine, after this Hot Stuff's going to be known as a P-24."

"I like our being a P-24," the pilot chuckled. "Just too bad we didn't get that son of a bitch."

"Maybe we didn't get him, but I bet they were shitting in their britches," Jacobson added.

"I sure as hell hope the Boss doesn't want to chase any more enemy fighters," Eisel implored as he gripped the twin .50s in the rear turret to right himself. "I left the turret doors open and came close to being thrown out."

After reaching their cruising altitude over the convoy, Shannon spoke over the intercom. "Maybe we didn't sink a sub this time out, but we sure as hell scared the shit out of a Heinie fighter."

In response, the entire crew nervously laughed over the intercom.

Four hours later at St. Eval, Shannon and his crew met with others who had flown patrol that day. The word quickly spread around the 330th that Hot Stuff was no longer a bomber, but a fighter, a P-24 no less. That evening at the O Club, the other officers slapped Shine on the back and toasted him on his fighter pilot skills.

The next morning, the crews of the 330th assembled in the briefing room. Major Cool informed them the preparations for the invasion of North Africa were well under way. *Operation Torch* as it was called was scheduled to take place within a week. He reminded the crews any information on the operation was classified and to be careful not to divulge anything about it. Cool congratulated the squadron in having done its job well in covering the Allied convoys and the RAF was going to assume the task. The 330th was to return to Alconbury. Although the squadron hadn't produced any definite results other than thwarting enemy fighters, it nevertheless had kept the U-boats off balance and contributed greatly to the Allied advance.

The crews were then briefed on their return flight to Alconbury. The Liberators were serviced and takeoff was scheduled for the next morning. Once back at their home base, the 330th was to have a few days of rest before assuming bombing missions over Europe.

"I look forward to our getting passes," Farley said. "After Shannon going after that Nazi fighter, I know we all could use a couple of days off."

"Do you think we could get passes to go to London?" McQueen asked.

"Not now," Rondeau replied. "Maybe once we get a couple of real combat missions under our belt, the brass will let us go to London. Right now, I'll just be happy to go to a pub and mix with the locals."

"Yeah, and by mixing, I bet you mean with women." McQueen grinned. "Sounds like a swell idea to me."

On November 2, although the weather was inclement the return flight to Alconbury was uneventful.

The ensuing four days at the 93rd's home base were filled with recreational activities such as softball, letter writing, card playing, and firing personal weapons at a makeshift range, and of course, the all-important passes into town.

CHAPTER 10

November 7, 1942
Fourth Combat
Mission: Brest

On November 7, Hot Stuff's crew along with eleven other of the 93rd's B-24 crews met in the mission briefing room. Major Compton uncovered the planning map. The Liberators were to fly from Alconbury to bomb Brest, France, to attack German submarine pens. The red ribbons on the map outlined the flight paths for the B-24s to fly south to Bath and turn west along the English southern coast and then south to Brest. Each plane was to carry four one thousand–pound bombs. The formation was to fly at twenty-eight thousand feet then descend to optimal bombing altitude as it approached the targeted U-boat pens.

Lt. Michael Phipps, the group intelligence officer, then briefed the enemy situation. Antiaircraft fire was expected to be moderate and there was a low probability the twelve B-24s would encounter any enemy fighter aircraft.

After a three-hour flight, the Liberators were over the target area. The formation was preceded by B-17s, which had stirred up a hornet's nest. By the time the 93rd's B-24s arrived over the target area the flak had become extremely heavy. Nevertheless, the dozen Liberators delivered their forty-eight bombs. However, masking of the target area by smoke and debris left by the B-17 attack caused the bombardiers of the 93rd to drop their payloads short of the U-boat pens.

As the dozen B-24s turned back out over Biscay Bay, they were attacked in anger by nearly twenty Luftwaffe fighters. Intense aerial combat ensued.

"Bogies at five o'clock," Rondeau shouted.

"I see them," McQueen yelled.

Eisel quietly and methodically swiveled the twin .50s in the tail turret to his left. He identified the incoming enemy aircraft as single-engine Me 109s.

Rondeau in the upper turret and McQueen on the portside began firing their .50s at the incoming enemy planes. Hot Stuff's fuselage was riddled with holes. Eisel patiently watched as two enemy fighters banked to attack at the tail section. He waited until the right moment and opened up. The pair of Luftwaffe fighters burst into flames and hurtled toward the sea.

"Three more Me 109s at eleven o'clock high," Shannon bellowed.

"I see them," Jacobson yelled as he swiveled his .50 slightly to his left and began firing.

Rondeau rotated his turret to meet the incoming threat. He squeezed the triggers, and his twin .50s began spitting out their lethal ordnance. Their combined fire from Hot Stuff interweaved with that of other B-24s in the formation caused one more of the enemy fighters to be destroyed. Another was hit and seen belching smoke as it limped back toward France. The remainder scurried back to their airbases.

Twenty minutes later, twenty unidentified fighters appeared from nowhere and attacked the 93rd's formation over the channel.

The flashing of their wing-mounted machineguns caught the attention of the homeward bound Liberator crews. The now skittish B-24 gunners poured out a protective curtain of .50 caliber machinegun fire.

"Jesus Christ, not more," Lentz lamented as the unidentified fighters closed in. "Bogies at two o'clock."

"I see them," Jake spoke into the intercom.

Jacobson, McQueen, and Rondeau let loose with their .50s. Heat emanated from the hot barrels of their automatic weapons.

Lentz stared at the unidentified aircraft as they drew closer. The supposedly enemy planes recognized the flight of B-24s as being American and ceased their attack. At the same time, Lentz recognized the unique shape of the fighters' wings as they pulled up and away from the Liberator formation.

"Stop firing, those are RAF Spitfires," Lentz shouted over the intercom.

Shannon broke radio silence and informed the other Liberators of the identity of the incoming fighters and the twelve B-24s ceased their barrage. After frantic tries, communication was established with the British planes. After listening to radio traffic between the American flight leader and the Spitfires, Shannon suddenly spoke into Hot Stuff's intercom. "I'll be damned. Those are Czech pilots." It was obvious the Czech fighters were scrambled to intercept what was perceived to be incoming enemy bombers. This was a clear case of a major screw-up.

McQueen bit into his D ration and chewed on the hard chocolate bar. He leaned on the .50 machine gun he named *Annie* and gazed out the open window at the Spitfires. "I thought they're supposed to be on our side."

Farley looked over at his fellow waist gunner. "Paul, shit happens. And don't you ever stop eating? You're nothing but a goddamned chow hound even in the middle of a firefight."

"Nothing like food to calm my nerves," McQueen retorted.

"Maybe, but when you toss your cookies, I end up smelling like puke."

Night was closing in and the "friendly" Spitfires escorted the 93rd's Liberators to the RAF base at Exeter in southwestern England. In the waning light, Shannon and Lentz could see the aerodrome had three runways; however, ground control directed the 93rd to use the only one suitable for the B-24s.

In less than an hour, all the bombers and fighters successfully landed in near darkness. Once on the ground, the Czech pilots emerged from the Spitfires and, in broken English, greeted their American allies as they climbed out of their B-24s. After a few rounds of drinks at the officers' club, all was forgiven.

At the bar, the Czech airmen lightheartedly criticized the American gunners as having poor marksmanship as demonstrated by the tracers missing the Spitfires. It was at this time the American officers informed their allies that every fourth round fired was a tracer, and they should take a close look at their fighters once it was daylight. The Czech officers couldn't believe it and left the club to see for themselves.

After returning to the club, the Czech pilots were believers as they found their aircraft would require major patchwork to cover the multiple .50 caliber holes in the wings and fuselages of the Spitfires. It was a miracle none of the Spitfires were knocked out of the sky.

The next day, Hot Stuff and the 330th flew back to Alconbury for a short break. While the aircraft were serviced and prepared for another mission the crewmen relaxed and waited.

CHAPTER 11

November 9, 1942
Fifth Combat Mission:
St. Nazaire

Early on the morning of November 9, the crews were awakened at 0400 as a prelude to the day's mission. In the briefing room, the large map depicted red ribbons leading to St. Nazaire on the French coast. A dozen B-24s from the 93rd were the only aircraft available for the mission. Hot Stuff was among them. The twelve planes were to attack the German submarine pens located there.

As dawn broke, Shannon started Hot Stuff's engines. The four one thousand–pound bombs had been loaded by the ground crew. Rondeau checked the engines' performance and informed Shine the Liberator was operating properly.

Upon receiving the signal to line up for takeoff, Shannon taxied Hot Stuff to the end of the runway and waited. The twelve B-24s lifted off in thirty-second intervals, Hot Stuff being the ninth.

At twenty thousand feet, the Liberators formed into their defensive groups of three. After three hours into the flight, two of the

BEFORE THE BELLE

B-24s aborted due to mechanical problems and the ten remaining aircraft continued toward the target area.

As Hot Stuff approached the St. Nazaire submarine pens, German 88 millimeter antiaircraft fire engulfed the group. As the Liberators flew through the moderate flak, the lead ship's bombs fell short of the target. Nevertheless, the lead bombardier led the following nine B-24s over the pens where they dropped their payloads. Aerial photography of the bombing would later show the one thousand–pound bombs scattered over the target with little effect.

Fortunately, the flak delivered by the German 88s had been for the most part ineffective. As the 93rd's bombers turned toward Alconbury, they were unchallenged by enemy fighters.

CHAPTER 12

November 11, 1942
Sixth Combat Mission: AntisubmarinePatrol

Two days later, on November 11, Hot Stuff was back on submarine patrol.

After six hours on station, the tedious mission had been uneventful. No U-boats had been sighted, and fortunately Allied convoys on that day sailed safely to Great Britain where they would unload their precious lifeline cargo.

"I think I'm going cross-eyed," Craighead griped as he peered through his belly gunner's position at the endless gray sea. "All I've seen is white caps and ships. I sure as hell would like us to see some action."

"Watch what you say, Joe," Farley said. "Your wish may come true."

Lentz let the binoculars hang on his chest. "You know what day this is?" he spoke into the intercom. "Today's Armistice Day. World War I ended on the eleventh hour of November 11 in 1918. And here we're at it again going against the Hun. Will those bastards ever give up?"

"Apparently, the German people fell for the crap Hitler was preaching, and now we're into another war with them," Gott responded as he looked up from the small navigator's table. "I have no doubt we'll beat the Heinies again. Hopefully, sooner than later."

Eisel pulled the binoculars away from his tired eyes. Instinct told him to look up from the tail turret. "Shit! Bandits at six o'clock high."

The otherwise routine patrol mission had been interrupted by five Me 210s. The twin-engine heavy fighters dove toward the vulnerable tail of the lone B-24. The Luftwaffe aircraft opened fire with their twenty millimeter cannon and 7.92 millimeter machine guns.

Rondeau climbed into the top turret and rotated the twin .50s to the rear and began firing.

Eisel, in his usual cool manner, aimed the rear turret's guns at the incoming Luftwaffe fighters. At the precise moment, he squeezed the triggers. The accurate fire from his twin .50s raked two of the approaching enemy aircraft. The planes burst into large fragments and smoke. A third Luftwaffe fighter broke out into flames and fell toward the sea. Eisel fired his twin .50s again, and an engine on the fourth fighter began smoking, and it lost altitude as it turned toward the French coast. The fifth Me 210 wanted no part of the fight and it too fled east toward the safety of its airbase.

"Goddamned good shooting, fellows," Shannon shouted into the intercom as he and the other crewmen watched the remains of three enemy fighters plummet toward the cruel icy sea. Two German airmen were seen bailing out of the third enemy fighter, their parachutes blossoming from their backs; a sure death awaited them in the frigid Atlantic waters if not expeditiously rescued.

"Eisel got the bastards, sir," Rondeau reported. "They came in too low for me. He saved our asses." The other gunners reported similarly.

"Well, if that's the case, congratulations, Eisel," Shine remarked. "We'll chalk you up with three victories." After a pause, he continued, "Ah, anybody hit?"

All crewmen reported that no one was wounded.

McQueen looked at the light beaming through the perforations in the fuselage. He stuck his gloved finger through one of the holes close to his head. He adjusted his flak helmet. "I'll be a son of a bitch. It's a goddamned miracle none of us was hit."

CHAPTER 13

November 14 and 17, 1942
Seventh and Eighth Combat
Missions: St. Nazaire Twice

At 1000 hours on November 14, Hot Stuff took off with eleven other Liberators for another run at the St. Nazaire submarine pens.

"How many goddamned times do we have to attack those U-boat pens?" Gott lamented.

"This is war, Jim," Lentz responded. "Like the old saying, *if at first you don't succeed, try, try again.*"

"Yeah, but going to the same place again and again is wearing a hole in my navigation chart," Gott said.

"I hope like hell, I can put those eggs in the pickle barrel this one last time," Jacobson fumed. "I'm getting tired of looking at the same aerial photos of those damned pens. They always look undamaged."

"Maybe this time, we'll get them for sure," Shannon spoke confidently.

As the formation neared the Brittany Peninsula, the aircraft took evasive action to avoid the heavy fire from the German 88s. The closer the B-24s got to the U-boat pens, the more intense the Nazi flak became. All the attacking planes penetrated the black clouds of exploding antiaircraft fire and dropped their bombs onto the twelve foot thick reinforced concrete roofs of the pens.

After the planes released their deadly ordnance, they banked right and dropped in altitude at a rate of one thousand feet per minute and headed into Biscay Bay. This was planned as a means to preclude enemy fighters from attacking the soft underbellies of the B-24s. The dozen Liberators made it safely to Exeter.

The next day, the 330th returned to Alconbury.

On November 17, St. Nazaire sub pens and nearby power plants were the high priority targets.

As the crews left the briefing room and headed for the trucks that would ferry them to their aircraft, McQueen quipped, "I'm beginning to feel flying missions against those Nazis at St. Nazaire is like visiting old friends. Only they never offer us a schnapps and a smoke when we come calling."

Jacobson chuckled, "Let's just say the *third time is a charm*, McQueen."

"I certainly hope so, Lieutenant," the waist gunner responded. "My side of Hot Stuff is getting to look like a slice of Swiss cheese."

The Liberators began to liftoff on that cold morning at 0930. They approached the target area from the north at eighteen thousand feet where the B-24s encountered heavy flak.

Hot Stuff shook and bounced as Jacobson tried to focus the bombsight through the turbulent air. As they neared the target, Shannon passed control of the Liberator to his bombardier. The target area was clouded over by smoke and debris left by a flight of B-17s only minutes before. Jake followed the lead B-24's bombardier, released his bombs and Hot Stuff along with the other Liberators made a run for Biscay Bay. Again, there was no encounter with enemy fighters, no losses and the 330th safely made its way back to Alconbury through miserable weather.

After the squadron's aircraft were positioned on the concrete aprons, the crews walked to the debriefing area.

McQueen sniffed the air. "Son of a bitch, I must really be hungry. I'll bet two bucks, I mean a pound, I smell doughnuts and coffee."

Farley laughed. "You're letting your stomach scramble your brain, again, Paul. Can't you think of anything but chow?"

As Hot Stuff's crew entered the large Nissen hut, they were greeted by four British women standing behind a makeshift plywood bar. They were dressed in blue uniforms emblazoned with red crosses. "Would you men like a fresh cup of Joe and a doughnut?" one of the smiling faces asked.

"Well I'll be a…" Farley blurted before Lentz's hand quickly covered his mouth. The copilot spoke for the crew, "Why yes, we sure as heck would enjoy a cup of your coffee," he pointed toward the tray containing the pastry, "and one of those delicious looking doughnuts."

Each of the smiling crewmembers hooked two or three doughnuts over grimy fingers of one hand; the other hand grabbed a hot cup of coffee.

McQueen spoke through a mouthful of the delicious fresh pastry as he looked at his fellow crewmates. "Never doubt my nose when it comes to sniffing out food."

Each crew munched doughnuts and sipped coffee while they waited to be debriefed by group staff officers. The results of the mission were inconclusive, and the staff would have to wait until the next day for aerial photos.

At the conclusion of the debriefing session, the crews stopped once more by the Red Cross coffee bar and helped themselves before returning to their Nissen huts.

The next morning after breakfast, Shannon, Lentz, and Jacobson joined the pilots and bombardiers in the debriefing room.

There they viewed aerial photographs projected on a large screen of the results of the attack on the St. Nazaire area from the previous day. It was clear the bombings conducted by B-17s had obscured the target just ahead of the B-24s, causing the Liberators' bombs to once again miss the target. One photo showed two bombs had straddled an unidentified vessel, possibly damaging it. Other than that, the mission was deemed unsuccessful for the 330th.

As Hot Stuff's officers left the briefing room, Jacobson showed unusual agitation. He pulled out a pack of Camels and lit up, a puff of smoke emanating from his lips as he spoke. "Those goddamned mission planners at Eighth Air Force keep making the same mistakes over and over again. When the hell are they going to learn having the B-17s go in ahead of us really screws up *our* bombing results. For once, we should go in first so we can see the target. I know we can do a better job if they'd only give us a chance."

"Well, Jake," Shine remarked, "I agree with you. But orders are orders. All we can do is bitch to Timberlake. Maybe if we do it enough, he'll be able to persuade the higher ups to change tactics."

Lentz pointed out, "I can think of one good reason why HQ wants us to follow the B-17s. Their cruising speed is slower, and we can easily catch up with their formation. Can you imagine if we led the raid?" He chuckled. "The B-17s would never keep up with us."

"Yeah," Shine said, "and by cruising faster at altitude, our B-24s will be more stable, and we wouldn't have the problems we have now of bouncing all over the place trying to maintain a close formation. After all, Timberlake's been preaching to keep our formation tight for better protection against the Jerries."

"Maybe someday, we'll fly missions only with Liberators and the whole problem will go away," Lentz responded. "Besides I'm getting tired of the B-17s stirring up the Nazi fighters for us to take on."

"I look forward to the day it'll be a B-24 only show," Jake said.

CHAPTER 14

November 22, 1942
Ninth Combat
Mission: Lorient

Before dinner on November 21, Hot Stuff's crew was informed that instead of antisubmarine patrol, they were to fly a bombing mission the next day. As per normal operating procedures, they weren't given any details about the mission until their briefing the next morning.

After an early morning rising and breakfast, eighteen of the 93rd's Liberator crews gathered in the large Nissen hut for their briefing. The dozen and half B-24s was the most the group could muster for the mission as a number of aircraft were either on antisubmarine patrol or were not considered mission ready. It wasn't until the cloth covering the map revealed the target for November 22—the submarine pens at Lorient. The same target area the group had scrubbed its mission on a month earlier due to cloud cover.

Colored tape depicted the ingress and egress routes to the heavily concrete-roofed sub pens. The flight paths were nearly identical to those the 93rd had flown on October 21. They were to fly southwest to the tip of England, turn south to a waypoint due west of Lorient, and then east to the target area and return. Updated blowups of aerial reconnaissance photos were displayed for the bombardiers' and pilots' edification.

Jake leaned over and muttered in Shine's ear, "Here we go again. Hope we can make good use of the bombs instead of wasting them in the Wash."

"I have a feeling this time will be different," the command pilot responded.

The group operations officer noted each bomber was to carry six one thousand–pounders; the heavy bombs were deemed sufficient to penetrate the pens' dozen feet of reinforced concrete. Light anti-aircraft fire and minimal encounters with enemy fighters were anticipated. The bombers were to fly at twelve thousand feet to the target area, but this time, instead of attacking the pens at low altitude, the Liberators were to climb to twenty-one thousand feet to bomb at high level. Takeoff was scheduled for 1000.

Following the briefing, Hot Stuff's crew, like those of the other seventeen Liberators, mounted trucks that ferried them to their aircraft. Many of the crewmembers had taken one last drag on their cigarettes before boarding the trucks—their last until after returning to Alconbury. As Hot Stuff's crew climbed aboard the Liberator, Shannon, Lentz, and Rondeau walked around the aircraft, making a quick visual check of the plane's exterior; satisfied, they climbed into Hot Stuff.

After Hot Stuff's engines were warmed up and operating properly, Shannon received the signal to form in line for takeoff. As per procedure, a flare was fired into the air and the first B-24 began rolling down the runway followed by the others in thirty second intervals. Col. Timberlake and several of his staff officers stood atop the Alconbury control tower and observed each heavily-laden Liberator as it slowly lifted off the runway and climbed into the cloud-filled sky.

BEFORE THE BELLE

Three hours later, the formation climbed to the planned twenty-one thousand feet. This time, the target was void of cloud cover and the bomb run continued as planned. No aircraft had aborted, and the raid was to be conducted by all eighteen Liberators.

The air in and around the formation began to fill with smoke and red flashes from flak. Hot Stuff bounced and swayed through the shock waves of the exploding ordnance that surrounded the aircraft. Several slivers of shrapnel penetrated the fuselage, but Shannon kept the Liberator on course. Once over the target area, he relinquished control of Hot Stuff to Jacobson who had the target area within his sight. When the bombardier of the lead B-24 named Ball of Fire released his bomb load, Jake and the other aircraft in the formation followed suit.

Jacobson kept an eye on the target area as he returned control of Hot Stuff to Shannon. This time, the formation's bombs hit the pens in good order and as a bonus a number of the bombs struck the nearby rail yards as well. Jake knew Ball of Fire's bombardier, Cristopolus "Kelly" Yenalavage had done well in leading the bomb run. "Goddamn, Shine, you were right about this mission. Looks like we really pounded the shit out of them this time."

As the formation turned to leave the target area, Hot Stuff's gunners scanned the skies for German fighters. They were not to be disappointed. Three Ju 88s rose in anger to meet the Liberators as they flew out over the Bay of Biscay. The three twin-engine heavy fighters chose to first attack the formation's lead aircraft Ball of Fire from its underbelly, inflicting damage to one of its engines. Combined supporting fire from the formation's .50s sent one of the Luftwaffe's Ju 88s plummeting into the sea. A second was damaged by the brutal fire delivered by the Liberators and headed for the French coast. After a half dozen passes at the 93rd's formation, the third enemy fighter had enough and scurried to safety as well.

Of the Liberators in the flight, Shannon took count, none had been lost. However, one had an engine shot out, and a number sustained moderate damage. He reduced Hot Stuff's speed and joined Ball of Fire to fly adjacent to the crippled plane in order provide covering fire for the damaged B-24.

As the formation drew near Alconbury, priority for landing was given to those Liberators, which had sustained heavy damage and had severely wounded crewmen. Among those B-24s was Ball of Fire. Fire trucks and ambulances scrambled to meet those aircraft immediately upon landing.

It wasn't until after Hot Stuff landed that Shannon and Lentz found out the situation on Ball of Fire. The pilot and a good friend of theirs, Howard Young, had sustained a severe wound to his arm below the elbow, one that would require amputation. The copilot, Cleveland Hickman, was wounded in the leg. It was the bombardier, Yenalavage, who climbed into the pilot's seat after Young was removed for medical attention and assisted Hickman with the rudders to fly the plane back to base. Hickman had never landed a B-24, but with Yenalavage's strong legs, they were able to successfully complete a hard landing and brake to a stop.

After the debriefing, Hot Stuff's officers bellied up to the bar along with those of the other Liberator crews who successfully flew the mission over Lorient. Shannon thought of his seriously wounded friend, cleared his throat, and lifted his glass of beer. "Gentlemen, here's to our good fortune. May Lady Luck continue to smile on us."

Through the hazy, cigarette smoke–filled Nissen hut, resounding responses were voiced.

Lentz, thinking of the increasing number of empty cots in the barracks cleared his throat and lifted his drink, "May I propose a toast to those who will no longer be with us."

CHAPTER 15

November 24, 1942
Tenth Combat Mission:
AntisubmarinePatrol

Two days later on November 24, Hot Stuff was assigned antisubmarine patrol over Biscay Bay. Six tedious hours had passed and the convoys the Liberator shepherded sailed unharassed by German U-boats.

"This is getting old," Gott muttered over the intercom as he scanned the dark gray seas from his station behind the bombardier.

"If nothing else, our being up here keeps the Nazi wolf packs from surfacing to charge their batteries," Jacobson replied. "They can't cover long distances underwater without running their diesel engines to charge their batteries. They must know we're up here waiting."

McQueen yawned and took a bite out of the D ration bar. He spoke through a mouthful of chocolate. "I'm going to be gray-headed and stoop-shouldered by the time we get to spot one of those Nazi bastards."

At that moment, Rondeau's voice emanated through Hot Stuff's intercom. "Two bandits at seven o'clock high."

"What are they?" Lentz asked.

Rondeau studied the silhouettes of the incoming fighters. He recognized the sleek single-seater with its two thirteen millimeter machine guns and four deadly twenty millimeter cannons. "They're Fw 190s. They're coming in fast."

Just then, the lead German fighter's twenty millimeter cannons fired. The explosive rounds began penetrating Hot Stuff's fuselage. Loud thumping sounds emanated throughout the B-24 as Rondeau and Eisel rotated their turrets to face the oncoming threats. Farley swiveled his .50 left and upward. Rondeau and Farley immediately began firing their machine guns at the two enemy fighters. Eisel waited.

"Son of bitch, they're fast!" Rondeau yelled into the intercom as he rotated his turret firing at the passing Focke Wulf fighter.

Eisel eyed the second intruder and opened up. The engine of the Luftwaffe aircraft burst into flames. As the aircraft began to plummet toward the sea, the pilot could be seen exiting the doomed aircraft, his parachute blossoming a few seconds later.

"Nice shooting, George," Farley shouted into the intercom.

The other Fw 190 turned to make another pass at Hot Stuff. This time the enemy aircraft chose to attack the soft underbelly of the B-24. Craighead swiveled his .50 in the direction of the attacker and squeezed the trigger. The tracers from the belly gunner's machine gun bracketed the climbing enemy fighter, several rounds penetrating the wing area and one hitting the cockpit.

The German pilot made another pass, twenty millimeter cannons blazing. Hot Stuff suffered damage to one of the large tail sections. Eisel fired his twin .50s at the oncoming bright yellow nose. His rounds failed to mortally damage the Fw 190. Apparently after this third pass, the Luftwaffe pilot decided the deadly fire from the B-24 was too much and he retreated back to the French coast.

"Jesus, those Fw 190s are really fast," Farley lamented as he watched the enemy fighter fade in the cloudy sky. "I could hardly take a lead on the bastards."

"I sure as hell hope the Jerries don't have many of those in the inventory," Rondeau said.

"Good shooting, guys," Shannon spoke into the intercom. "Anyone been hit?"

All the crewmembers reported in; they were uninjured.

Shannon felt control of the rudders was too mushy. "Eisel, what damage did we suffer on the tail section?"

The tail gunner looked left and right. "Our starboard tail has two big holes in it. The portside rudder also has a bunch of small punctures. Other than that, the tail section looks solid."

"Okay, but keep an eye on the tail damage," Shine responded. "How's the fuselage?"

"We've got a bunch of good-sized holes in the skin," McQueen reported. "But I don't see any damage to the frame."

Rondeau scanned the upper engine and wing areas. "There are a bunch of holes in the wings, but I don't see any fuel or oil leaks and the engines look like they're functioning properly."

"That's good news," the pilot responded. He wriggled the controls a bit, and Hot Stuff slowly responded. He looked at Lentz. "We should be all right until we're relieved in about another hour or so. When we get back it looks like the ground crews will have their hands full patching *her* up. And after this latest encounter, I think we all deserve some well-earned time off."

A number of elated voices could be heard over the plane's intercom.

CHAPTER 16

London Leave

After returning from their antisubmarine patrol mission and the encounter with the Fw 190s, it was determined repairs on Hot Stuff would take several days. While the work was to be done on the Liberator, Col. Timberlake and Major Cool agreed with Shannon to give Hot Stuff's crew three-day passes to go to London; their first opportunity to visit the big city. They donned their "best" uniforms and polished their shoes. The enlisted men were inspected and then briefed. They were to be on their best behavior while in London as they were considered "guests" in an Allied country. They were trucked along with other crews on pass to Huntington Station where they boarded a train. As was normal for late November in England, the weather was gloomy, and all the men carried raincoats along with overnight bags. As the train pulled away, Jeffers waved to Mr. Walker the stationmaster on duty; the husband of the woman who did his laundry smiled and waved back.

During the train ride, Hot Stuff's crew observed the changing countryside in the intermittent rain. It gradually evolved from farms and green fields dotted with sheep to small villages and finally to the cluttered buildings of the big city. After the three-hour trip with numerous stops along the way, the train pulled into a nondescript crowded station in central London. The officers detrained and went their separate ways not to rejoin the enlisted men until the end of the pass period.

Like other cohesive B-24 enlisted crews, McQueen, Eisel, Farley, Rondeau, Craighead, and Jeffers stuck together while in London.

Their first impression of the city was the destruction brought about during the *Blitz*, the name the Brits gave the nightly attacks by German bombers. During the period September 7, 1940, and May 21, 1941, the Luftwaffe had attacked London seventy-one times. More than one million homes had been destroyed or damaged, leaving three hundred seventy-five thousand homeless and nearly twenty thousand killed. All along the Thames River, most of the buildings had been leveled. Famous landmarks that suffered damage included Buckingham Palace, Westminster Abbey, and the Chamber of the House of Commons. Although St. Paul's Cathedral was surrounded by bombed-out buildings it somehow escaped damage. Government buildings were heavily sandbagged, and many windows were X-taped to prevent shattering during sporadic air raids that continued during what Londoners called the "lull."

Everywhere they went, the streets were packed with Londoners intermixed with uniforms from nearly two dozen Allied nations; among them, the six American airmen identified Australians, New Zealanders, Poles, French, Canadians, Indians, and Belgians by their shoulder patches. During midday, parks were filled with office and factory workers picnicking on lawns. In the parks, children who had not been among the thousands evacuated to the countryside to be kept out of harm's way during the *Blitz* enjoyed games and amusement rides. Sections of city parks were set aside for vegetable gardening to support meager food supplies. Ration coupons were required for purchases of food, clothing, and many other necessities. In spite of the wartime conditions, the city's population maintained an air of cheerfulness.

While in London Hot Stuff's enlisted men stayed at the Regent Palace, a very upscale hotel located on a triangular site on the north side of Piccadilly Circus. Upon entering the hotel, the airmen walked into a circular lounge lined with marble under an elaborate ceiling that formed a shallow circular dome. The airmen stared wide-eyed at the opulent surroundings as they walked through the vestibule to the reception desk.

The relatively high pay the American military received in comparison to their British counterparts permitted them to stay at such affluent accommodations while on pass. Like many American soldiers, Hot Stuff's enlisted men toured the city. Most sites such Westminster Abbey, Parliament Building, and Madam Trousseau's Wax Museum were within easy walking distance from the hotel. They ate at pubs and fraternized with local unattached women. Due to the scarcity of meat, all meals were bland and inexpensive, costing between two and six pence each.

Because London was under such severe nightly blackout conditions, Hot Stuff's crewmen found it somewhat difficult to get around the foggy, rain-shrouded streets in the dark. When darkness fell over the city, the disciplined Londoners complied with strict blackout regulations. The streets were dark as street lights were not illuminated. Windows and doorways of buildings and homes were covered with heavy dark drapery. Air raid wardens patrolled the streets to ensure compliance with regulations that included a curfew imposed for many during hours of darkness. The few vehicles that roamed the streets at night had blacked-out headlights that could not be seen from the air, but emitted a low beam on the pavement sufficient for drivers to see ahead. Needless to say, driving and walking along the darkened thoroughfares were precarious.

On their last night in London, Hot Stuff's six young enlisted men went in search of a friendly pub. Eisel was known to be the real drinker in the crew.

"George, we can't see shit in all this heavy fog," Rondeau said. "How about leading us with your nose to a friendly pub. We all need something to eat and drink to celebrate our last night in London."

The tail gunner retorted, "Just so happens I can smell a pub from here. Follow me!"

At the stairs leading to an underground establishment, Eisel spread the heavy blackout drapes. Once inside, they were greeted with heavy smoke-laden air, the sour odor of spilled ale, loud music from a small band, and boisterous conversation. The pub was packed to overflowing with patrons. Hot Stuff's crewmen had to elbow their way through the throng to get to the bar where they shouted their orders for pints of warm ale.

"Now if we could find a table and a few lasses in this mob," McQueen shouted over the din.

"Let me take a look around," Eisel said as he plowed through the crowed room.

McQueen motioned for the bar keep. The ruddy-faced balding rotund man in shirt sleeves leaned forward and cupped a hand over his ear in order to hear what the Yank had to say.

"This is our last night in London, and we want six pints of your best ale," the army sergeant shouted.

A minute later, the man behind the bar set six tankards in front of McQueen. "That'll be twelve pence, Yank."

As McQueen counted out the British currency, he asked the man about his limp.

"Oh that. It was at Flanders back in '14 when I lost my left leg just below the knee. A Hun artillery shell exploded near our trench. I was one of the lucky ones."

McQueen and the other four sergeants at the bar lifted their mugs. "Here's to the luck of the draw, ah… What's your name?" the waist gunner asked.

"Me name's Clive."

McQueen reached across the bar and took Clive's hand and shook it. "My name's Paul. Glad to meet ya." The waist gunner introduced his fellow airmen. "How about our buying you a pint, Clive?"

"Mighty considerate of you, Chaps. I think I will draw myself a pint."

Rondeau looked around and saw several British soldiers and airmen. He motioned for them to come to the bar. "How about you fellows joining us for a drink? It's on us!"

Four British servicemen sidled up and shook hands with the Americans. One exclaimed, "Be glad to join you *Yanks* from across the pond."

It wasn't but a few minutes later, and Eisel, with drink in hand, returned to the bar with a female companion in tow. "Follow us, we've got a table in back, and five ladies are anxiously awaiting your arrival."

One of the British servicemen hoisted his pint of ale in a salute to the Americans, "Cheerio, Yanks!" He turned to his fellow soldier. "As they say, these American chaps are overpaid, oversexed, and OVER HERE!"

Air raid sirens wailed as the Hot Stuff crewmen were introduced to the women at the table. For about a minute, the band stopped playing, and the noise level dropped to a murmur as antiaircraft guns fired at the approaching German bombers. Although there had been what was known as a "lull" in the intensity of the bombing of London by the Luftwaffe after May of 1941, the Germans still persisted in conducting sporadic raids on the city. Exploding bombs slowly approached their location. A detonation nearby shook the building. Dust fell from the ancient ceiling and the lights flickered, but remained lit. McQueen noticed a sign on the pub wall and grinned at the droll British humor.

During an air raid, lights will be extinguished.
No one will be permitted to enter or leave.

In event of a direct hit, this pub will close immediately.

"Hope like hell this place won't have to close," the waist gunner nervously chuckled.

No sooner had the words left his mouth the band struck up "God Save the King" and conversation rose to its previous ear-splitting level. All activity resumed as the proprietor ignored the warning on the sign on the wall and kept the lights burning. The band, consisting of mostly middle-age men, continued to play throughout the air raid.

Moments later, the explosions ceased, antiaircraft guns went silent, and all clear sirens blared. No one inside the pub seemed to notice.

Four hours later, Hot Stuff's sergeants held each other up as they staggered in the dark to the Regent Palace Hotel for a few hours of sleep before returning to the train station.

Daylight streamed through the rain-smeared hotel windows. "Stop that damned pounding, Ken," McQueen groused.

Jeffers moaned. "It's not me," he uttered to his hotel mate. "It's the goddamned door." He shouted, "Go away, no one's here."

A voice from behind the door announced, "Time for you Yanks to check out. It's after noon."

After a few minutes of silence, McQueen's eyes snapped open. He glanced at his watch. "Goddamn! Get it together, Ken, we've got less than an hour to catch our train back to Huntington Station."

The end of the three-day pass period had arrived and Hot Stuff's sergeants gathered at the station platform where they had arrived. All of them looked hung-over and bleary-eyed as they boarded the train for the return trip to Huntington Station.

As he took a seat in the compartment, McQueen glanced out the window and nudged Farley. "Would you look at that?" They saw Lentz, Gott, and Jacobson smiling a few feet away from Shannon who was ardently saying farewell to a gorgeous redhead.

"Whatever Shannon's got, I sure as hell want some," McQueen sighed. "That dame is really keen. Even the other officers look jealous."

The shrill locomotive whistle pierced the fog-bound station. Lentz tapped Shannon on the shoulder. "Shine, the train is starting to leave."

Lentz, Gott, and Jacobson jumped on the moving train.

Shine gave his female friend one last kiss and ran for Lentz's outstretched arm. The copilot's strong right arm lifted Shannon off the platform and into the now accelerating train.

Jacobson slammed the exterior compartment door closed and exhaled. He looked at Lentz. "That was too damn close. This is the last train out for today. Shine would have been in deep shit if he was late reporting in."

Lentz patted the Hot Stuff's command pilot on the shoulder. "You didn't introduce us. She's a real Sheba. What's her name?"

Shannon stared out the window as the train accelerated out of the station. "Her name's Helen. And by the way, her sister's Fifth Avenue, a real class act. You'd like her."

During the three-hour return trip, they all slept. The trainmaster awakened them only minutes before they reached Huntington Station. As they detrained, they donned their raincoats to ward off the chilly drizzle and walked to the trucks that were waiting to take them back to Alconbury.

Rondeau buttoned the collar of his raincoat and looked up at the dark gray sky before he climbed into the rear of the truck. "This is a hell of a way to end our three-day pass."

CHAPTER 17

Flying South

It was December 6, 1942, and Hot Stuff had not flown a mission since its crew had returned from London. Repairs had been made to the Liberator, and the crew was itching to get back into action. Since the weather at Alconbury had disintegrated into day after day of rain, cold, and fog, the 93rd had been grounded. The ever-present mud made life all the more miserable for all the flight crews. McQueen and his fellow enlisted crewmembers, with nothing to do sat in their new Nissen hut played cards, wrote letters, and griped about the inactivity and long hours of boredom.

"Sure miss that last night we had in London," Craighead moaned as he adjusted his poker hand.

"How do you spell *miserable*?" Jeffers asked.

Eisel took his eyes off his poker hand and looked at the quiet radio operator scribbling away on a pad of paper. "Who the hell you writing to this time, Ken? You must be running out of relatives and friends to write to by now."

"Just want to keep the folks at home aware of the major sacrifices we're making over here."

"Keep up the good writing," the tail gunner said. "We want everyone back home to know how miserable and unappreciated we are. And don't forget to tell them how shitty the weather is. And by the way, *miserable* is spelled m-i-s-e-r-a-b-l-e."

"Thanks, and don't worry, I've already told them how crappy our life is again and again in my letters," Jeffers said.

"Eisel, get back to the game, goddamn it," McQueen demanded. "I want to win back all that money you took from me last night."

The officers spent their days in their mess playing pool and cards as well as bellying up to the bar. The miserable weather was so depressing that the crews were becoming lethargic.

Lentz glanced out the window of the officers' mess. "Jesus Christ, will it ever stop raining in this desolate country?" He looked at the Betty Grable calendar on the wall. "Tomorrow is the first anniversary of when the Japs attacked Pearl Harbor. Besides going to London for three days, all we've done is sat on our asses for the past two weeks."

Suddenly, the boredom was shattered by the ringing of the telephone in the large Nissen hut. One of the group's staff officers picked up the receiver and handed it to Col. Timberlake. The group commander listened for a moment and responded with "Yes, sir!" He spoke to his operations officer, and within seconds, he and his staff hurriedly left the building.

"Looks like something big is in the wind," Shine commented. "I never saw those staff guys move so fast. Maybe we're going to get back into the war after all, John."

Lentz glanced out the window once again. "Think you're right, Shine. Can you believe it? The weather is starting to clear." He walked over to the calendar and slapped Betty Grable's butt for good luck as he had done prior to all Hot Stuff's missions.

After a quarter of an hour, the phone erupted again. The mess NCO shouted out, "Colonel Timberlake wants all crews of the 328th, 330th, and 409th squadrons to assemble in the briefing room immediately."

BEFORE THE BELLE

"Finally some action," Jacobson extolled as he grabbed his crushed service cap. He gulped down the last of his beer and tore the Betty Grable calendar off the wall. "Come on, babe, we're on our way to glory."

When the crews of the three squadrons were seated, Col. Timberlake mounted the briefing stage. "We're to rapidly deploy from Alconbury to a yet to be determined location. The duration of our mission is expected to be ten days. We're going to leave the ground crews behind. Only a few maintenance and administrative specialists will accompany us. You're to take only the clothes on your back, a change of underwear and socks, and personal items."

Timberlake pointed to a location on the large map of England. "We're to start immediate takeoffs for Exeter in Land's End on the southwest tip of England. There we'll refuel and get a detailed briefing on the mission." He then turned the hastily assembled meeting over to Major Compton who provided the necessary details for their short flight.

Later that day, twenty-four Liberators of the 93rd landed at Exeter for refueling. While there, the crews received a final and more detailed briefing. The operations officer pointed at the huge map in the briefing room. It displayed the route of their mission. They were to fly south, low over the Bay of Biscay, follow the coast of France in order to avoid encounters with enemy aircraft, and pass over the Straits of Gibraltar. Their destination was Tafaroui, an old French navy aerodrome near Oran, Algeria.

Gott and the other navigators were issued British maps based on the metric scale. Because the altitudes were in meters instead of feet, this was to later prove fatal for one of the flight crews.

With their final destination being Algeria, the crews expected to find wine, exotic food, and harem girls to greet them when they landed.

As Hot Stuff's crew filed out of the briefing room, McQueen slapped Eisel on the back. "I can't wait to get my hands on one of those beautiful Algerian belly dancers."

"You'd better hope those belly dancers don't have crazy boyfriends with big curved swords." Eisel quipped. He looked down at McQueen's groin. "I've heard that they'll cut off your body parts if they get real mad."

"Ouch," Jeffers said as he grabbed his crotch.

All the crews were fed and bedded down in Nissen huts for the night.

Before daybreak, the crews of the three squadrons were rousted from their sleep. After a hot breakfast, the twenty-four Liberators took off and headed south for North Africa; it was December 7, the anniversary of the Japanese attack on Pearl Harbor.

Timberlake, in the lead serial of the first squadron to takeoff, led the B-24s south along the French coast and then over Portugal. As the aircrews had been briefed, they were careful to avoid any incursion over Spanish territory in order to avoid antiaircraft guns and fighters from that Fascist country. When the southern coast of Portugal came into view, the formation reached the waypoint where they turned east, flying over British-controlled Gibraltar and parallel to the North African Mediterranean Coast. At the appropriate waypoint Timberlake's flight of eight Liberators turned south and landed at Tafaroui aerodrome near Oran, Algeria, just before dark.

The 330th was the last squadron to takeoff, and Hot Stuff was among the last to have "wheels up."

During the flight, Shannon and Lentz discussed why they were being rushed to North Africa.

"Shine, do you think the Allied landings in *Operation Torch* have turned to shit?" Lentz asked. "Could that be why we were ordered to North Africa on short notice? To bolster our army's ground effort?"

"John, you know as much as I do. I have to think our guys are doing okay, but they need our support. Maybe we're going to help finish off Rommel. Who knows?"

BEFORE THE BELLE

Hot Stuff's squadron trailed the other two. As their formation turned after overflying Portugal, they could see Gibraltar in the distance. As the aircraft began to cross over the British territory at fourteen thousand feet, they began to encounter heavy flak.

"Christ, I thought the Brits were on our side," Lentz shouted. "Can't they tell the difference between an American or Axis plane?"

Shannon gripped the controls as Hot Stuff bounced and slipped sideways through the puffs of black smoke and shock waves. "Either they didn't know we were coming or those are the goddamned Spanish firing at us."

"I didn't know flak could get this bad," Gott said as his gloved hands gripped the small navigator table.

Eisel shouted into the intercom, "This is worse than that ballbuster roller coaster at the Ohio state fair. Glad my stomach's empty."

McQueen had just swallowed a stone hard chunk of D ration. His stomach rebelled, and he threw up on Farley.

"Aw, shit, Paul, not again. Why didn't you upchuck in the bucket I brought?" The smell began to make him sick as well and he raised the bucket to his chest.

Almost as quickly as it had begun the antiaircraft fire faded away and Hot Stuff's flight path smoothed out. However as dusk emerged the 330th's formation had broken up. The individual Liberators continued on toward their destination.

The arrival of the 93rd BG at Tafaroui was completely unexpected. No arrangements had been made by Allied forces there to accommodate the landing of the B-24s. As darkness closed in, rapidly deteriorating weather began to cover the small mountains that surrounded Tafaroui, and the follow-on crews found it difficult to locate the airfield. The runway had no lights, and with the murky conditions, Timberlake was concerned the incoming aircraft could meet with disaster. He quickly arranged for kerosene pots to be lit along one side of the strip as an aid to landing.

"Where are we, Jimmie?" Shannon asked the navigator after he banked Hot Stuff into a circular flight path.

As Gott looked out the small side window into the cloudy darkness, he pointed down. "The field has got to be right below us, Shine. I'm goddamned sure of it."

Rondeau checked the fuel gauges, tapping them with his gloved finger. "We're going to land very soon whether we want to or not. We're damned close to running on fumes now."

Like other aircraft in the 330th, Hot Stuff circled several times when suddenly, one by one, kerosene-fueled flare pots illuminated one side of the runway. But which side?

"Goddamn, there it is!" McQueen yelped. "Can't wait to meet those beautiful dames in those see-through harem duds."

"This could be tricky, Shine," Lentz commented. "We don't know which side of the runway the lights are on."

"I'm betting the lights are on the left. Here we go." Shannon aligned the Liberator nose with what he hoped was the runway, pushed forward on the controls, and decreased engine speed.

Lentz lowered the landing gear and murmured, "In God we trust."

At that moment, Timberlake's voice crackled over the radio command net. "Land to the right of the lights."

After the nine-hour flight from Exeter, Hot Stuff's wheels touched down, and Lentz exhaled. "Son of a bitch, you're lucky, Shine. I bet we didn't have enough fuel to make another pass over the field."

Hot Stuff and six other aircraft of the 330th were among the last to land just as the weather closed in around Tafaroui. There were no survivors when one of the squadron's Liberators crashed into a nearby mountain. It was believed the altitudes on the British metric map might have been misread by the tired navigator as feet instead of meters.

CHAPTER 18

Tafaroui

The 93rd,, still an Eighth Air Force, asset was now attached to the Twelfth Air Force, which supported *Operation Torch*, the name given to the Allied landings in North Africa. The air field at Tafaroui was located along the Mediterranean near the city of Oran. The field itself was situated on an open plain between east-west ranges of the Atlas Mountains.

The B-24s were in the minority of the Twelfth Air Force as the preponderance of the heavy bombers consisted of B-17 Flying Fortresses. The 93rd was given the mission of attacking the rear elements of Field Marshal Rommel's German Afrika Korps. The Axis forces had to be destroyed in North Africa in order for the Allies to secure a base of operations for attacking Europe from the south.

The tired aircrews of the 93rd BG found themselves billeted in old gray barracks that reminded them of French Foreign Legion movies. The base at one time had been a cadet training station for French naval aviators. It was now a derelict, its buildings crawling with bedbugs and fleas. The flight crews were issued beds with straw mattresses teeming with the vermin.

McQueen stared at the wall above his assigned bed. He motioned to the tail gunner. "George, bring that kerosene lamp over here."

In the flickering light, McQueen leaned closer to the wall and inspected his bed. "Jesus Christ, the wall and the mattress are moving. There's no way I'm laying down with all those bugs. As dirty as it is, I'm sleeping on the floor tonight."

After a near sleepless night, Hot Stuff's gunners, radioman, and flight engineer decided to bed down inside their aircraft for the duration of their stay at Tafaroui.

There was no sunshine. Once again, foul weather greeted the 93rd as the North African region was saturated with rain, which quickly turned the dry soil into mud. The runways were not suitable for the heavy four-engine bombers. There were no paved parking aprons for the aircraft and no maintenance facilities. When the heavy rains set in, the crews slept under their Liberators. It seemed every man had developed a cold. The miserable conditions dragged on for three days.

"I thought we had left the shitty weather in England," McQueen groused. "I can't believe things could get any worse."

Farley responded, "Give it time, Paul. I'm sure the army's got its best men trying to locate a worse shit hole for us to fall into."

Rondeau walked up to the other enlisted crewmen. "Here's a little news that will make your day complete."

"What do you mean?" Farley asked.

"We're not going to get paid until we get back to England," the flight engineer replied.

"Aw shit," Craighead moaned.

"Don't worry about it," Rondeau said, "we're only going to be here for about ten days. That means we should be back by payday at the end of the month. Besides, everything we need is free for us like smokes and chow. Just in case, hold onto whatever lettuce you have left from last payday."

CHAPTER 19

December 13, 1942 Eleventh Combat Mission: Bizerte

Four days after arriving at Tafaroui, Timberlake received orders for his group to conduct a bombing raid on Bizerte. On December 12, the skies cleared; however, the ground was saturated with rainwater, which caused ever deepening mud. Col. Timberlake advised Twelfth Air Force that it was dangerous to take off, but he was nevertheless ordered to conduct his assigned mission.

With minimal ground support, each crew had to load bombs, fuel the aircraft, and arm the machineguns.

Hot Stuff's six enlisted crewmen formed a human chain, passing five-gallon cans of aviation fuel from the back of a two-and-a-half–ton truck up onto the wing. At the end of the chain, Rondeau repeatedly poured the precious gasoline into the embedded wing tanks.

As he passed an empty gas can back to McQueen, Rondeau looked at the growing pile of empty containers, "You know, Paul, if the army ever wants us to build a goddamned pyramid in the desert, we'll know how."

"Hot Stuff's got to be the thirstiest plane in the squadron," Jeffers said. "At the rate, I'm going my arms will extend to my knees and this war will be over."

"I know we're going to need new uniforms with longer sleeves," McQueen said as he looked at his bare arms exposed through the unbuttoned cuffs of his khaki shirt. "I know my arms are getting longer."

"Well, one thing, at least we've got the bomb bay loaded with five hundred pounders," Farley said. "I'm glad these sorry bastards left wagons to cart the bombs and hoist them up into the plane. Can you imagine us carrying those heavy bastards?"

"Yeah," Rondeau said. "Let's be thankful for the little things in life."

Following the mission briefing, the gunners loaded the ammo boxes with belts of .50 caliber ammunition. "Jesus, this ammo's heavy," McQueen remarked.

"Look at it this way, Paul," Eisel retorted. "At least we won't be caught reloading those goddamned thirty-six-round drums while those Nazi bastards are shooting at us."

"Now I can give one of those Heinies *the whole nine yards*," Farley boasted.

"What the hell do you mean by *the whole nine yards*, George?" McQueen asked as he loaded a belt into his .50 and pulled back on the receiver.

"Well, it's what I hear fighter pilots say when they use up all their ammo going after a target," the waist gunner responded. "That's the length of the .50 caliber ammo belt loaded on their planes."

Minutes later, the group's twenty-three Liberators, engines running, lined up on the muddy field and waited for the signal to take-off. They were to depart in thirty-second intervals.

While attempting to taxi onto the runway, one of the Liberators dove knee-deep in the mud and collapsed its nose wheel. The Liberator's frame was severely damaged. With no decent maintenance equipment available, the B-24 named Geronimo never flew again. Not wanting to lose any more aircraft to runway mishaps, Timberlake convinced Twelfth Air Force headquarters that the mission for that day should be cancelled.

On December 13, the 93rd found itself back in the war. The crew of Hot Stuff, along with the remaining other twenty-one B-24s, were to fly a mission against the docks and harbor at Bizerte, the northern most African city on the Mediterranean.

Eisel was temporarily assigned as the tail gunner on the Liberator named Ambrose, piloted by Shine's best friend, Lt. John (Packy) Roche. Ambrose's usual tail gunner was medically incapable of performing his duties. The tail gunner from the crippled Geronimo sat in Hot Stuff's tail.

As Hot Stuff gained bombing altitude and leveled off for its position in formation, Shannon spoke over the intercom. "Okay, guys, we're on way. Let's make it good. Gunners, stay alert for enemy aircraft."

In the warmer high altitudes of North Africa, the gunners found they could get away with wearing only their leather flight jackets over coveralls. "Glad we don't have to wear those bulky sheep-lined high-altitude suits," Farley said as he flapped his arms in the air. "So much easier to move around."

"Now if only we could have a couple of cold beers while we're cruising the Mediterranean," McQueen quipped as he looked out the open window at the blue water below.

Three hours later, the target area loomed ahead. The twenty-two Liberators maintained their layered formation as they approached the harbor area. The lead B-24 was to drop its bombs first, and the bombardiers of following Liberators would direct their bombs onto the detonations on the ground.

Shannon and two of his fellow squadron pilots, Kunze and Roche, known as the "Terrible Three" decided to fly lower than the other Liberators in the flight to make a more precise bombing run over the target. As soon as they approached the lower altitude, the three B-24s began receiving very heavy ground fire from the air defenses surrounding the Axis-controlled port. Midair explosions and flak encompassed the moving air space occupied by the Terrible Three's bombers. The three Liberators flew into what seemed like a black cloud filled with red flashes.

Roche's B-24, named Ambrose, was hit in the fuel line but continued the bomb run. Following the raid, Roche managed to keep his aircraft in formation as far as Bone, Algeria. There the engines went dead when the fuel tanks ran dry. He made a dead stick landing previously thought impossible with a heavy bomber. The landing would have been successful had there not been a gully halfway down the field. The nose wheel caught in the ditch and broke Ambrose's back killing three crewmen. Eisel, who had been the tail gunner on loan from Hot Stuff, survived the crash.

Local Algerians descended upon the crash site, seeking to steal anything of value from the damaged aircraft and the dead crewmen. Roche pulled his .45-caliber pistol and maintained guard over the plane and the deceased crewmen throughout the night. The distress signal from Ambrose just before it crash-landed alerted friendly forces who arrived on the scene the next morning and the Algerians faded into the desert.

Kunze's aircraft, Big Dealer, completed the bomb run as well, but was badly shot up. In spite of the damage, Big Dealer successfully returned to Tafaroui with the remaining Liberators.

When not at his radio, Jeffers often sat between Shannon and Lentz. He dreaded the hair-raising, loud whooshing sound that accompanied the shock waves from the aerial detonations, which shook and bounced Hot Stuff. As their aircraft flew into the black clouds and red flashes of antiaircraft fire, metal fragments from a nearby exploding projectile penetrated the starboard side outboard engine.

Shannon quickly "feathered" the engine by cutting its fuel supply in order to keep it from catching fire. The two pilots struggled to keep the aircraft in formation on the three remaining engines.

Hot Stuff's erratic movements made Jacobson's job all the more difficult. He focused the bomb sight. "I've got the target," he said.

"She's all yours, Jake," the former fighter pilot spoke over the intercom. His hands released control of the Liberator to the bombardier.

Despite the bouncing and the loss of one engine, Jacobson managed to control the aircraft with the bombsight and focus on the target area. He opened the bomb bay doors, and as the crosshairs aligned with the target, he released the bomb load. "Bombs away!"

The release of the six thousand–pound load caused Hot Stuff to rapidly rise. Shannon immediately took control of the aircraft in order to avoid a mid-air collision with other Liberators.

"Let's get the hell out of here," he said as the formation turned out over the Mediterranean and began its flight back to Tafaroui. Rondeau examined the fuel gauges and saw gasoline was leaking from the line leading to the damaged engine. The flight engineer quickly shut it down and reported his action to Shannon. Limping on three engines, Hot Stuff fell out of formation.

"We're all alone now," Shannon spoke over the intercom. "Keep a sharp eye out for enemy aircraft."

Beads of sweat broke out on McQueen's forehead. "As much as I hate that Tafaroui shit hole, I'd rather live there than die up here." He nervously pulled back on the .50's bolt several times, ejecting unspent cartridges. "Jesus, I can't wait to get back and have a cigarette."

He and the other gunners scanned the skies for enemy vultures looking to take advantage of a wounded bird. Hot Stuff's crew barely spoke over the intercom on their return to base. Fortunately, no enemy aircraft were sighted. Hot Stuff approached Tafaroui an hour after the other B-24s.

Because of Shannon's quick fighter pilot instinct and handling of the controls, Hot Stuff landed safely on three engines. None of the crew was injured during the mission, although fading sunlight beamed through multiple holes in the fuselage.

Instinctively, upon exiting the aircraft, each smoker pulled out a pack of cigarettes and lit up. McQueen looked at his Chesterfield. "God, this tastes so good."

"Give me one of those!" Rondeau demanded.

The waist gunner watched as the flight engineer took a cigarette from the pack, lit up, and inhaled deeply. "When in hell did you start smoking?" McQueen challenged.

"Right after that goddamned mission!" Rondeau coughed as he exhaled a cloud of smoke. "Jesus, this tastes great."

"We were really lucky to get back to base without Nazi fighters coming at us," McQueen commented.

"It's flying through that damned flak that scares the shit out of me," Jeffers said as his shaking hand held a match to the Lucky Strike dangling from his quivering lips. "We can't take evasive action or defend ourselves against it. We have to fly right through that hell to the target, and it gives me the heebie jeebies."

Eisel exhaled a cloud of smoke. "That's why I like being on the .50s. Unlike flak, Jerry fighters are a personal thing with me. I can shoot back at them. It's just between me and the Nazi. Sort of like a duel in the Old West."

That night, the crews of Hot Stuff and Big Dealer assisted the few available maintenance personnel in cannibalizing the never to fly again Geronimo still lodged knee deep in mud along the run-

BEFORE THE BELLE

way. As they removed engine parts and sheet metal from the crippled Liberator, the crews of the remaining flyable nineteen B-24s of the 93rd BG prepared to take off to attack Bizerte once again the next morning. Wanting to get back in the action, the crews of Hot Stuff and Big Dealer worked feverishly with maintenance personnel to make the necessary repairs.

The morning of December 14, the crew of Hot Stuff watched as the Liberators took off to attack Bizerte once again. Six hours later all nineteen of the B-24s returned safely to the base.

Shannon and his crew attended the debriefing where they learned the group had made several successful bombing runs on docks and railroad yards. In addition to moderate antiaircraft fire, the crews encountered Fw 190 and Me 109 fighters for the first time in North Africa. The close formation of the B-24s Col. Timberlake had advocated proved its worth as the group successfully defended itself and all aircraft returned safely with no personnel injuries.

As the enlisted members of Hot Stuff left the briefing room, Rondeau pointed into the air with both hands. "I would have loved to have given those Heinies a taste of my twin .50s. Bet I could have sent a couple of those Nazis to hell."

McQueen slapped Rondeau on the back. "How about a little wager on who downs the next Jerry?"

Farley reached into his pocket and pulled out several British Pounds. "I'll bet you both a pound I get the next bastard," he ventured.

"I'll take a piece of that action," Craighead said. "How about all of us pooling a pound each and the first one to knockoff the next Jerry gets the pot."

"When Eisel gets back, he'll want in on this," Rondeau said.

"The more the merrier," McQueen quipped.

Filled with bravado, Hot Stuff's gunners reached into their pockets and flashed the cash.

"Wait a minute," McQueen blurted, "who's going to hold the pot? I sure as hell can't trust any of you guys with it."

After a few moments of silence, Craighead piped up, "How about giving it to Jacobson?"

After a short discussion, the gunners all agreed and went in search of Hot Stuff's bombardier.

Later as they bedded down in Hot Stuff for a few hours' sleep, Rondeau quickly sat up and remarked, "Wait a minute! Jacobson's the nose gunner. What if he gets the first kill?"

"Aw, shit," McQueen said, "you're right."

After a few moments of silence, Farley piped up, "Tell you what, we just tell Jacobson the money's strictly for full-time gunners and not part-time bombardiers, unless he wants to kick in another pound himself."

"Good idea, George," McQueen yawned. "We'll tell him first thing in the morning. Now let's get some shut-eye. We've got to finish up repairing the engine tomorrow."

CHAPTER 20

New Engine

At a hasty briefing the next morning, the aircrews received word the group would once again be moving. This time, some 1,400 miles further east to a place called Gambut Main in Libya. The 93rd would fly to their new base under the cover of darkness in order to conceal their movement from the enemy.

Farley leaned over and murmured into McQueen's ear. "I got to give the army credit. It only took them a couple of days to locate a worse shithole than Tafaroui. It's got to be so bad they want us to arrive in the dead of night so we can't see how shitty it is."

"Aw, George, look at the bright side," McQueen said. "I just know those harem girls will be waiting for us there."

"Sure," Craighead said. "And I know a bridge in Brooklyn that I'd like to sell you."

After the briefing, Shannon and Hot Stuff's other officers sat around a scarred wooden table, its surface covered within numerable cigarette burns. They had just finished their breakfast of cold C and K rations and the table was littered with half-filled tin cans and cardboard boxes. Shine puffed on a Lucky Strike from a C ration box.

"Let's hope the maintenance guys can get that engine repaired today," Shine said. "I sure as hell hate to be left behind when the group takes off tonight."

"Yeah," Gott agreed. "But I wonder how Ambrose's crew is doing out in the desert? Scuttlebutt says they crashed trying to make a dead stick landing."

Lentz looked at Shannon. "That's damned near impossible with a heavy bomber. I sure as hell hope Eisel is okay and can join us before we move."

"Maybe he'll be able to join us later on," Shine said.

Lentz blew a smoke ring into the dusty confines of the old French officer's barracks. "We're lucky to have Geronimo for cannibalization. I overheard Major Compton say as long as we're in North Africa, we'll have to get along without replacement B-24s, new crewmen, and even spare parts. Not good."

Just then, Jacobson broke into hysterical laughter. "Jake, what the hell is so funny?" Gott asked.

The bombardier then related how the gunners had wagered a pound each, and the total would go to the first one to shoot down the next Nazi fighter. "And they gave the money to me to hold for the winner. I even coughed up a pound to be in the running. I know I'll never win it. When I was in gunnery school, I couldn't hit the broadside of a barn with the .50."

Just before noon, the flight engineer wiped the oil off his hands and sat in Hot Stuff's pilot seat. He shouted out the open side widow. "Clear!"

Shannon, along with the rest of the crew and squadron maintenance personnel, stood back and watched as Rondeau fired up the three good engines to ensure sufficient electrical power would be available to turn over the repaired engine. After the three engines were running, the blades of the repaired starboard engine slowly began to rotate. The engine coughed black smoke and the blades slowed to a standstill.

"Come on, you bitch," Rondeau shouted as he started the engine once more. Again, the propeller slowly rotated, but the engine failed to start.

Shannon shook his head and slapped his crushed service cap against his leg. A voice in his head screamed: *Come on, Hot Stuff, don't let us down now. We barely even got into the war. It can't end like this.*

The crew shouted encouragement. McQueen cupped his hands near his face and yelled at Rondeau. "Give it another go, Grant! How in the hell am I going to win that bet on getting the next Nazi fighter if Hot Stuff refuses to get off the ground.?"

Rondeau looked down at his crewmates and nodded. He grimaced and patted the instrument panel as he tried to start the repaired engine once more. "Come on, come on."

The blades slowly turned, and the engine again belched black smoke heavily laden with gasoline fumes. Miraculously Hot Stuff came to life, the repaired engine roaring. The crew jumped up and down, slapped each other on the back with their oily hands, and shouted words of elation.

"Son of a bitch, like my Mama always said, 'Third time's the charm'," Gott laughed as he watched the repaired engine continue to run smoothly.

Lentz shouted as he patted Shannon on the shoulder. "Goddamn it, Shine, we're back in the war!"

Shannon stood speechless as he stared at the running engine, and the aluminum patches on their aircraft. His thoughts were more subdued than the rest of the crew. *We're wounded, baby, but we can still deliver a punch. Thanks, Geronimo, for sacrificing your chance at glory for ours.*

CHAPTER 21

Gambut Main

Darkness was setting in on December 15 as the crews of the 93rd made last-minute checks before starting their engines. The plan was for the 93rd BG to take advantage of the current fair weather and fly out of the mountainous area of Algeria in a bright moonlit night. The group was to take off in serials of three planes each in order to provide mutual protection from German night fighters while passing over enemy territory. Ground and administration personnel as well as Geronimo's crewmen were spread among the twenty-one aircraft.

Just as Hot Stuff began to roll, the headlights of a speeding truck could be seen approaching the airstrip, its horn blaring. Out jumped the surviving crewmen from the now derelict Ambrose. They climbed aboard the B-24s waiting to take off.

Eisel limped up to Hot Stuff. At the portside of the aircraft, he shouted over the roar of the idling engines at Shannon, his left thumb extended in hitchhiker fashion. "Going my way, Lieutenant?"

"Always room for one more, Eisel." Shine smiled as he yelled through the open cockpit window. "Climb aboard!"

As Eisel made his way through the rear of the aircraft, his crewmates slapped him on the back, and shook his bandaged hand.

"You're one lucky bastard to have survived that crash," McQueen declared. "Glad to have you back with us!"

After a seven-hour flight, they reached their new base at Gambut Main in the Libyan Desert thirty miles southeast of the Mediterranean coastal city of Tobruk. All twenty-one aircraft landed without incident as the landing strip was clearly visible in the bright moonlight. Hot Stuff and its sister aircraft were now only four hundred miles from Rommel's lines. So close, they were within range of enemy aircraft. The group was now the most forward Allied heavy bomber unit in North Africa.

Shannon decided the crew should sleep on the aircraft until daylight. An hour later, the sun rose on December 16. Hot Stuff's crew jumped down onto the desert floor. They looked around at their surroundings and sighed. Gambut Main was nothing but wasteland with a steel mesh landing strip and one metal building. Parking for the aircraft was off the runway on the bare desert floor. As far as the eye could see the area around Gambut Main was littered with destroyed enemy and friendly aircraft and vehicles.

"This place looks the like junk yard at the edge of my home town," McQueen commented. "Kinda makes me feel homesick."

"You gotta be shitting me," Farley laughed. "I thought you came from a nice town in upper New York."

"Don't be a wise ass," the waist gunner retorted. "That junkyard was one of my favorite playgrounds when I was a kid."

Hot Stuff's crew found the few antiaircraft positions manned by British troops were the only other signs of civilization. The sandbagged forty millimeter Bofors antiaircraft guns and search light sites were strategically located at various points along the runway.

"Goddamn, George, you were right," Craighead said to the waist gunner. "HQ really went out of their way to find a worse shit hole than Tafaroui." He shielded his eyes and pointed toward one of the British protective positions. "At least there seems to be some

Tommies in the area, but I don't think we'll find any friendly towns nearby like we had in Alconbury."

Farley chuckled as he gazed out into the open desert and slapped McQueen on the back. "When do those harem girls arrive, Paul?"

Upon completion of the move, the group was now attached to the Ninth Air Force. With the arrival of the 93rd BG it had expanded to 1,100 aircraft of all types since the British had whipped Rommel's Afrika Korps at the October battle of El Alamein 120 miles west of Alexandria, Egypt. The Allied aircraft were to oppose the two thousand planes the Axis Powers had based in North Africa.

Shortly after the sun had risen and the heat began to climb dust clouds could be seen approaching from the north. British trucks rolled in from out of nowhere and stopped near where Hot Stuff was parked. Soldiers in khaki shorts, shirts, and flat helmets deposited tents, cots, and blankets onto the sand. The Brits then mounted their trucks, turned around, and disappeared into the desert.

"Can you beat that?" McQueen declaimed. "Not even a goddamned 'hello' or a 'good-bye.' They just drive in, dump this crap and drive off."

Craighead stared at the dust of the retreating trucks. He took a swig of warm stale water from his canteen. "Son of a bitch. When are we ever going to get a shower and a hot meal?"

"Quit your bitching, Joe," Rondeau said, "and let's get busy putting up our tents. We need a place to get out of this goddamned sun and blowing sand."

"At least we have cots and clean blankets," Jeffers said as he examined an army issue blanket. "This is more than we had when we first landed at Alconbury."

"Yeah. And no bugs like we had at Tafaroui, at least not yet." Rondeau remarked as he watched a scorpion scurry across the sand.

BEFORE THE BELLE

"Jesus Christ," the flight engineer shouted as he stomped several times on the desert denizen. "That one was almost big enough to throw a saddle on."

McQueen looked down at the flattened scorpion. "Nice footwork, Grant. Well, at least that's one that won't be cuddling with any of us tonight."

Hot Stuff and the other Liberator crews erected raggedy off-white tents over the sand. There were no mess and bathing facilities. The men had to relieve themselves in the open. The crews were to subsist on C rations, canned spam and beans, along with dehydrated cabbage. They cooked dry food in alkali water drawn from a shallow well that had to have been in the desert since before the Crusades. Potable water at Gamut was taken from a well dug by the Royal Engineers of the British Eighth Army. Due to the low level of water in the well, each man was allowed to fill his canteen once a day. That meager amount of water was to be used for drinking and brushing of teeth. Shaving and bathing were out of the question. Several wells were discovered that had tainted water but were deemed safe for laundry use.

Mission briefings were conducted outdoors with maps spread over blankets on the sand. Rocks held down the map corners to keep them from being disturbed by the occasional gust of wind. Major Compton read notes decrypted from radio messages received from Ninth Air Force and used a branch of a tree as a pointer. It was obvious with the lack of niceties that were available in England everything at Gambut Main was going to be kept extremely informal and primitive.

Gambut had no weather forecasting capabilities. The 93rd relied on coded radio forecasts from headquarters in Alexandria which were usually garbled by the enemy or disrupted by weather. Further, any forecast they received was usually twelve hours old and useless. Sometimes the rain and dust storms lasted several days and deposited dust on food, drinks, clothing and beds, and unfortunately engines and thermostats.

The first such sandstorm they endured lasted three days. The group huddled in their tents, the only shelters they had for protection from the biting grit. Everything was covered with a fine powdery dust—crewmen, aircraft, food, and bedding. The only time they emerged was for the necessities of life; food, water, and visits to the latrine, now nothing more than a slit trench.

Jeffers scraped off a thin layer of grit from his open can of spam. As he chewed the meat, his teeth scraped against the minute sand particles. "One thing for sure, this ain't like Grandma's oatmeal."

Rondeau sipped from his canteen in hopes of washing down the grit-laden mouthful of canned beans. "Reminds me of when my older sister made me take a bite out of one of her mud pies."

"What I wouldn't give for a nice cold glass of beer right now," Eisel lamented.

Before the 93rd had flown to North Africa, specialists were on hand to maintain the bombsights and armorers the weapons. Across the airfield, the bombardiers used the downtime to hold classes on the cleaning and maintenance of the sensitive Norden bombsights. Gunners likewise held sessions on the proper care and cleaning of the .50 machineguns. Cleaning of the .45-caliber pistols was the responsibility of each crewmember.

Lentz sat on his cot in the tent he shared with Hot Stuff's other officers. On a rag-covered stack of C-ration cartons, he carefully laid out the disassembled parts of his .45. "Goddammit, I just cleaned this thing and wiped it dry. Now it's covered with dust again. I sure as hell hope it works when I'd need it."

"They set up a small range at the end of the runway," Gott said. "What do you say we go down there and fire off a couple of magazines?"

"Do you think we can see the targets through this storm?" Lentz asked.

"Hell, I don't know," Jacobson said. "If nothing else, we can check to see if our side arms work properly, even if we don't take them on missions. You going, Shine?"

Shannon took a small swig from his canteen. "I've eaten enough sand just sitting here in this tent. I'll be here when you guys get back."

The three officers, rags covering their faces, trudged through the biting sandstorm toward the small makeshift weapons range. Once there, they shot at empty C-ration cans filled with sand as the strong wind would easily blow the empty tins away.

Having fired only one magazine, Gott wiped grit from his eyes and exclaimed, "Enough of this crap. I'm going back to the tent."

"I'm with you, Jim," Lentz said as he lifted his face covering and spit sand away from the wind.

The three officers trudged back to their tent. "That wasn't very smart," Jacobson remarked. "Shine was right in not joining us."

CHAPTER 22

December 17, 1942 Twelfth Combat Mission: Sfax

By the predawn hours of December 17, the storm had passed and as the men of the 93rd emerged from their sand-swept tents, they were greeted with calm winds, clear skies and a blistering sunrise. Orders had been received from Ninth Air Force to conduct a special night mission to bomb Axis ammunition and petroleum facilities at Sfax, a port city on the central east coast of Tunisia. By depriving Rommel's Afrika Korps of vital supplies, the British Eighth Army could continue its westerly advance across Libya.

Col. Timberlake and his staff officers pondered their precarious situation in North Africa; there were no spare parts, no replacement aircraft, and no replacement crews in the pipeline. To conserve the group's resources something had to be done. The decision was made that no more than twelve of the group's Liberators were to fly missions as long as the 93rd was still in North Africa. Those aircraft left behind would have maintenance and repairs performed on them, and the crews would rest. Those assets would then be available for rotation into follow-on missions.

In preparation for the special mission to Sfax, the crews of the participating twelve B-24s, Hot Stuff among them, cleaned up their aircraft, pulled maintenance on engines and weapons, and loaded bombs. By sunset, the crews and bombers were ready for takeoff.

Sitting in Hot Stuff's darkened flight deck, instruments glowing in the shadowy confines, Shannon waited for the signal flare to start engines. Next to him, Lentz sat staring straight ahead. Rondeau sat behind the copilot monitoring the fuel gauges.

"You know, we're damned lucky to have completed eleven combat missions so far," Lentz pondered.

"And with no combat injuries to our crew," Shine responded. "Could be Hot Stuff must have good luck built into her."

"After that hellish flight back to Tafaroui on three engines, no doubt Lady Luck flies with us," Rondeau added as he checked the illuminated fuel gauges.

At 1900, a red flare shot into the darkened sky. Hot Stuff's engines along with the other eleven aircraft came to life. Ground crewmen lit cans of kerosene along one side of the runway. A second flare announced the time for takeoff by the first B-24. All others followed in thirty second intervals. Shine's aircraft was number nine in line with "wheels up."

As each aircraft took to the skies, the Tommies manning the antiaircraft positions along the runway could be seen in the light of the flaming kerosene runway markers waving their flat helmets in the air. Only the ground personnel could hear the Brits cheering as the B-24s lifted off to attack the Axis supply dump at Sfax. Unknown to the aircrews at that time, the Tommies took count of every Liberator that took off and then compared the number with those that returned. The number of Liberators for this mission was twelve. The Brits habitually began to do this for every mission. If the returning number of Liberators was less than what took off, they would express their condolences to the 93rd's surviving crews.

The eight hundred mile flight from Gambut Main was the 93rd's first combat mission from that location. The dozen Liberators flew over the darkened waters of the Mediterranean in order to avoid enemy aircraft. Sitting in the darkness, Hot Stuff's gunners alternated between napping and scanning the skies for hostile night fighters.

"Jesus Christ, this is so goddamned boring," McQueen mumbled as he gnawed on the stone-hard D ration chocolate bar. "If we had some light we could play poker."

"Thank God we can't do that," Farley declared. "Between you and Eisel, you've taken enough of my hard-earned pay."

In the dim light over his small chart table, Gott alerted the crew. "We're about twenty minutes out."

"Gunners, stay alert," Shannon ordered. He glanced at his watch. It was a few minutes after 2300. The headwinds had been negligible and there should be more than sufficient fuel for the return flight to Gambut Main.

The starlight illuminated the sea below as Jacobson began adjusting the bombsight. "There's sufficient light and I shouldn't have any problem locating the target area."

As the twelve B-24s approached Sfax, they were unchallenged by antiaircraft fire.

"We're there, Jake," Shine said to the bombardier. "You're flying the plane."

"Got it!" Jacobson replied as he took control of the B-24. "I can see the ammo and fuel dumps now."

The bombardier opened the bomb bay doors. He watched the red-orange detonations from the bombs released by the lead aircraft. When the crosshairs of Hot Stuff's bombsight met the target area, his gloved finger flipped the release switch. "Bombs away!"

As Jacobson closed the bomb bay doors, Shannon took control of the Liberator.

The waist gunners peered through the side window openings and watched the detonations of the deadly ordnance. The exploding fuel and ammunition on the ground illuminated the Liberators in a bright orange glow.

As the aircraft turned back toward the sea, Eisel had full view of the bombing results. His voice emanated through Hot Stuff's intercom. "Nice going, Lieutenant. Right in the pickle barrel!"

"That ought to slow down Rommel for a while." Lentz remarked.

"So far we've been lucky," Shannon said. "No flak and no Luftwaffe. Let's hope we have a free ride home."

"I see a bunch of what looks like fighters," Rondeau warned.

"Where are they?" Shine asked.

"They're at nine o'clock high. You can make out the flaming exhaust from their engines."

"I see them," Farley shouted as he pulled back on the bolt of the .50. "Don't know what type of fighters they are, but they're single engine."

The first of the enemy fighters swooped down over the Liberator formation, its cannon blazing. All of the B-24s began answering the challenge and the duel began.

"They're Me 109s," Eisel shouted as he squeezed the triggers of his twin .50s. "You can just make them out in the starlight."

Thumping sounds reverberated throughout Hot Stuff's fuselage as several rounds from the enemy's twenty millimeter cannons penetrated the aluminum skin. The gunners' adrenalin surged as they ignored the irritation and aimed their machine guns at the enemy aircraft's exhausts illuminated in darkened sky. One of the attacking Messerschmitt's flew into McQueen's sights; the waist gunner squeezed the trigger. The fighter's engine burst into flames and the aircraft began a downward spiral.

The sky was illuminated with tracer bullets from both friend and foe. Two more mortally wounded Messerschmitts lit up the midnight blue sky as they plummeted toward the desert floor. Lentz scanned the chaos all around. "As you were saying about a free ride tonight, Shine? Jesus, it looks like we're in the middle of Fourth of July fireworks."

"Guess I spoke too soon, John," Shine smiled. "Nice shooting, McQueen."

Suddenly the sky was calm; the enemy intruders had enough of the withering fire from the B-24s and fled the scene. The Luftwaffe had lost three of their aircraft and most importantly their highly trained pilots. Fortunately, none of the 93rd's Liberators was seriously damaged due to their adhering to Col. Timberlake's insistence on flying in tight formation of three aircraft for mutual protection.

Three and a half hours later, the kerosene-filled cans began to illuminate the side of Gambut Main's steel mesh runway. One by one the Liberators landed. The Tommies counted the number of returning aircraft. When the wheels of the twelfth bomber touched down, a cheer reverberated through the chilly predawn air. All aircraft and their crews had returned safely.

After the post mission briefing, the antiaircraft Tommies greeted the returning American Liberator crewmen with "We knew you'd make it, chums!"

McQueen smiled as he held out his hand to Jacobson. "Looks like I won the pot, Lieutenant."

The other gunners groaned as the bombardier handed over the six pounds to McQueen. Jacobson looked at the other gunners. "Since you were the next gunner to shoot down a Nazi fighter, you won the bet fair and square."

"You lucky son of a bitch," Farley grumbled. "If that bastard had been on my side, I'd be collecting the lettuce now."

"Tell you what!" McQueen said. "Next time we're in a bar, I'll buy you all a round of drinks."

CHAPTER 23

December 21 and 22, 1942 Thirteenth and Fourteenth Combat Missions: Sousse and Tunis

It didn't take long for German intelligence to locate the 93rd's new base of operations. Before the group's next mission, Gambut Main began to receive frequent night-time bombing and strafing by Axis bombers. Each air raid was preceded by a hand-cranked siren warning, which echoed mournfully across the Libyan Desert. All personnel took cover in slit trenches dug adjacent to their tents. The entire base was kept under strict blackout conditions. The only illumination was during air raids when British searchlights sought out aerial targets for their forty millimeter Bofors antiaircraft guns.

Timberlake ordered a widespread parking of the B-24s to lessen chances of being damaged in mass during air raids. A lesson relearned from the Japanese attack on Pearl Harbor a year earlier. By keeping the Liberators parked as far apart as possible, any damage inflicted during the raids would be minimal and quickly corrected before the next mission.

After three nights of nightly harassment by the Luftwaffe, the 93rd's crews were itching to get back at the Jerries. They were not to be disappointed.

Since the raid on Sfax, the Liberator crews had rested, pulled maintenance and necessary repairs, and kept themselves occupied by playing sports such as volleyball. On the morning of December 21, the group received a coded radio message with orders to conduct their first mission over Sousse, another important eastern Tunisian supply port some seventy-five miles north of Sfax. Like the raid on Sfax, the mission was to be conducted at night. They were to attack the harbor's rail yards and docked merchant shipping.

After their briefings, the crews anxiously refueled the B-24s, loaded each plane with twelve five hundred–pound bombs and ammo for the machine guns. By nightfall, the aircraft were ready and waiting for the signal to take off.

Onboard *Hot Stuff*, the crew waited in the dark as the engines warmed up. At 2000, a white flare signaled for the dozen Liberators to line up and begin to takeoff in thirty-second intervals.

Eisel sat on the floor between the waist gunners as Shannon taxied the Liberator into the line of aircraft. "You know what?"

"What?" Craighead yelled over the drone of the engines.

"The past two weeks have been the longest ten days of my life," the tail gunner bemoaned. "I thought we were going to be back in England by now."

"Goddamned, you're right, George," Farley exclaimed. "I wouldn't mind being in Alconbury gulping down a warm ale right about now."

"Well, so much for the higher-ups' shitty planning," McQueen quipped. "Look where we ended up after Tafaroui."

BEFORE THE BELLE

The entire crew laughed over the intercom at McQueen's witty remark.

As the B-24 ahead of them began to roll down the runway, Shannon taxied Hot Stuff to the runway's end. Lentz counted off thirty seconds on his watch. At the precise moment, he said, "Let's roll!"

Shannon pushed the throttles forward, released the brakes, and the heavy bomber slowly picked up speed. As the ground speed began to lift Hot Stuff's wings, he and Lentz pulled back on the controls and the B-24 gradually climbed into the night sky.

The estimated time for the eight hundred–mile flight was just over three hours. Headwinds were forecasted to be calm, and the formation was expected to be over the target area a few minutes before midnight. Antiaircraft fire was anticipated to be moderate, and enemy fighters were not expected to challenge the raid.

After three hours in the air, Gott announced they would be over the target area in twenty minutes. The gunners had been on alert for the past hour, scanning the darkened skies for uninvited guests. So far, intelligence had been correct, and no enemy fighters had been encountered.

"I don't think the Luftwaffe is very smart," McQueen blurted. "They always seem to come for us *after* we bombed the hell out of them. You'd think after all this time they'd come up to meet us *before* we unload on them."

"McQueen, never thought about it that way," Jacobson responded. "Glad you're not on their side."

"I'm too goddamned smart to be one of those goose-stepping bastards, Lieutenant," the waist gunner said.

"Let's get back to what we're getting paid to do," Shannon ordered. "I can see the harbor ahead of us. Everyone get ready."

Jacobson began adjusting the bombsight he had meticulously maintained under the primitive conditions at Gambut Main. He focused the lens. The ships and rail yards became clear in the bright starlight.

At that moment, flak from antiaircraft guns began to fill the sky. Hot Stuff and the other eleven Liberators were surrounded by lethal red-orange bursts. The aircraft bounced and swayed as Shannon struggled to keep the B-24 in close formation.

"Looks like intelligence was a little off," Jeffers remarked as he held on to the small table in front of the radio set. "I thought flak was supposed to be moderate. This shit is really heavy."

"I agree, Ken," Rondeau said as he sat behind the pilots staring through the cockpit's Plexiglas. "It looks like we're flying through hell."

McQueen clung to the machine gun, and the fuselage trying to keep his balance through the extreme turbulence as he stared wide-eyed at the brilliant flashes engulfing the formation. "Hope like hell we don't run into *heavy* flak."

"Cut the chatter, stay alert for enemy aircraft," Shine ordered. "You got the target area yet, Jake?"

"Clear as a bell, Shine," the bombardier responded.

"She's all yours," the command pilot said as he released control of Hot Stuff to the bombardier.

Jacobson took control of the Liberator as the plane shook violently. He opened the bomb bay doors and calmly waited until the quivering crosshairs covered the docks. The gloved hand pressed the release switch, and the five hundred–pound bombs fell away from the aircraft. "Bombs away! Let's get the hell out of here!"

"I've got the controls," Shine shouted. In spite of the shock waves from flak, he kept the plane in its position as the formation of the twelve B-24s slowly turned back toward Gambut Main.

For the next hour, Hot Stuff's gunners nervously scanned the darkened skies for enemy fighters. None rose to meet them.

They relaxed a bit after another half hour, but the memories of the Messerschmitts over Sfax kept them wary.

The horizon to the east was becoming purple when Hot Stuff's wheels touched down on the Gambut Main's kerosene-lit runway. All aircraft returned safely in spite of the heavy flak over Sousse. The British antiaircraft crews cheered each plane as it touched down.

At the debriefing, Col. Timberlake was pleased with the results of the mission. He rated the result of the night attack on Sousse as above "good" and reported same to the Ninth Air Force.

The next day on December 22, Hot Stuff and eleven other Liberators participated in another night mission, this time over Tunis where they attacked the harbor area hitting ships, barracks, rail yards, and docks. They encountered only light flak and no enemy fighters. The dozen B-24s returned to Gambut Main safely.

The next two days, a howling sandstorm descended on the base. The crews again sat huddled in their tents, trying their best to keep the dust and grit from entering. As if by divine intervention, the sandstorm blew itself out, and Christmas Eve evolved into a clear and star-studded night.

Other than the group chaplain conducting outdoor services, Christmas Day observances were, for the most part, nonexistent at the desert base. Not to be without some holiday spirit, Farley and McQueen wandered out into the desert, careful not to tread into areas marked as being laced with mines. There they found the remains of a dead tree of unknown origin. They returned with smiles on their faces and implanted the dried trunk into the sand at the entrance to their tent. Empty C-ration cans were hung from the few remaining branches of the scrawny five foot tree. They stood back and inspected their handiwork. Their fellow tent mates complimented the waist gunners on their Christmas décor.

"Well the OD cans are the closest thing we have to putting green on this thing," McQueen observed. "Now what are we going to celebrate with?"

Craighead announced, "I hear they're grilling some spam over an open fire at the mess tent. The burnt parts might have a different taste. At least it might go better with the cold beans."

With that, the six crewmen plodded the two miles to the end of the runway where the mess tent was located.

CHAPTER 24

December 26, 1942 Fifteenth Combat Mission: Tunis

The day after Christmas Hot Stuff participated in another mission over Tunis; this time, a daylight raid. The mission consisted of attacking the harbor and merchant shipping.

Hot Stuff had been in the air for just over an hour when McQueen looked down at Craighead. "Joe, you've been awfully quiet. What's eating you?"

"Ever since we ate that burnt spam yesterday, I was thinking of my mama in the kitchen peeling potatoes for our Christmas dinner. She'd always ask me to taste the cranberry sauce to see if it was too tart. Then she'd ask me to mix sugar into the serving bowl until the sauce was just right."

Craighead rubbed his eye and turned away from McQueen. "It's been two years since I had Christmas dinner at home."

"Yeah, I can see my whole family gathered around the big dining room table," the waist gunner said. "Everyone would be there: my folks, brothers and sisters, grandparents, uncles, aunts, and cousins. The whole damned family. I can just taste that turkey now.

"After dinner, we'd wash the dishes and settle in the living room. Everyone got one present. We didn't have much money, so a lot of the gifts were handmade."

Farley cleared his throat. "I always got two helpings of dessert after Christmas dinner. My piece of pumpkin pie and since Uncle Fred always fell asleep in the chair before dessert, I ate his too."

"I wonder if I'll ever see Christmas at home again," McQueen wistfully murmured.

Except for the periodic squawking of radio traffic among the bombers, Hot Stuff's crew remained unusually quiet for the next two hours.

The melancholy silence was shattered by Gott. "Shine, we're about thirty minutes out."

"Okay, everybody be on the lookout for enemy fighters. Gunners, test your weapons."

After each gunner fired off a few rounds, five pairs of eyes searched the skies around the formation.

Lentz looked out at the distant harbor. "It looks like we were never there five days ago."

"That was a night raid," Shine uttered. "We never got a good reading on how well we did. This time, we should do much better in daylight. Jake, can you see the target?"

The bombardier leaned forward and gazed through the Plexiglas. "Clear as a bell, Shine," Jacobson responded as he began adjusting his bombsight.

Minutes later, the sky in front of the Liberator formation erupted with red flashes and black smoke. As Hot Stuff entered the treacherous flak-filled sky, the flight deck was filled with the whooshing sound of exploding antiaircraft fire.

BEFORE THE BELLE

In the rear of the aircraft, Farley commented, "That sharp cracking sound reminds me of large firecrackers all going off at once. Almost like the Fourth of July back home."

As Lentz gripped the control wheel to help Shannon steady the violent tremor of the B-24, he commented, "Never could understand why the crew in back doesn't hear the same sounds from the flak as we do."

"Jake, you ready?" Shine asked.

Jacobson opened the bomb bay doors and focused on a cluster of enemy ships. "Got the target, Shine."

"You've got control."

The bombardier adjusted Hot Stuff's flight path until the bombsight crosshairs were overlaid on three ships moored in the harbor twenty thousand feet below. As he had done so many times before, his gloved hand toggled the bomb release switch. "Bombs away!"

With the release of the five one thousand–pound bombs, Hot Stuff slowly rose toward the scattered clouds. Jacobson relinquished control to Shannon.

As the dozen Liberators turned out over the Mediterranean, the flak diminished. No enemy fighters rose up to meet them.

The raid was rated "good" as aerial photos showed the 93rd's Liberators had sunk numerous Axis merchant vessels; however, swifter enemy combat ships escaped damage as they ran for safety in open waters.

Unlike B-17s, the B-24s had the extended range to carry the five one thousand–pound bombs needed to sink enemy shipping in Tunisia. The most dangerous aspect of the long-range missions from Gambut Main to Tunisia's coastal cities was the B-24s being unescorted by fighters for over five hours.

The 93rd's missions were frequent and assigned with little prior warning. Now with all the missions being conducted in daylight, they were timed in such a manner that in one day the B-24s could conduct a mission, return to base, be rearmed, serviced, refueled, and ready for the next day's flight by 2300. In the interest of needing to keep wear and tear on the aircraft and crews to a minimum training was essentially nonexistent.

The dreary post-combat grind was hard on both men and machines. However, the group nonetheless relentlessly persisted. The 93rd was now down to twenty-one bombers, and several were questionable as to combat worthiness. After nearly three weeks in North Africa, there still would be no replacement aircraft, spare parts, or crews. Given this dire situation, the B-24s named Ambrose and Geronimo proved to be fortuitous in that crew chiefs and mechanics flew back and stripped those aircraft for much-needed parts, and they were ready to do the same with any other crippled Liberator they could find.

CHAPTER 25

December 27, 1942 Sixteenth Combat Mission: Sousse

There was no rest for the weary. The next day on December 27, Shannon and his crew were bound for Sousse again, this time in daylight. With eleven other Liberators they were to repeat the December 21 mission with attacks on Sousse port facilities and shipping.

After three and a half hours, Gott announced, "The target area should be dead ahead."

Shine gazed through the Plexiglas. "I see the harbor now. Looks like some smoke still lingering after our last mission. Jake, you see the target?"

"Got it, Shine."

"Looks like the Luftwaffe is late again," McQueen blurted. He leaned forward to get an expansive view of the sky from Hot Stuff's starboard side. "Not a Kraut in sight."

"You and your goddamned mouth full of gobbledygook, Paul," Farley screamed. "The bastards are closing in on us fast from ten o'clock. Do you see them, Grant?" He pulled back on slide chambering a round on his .50.

Rondeau traversed the upper turret to his left and took aim at the yellow-nosed Me 109s bearing down on the formation.

Just then the entire sky surrounding the dozen Liberators erupted into red flashes and smoke from the German antiaircraft guns. Hot Stuff's crew was so engaged in dealing with enemy aircraft and completing their mission that the there was no time to feel fear. The familiar whooshing sounds and Hot Stuff's violent shaking from the deadly aerial explosions all around them, although unnerving became background racket. The ever-present fear patiently waited until the mission was completed.

"Our last visit to Sousse must have really pissed off our hosts," Lentz observed as the enemy fighters swarmed through their own flak. "Those bastards are really gutsy flying through this shit."

"Ready to take over, Jake?" Shannon asked.

"Let me have it," the bombardier replied.

"It's all yours."

Jacobson opened the bomb bay doors. He maintained his composure through Hot Stuff's violent shuttering as he focused on the lead aircraft's bomb delivery. At the precise moment, his gloved hand toggled the switches releasing the five one thousand–pound bombs. "Bombs away! Let's get the hell out of here, Shine."

Shannon as always maintained close formation with the other Liberators. As he banked Hot Stuff toward the Mediterranean, he watched the Me 109 pilots brave the flak in their attempts at shooting down the 93rd's B-24s. To his left two of the enemy fighters blew apart in the maelstrom of the antiaircraft fire from below and the .50s firing from the B-24s.

Once over the open water, the ground fire ceased, but the enemy fighters persisted by chasing after the Liberators. Their tactic was to attack the vulnerable tail and underbelly of the trailing B-24s, Hot Stuff among them.

Eisel's pair of machine guns waited patiently through all of the aerial combat until this moment. This was the first time the approach of the enemy aircraft came within his view. As the first yellow-nosed enemy fighter appeared within his sight, he held his fire. Out of the corner of his eye, he could see the orange tracers pass by Hot Stuff's twin tails. He estimated the closing range to the incoming target. Eisel hesitated until a voice in his mind whispered, "Now!" Then his gloved fingers squeezed the triggers of his twin .50s. It took only a short burst and the lead German fighter disintegrated. Eisel instinctively ducked as parts of the Me 109 blew past his turret.

Eisel sat up and rotated the turret to take aim at a second incoming threat. Fire from Hot Stuff's tail turret blazed, the tracers enveloping the Nazi fighter. The enemy plane dove away and flew toward the Tunisian coast, trailing black smoke.

The remaining enemy fighters broke off their attack and returned to base. Although some of the B-24s were damaged, the dozen aircraft were able to maintain formation on their return to Gambut Main.

For several minutes, Hot Stuff's intercom was silent. As the pulse rate of each man began to slow, the realization of what they had just survived began to overwhelm their senses.

Craighead pulled back from his .50 and looked at his gloved hand. It was trembling violently. Sweat broke out on his forehead.

Lentz stared at the holes in the Plexiglas windshield as air rushed through punctures. "Jesus Christ, that was the worst yet."

Shannon shook himself out of his reverie. "Anybody hurt? Damage report."

The men looked around at their crewmates and the minute holes in the fuselage. Again, good fortune smiled on Hot Stuff. Miraculously, unlike other aircrews in the formation, none of Shannon's men were wounded.

McQueen quipped, "A few more small holes back here. The skin is starting to look like a slice of Swiss cheese, but we're holding together."

Eisel reported the twin tails had some small holes, but nothing major.

Rondeau checked the instruments and looked out the upper turret at the wings. The four 1,200 horsepower engines were running smoothly and there were no fuel or oil leaks. The gauges indicated there was sufficient fuel to easily make the return to base. He smiled and reported to Shannon. "Lieutenant, everything's hunky-dory here."

"Looks like George got a couple of the Jerries as we left the target area," Craighead reported. "And from here in the belly, I saw several of the Nazis go down over the harbor. All our gunners were really cooking with gas."

"Timberlake was right again about keeping the formation tight," Lentz stressed. "That's why he's above my pay grade. Our combined firepower along with the German antiaircraft fire really did some damage to the Luftwaffe today."

"And we walloped the hell out of the harbor area again," Jacobson pointed out. "At the rate we're going, Rommel's war machine is going to slowly grind to a screeching halt. A few more days like this and our guys on the ground will push the bastards out of North Africa."

Shine nodded as he spoke to the entire crew. "You guys did a great job today. We completed our mission, and we're still in one piece."

It was 1730 when the first of the returning Liberators touched down at Gambut Main. The Brits on the antiaircraft guns nervously counted as each B-24 taxied off the runway. Twelve took off at 1000 and twelve returned almost eight hours later. They waved their helmets overhead as they cheered. Some ran toward the bombers to personally welcome the crews back.

CHAPTER 26

Enemy Air Raid on Gambut Main

Shortly after the Liberators had returned from the December 27 raid on Sousse the Luftwaffe attacked Gambut Main once again in darkness. The 93rd's personnel heard the wail of the air raid siren and dove into shallow trenches. Seconds later the drone of approaching enemy planes could be heard. As per standing operating procedure, the B-24s were spread over a vast area to preclude mass damage. This time the expected bombs never fell. Only sporadic machinegun fire strafed the airstrip.

As the Tommies' searchlights lit up the skies, Royal Air Force night fighters intercepted the Axis aircraft over the base. The 93rd's personnel were treated to a dazzling display of tracers zigzagging across the darkened desert sky. On this particular occasion a British fighter shot down a Nazi bomber. The enemy plane burst into flames lighting up the midnight sky as it plummeted to earth.

Fifteen minutes later the all-clear signal was given and the airmen emerged from the trenches. As from past experience they were not surprised at how little damage the Luftwaffe had inflicted.

Farley walked out onto the dark airstrip. "Ouch. Goddamn it, I must have stepped on a scorpion."

McQueen bent down and picked up a four-pointed steel spike. "I'll be damned, here's your scorpion, George."

The dim moonlight revealed the area had been littered with thousands of the spikes. Gott picked one up. "Looks like the Huns are running short on armaments. That's probably why they didn't bomb us this time. Maybe our attacking their ports is doing some good."

Shine examined one of the spikes. "Gotta give them credit, they're clever. They're planting these in hopes of shredding our tires and grounding our planes. We'll have to clear the airstrip before we can takeoff."

At daybreak, Col. Timberlake had all the men on the airstrip doing the back-breaking work of clearing it of the dangerous spikes. He turned to his operations officer, Major Compton, "We can't keep this up for any length of time as it screws up our ability to schedule missions. Why don't you see if we can hire some locals to do the cleaning up for us?"

CHAPTER 27

December 29, 1942 Seventeenth Combat Mission: Sousse

The next day the 93rd was ordered to bomb the Sousse harbor installations for a third time, specifically docks, rail yards, and barracks. After the usual briefing off the map on the desert floor the twelve designated crews climbed into their aircraft.

Farley watched as McQueen tried to clamor into Hot Stuff. "What the hell's wrong with you, Paul?'

"Christ, my back is killing me. Give me a push. I'm only twenty-three, and I feel like I'm older than my grandfather. That policing up of the spikes the Jerries dropped on the runway was worse than any police detail I was on in basic training. I hated picking up cigarette butts around the barracks, but this took the cake."

"No reason to snap your cap over it," Farley grunted as he shoved McQueen into the hatch. "We had to get it done if we were ever going to stay in this war. We couldn't let those bastards take us out of the fight."

Craighead followed Farley into the aircraft. "Look at the bright side, guys. I overheard Col. Timberlake is going to pay locals to pick up those spikes if the Nazis try that trick again."

Just over an hour into the flight, the British fighter escort had reached their maxim range and turned back. McQueen watched as the P-40s faded to the east. "Well, it looks like we're back in the meat grinder again."

"Gunners, test fire your weapons," Shannon ordered. "Save your ammunition for the Jerries."

Remembering the last mission over Sousse, each gunner pumped several rounds into empty space, ready to face another Luftwaffe onslaught. All gunners reported their weapons functioned properly.

"This baby is red hot and ready to go," Farley exclaimed. "I did a killer-diller job cleaning it last night."

Craighead looked up from the belly gunner's position. "I feel it in my gut my time has come to blow the shit out of one of those Jerry hot shots."

The third mission over Sousse turned out to be like watching the same movie twice. The extremely heavy flak was mixed with daring German pilots flying through their own antiaircraft fire to attack the dozen B-24s. The 93rd's Liberators persisted. The bombers maintained formation through the aerial barrage while creating a protective umbrella with their relentless machine gun fire. It reminded one of swatting a swarm of mosquitoes while trudging through a Louisiana swamp. In the maelstrom the group's bombers successfully dumped their lethal loads on the target area and turned toward the Mediterranean.

Just like on the previous mission over Sousse, the antiaircraft fire diminished and the Luftwaffe came at the formation with a vengeance.

"Christ, they're more of them and they're all over us," Lentz exclaimed as he rotated his head in all directions. "Twelve o'clock! Two o'clock! Nine o'clock"

The gunners could feel the heat of the .50s blowing back into their faces as they fired repeatedly at the incoming harbingers of death.

"Joe, one at seven o'clock low," Eisel shouted into the intercom. He looked up as he aimed his twin .50s at another enemy fighter, this time diving from five o'clock high trying to attack the vulnerable tail section. Again, the tail gunner rotated his turret and waited. Now! The twin .50s spat out their lethal message. A wing section of the Me 109 broke off and the enemy aircraft spiraled downward just feet away from Hot Stuff.

The belly gunner responded, "See him." He opened fire at the rising threat as bullets from the ascending Me 109 slammed into the soft underbelly of Hot Stuff. The enemy plane veered off, its engine catching fire. "Got the son of a bitch."

Shannon looked down to his left and saw the flaming enemy plane plunge toward the sea, the pilot bailing out. "Nice shooting, Craighead. Chalk one up for you."

The belly gunner was elated to have scored his first confirmed aerial victory.

Another enemy fighter dove at Hot Stuff's tail section. Eisel took aim and squeezed the triggers. Several rounds fired and then nothing! He frantically pulled back on the receivers several times. He had run out of ammunition during the frantic onslaught. He watched as the Nazi pilot turned for a second run at the B-24. What to do?

The tail gunner then remembered an incident told to him by a gunner from another one of the squadron's Liberators. When that gunner's .50s were out of ammo he told Eisel he was frantic. In desperation he reached for a flashlight and began blinking it on and off feinting gunfire. This deception worked beautifully; the enemy fighter banked and made for safe haven.

Eisel quickly reached for his flashlight and as the German fighter dove at Hot Stuff, he aimed the flashlight and rapidly flicked it on and off hoping the enemy pilot would believe he was facing deadly machine gun fire. The trick worked! The Me 109 peeled off without firing a shot and headed for the safety of its base in Tunisia. Was the enemy fighter out of ammo or low on fuel? No one would ever know for sure. Regardless Hot Stuff survived to fight another day.

Within minutes, the entire engagement was over. The only sound within the confines of Hot Stuff was the drone of her engines mixed with air rushing through the open windows and minute holes in the fuselage. The enemy aircraft retired from the aerial combat as they had either expended all their ammunition or were running low on fuel.

As per all combat missions, Shannon requested the crewmembers report on any casualties and on damage to the aircraft. Again, the fates smiled on Hot Stuff; no one had been wounded and although a few new minor holes had been added to the fuselage the Liberator was deemed airworthy.

Three hours later the twelve Liberators landed at Gambut Main. Hot Stuff's crew deplaned, all talking at the same time as they reached for their smokes and lit up.

"There were so many goddamned Jerries up there I almost ran out of ammo," Farley spoke as he exhaled a cloud of smoke. "Seems like anywhere I pointed my .50 I couldn't miss. Reminded me of a shooting gallery at the traveling carnival back home."

"I did run out of ammo!" Eisel exclaimed. "Jesus, I almost shit in my pants when that Nazi dove straight at me and all I could do was stare at the bastard's blazing guns."

"What happened?" McQueen was shocked. "That son of a bitch could've done us in."

Eisel smiled as he deeply inhaled his Chesterfield. "The bastard came around a second time. That was his mistake. It gave me time to think. I reached for my flashlight and when the son of a bitch came at me again, I aimed it at him flashing on and off as fast as I could. I hoped from a distance that the flashing would look like my .50s firing at him."

"And?" Craighead asked, his eyes open in amazement.

Eisel coughed and laughed. "Well, it worked. We're all still here. The bastard peeled off and ran for home."

"That's the damnedest thing I ever heard, George," McQueen extolled. He took a deep draw on his Lucky Strike. "You can damn well bet I'll remember that trick! That was really quick thinking."

"Well, to tell you the truth," the tail gunner confessed, "I didn't just think it up. I overheard another tail gunner tell the story about his using a flashlight to fake machine gun fire when he ran out of ammo. So I grabbed my flashlight, aimed it at the Jerry and started flashing it."

Rondeau looked at the other crewmembers. "We're all glad it worked." He turned to Craighead and slapped him on the back. "Joe, you were really cooking with gas today. Nice shooting. You got your first Nazi."

CHAPTER 28

Happy New Year

On New Year's Day 1943, Gambut Main was engulfed in a severe sandstorm that lasted three days. The crews had to stay sheltered in their tents where they played cards, ate and slept.

Through the fog of dust within the confines of the tent Eisel looked around at his fellow poker players, shuffled the deck and sneezed. "Ante up, gentleman, five-card stud." After seeing the pot was correct, he dealt out the hands.

Four players sat on a blanket spread atop the sand floor. Rondeau was asleep on his cot and Jeffers sat writing a letter home.

McQueen chewed on a D-ration chocolate bar as he arranged his cards. After a moment of assessing his hand, he exclaimed, "I bet five pence."

The others wanted to see what he held and matched the bet.

"Read them and weep, boys," McQueen chortled as he showed two pair.

Craighead and Farley slapped their cards down on the blanket. "Dammit, Paul," the belly gunner lamented, "you're the luckiest son of a bitch I know."

McQueen reached out and began dragging the pot toward himself when Eisel piped up, "Not so fast, Paul." He then flashed three of a kind and smiled.

"Why you, bastard, you misdealt the cards," McQueen shouted as he lunged at the tail gunner.

Jeffers dropped his pencil and grabbed McQueen by the shoulders. "Paul, let's not start a fight among ourselves. Save it for the Jerries."

McQueen froze in place and looked Eisel in the eye and sighed, "Sorry, George. Must be this goddamned sandstorm and waiting for some action that's getting to me."

"Forget it, Paul," Eisel said. "You'll win it back in no time." He slammed the cards down in front of McQueen. "Besides, it's your deal."

The Consolidated B-24D Liberator, 1942. Public Domain.

The *Hot Stuff* crew. Front Row: Sgts. Grant Rondeau (Engineer and Top Turret Gunner), Joseph Craighead (Belly Gunner), L. F. Durham (Tail Gunner substituting for George Eisel), Paul McQueen (Waist Gunner), Kenneth Jeffers (Radio Operator), George Farley (Waist Gunner). Second Row: Lt. Robert Jacobson (Bombardier), Capt. Robert Shannon (Pilot), Lt. James Gott (Navigator), Lt. John Lentz (Copilot). Courtesy of Kelly (Jacobson) Treybig, Jacobson's daughter.

Flight record of 1st Lt. Robert T. "Jake" Jacobson, bombardier on the B-24 Liberator *Hot Stuff.* All of his missions were on *Hot Stuff.* Courtesy of Kelly (Jacobson) Treybig, Jacobson's daughter.

Aerial view of Grenier Army Airfield, New Hampshire, 1942.
Courtesty of New Hampshire Aviation Historical Society.

View of barracks and officers' quarters, Grenier
Army Airfield, New Hampshire, 1942. Courtesy of
New Hampshire Aviation Historical Society.

View of Officers' Club, Grenier Army Airfield, New Hampshire, 1942. Courtesy of New Hampshire Aviation Historical Society.

Navy Lt. Harry W. Byron, flight instructor and ferry pilot, 1942. Courtesy of Betty Byron, Harry Byron's daughter.

Florene Watson, flight instructor and ferry pilot from Women Auxiliary Ferry Squadron (WAFS), later known as Women Airforce Service Pilot (WASP). Florene later became commander of the WASP. Courtesy of Knight Kappers.

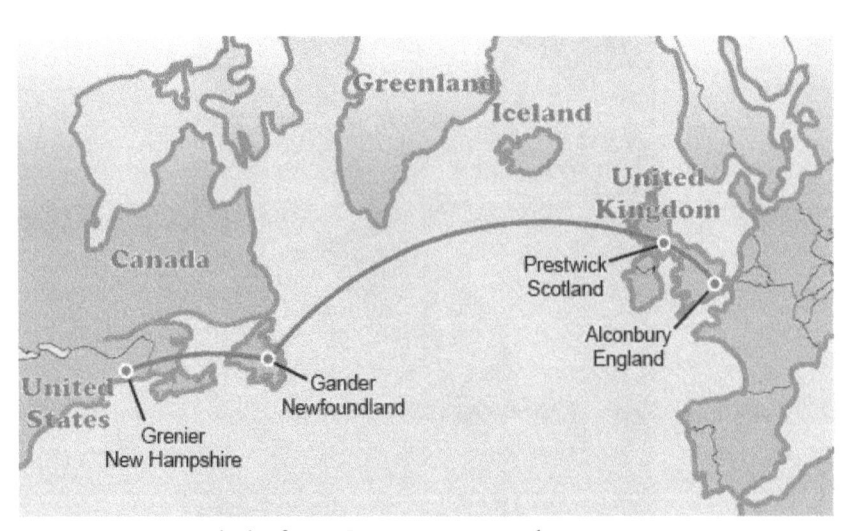

Flight from Grenier Army Airbase, New Hampshire to Alconbury Royal Air Force (RAF) aerodrome, England. Courtesy of Jim Lux.

Aerial view of RAF Alconbury aerodrome, 1942. B-24 Liberators of the 93rd Bombardment Group are parked on the runway. Public Domain

B-24 Liberator *Hot Stuff* on its third combat mission while flying over the Bay of Biscay on antisubmarine patrol. Courtesy of Don Morrison, 93rd Bombardment Group Assn. Historian.

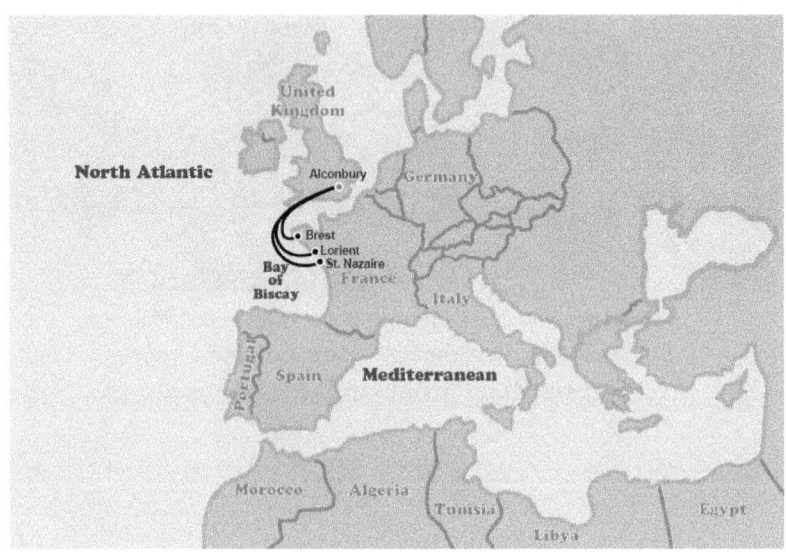

Flight paths of combat missions flown from Alconbury RAF aerodrome. Courtesy of Jim Lux.

The most often encountered enemy fighter was
the German Messerschmitt Me 109. Courtesy
of National Archives and Records.

German heavy fighter Messerschmitt Me 210.
Courtesy of National Archives and Records.

German heavy fighter Junkers Ju 88. Courtesy of National Archives and Records.

British Spitfire fighter flown by Czech pilots who mistakenly attacked 93rd Bombardment Group B-24s returning from a mission. Courtesy of National Archives and Records.

German Focke Wulf Fw 190 fighter often encountered during bombing missions. Courtesy of National Archives and Records.

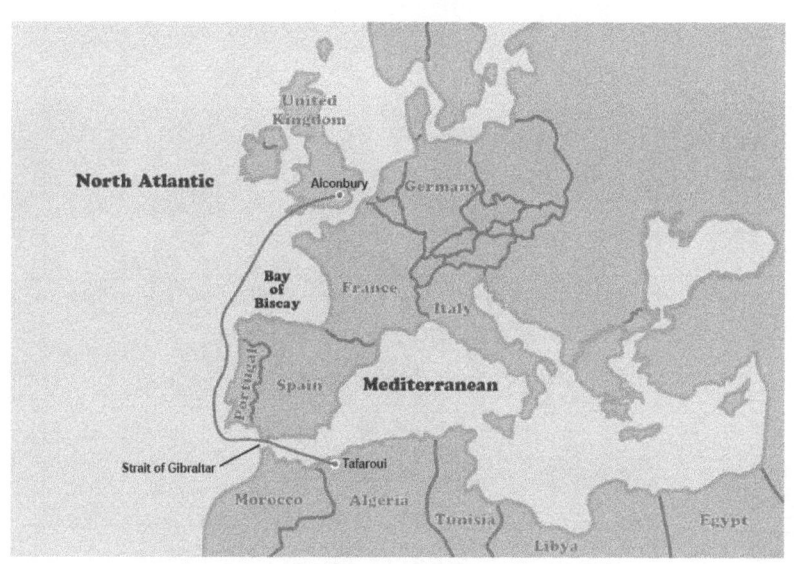

Flight path from Alconbury RAF to Tafaroui, Algeria, North Africa. Courtesy of Jim Lux.

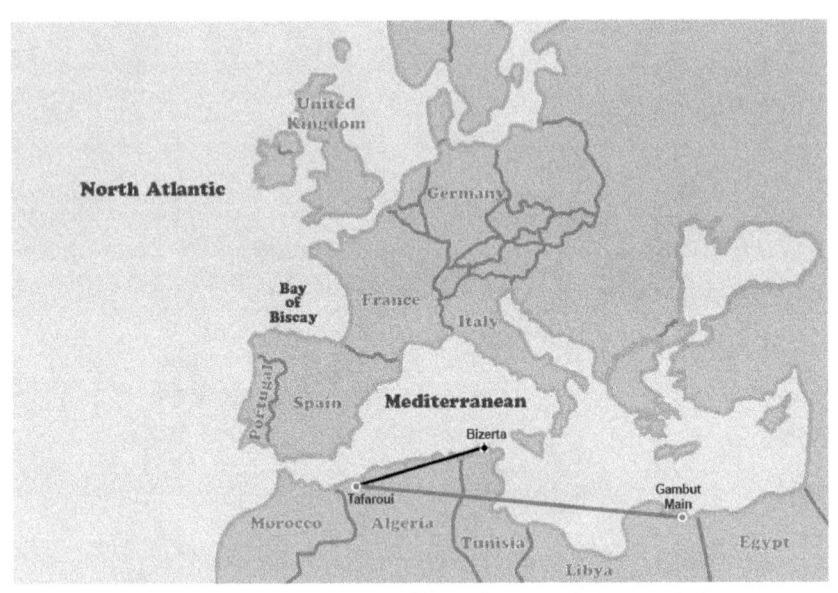

The only combat mission flown from Tafaroui and the flight path to Gambut Main, Libya. Courtesy of Jim Lux.

British 40 mm Bofors antiaircraft gun of the type that defended Gambut Main. Courtesy of Knight Kappers.

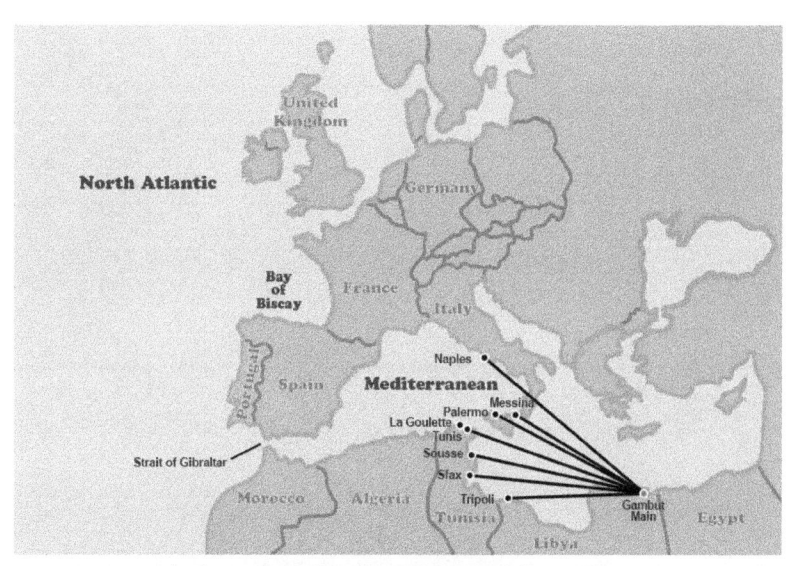

Flight paths of combat missions flown from
Gambut Main. Courtesy of Jim Lux.

B-24 Liberator *Hot Stuff* officers in British uniforms
while in North Africa. From left to right are bombardier
Lt. Robert "Jake" Jacobson, copilot Lt. John Lentz
and pilot Lt. Robert "Shine" Shannon. Courtesy of
Jackie (Lentz) Broome, daughter of John Lentz.

American-made P-40 fighter flown by British pilots in
North Africa. Courtesy of the Australian War Memorial.

World leaders President Franklin D. Roosevelt and Prime Minister Winston Churchill in the foreground with staff officers at the Casablanca Conference, January 14-24, 1943. General Henry "Hap" Arnold, Chief of U.S. Army Air Corps is standing on far left. General George Marshall, U.S. Army Chief of Staff is standing behind President Roosevelt. Lt. Gen. Frank Andrews is standing on the far right. During the conference, Andrews was appointed Commander of all U.S. Forces in the European Theater of Operations. Courtesy of the U.S. Department of State Office of the Historian.

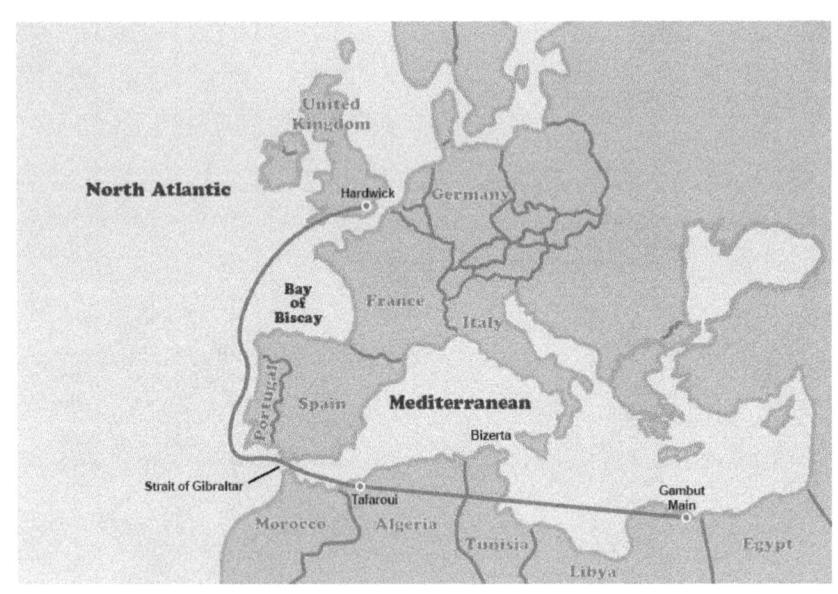

Flight path from Gambut Main to Hardwick RAF aerodrome, England. Courtesy of Jim Lux.

Aerial view of Hardwick RAF aerodrome, 1943. Public domain.

Flight paths of combat missions flown from
Hardwick RAF. Courtesy of Jim Lux.

Robert "Shine" Shannon shortly after being
promoted to captain. Courtesy of Jim Lux.

Lt. Gen. Frank Andrews and aide Lt. Col. Fred Chapman in England sometime before the final flight. Courtesy of Malinda Bailey Hayes, Chapman's niece.

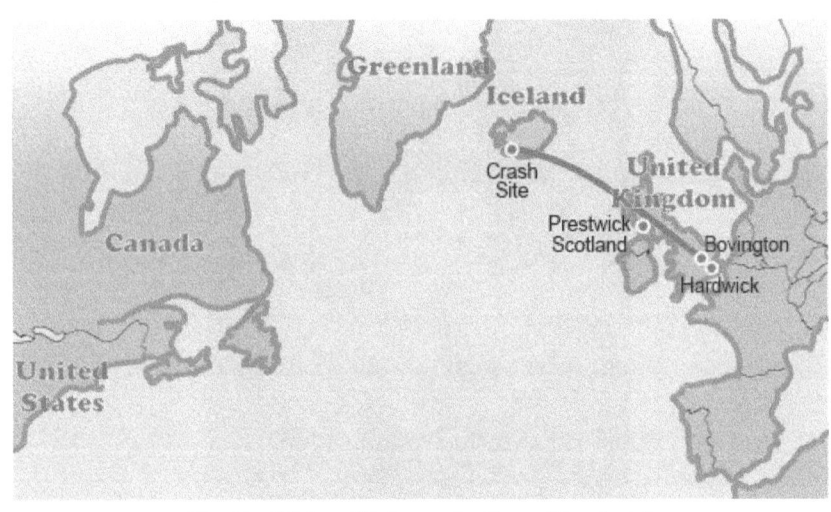

Hot Stuff's last flight paths from Hardwick RAF to Iceland. Courtesy of Jim Lux.

Remains of *Hot Stuff's* tail section at crash site where Sgt. George Eisel was found alive. Public Domain.

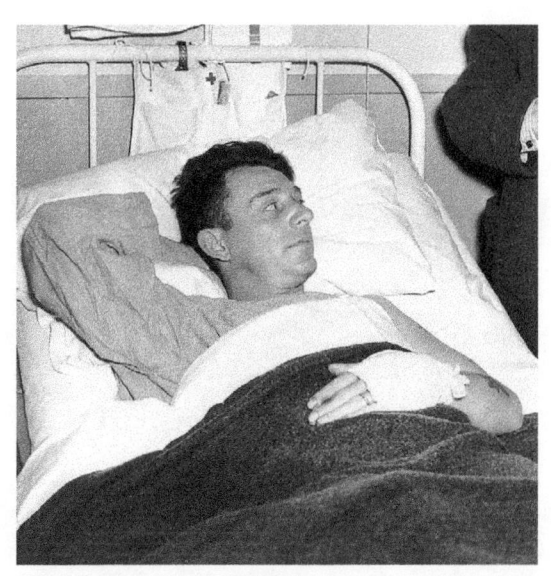

Sgt. George Eisel and only survivor of the *Hot Stuff* crash in Iceland. Courtesy of Diane and Dick (Eisel's second cousin) Brooker.

Burial at Fossvogur Cemetery in Reykjavik, Iceland. Courtesy of Malinda Bailey Hayes, Lt. Col. Fred Chapman's niece.

Artwork completed for a Time Magazine cover showing Lt. Gen. Frank Andrews as Commander of U.S. Forces in Europe superimposed over a map of Europe with potential invasion routes depicted behind him. Courtesy of Jan Andrews Clark, Gen. Andrews' granddaughter.

William Gros, former radio operator on *Eager Beaver* and good friend of Kenneth Jeffers, radio operator on *Hot Stuff.* Courtesy of Jim Lux.

Bombardier with Norden bomb sight. Public Domain.

B-24 Liberator gunner wearing high altitude gear and flak helmet. Courtesy of Knight Kappers.

Lt. Gen. Frank Maxwell Andrews, commander of all U.S. Forces in the European Theater of Operations at the time of the fatal crash. Courtesy of National Museum of the United States Air Force.

B-24 waist gunner in high altitude gear. Public domain.

Lt. Robert Jacobson, Hot Stuff's bombardier. Courtesy of Kelly (Jacobson) Treybig, Jacobson's daughter.

Hot Stuff officers with other officers from the 93rd Bombardment Group in North Africa. Second from left: Lt. Robert Shannon (pilot); Third from left: Lt. John Lentz (copilot); Fourth from left: Lt. James Gott (navigator); and Fifth from left: Lt Robert Jacobson (bombardier). Courtesy of Jackie (Lentz) Broome, daughter of John Lentz.

CHAPTER 29

January 5, 1943 Eighteenth Combat Mission: Sousse

On the morning of January 5, the brilliant hot desert sun edged over the horizon immediately incinerating the cold night air. The day before, the 93rd had received orders from Ninth Air Force to bomb the Axis stronghold of Tunis. This was intended to support the advancing British Eighth Army as it moved west.

Munching on C rations and sipping precious water from canteens, the aircrews huddled around the map lying on a blanket. Major Compton briefed the details of the day's mission. As always, should the primary target area be socked in, the secondary target was Sousse, an important port on the east coast of Tunisia.

British P-40s operating out of forward bases were to meet the 93rd's B-24s and provide air cover against enemy fighters for half of the eight hundred–mile flight to Tunis. After that, the Liberators were to be on their own.

A dozen Liberators were to conduct the raid, Hot Stuff among them. The planes had been refueled, rearmed, and bombs loaded the night before. All was ready.

After a preflight check of Hot Stuff, the crew climbed aboard the aircraft. Shannon received the signal to start engines and after warm-up taxied the B-24 to sixth in line for takeoff. At 1100, a flare was shot into the air and the bomb-laden Liberators took to the skies in thirty-second intervals.

Moments later the aircraft assumed their positions in the mass formation. An hour later, Eisel recognized the profile of the American-made P-40s and shouted through his oxygen mask, "I see the Brit P-40s at five o'clock high. They're coming on fast."

At that moment, the pilot of the lead bomber established communications with the escort fighters. Shannon and Lentz listened with interest as the Brit squadron leader announced their arrival. "Hey you Yanks down there, we're here to clear the sky of the Jerry infestation."

Lentz glanced at his watch. "Can you beat that? Our escort is right on time." He looked over his right shoulder and counted eight friendly fighters.

Jeffers, sitting just behind the pilots, pointed through the windscreen. "Goddamn, here comes trouble. Looks like our friends arrived just in time."

A half dozen German Me 109s were heading straight for the formation. A disembodied voice with a strong British accent permeated the airwaves. "The game's afoot. Talley ho, chaps."

The crews of the B-24s were about to be entertained by the dogfights that ensued all around the formation. "Gunners, choose your targets carefully," Shannon ordered. "We don't want to knock down friendlies."

"Would you look at that?" McQueen blurted as he watched a pair of P-40s attack one of the enemy aircraft. In turn, each of the British fighter's six .50 Browning machine guns raked the German plane, causing it to explode into a ball of fire, flaming debris falling to earth. There was no parachute.

Farley looked up as another Me 109 began belching smoke, the pilot bailing out. "Damn, those Brits are good." As the crippled aircraft began to succumb to the pull of gravity, he saw the Nazi pilot's parachute blossom over the Libyan Desert. "Lucky bastard."

Shannon watched the aerial duel with envy. It reminded him of the 1933 movie *The Eagle and the Hawk*, a film about Royal Air Force pilots in WWI he had watched growing up. The old feeling came back. *Goddamned, as much as I love flying bombers, just once more I'd like to feel my pulse quicken as I have one of those Nazi bastards in my sights and squeeze the trigger.*

It was all over within minutes. The P-40s, although somewhat slower than the Me 109s, dove on the enemy aircraft and cut their number down by two; the remaining German fighters had enough from the Brit escort combined with the blistering machine gun fire from the Liberators and scurried back to their base. The Brits had done their job well, none of the Liberators suffered major damage.

Thirty minutes later, the British fighter escort had reached its maximum range and radioed "Good hunting, Yanks" to the 93rd's bombers and turned back toward their base. Now the Liberators were on their own.

"This isn't over yet. Gunners stay alert," Shannon ordered.

After another hour of flight, Gott announced over the intercom, "We're about twenty minutes out."

As Hot Stuff approached Tunis, Jacobson began to adjust his bombsight. He shook his head. The entire target area was obscured by clouds. The flight commander ordered the formation to turn toward the secondary target at Sousse a few minutes flying time to the southeast.

As Hot Stuff approached the secondary target area the cloud cover cleared and the eastern Tunisian harbor came into view some twenty-one thousand feet below. Unlike previous missions over Sousse, antiaircraft fire was sparse. Ignoring the flak, Jacobson adjusted the bomb sight and opened the bomb bay doors. After Shannon handed control of Hot Stuff to Jake, the bomb sight crosshairs aligned with two freighters and the bombardier released the five thousand–pound load. A few moments later, the 93rd denied the Afrika Korps of much needed war supplies as several ships, wharves and warehouses exploded sending plumes of flames and smoke into the harbor sky.

The mission on the secondary target completed, the Liberators turned and headed back to Gambut Main. Suddenly enemy fighters rose to engage the B-24s. During the half hour conflict one Liberator, Eager Beaver suffered significant damage.

Jeffers listened in on the command net as he learned the crippled aircraft had sustained damage to fuel lines and one wing and could not make it back to Gambut Main. Eager Beaver diverted to Malta some two hundred miles to the east for repairs. "Son of a bitch, my buddy Bill Gros is the radio operator on that plane."

"Hope they make it okay," Gott remarked as he scanned his charts. "The air strips there are really short."

"It's good the Heinie fighters didn't come up to pursue us," Lentz observed. "That'll give Eager Beaver a better chance to make it to Malta."

"I can't believe it," McQueen said, "the Nazi fighters didn't come after us."

Farley bragged, "Probably scared the shit out of them the last time we were here. Didn't like the taste of our .50s."

"Bet our bombs are blowing their ammo and fuel dumps sky high," Rondeau added. "Can't fly without gas and can't shoot if you don't have ammo."

It was after 1900 when the last of eleven Liberators touched down at Gambut Main. In the darkness the Brit antiaircraft gunners were dismayed that one of the B-24s was missing.

CHAPTER 30

Cairo Adventure

The entire 93rd had worn the same clothes night and day for weeks and the uniforms had become tattered and torn. They had left England only with a change of socks and underwear which they managed to periodically rinse out in alkaline water drawn from the ancient well.

Fortunately a British quartermaster was available to issue British battle dress uniforms to the Americans. However, footwear was not available. The Americans' shoes now well-worn were for the most part kept together with wire and twine. All the aircraft needed extensive repair and the aircrews, as tired as they were, were required to assist the meager ground crews, sometimes working in a deluge of rain or blowing sand.

Since there was a shortage of ground transportation to the mess tent two miles distant, the crews ate C rations on the flight line. Maintenance of the Norden bomb sights proved to be a full time job for bombardiers. Regular classes were held among the bombardiers to instruct them on how to keep the sensitive bombsights in operational condition. While in England this was the work of skilled technicians. Without those technicians, the aircrews had to perform ground crew tasks which included stripping their own weapons, loading bombs and ammunition as well as filling the aircraft fuel tanks using five-gallon cans.

On the morning of January 6 Rondeau knelt as he bound up his well-worn shoes with wire that had once secured C ration boxes. "Look at this. This wire is the only thing that's holding my shoes together."

"I'm stuffing cardboard from C-ration boxes into my shoes to cover the worn soles," McQueen countered.

"I'm glad the Brit quartermaster came out here and gave us some of their battle dress uniforms," Jeffers said. "At least we're not dressed in those filthy rags we've been wearing for two months." He looked down at his feet. "Too bad the Brits couldn't issue us some new shoes."

"Jesus, what I wouldn't give to take a shower and shave," Eisel commented. "We haven't been cleaned up since we left Alconbury. I hate putting on that clean Brit uniform over my dirty body."

"Yeah," McQueen lamented as he stroked his month old beard. "Guess we don't smell too good either."

Just then Shannon approached the tent housing Hot Stuff's enlisted men. The men stood as he entered their shelter from the hot sun.

"As you already know Col. Timberlake was able to arrange for the group to go to Cairo for a little leave," Shannon pointed out, "and we're rotating crews as not to disrupt mission capability."

"We already know that sir!" Rondeau exclaimed. "When do *we* go?"

"That's why I'm here," Shine smiled. "We drew the long straw; we fly to Cairo this afternoon."

The six enlisted men jumped up and down slapping each other on the back, dust billowing from their uniforms.

"Cairo and dancing girls, here we come," McQueen shouted.

BEFORE THE BELLE

On the late afternoon of January 6, Hot Stuff and another B-24 from the 93rd circled over the pyramids and sphinx. Shannon spoke over the intercom. "Now that's a sight we'll always remember."

Eisel took motion pictures of the sight below using the last of the film in the camera he had purchased when they had been at Page Field in Florida. "This's got to be better than anything I've ever seen in history books."

Minutes later, the two Liberators landed at the aerodrome at Fayid on the outskirts of Cairo. As Hot Stuff rolled to a stop on the concrete apron and its pilots shut down its engines, a jeep and a six-wheeled three-quarter-ton weapons carrier roared to a halt alongside.

After Shannon, his crew and a few ground personnel stepped onto the hardstand a British army corporal, clad in khaki shorts and shirt dismounted the jeep and saluted Shannon. His eyes swept over the filthy, bearded Americans.

"I understand you chaps are from Gambut Main. I've been instructed to take you to your accommodations in Cairo."

Shannon returned the salute and smiled. "We are that, Corporal. Lead on."

The British NCO sat behind the wheel of the jeep while Shine sat in the passenger's seat and the other three officers swarmed into cramped confines of the rear. The enlisted men squeezed themselves into the open truck driven by a British private. Eisel's right leg was still hanging over the tailgate of the weapons carrier when with a screech of tires both vehicles raced for the aerodrome gate. The passengers grabbed whatever they could to keep from falling out. Shannon braced himself in his seat wide-eyed as his right hand gripped the jeep's windshield.

For centuries the ancient city had been occupied by foreign armies. Now it was dominated by British and Allied forces. The city was slowly becoming a mix of white-washed buildings reminiscent of Biblical times and the more colorful twentieth century edifices. Everywhere the streets were congested with a combination of Egyptians and foreign soldiers of every description. Camels, carts, bicycles, taxis and military vehicles choked every passable thoroughfare. After a forty-five-minute horn-blasting, hair-raising ride through the streets by the maniacal Brit drivers the vehicles screeched to a halt at the entrance to the elegant Shepheard Hotel.

The edifice was strategically located on the banks of the Nile River in the heart of Cairo. It was situated within walking distance of historical attractions and the commercial district. To the hotel management and staff, nothing was too good for its American guests.

As the enlisted men jumped out of the truck, McQueen quickly lit a Lucky Strike with a trembling hand and looked at his fellow waist gunner. "Jesus, George, the way that Brit drove scared the shit out of me."

"I can't believe we came so close to dying," Farley remarked as he tried to steady himself on wobbly legs. "Paul, gimme one of those butts."

"You see how close we came to hitting those camels? And trucks?" Jeffers exclaimed with a cigarette dangling from his quivering lips. "And I sure as hell don't know how we squeezed through the jammed-up traffic snarl in the center of town, never slowing down."

Rondeau, the now dedicated smoker, took one of McQueen's cigarettes and lit up. "These Brit drivers must be on the Nazi payroll. I've never been so goddamned scared in my life and that includes all the shit we flew through on the bombing raids. You'd think they're trying to kill us?"

The British Corporal dismounted and announced. "We have arrived, chaps. Hope you Yanks enjoy yourselves. Go on in, they're expecting you."

Shannon looked at his right hand. It was still frozen into the windshield death grip even though he had leaped from the jeep before it had come to a complete stop. He shook his hand to increase circulation as he stared at the opulent facade. He exhaled realizing he had just survived a near death experience and was lucky to be standing on solid ground. "Well, we made it."

"This is the fanciest goddamned hotel I think I've ever seen," Craighead expounded with his mouth agape. The men stood in awe as they stared at the magnificent edifice. The belly gunner turned toward Shannon. "Lieutenant, do you think they dropped us off at the wrong place? This looks like something for top brass."

"No mistake," Shine said as he wiped the perspiration off his forehead with a shaking hand and exhaled. "Our orders are for us to stay here for three nights, do some touring, shopping and just plain enjoy ourselves." He looked at the bearded sunburnt faces surrounding him. "We made it this far, let's do as ordered and really enjoy ourselves."

Taking a deep drag on his cigarette McQueen blurted, "I can't believe it! Maybe we'll be able to see some of those beautiful dancing girls after all."

Once checked in, the officers were given individual rooms and the enlisted men were assigned two to a room. Before proceeding to the elevator, the concierge greeted Hot Stuff's crew. After a quick onceover glance at the grubby group and a sampling of the odor emitting from the airmen he crinkled his nose and in haughty English suggested they leave their clothes outside their doors for laundering after they retired for the night. He assured the men their uniforms would be delivered clean by the next morning. The hotel barber shop was at their disposal.

Shannon told the men to get cleaned up and meet him at the barber shop in an hour. "Remember fellows, we're American guests here and you will look and act accordingly." With that the crewmembers took their room keys and headed for the elevator.

As Lentz unlocked the door to his room, he whistled and looked at Shannon down the hall. "Shine, would you take a look at this? I'll bet the Edgewater Beach Hotel in Chicago isn't this nice."

"See you in the barber shop," Shannon kicked the door of his room closed and started peeling off his uniform.

Farley and McQueen entered their room. "I've got dibs on the tub first," McQueen announced.

"Wait a minute, I'll flip you for it," Farley countered.

McQueen won the coin toss and settled in the hot water and sighed. He looked at a bottle standing on a table near his arm. The label was in a foreign language, possibly French. "What the hell is this stuff?"

He opened the bottle and smelled the contents. "Wow, this smells good." He poured half the contents into the stream of hot water spewing from the tap. Within seconds, he disappeared into a cloud of quivering bubbles. He leaned back, lit a Lucky Strike, and sighed as his fingers popped bubbles. "Hey, George, this is the life."

Farley looked into the bathroom and laughed. All he could see was what appeared to be a lit cigarette taking a bubble bath. "Wait'll I tell the guys about this."

After bathing, the men descended to the hotel barber shop. There they were treated to haircuts, shaves, and manicures. As far as the Brits were concerned, nothing was too good for the Yanks. From there they advanced to the hotel bar.

During their three day stay at the Shepheard Hotel, the crewmembers discovered if they left their clothes by the door to their room at night, the garments would be found cleaned and neatly laid out the next morning. Since the crew had not been paid since leaving England they were issued local currency from a fund established by combined Allied governments.

During the day Hot Stuff's officers toured the city and its outskirts. The highlights of their visit was strolling through the Cairo

BEFORE THE BELLE

museum and traveling by military vehicles to view the pyramids and sphinx from ground level. In the late afternoons Shannon and Hot Stuff's officers congregated on the Shepheard's terrace overlooking the Nile. There they sat on wicker chairs sipping drinks while watching the river traffic. At night they dined at the hotel and local restaurants, and strolled through the alleyways and bazaars looking for souvenirs and gifts. In one of the bazaars, Shannon entered an exotic perfumery. Lentz watched as his command pilot sniffed various samples. "Who's the lucky girl this time, Shine? Must be that redhead in London."

Shannon continued to enjoy the fragrances and then held up a small uncapped bottle. "Wrong. This is for my best girl back in Iowa." He turned to the proprietor and indicated the small bottle he held in his hand was his choice. A somewhat larger version was gift wrapped in brightly colored paper and tied with a bow.

During the day Hot Stuff's enlisted men strolled through the local bazaars, some buying trinkets and souvenirs. At one shop, they found leather goods.

"Shoes!" Jeffers exclaimed. The crewmen bounced off each other trying to get into the narrow shop entrance. After fitting and haggling with the shopkeeper, all six of them were shod in new soft leather boots.

Eisel looked down at his new footwear. "They're not exactly issue, but they're a hell of a lot better than what we had. Besides, who's going to give a damn?" Their old shoes were left lying on the well-worn Persian carpet that covered the dirt floor.

In the evenings, they went to local restaurants where they enjoyed local cuisine and were treated to performances by belly dancers. "I just knew before we left North Africa we'd see those beautiful harem women," McQueen blurted as he stuffed pieces of lamb and rice in his mouth with his fingers.

After dinner, the six enlisted men found their way to some bazaars where there was lively X-rated entertainment.

On the evening of January 9, Hot Stuff returned to Gambut Main. All of the men exited the aircraft clean, well-rested, and in good spirits. They were more than ready to get back into the war. Like the crew, Hot Stuff was also ready for combat. She had been cleaned, patched up and had maintenance performed on her by ground crews while in Cairo. In addition to maintenance auxiliary fuel tanks had been installed in the forward portion of the right bomb bay. The fuel tank modification would extend the range of the B-24s by some three hundred miles.

As Shannon walked with his copilot to their tent he remarked to Lentz, "Something's up with the additional fuel tanks, John. I'll bet we can expect the Ninth Air Force to have us fly missions beyond North Africa."

"I can't argue with you on that, Shine.

Jeffers looked around the base and noticed Eager Beaver had rejoined the 93rd after diverting to Malta following the last mission over Sousse. He anxiously sought out his friend Bill Gros.

The sun was approaching the horizon when Jeffers found Eager Beaver's radio operator sitting in his tent. "Jesus, glad to see you're in one piece, Bill."

"I feel like I'm damned lucky to be back at this desert hell hole," Gros laughed as the two shook hands and slapped each other on the shoulders.

"What happened?" Jeffers asked.

"Well, for starters, none of us were wounded. But when one of those Jerry fighters hit Eager Beaver he got us right on the fuel lines and one wing. Don't know what would have happened if those Nazi buggers had chased after us.

"With the fuel leaking the goddamned plane smelled like the inside of a gas tank. Since we didn't have to worry about Nazi fighters, we were scared shitless the heat from the engines would set us on fire. Then we started to run out of fuel and didn't know if we could make it. The fuel gauges read empty. We started to get ready to bail out, but shot down that idea when we found out the life raft was ripped to shreds from flak. I got to tell you that was a pretty goddamned hairy flight to Malta.

"I was able to send a distress signal to Malta. Little did I know what a lucky message that was or we would have flown right into friendly antiaircraft fire.

"When we decided to divert to Malta, we found out there were two airports that handled only fighters. We went to Luqa, which was long enough for twin engine aircraft, but not for four-engine planes. The short runway was on a downhill slope and filled with craters from enemy attacks. To make it even worse, there was a deep quarry at the end of the runway.

"It was so dark, our pilot Lieutenant Rinehart couldn't see the ground. He told me to radio them to turn on the runway lights and luckily they did. Over the intercom Rinehart told us we may be landing right into a nest of Nazis, but we had no choice. We were out of fuel, the plane was damaged, and we had to land.

"Got to give Lieutenant Rinehart credit. That landing field on Malta was really short. He put Eager Beaver down at one end of the runway and we were cruisin' for a brusin' trying to keep from running into a bomb crater. We were lucky to stop rolling when we did. Our nose hung over the edge of the quarry at the end of the runway. It gave us all the heebie-jeebies.

"Rinehart turned Eager Beaver around in case we had to make a quick getaway. He had his hands on the throttles ready burn rubber. The whole crew was really sweating it. Let me tell you, Ken I was almost ready to upchuck. We were never so glad to see the Brits in their blue RAF uniforms in our lives. By the luck of the draw we had landed on an airstrip in RAF hands."

"Jesus, that's wild!" Jeffers exclaimed.

"We found out we got there on a wing and a prayer. We were only a couple of gallons from crashing into the sea.

"The Brits there had never seen a B-24. After inspecting the damage, they were a hip bunch of guys and immediately set off to make repairs. Our flight engineer showed them what to do and they did a bang-up job on Eager Beaver."

"How long were you there?" Jeffers asked.

"Three days. The Brits treated us like real heroes. Even though they were next to starving, they shared what food and money they had."

"You look all spruced up. Haircut, shave and clean clothes," Jeffers commented.

"Oh, that. We found out the *O. Henry*, a US Liberty ship was docked in the harbor and the Brits took us down there. Those merchant marines took care of us. We ate fresh food, none of that canned stuff we choke down here at Gambut Main. We showered and their barber gave every crewmember a haircut and a shave. And get this; they had real toilets that flushed. We slept on clean sheets for three nights and they loaned us clean threads to wear while they laundered our filthy Brit uniforms. Got to say we were on cloud nine for three days."

Jeffers patted Gros on the shoulder. "Well, it's good to see you in one piece, Bill. I was worried I'd never see you again."

CHAPTER 31

January 10, 1943 Nineteenth Combat Mission: La Goulette

The morning of January 10, eleven tired and filthy crews munched on C rations and sipped tepid water from their canteens. They stared at Hot Stuff's clean, well groomed crewmen in bold face jealousy. Shannon's men were more than ready for combat. In the ever increasing desert heat the assembled bomber crews stood around a map spread out on the blanket. Col. Timberlake announced the target for the day's mission was Bizerte. The outdated weather forecast they had received reported cloud cover may obscure the Bizerte area and La Goulette, a small Axis-held island off Tunisia that served as an Axis supply depot, was selected as a secondary target.

The operations officer presented details from aerial photos taken several days earlier by British reconnaissance aircraft. Both target areas were high priority as they were key Axis supply points. The staff officer looked at his watch; takeoff was 1100.

Hot Stuff joined the eleven other Liberators shortly after reaching cruising altitude. The formation encountered extremely heavy headwinds.

Rondeau monitored the fuel gauges. "Lieutenant, we may have a problem getting back. These headwinds are causing us to consume too much fuel. I hope we'll have enough to get back to base."

Shannon spoke over the intercom to his navigator, "Jimmie, what do you think? Can we make it okay?"

"By my calculations, we'll burn up every drop of fuel in the tanks, but with a little luck I bet we'll make it. We should be over Bizerte in a few minutes."

"I have no doubt when we turnaround the tailwinds will carry us home," Shannon prophesied.

At that moment a message was received by Jeffers. The weather forecast for Bizerte had been incorrect. Cloud cover shrouded the primary target and the formation was to attack the facilities on the small Axis-held island of La Goulette in Tunis's harbor.

As the formation continued on toward the secondary target, the cloud cover cleared. "We've come all this way; just as well do some damage while we're here," Shannon said.

Little antiaircraft fire was received as the dozen bombers pummeled the supply depots on the Mediterranean island off Tunis. No aircraft were lost during the raid and dusk began to fall as the Liberators turned toward Gambut Main.

In spite of the difficulty in trying to land at night, Hot Stuff and ten other aircraft landed safely. Shannon's crew wearily stepped out of the B-24's confines after the long flight. All of them lit up except Rondeau. He climbed onto the port wing a stick in hand and poked it into the fuel tank. "Jesus Christ, we just made it! There's nothing in *her* but fumes."

Rondeau jumped down and bummed a cigarette off Eisel. "God, I need one of those."

At the lantern-lit debriefing, Shannon noticed there were fewer officers gathered. It was at that moment the group's operations officer informed them on the return trip Big Dealer had run out of fuel trying to find the base. The last word he had was the pilot attempted a dead stick landing in the desert and the B-24 crashed several miles away on the Egyptian border. Four crewmembers perished.

In the kerosene lamp light Col. Timberlake slowly shook his head. The 93rd in North Africa was now down to nineteen aircraft, some of them questionable as to being mission capable. With no replacements for aircraft, crews or parts, the group somehow managed to maintain operational effectiveness. This was due to every man knowing he had to put forth maximum effort far beyond that which would be expected of him.

While living in Libya, the crews were able to enjoy life a bit more. Between missions, they played baseball, drank American beer and repaired Italian Fiat automobiles. One crewmember raced around the desert on a captured German motorcycle. Two captured enemy fighters, a Messerschmitt 109 and Junkers 88, were repaired and put into flying condition by the 93rd's crews. Both planes had their German markings painted over with white stars and were planned to be used to shuttle between Gambut and the Delta near Alexandria, Egypt.

CHAPTER 32

January 13, 1943
Twentieth Combat
Mission: Sousse

On January 13, the third day after the La Goulette raid, the Ninth Air Force ordered the 93rd to target Tripoli. As before, the mission was to inflict as much damage on Rommel's supply depots as possible. This was in support of the westward progress of the British Eighth Army. For this mission the 93rd scraped together a dozen mission-worthy Liberators, Hot Stuff among them.

The briefing routine was the same; crewmembers gathered around the map spread on the sand. The operations officer read from notes on a clipboard. "If the weather is crappy over Tripoli, you're to continue to your secondary target. And yes, it's *Sousse* again."

A mournful groan emanated from the assembled crews. "I can't believe Sousse is the secondary target. Between us and the Brits bombing that place over and over again, there shouldn't be anything left," Eisel commented.

McQueen turned toward Farley. "Bet you two pounds we go to Sousse and pound it back into beach sand."

The waist gunner replied, "You're on, Paul. There's no way we're going to miss Tripoli *this* time."

Three hours into the mission, word was passed across the intercom Tripoli was socked in. They were going to proceed on for another hour to bomb port facilities at Sousse. Farley sighed through his oxygen mask, looked at McQueen's outstretched glove and slapped two pounds into it. Not a word was spoken between the two.

As the dozen B-24s approached the port city, moderate antiaircraft fire began to fill the path in front of the formation. While Hot Stuff bounced up and down through the flak's shock waves, Jacobson adjusted his bombsight. "I'm beginning to feel like the Fuller Brush man standing in the doorway, a hostile glaring housewife ready to slam the door in my face."

"You ever sell anything door to door, Jake?" Gott asked.

"No. But I remember my mom getting rid of all kinds of salesmen selling everything from Bibles and vacuum cleaners to brushes," the bombardier replied. "We know the Nazis below don't want what we're offering."

When the harbor facilities came within the crosshairs, Jake released the bomb load. "Bombs away!" Shannon took control of the aircraft and the formation flew back to Gambut Main. There were no enemy aircraft sighted and all of the 93rd's Liberators returned safely.

CHAPTER 33

January 15, 1943
Twenty-First Combat
Mission: Tripoli

Two days later on the morning of January 15, a dozen crews gathered around the map on the sand for a routine briefing by Col. Timberlake and Major Compton. As the British Eighth Army advanced toward Tripoli, the Axis-held city was a high priority target for the Ninth Air Force. Since Hot Stuff was considered to be one of the more mission worthy aircraft, Shannon and his crew stood looking down at the map. Aerial photos of the harbor area and docked vessels were passed among the pilots and bombardiers. It was crucial that Rommel's logistical support was interdicted.

The Liberators took to the air at noon. As they drew closer to Tripoli, the formation was joined by British P-40s. No enemy aircraft rose to challenge their approach. Shortly after the escort fighters turned back to support British ground forces, the B-24s came under heavy antiaircraft fire. Regardless, the formation pressed on and delivered its lethal load on the harbor hitting vessels and shore areas.

Eisel looked down from his rear vantage point as the formation turned toward Gambut Main. "Looks like we really pounded the shit of those bastards again." He captured the flames and smoke twenty-two thousand feet below with his movie camera.

None of the Liberators left the target area unscathed; however, one of the Liberators suffered a direct hit from the flak. Shannon dropped back to provide covering fire should enemy fighters try to take advantage of the crippled B-24. Fortunately, no Axis aircraft rose to the occasion.

An hour after leaving the target area, Hot Stuff's crew watched as four men bailed out of the stricken bomber. To their knowledge, the blossoming parachutes dropped into friendly territory. The remaining six crewmen stayed with the severely damaged Liberator all the way back to Gambut Main and the pilots were able to successfully land the aircraft. The plane was deemed unrepairable and provided spare parts for lesser damaged Liberators.

Timberlake's group was now down to eighteen aircraft, a few no longer deemed mission capable, six less than when it left England over a month earlier.

The next day, the 93rd received word that the four men who had parachuted out didn't survive.

CHAPTER 34

January 17, 1943
Twenty-Second
Mission: Tripoli

After chowing down on C rations on the morning of January 17, twelve of the group's crews, Hot Stuff among them gathered in the now searing hot sun for the briefing on the day's mission. Col. Timberlake and his operations officer pointed to Tripoli as the targeted area. Photos from aerial reconnaissance aircraft were passed around. As successful as the previous mission had been there still was work to be done. The specified targets consisted of several ships in the harbor.

The night before, the selected crews had already prepared their Liberators for the mission; fuel tanks filled, bombs uploaded and machine gun ammunition loaded. Takeoff time was set at 1130. As per all missions, Shannon received the signal to start engines and to taxi *Hot Stuff* into its place in the line of waiting B-24s. Again the aircraft took off in thirty second intervals. After the group formed into four elements of three aircraft each, the Liberators headed west.

Unfortunately the bombers encountered strong head winds and their flight time to the target area was five hours.

Three hours into the flight Lentz mumbled through his oxygen mask. "With these goddamned headwinds, it seems like it's taking us forever to reach our target."

Buffeted by the winds, Hot Stuff bounced up and down and Shannon and Lentz struggled to keep in formation.

"By my calculations, it'll be another two hours before we reach Tripoli," Gott said.

Farley looked over his shoulder at McQueen. "You're not going to get sick all over me again, are you, Paul? It's been a while."

A slightly green face turned to the fellow waist gunner. "Don't worry, George, I didn't eat too much before takeoff. So far so good."

"Let's hope so. I can only take so much of your puke before I spill my guts," the left waist gunner replied. "How are you doing in the tail, George?"

Eisel grunted in his oxygen mask as the plane dropped several feet and immediately bounced upward. "Just like when I was a kid on the roller coaster at the state fair with a belly full of hot dogs, the C-ration crackers and peanut butter are staying down."

Two hours later upon signal from the lead aircraft Hot Stuff's bombs hit the designated Axis merchant shipping in Tripoli. The B-24's gunners reported their bombs landed at the north end of the Spanish Mole and on the town. Enemy flak was the heaviest the 93rd had encountered since arriving in North Africa. Many of the aircraft sustained punctures in fuselages from the flak, but none were seriously damaged. Once the Liberators banked to return to base, they had several enemy aircraft in pursuit. Of those fighters, two Messerschmitt 109s bore down on Hot Stuff.

Lentz looked up to his right. "Bandits at two o'clock." He confidently waited for Rondeau in the top turret to fire the twin .50s at the attacking fighters.

"I see them," McQueen shouted as he turned his .50 toward the threat and began firing.

Lentz's eyes grew wide as the yellow nose of the lead fighter drew closer, its guns blazing away. "Goddamn it, Rondeau that son of a bitch is right on top of us! Fire!" He ducked away from the hail of 20 millimeter cannon fire that slammed through the cockpit area. One round exploded behind Shannon's seat in the cockpit.

Shine's fighter pilot instinct took control as he instigated evasive action, careful not to come too close to other aircraft in the tight formation.

Gott turned toward Lentz, "Rondeau's been hit!"

Lentz started to get up from his seat. "Stay put, John," Shannon ordered. "I need you here in case something happens to me." He spoke over his shoulder to the radio operator who sat just behind the copilot during bombing runs. "Jeffers, go man the turret."

"I'll check on Rondeau," the navigator shouted. When Gott knelt beside the flight engineer he found there was no blood. Rondeau had not been wounded, but was unconscious from lack of oxygen. The navigator grabbed the portable oxygen bottle and placed the mask over Rondeau's face. A few moments later, the airman began to regain consciousness. Gott gave the bottle to the aircraft engineer, "Here keep breathing on this for a while." The navigator inspected the flight engineer's oxygen line and found it had been severed by enemy fire. He managed to repair it using adhesive tape from the first-aid kit.

The withering fire from the formation's .50s drove away the attackers.

Moments later when it appeared, Hot Stuff was out of harm's way, Shannon spoke over the intercom. "Anybody hit?"

Each crewmember checked in over the intercom they were okay.

Shannon then gave the controls to Lentz and looked behind his seat. The fuselage was riddled with holes, but a colorful package stood unharmed. "Whew, glad that expensive bottle of perfume I bought in Cairo survived."

"Maybe that's a sign of good luck," the copilot added.

Night had fallen shortly after the group had turned back to Gambut Main. Fortunately, the weather remained clear and the last of the planes landed safely in full moonlight by 2100.

Following the raid, Hot Stuff along with several of the group's Liberators were ordered to stand down for maintenance and repairs. The crews were left to their own devices playing baseball, taking joy rides on captured German vehicles, writing letters and playing cards.

The remainder of the group was assigned missions to bomb Sousse on January 19. The flak over the harbor area was light. The principle target was a large German ship, but the bombs missed it. However, the docks were left in flames. Six Me 109s attacked the group following the bomb run and some Liberators sustained minor damage. Four of the enemy fighters were shot down. The B-24s returned to base by 1800.

CHAPTER 35

Courier Flight to Alexandria

On January 20, the day after the B-24s returned from their mission to Sousse, Col. Timberlake called Shannon aside and ordered him to fly a courier mission to Ninth Air Force at Alexandria, Egypt. Shine was to carry reports on mission results to HQ and return with intelligence information on target areas for future missions.

Because Shannon was a former fighter pilot, Timberlake chose him to convey the documents in a captured German Me 109s that had been repaired by crewmen. The fighter now sported a white star where once the iron cross was fixed. Shannon was to takeoff at 1000 on January 21 and return the next day.

Hot Stuff's pilot sat in the captured fighter and familiarized himself with the controls. When he felt comfortable with the instruments and controls, he revved up the engine. Rondeau and a ground maintenance technician stood by with fire extinguishers. When Rondeau gave Shine the "okay" salute, the former Nazi fighter began to roll onto the runway. Seconds later, the fighter was airborne once again.

Compared to the P-40 Shannon was surprised at how agile and light the captured fighter felt. It responded rapidly and was so easily maneuverable. He felt the old fighter pilot excitement as he put the Messerschmitt through its paces.

Hot Stuff's crew and ground personnel watched as Shannon put on an impromptu air show for entertainment. There was a lot of laughing and back slapping as they hooted and congratulated themselves on the great job they did in restoring the German aircraft into flying condition.

Shine made several touchdowns and takeoffs to ensure the aircraft was safe for flying. After he parked the Me 109 and shut down the engine, the spectators ran up alongside the fighter and cheered.

Shine stood on the wing, doffed his crushed service cap and bowed. He looked around at the smiling faces. "Fellows, I now pronounce this fighter airworthy."

On the morning of January 21, Shannon finished a breakfast of canned spam and crackers. He strolled over to the group's operations officer to plan his flight route. He estimated it would take him about an hour to fly the three hundred miles to the east. While there, Col. Timberlake handed Shine a flat leather briefcase. "Make sure you take this to Ninth Air Force intelligence, and before you return, pick up aerial reconnaissance photos and any intelligence information they can provide for future missions."

Shannon took the briefcase, casually saluted his commanding officer, and headed for the parked Me 109. A back seat for a passenger had been configured in the captured aircraft. Shine had decided to take his copilot with him to Alexandria. He met Lentz who stood by the fighter's wing wearing his parachute, a smile and a headset over his service cap. Rondeau helped Shine strap on his parachute. Moments later at 1000, the agile aircraft leaped off the runway and took to the sky.

Lentz had never flown in a fighter before and was exhilarated by the rapid takeoff and climbing speed of the small aircraft. He spoke to Shannon over the makeshift intercom, "Wow, Shine, now I know what it's like to be a fighter pilot. Don't you miss it?"

"Yeah, that feeling is always with me. But I enjoy the challenge of flying Hot Stuff more."

Just over an hour later, Shannon landed the Me 109 at a nondescript airstrip on the outskirts of Alexandria. After climbing out of the cramped confines of the fighter, the two pilots stretched their legs and looked for ground transportation to take them to Ninth Air Force Headquarters. Shannon carried the small leather briefcase under his arm as he and Lentz walked toward a parked jeep with an American soldier sitting behind the wheel. They were driven to a nondescript concrete building where Shine handed the pouch to a staff officer.

While at the base, they made their way to the officers' mess for the noon meal. It was the first time since Cairo they enjoyed hot food consisting of fresh eggs cooked to order, bacon and toast with jam. Later they were shown to transient officers' quarters where they showered and shaved. They rested and wrote letters home until it was time to meet at the officers' mess for drinks and dinner.

The next morning after a leisurely breakfast, Shannon and Lentz walked over to HQ. There Shine signed for the intelligence documents before the return flight to Gambut Main.

After the hour-long flight to Gambut, Shannon handed the leather case to Major Compton. It was at this moment Shine and Lentz were told about the third raid to Tripoli that had been conducted while they had been in Alexandria. The mission had been called back at the last minute because the city was supposedly in Allied hands. However, one flight of three of the group's Liberators hadn't received the recall message and had bombed the city.

Col. Timberlake was concerned the bombs from those three B-24s may have inadvertently fallen on Allied ground troops. It was not until nightfall that his concerns were laid aside. Allied troops had arrived at the outskirts of the city, not within, and did not sustain casualties because of the bombing.

CHAPTER 36

January 26, 1943
Twenty-Third
Mission: Messina

The dispatches Shannon had carried back from Alexandria denoted a shift in the Ninth Air Force's target areas for the 93rd. With the complexion of the ground situation in North Africa beginning to favor the Allies, Col. Timberlake received orders to begin bombing of Italy and Sicily. Fortunately, the group had been given over a week to prepare for the long missions across the Mediterranean. Several planes had been dispatched to Alexandria for sorely needed maintenance, repairs and upgrades. During this time the remainder of the group's operational Liberators had been retrofitted with auxiliary fuel tanks in the right bomb bay further extending the range of the bombers.

On the morning of January 26 fourteen of the group's Liberators were considered mission capable. Of those twelve were chosen for the day's mission, Hot Stuff was among them. The dozen crews gathered around the map spread on the desert floor. This time the group's route ranged west by northwest out across the Mediterranean. Col. Timberlake informed those present for the first time since arriving in North Africa, the mission target was on the continent of Europe; they were to bomb the harbor of Naples, Italy. Excited chatter erupted among the crewmen.

That morning the operations officer briefed the details of the plan. The formation was to arrive over the target area at dusk leaving sufficient light for bombing. The purpose was to return in darkness thereby reducing the probability of attacks by enemy fighters. Should Naples be obscured for some reason, the secondary target was the port area of Messina, Sicily. Each B-24 was to carry five one thousand–pounders. Takeoff time for the nine hundred–mile flight was scheduled for 1400.

Ninth Air Force directed that photos of the bombing results be taken since this was the first mission onto the European Continent from North Africa. The operations officer handed Shannon the cumbersome K-20 camera. "You'll be at the end of the formation and in the best position to take after-action aerial photos."

A few minutes later, Shine gave the encased ten pound camera to Jeffers. "Here. Learn all you can about using this thing in the next two hours. You're now Hot Stuff's official aerial photographer whenever they hand us the camera."

"Yes, sir," Jeffers responded with a stunned look on his face.

McQueen slapped Jeffers on the back. "Congratulations, Ken. When the war's over you can get a job with *Life* magazine."

Jeffers opened the leather camera case, pulled out the technical manual and sighed. The radio operator walked slowly back to his tent, open manual in hand and the camera case strap slung over his shoulder.

As Jeffers sat on his cot in the hot tent, he mumbled, "I don't know a goddamned thing about cameras. I couldn't even take a decent picture with a Kodak box camera." He then dug deep into the K-20's manual. Just then he remembered his fellow radio operator Bill Gros who had taken aerial photos from Eager Beaver. Within minutes he sought out Gros. After an hour of discussion, Jeffers felt confident he was up to the task.

Upon signal, Hot Stuff's four Pratt & Whitney 1,200 horsepower engines roared to life at 1355. The engines had well over 300 hours on them; well beyond the time limit for overhaul. The nearly flawless performance of the engines in spite of minimum maintenance in the dust and sand of North Africa was evidence of their durability.

Upon the firing of a flare by the group's operations officer, the routine lining up of the dozen aircraft on the runway began. Hot Stuff was eleventh in line. Another flare signaled takeoff time for the first B-24 to roll down the runway. As per plan, the remaining eleven Liberators rolled in thirty-second intervals.

As they climbed to cruising altitude, the flight formed into four sets of three aircraft each.

Shannon spoke through his oxygen mask into the intercom. "Today's a swell day for us. We've helped push the Axis forces back in North Africa and now we're going to hit them on their own turf; where it really hurts."

"I overheard we have one guy in the group who came from Naples, and he's really upset," Lentz commented. "You can understand how the guy feels if you think you'll be bombing your own family."

"Not too much different from our own Civil War where brother fought brother," Jacobson sighed.

"Yeah, that's really something to think about," McQueen added.

After four hours in the air bucking strong headwinds there was no way the bombers could reach Naples before it was shrouded in darkness. The flight leader of the formation determined they would divert to their secondary target of Messina.

Dusk was already approaching when the 93rd's Liberators sighted Messina's harbor area. The formation began receiving moderate flak as the bombardiers sighted their targets.

Shannon spoke to Jeffers over the intercom. "Jeffers, don't forget to take aerial photos of the effects of our bombing."

"Got it, Lieutenant." The radioman pulled the large K-20 camera from its case and hung the camera strap around his neck as he crawled to the open bomb bay. There still was sufficient light to take decent photos.

As the B-24s released their lethal ordnance in train, the one thousand-pound bombs fell onto the town, a merchant vessel steaming out of the straits, nine vessels near the coast and four within the Messina basin.

As the bombs were released, Jeffers crawled to the open bomb bay. He followed his friend Gros's advice. To keep from falling out he knelt against a ten inch board he wedged between his knees and the forward bomb bay stanchions. He leaned over the yawning precipice and focused the lens. He was surprised how clear the image was through the eyepiece. He snapped a picture and repeatedly wound the film and snapped more. As he wound the film to snap one last photo, Hot Stuff was severely jostled from the turbulence created by flak.

Farley watched the radioman shift his weight to compensate for the aircraft's erratic movements in order to take yet another photograph. He let go of his .50 as he stared at Jeffers, but there was no way he could safely cross the nine-inch catwalk over the open bomb bay.

McQueen shook his head. "Son of a bitch, Jeffers, get back from the bomb bay."

Just then a close aerial explosion caused Hot Stuff to bounce violently.

Jeffers let go of the camera as he tried to grab anything to keep himself from falling out. The heavy camera hanging from his neck pulled him down toward the abyss. Just as he was about to fall, a pair of hands grabbed Jeffers' parachute harness from behind and pulled him to safety.

"Think that's enough picture taking for now," Rondeau declared. "Lieutenant, you can close the doors now."

"Good catch, Grant," Farley shouted over the intercom.

Jeffers's heart was beating like a snare drum and perspiration poured down his face. "Thanks, Grant. Thought I was a going to end up in a prisoner of war camp." He gasped as he sat back down on the metal stool in front of the bank of radios.

McQueen quipped, "Ken, look at the bright side, you could have had a great Italian dinner tonight."

In spite of the near tragic loss of Jeffers, the radioman was able to capture the successful results of the bombing on film.

As the Liberators turned to fly the nine hundred mile route back to Gambut Main, only one plane sustained damage and that consisted of some perforations in the wingtip from flak. No enemy fighter aircraft rose to challenge the formation.

On the long return flight to North Africa, Hot Stuff's gunners were able to stand down. In the dim interior light Craighead set up the poker board and McQueen and Farley sat while Eisel dealt out the poker hands. After an hour of listless card playing, they gave up and one by one fell asleep leaning against the fuselage.

The returning Liberators had to land in the dark at Gambut. The runway had one row of lights that marked its length. The radio beacon which provided direction for the last few miles was jammed by the enemy.

It was just before midnight when the first Liberator's wheels touched down on the steel mesh runway. All aircraft returned safely to Gambut Main with no casualties and only one Liberator slightly damaged.

CHAPTER 37

January 30, 1943
Twenty-Fourth
Mission: Messina

Late the next morning, Shannon once again flew the Americanized Me 109 on a courier flight to Alexandria, Egypt with the film from the raid on Messina. This time he took Jacobson as his passenger.

The bombardier found the flight to be exhilarating as the pilot put the swift aircraft through its paces. Jake spoke through the makeshift intercom. "Shine, I had no idea how much fun flying a fighter can be. Don't you miss it?"

"John said the same thing, but like I told him the thrill doesn't match piloting Hot Stuff."

After an uneventful one-hour flight they landed at the base which housed the Ninth Air Force Headquarters. Shannon parked the plane on the apron and the two climbed out. A jeep pulled up to the fighter. Within minutes they were within the confines of the headquarters building.

While the film was being developed, Shine and Jake sat at a table covered with white linen. A waiter brought sandwiches and cold

BEFORE THE BELLE

Coca-Cola. "Now this is what I call real living," Jake commented as he bit into his lunch and took a long swig of the soda. "Not since our trip to Cairo have I enjoyed a meal so much."

Three days later on January 30, the 93rd was ordered to return to Messina. The aerial photos Jeffers snapped were compared to earlier intelligence photos. The results indicated their next target was naval storage facilities at the north end of the city's harbor. Again, a dozen Liberators were selected for the mission. Attacking targets in Italy continued to be planned for afternoon takeoffs so the Liberators could arrive at the targeted areas before dusk. The aircraft were to fly at four thousand feet to evade enemy fighters and then climb to bombing altitude ninety minutes before reaching the initial point for making the bomb run.

Hot Stuff was considered to be one of the more mission capable aircraft in the group and for this mission it was selected to be one of the three lead bombers. Upon seeing the signal flare at 1430, Shannon pushed the four throttles forward and the Liberator began to roll. Seconds later they were airborne and within minutes the dozen aircraft were in tight formation bound for Sicily.

After bucking mild headwinds for three and a half hours, the port city loomed in the distance. Following the lead B-24, Celhalopodus, Hot Stuff and the other ten Liberators delivered their five one thousand–pounders in train on shore installations, the middle of the town and on nine vessels near the coast.

Flak was light and as the American bombers banked out toward the Mediterranean, the only aircraft to sustain any damage was Celhalopodus. No enemy fighters were encountered on the mission.

Jeffers looked back out the small side window as Messina disappeared in flames and smoke in the approaching darkness below. "Glad it wasn't me taking those aerial photos. I've had my fill of looking down the devil's throat."

"Looks like we kicked the shit out of them again," Eisel spoke into the intercom. "Messina's fire department's going to have a busy night at the docks."

Four hours later Hot Stuff's wheels touched down at Gambut. As the crew deplaned in the moonlit desert, a pilot from another Liberator invited Shannon and his men to the mess tent for a post mission celebration.

Shannon removed his crushed service cap and ran his fingers through his hair. "I'm bushed. Can't we make it another time?"

The pilot smiled. "Come on, Shine. You and your crew deserve this."

Shannon looked at his crew standing in the moonlight. "Well, okay. But let's make it quick, we all need sack time."

When Hot Stuff's crew arrived at the mess facility, each one was handed a cold bottle of beer. The surprise was greeted with lots of laughing, backslapping and lighting up of cigarettes. The mess tent was inundated with clouds of tobacco smoke and riotous chatter.

"How did we get ice cold beer out here?" Shannon asked his host.

The two pilots clinked their beer bottles and the host pilot laughed. "While you guys were on a mission, we flew to Cairo for some quick engine repairs and stayed a couple of nights at the Shepheard. Before leaving we requisitioned a vacant bath tub, filled it with ice from the hotel bar and loaded it into our bomb bay. We also brought back a dozen cases of beer, compliments of the Shepheard bar."

"Jesus," Shine replied. "What a keen idea. Wish I'd thought of that when we were in Cairo. How the hell did you sneak a tub full of ice out of the hotel?"

"First, we requisitioned a tub from one of our rooms the night before we left. Then after midnight when the lobby was deserted we lugged it out to a truck in the parking lot and covered it with a canvas. You know, it's surprising what a little money can do. We bribed a hotel employee to open the bar's storage room. We requisitioned twelve cases of beer and loaded it onto the truck.

"Then this evening just before we left the hotel for the airbase we carried buckets of ice from the bar's ice maker to the tub on the back of the truck. Before anyone could stop us we hauled ass out of there. The cold night air slowed the ice's melting. When we reached cruising altitude, the cold air refroze the water until we landed at Gambut." The pilot gestured at the tub still a quarter full of beer bottles in the chopped ice. "And there you have it."

Just then Timberlake entered the mess tent. The noise in the canvas structure faded to a whisper, all eyes on the 93rd's commander. His face stern, he quietly walked up to the tub, looked down and helped himself to one of the bottles. "I commend your ingenuity, gentlemen. There's no doubt this mission required precise planning and execution." He opened the bottle of beer, took a swig and continued. "However this type of midnight requisitioning has got to stop. After all we need to keep on good terms with the Shepheard Hotel." He then broke into laughter.

CHAPTER 38

February 7, 1943 Twenty-Fifth Combat Mission: Naples

By the end of January 1943 all of the 93rd's bomber crews were exhausted and their B-24s were showing wear and tear. The routine was becoming monotonous; a mission one day, sack time the next. In between some of the men played baseball, others played cards and wrote letters. Somehow American beer and Coca-Cola managed to be trucked in along with C rations, bombs, gasoline and machine-gun ammo. Sandstorms often impacted missions and baseball. Some mechanically inclined men spent hours repairing Italian vehicles which proved to be of great use since the group suffered a shortage of issue vehicles to traverse the expanse of Gambut Main.

At midmorning on February 7, the crews of Hot Stuff and eleven other B-24s received a briefing in the open as they had ever since their arrival at Gambut Main. Their target was the harbor facilities at Naples. For this mission Hot Stuff was designated the lead bomber.

BEFORE THE BELLE

En route to the target area, the 93rd was joined by B-24s from the 98th and 376th groups flying out of the aerodrome at Fayid, Egypt. It was to be one of the larger bombing raids from North Africa.

After just over five hours, the Italian port city loomed in the distance. The gunners on the bombers were on alert for enemy aircraft. The formation approached the target area at twenty thousand feet. The flak was moderate.

Jacobson methodically took control of Hot Stuff from Shannon and guided the aircraft over the target area. He flipped the switch that opened the bomb bay doors. He aligned the crosshairs on his bombsight and selected the bomb racks to release in fifty foot intervals. His gloved hand toggled the bomb release switch. "Bombs away!"

A few seconds later, he observed two enemy merchant vessels being damaged with 500 pound bombs. Control of Hot Stuff reverted to Shannon and they and the other eleven Liberators of the 93rd began their return flight to Gambut Main. It was at this moment, they watched in horror as a Liberator from the 376th took a direct hit severing the portside wing from the fuselage. The separated wing with its two engines still running made a slow revolving descent toward the harbor. The doomed bomber began a slow downward spiral through broken clouds.

"Bail out! Bail out!" Farley shouted through the open window on Hot Stuff's portside.

McQueen stood next to Farley and looked down at the tragedy. "Get out, goddammit!"

As the mortally wounded aircraft disappeared into the clouds, no parachutes were observed. Hot Stuff's crew was silent. Ten more empty bunks. How lucky they were to have survived another mission.

Although no enemy aircraft rose to challenge the B-24s, the gunners maintained vigilance until the 93rd was well out to sea.

"My hands are still shaking," McQueen bemoaned. "Why didn't those guys bail out?"

"When the fuselage is spiraling like that it's near impossible to get out even if they were able to open the bomb bay," Lentz responded.

"Could be some of the crew were too wounded to jump," Jacobson added.

Just before midnight the 93rd's dozen Liberators returned safely to Gambut.

The next two days the crews stood down. They rested, played games and pulled maintenance on the aircraft.

CHAPTER 39

February 10 and 20, 1943 Twenty-Sixth and Twenty-Seventh Combat Missions: Palermo and Naples

On February 10, the lull in the action was interrupted when the 93rd was called upon to bomb Palermo, Sicily. Hot Stuff, being one of the fourteen mission-capable Liberators in the group was selected to participate with eleven other B-24s. The principal targets were a chemical factory and an industrial area. The group's bombers were to once again be joined by Liberators flying out of Fayid, Egypt.

After three hours into the mission, Shannon heard over the command net that the bombers from Fayid aborted due to bad weather. It fell upon the 93rd to complete the mission alone. The dozen Liberators bombed various targets, each aircraft dropping nine five hundred pounders in train. The chemical factory was left in ruins as well as was the surrounding industrial area.

Fortunately, there was minimal antiaircraft fire and no enemy fighters were encountered. The twelve aircraft returned to Gambut

Main without loss. As was habit, the Brits manning the airbase's antiaircraft guns counted the returning planes and were relieved to find there were no losses.

Hot Stuff did not participate in a follow-on bombing mission on Naples. At the debriefing, Shannon and his crew were saddened to hear the group had lost two planes and crews, something the antiaircraft crews already knew. Now only sixteen Liberators comprised the 93rd Bombardment Group in North Africa.

Lentz shook his head. "That'll be twenty more cots that will be empty tonight. I feel like we keep losing members of our family."

Shannon's voice, choked with emotion, murmured, "They all died cloaked in glory."

Of the remaining sixteen Liberators in the 93rd, some were barely operational.

On the afternoon of February 20, the 93rd attacked Naples a third time. It was rough. The Germans had moved in after the first bombing and they were waiting for the Liberators. Antiaircraft fire was very heavy and several of the bombers were hit and two were lost.

After the mission Jeffers sought out his friend Bill Gros the radio operator on Eager Beaver who's Liberator was near the two doomed B-24s. Gros related how he felt when he watched in total shock as the two planes went down. With watery eyes he told Jeffers their mutual friend Bob Woody, another radio operator, went down with one of the planes.

Jeffers put his hand on Gros's shoulder. "Jesus, Bill, I'm so sorry to hear about Woody. Why is it the good guys seem to pay the price in this goddamned war?"

CHAPTER 40

Farewell to Gambut Main

On the morning of February 23, Col. Timberlake assembled the 93rd within the old sheet metal hangar, the only building at Gambut Main. It was a red letter day for the group. The odyssey to North Africa was about to end. He announced orders had been received for the group to return to England and rejoin the Eighth Air Force.

The two hundred men standing around the group commander broke into cheers and excited chatter.

"We're going to return to England by way of Tafaroui," Timberlake continued. "Takeoff time will be midnight. There will be no formation; each plane will be on its own. Once the last plane is in the air, Gambut Main will close as an Allied airbase."

Another round of cheers erupted from the gathering. Timberlake waited for the rejoicing to die down and continued. "Instead of our final destination being Alconbury, we'll be flying into a brand new airbase—Hardwick, north of London. Oh, and by the way, we'll all receive back pay once we get there."

Following Timberlake's announcement, the various pilots and navigators anxiously gathered around a map on the ground where the group's operations officer briefed them on their route. The plan was for the individual aircraft to retrace the flight path the group flew from Tafaroui to Gambut Main. By flying in darkness the chance of being challenged by Axis fighters would be minimized. The planes were to takeoff in two minute intervals.

The crews and ground personnel anxiously spent the rest of the day packing and preparing the remaining fourteen B-24s for the long 1,100 mile flight to Tafaroui. During their preparations the American airmen also took time to say farewell to the Brits who manned the Gambut antiaircraft positions. They gave their "cheerleaders" what cigarettes, beer and other comforts they no longer required or could not take on the planes. The Brits had become "chums" with many of the men in the 93rd and sweated out the twenty-three missions the group had flown out of Gambut. Hot Stuff participated in sixteen of those missions as well as one more out of Tafaroui.

Some of the Brits had been in North Africa for two years and longed for their homeland. As a sign of friendship the Americans agreed to carry greetings, parcels and letters back to England for the contingent of "The Desert Rats" that protected the airbase. Once the 93rd left Gambut Main, the Tommies were to redeploy elsewhere in the British Eighth Army.

At midnight Timberlake's Liberator Teggie Ann roared down the runway at Gambut Main for the last time. The Brits at the anti-aircraft positions shouted messages of good luck and waved their helmets in the air; not unlike they did when the 93rd flew combat missions out of the airbase.

Of the twenty-four Liberators that left England two and a half months earlier, only fourteen survived. More important than the aircraft lost were the crewmen who would never return.

Before taking off, each of the 93rd's Liberator crews helped cram ground personnel, survivors of lost aircraft and gear onboard. A half hour after Timberlake's Teggie Ann had departed, the last B-24 had "wheels up."

BEFORE THE BELLE

Hot Stuff was the twelfth Liberator to takeoff into the darkness bound for Tafaroui. Like all the 93rd's airmen, those aboard Shannon's B-24 were with mixed emotions; anxious to leave and return to civilization and sad thinking of those who would not be going back with them.

"You've been awfully quiet, Paul," Farley said to the other waist gunner. "What's eating you?"

"Did you hear what the 'old man' told us?" McQueen answered. "We're going to Hardwick, a new airbase north of London. Do you know what that means?"

"What?" Farley responded. "Paul, a new airbase is a new airbase."

"No, no." the waist gunner said. "You don't get it, George. Remember just when Alconbury was starting to become livable they sent us to Tafaroui and then Gambut Main; one shit hole worse than the one before. Knowing the brass, Hardwick has got to be the worst yet. Just the name makes it seem crappy."

"Wait a minute, Paul. We're going back to civilization and Timberlake did say Hardwick's north of London. Think of it. The big city and great times. Bet you two pounds you're all wet," Farley responded.

"You're on, Buddy," McQueen asserted.

"I'll take some of that action," Craighead said. "I'm betting Hardwick is going to be a swanky place."

"Okay, Joe," McQueen boasted. "I can take your money too."

"That's enough, you guys," Shannon spoke over the intercom, "cut the chatter and stay alert. Before any bets can be collected remember we've got to get back to England."

Seven long hours later, Shannon heard over the command net that Northwest Africa was socked in. The chances of the fog burning off before the 93rd's Liberators ran out of fuel weren't good. To make things worse the radio range system at Tafaroui was inoperative.

The pilots had two choices. The first was to continue another two hundred miles to Gibraltar in hopes of not running out of gas and finding clear weather. The second was to circle above Tafaroui until the fuel ran out in hopes the fog would clear. They all chose to try landing at the old French airbase near Oran, Algeria.

Not knowing how long they would be aloft the 93rd's crews began jettisoning excess weight in order to reduce fuel consumption. Even the load of fresh eggs on board Timberlake's Teggie Ann that had been purchased for a celebratory breakfast at Tafaroui was sacrificed. However, the precious cargo of mail and gifts from the Brits to their families were considered sacred and remained onboard the B-24s.

A few of the Liberators, guided by controllers in the airbase tower, took a chance and flew at treetop level searching out the runway. They managed to break through the low clouds and successfully touched down. Two of the B-24s came close to colliding as they vied for air space while landing at the socked-in airbase.

"This shit is like pea soup," Lentz commented as he gazed out of the windshield. He then looked at the fuel gauges. "We'd better find Tafaroui soon or else Hot Stuff turns into a glider."

"Where the hell are we?" Shannon asked Gott. "We can't keep flying around in this goddamned crap forever."

"Shine, I've checked and double checked; I'm sure we're right over Tafaroui," the navigator responded.

Just then, a shadow appeared through the clouds on Hot Stuff's portside. Shannon looked to his left. An American twin engine military transport aircraft loomed on his port wing tip.

An unfamiliar voice emanated over the command net. "We heard you guys needed some help. Stick with me, I'll guide you down."

"Where the hell did he come from?" Lentz asked as he looked to his left.

"I don't care," Shine responded. "If he could find us in this crap, I'm sure he can lead us down."

Shannon spoke to the unknown C-47 pilot over the command net, "Okay, lead the way." He kept his port wing as close to the transport plane as possible as they descended.

The daring C-47 pilot led Hot Stuff down through the murky mist and suddenly the runway appeared in front of the Liberator. "You're on your own now," the unknown pilot said. "Have to go back up and search for others."

"Thanks for your help," Shannon radioed back.

As Hot Stuff descended toward the Tafaroui airstrip, the transport plane disappeared up into the low hanging clouds.

At the moment, Hot Stuff's wheels touched the runway surface excited chatter broke out on the intercom. They had successfully negotiated the first leg of their journey back to England.

Timberlake counted the Liberators already on the ground and those that continued to touch down at Tafaroui. They had come so far and he didn't want to lose any more planes and crews. Several landed with only a few gallons of fuel remaining in the cells. In the end there were thirteen planes on the ground. Bad Ass was missing. The group commander feared for the worst. It wasn't until much later when British agents reported the Liberator had run out of fuel and was forced to land in Spanish Morocco. The crew was alive but was now interned for the duration by the Fascist Spanish Government.

Considering the crude living conditions the group endured during the two and a half-month stay in North Africa, Timberlake was pleasantly surprised at the overall good health of the men. The two medical kits brought from England were found to be sufficient to care for the wounded.

During the twenty-five missions the 93rd conducted while in North Africa, the group handed out its share of punishment to Rommel's Afrika Korps and its Italian ally. This included: the sinking of seven enemy merchant vessels and damaging numerous others; the shooting down of twenty enemy aircraft and crippling countless others; the destruction of untold numbers of shore installations; the destruction of enemy fighter bases along with parked planes; and the demolishing of rail lines, bridges, and rolling stock.

During their last month in North Africa, the 93rd was visited by a number of high-profile dignitaries. The informal stopovers consisted of passing among the members of the group, shaking hands and commending them for the splendid job they were doing to thwart the Axis forces in North Africa.

Among the distinguished visitors were General Harold Alexander, Allied Middle East commander in chief; General Henry (Hap) Arnold, chief of the United States Army Air Force; General Bernard Montgomery, commander of the British Eighth Army; Major General Carl Spaatz, commander of US Air Operations in the United Kingdom; Major General Lewis Brereton, commander US Ninth Air Force; and Lieutenant General Frank Andrews, now commander of US Forces in the Mediterranean.

General Andrews was already known to members of the 93rd as the group was under his command while it conducted antisubmarine patrol duty off the coast of Florida six months earlier. Unknown at the time of his visit Andrews was soon to be notified by General George Marshall, the Army chief of staff, he was to assume command of US Forces in the European Theater of Operations. The 93rd would once again be under Andrews' command.

CHAPTER 41

Return to England

Tafaroui was socked in for almost two days. During that period, the 93rd rested and prepared the thirteen B-24s for the flight to Hardwick.

The weather forecast for February 27 proved favorable and the group operations officer briefed the crews early that morning. The route back to England was a reverse of that taken to Tafaroui. The planes were to fly over Gibraltar and then once out over the Atlantic they were to turn north toward Land's End, the southwestern-most tip of England. In order to avoid friendly antiaircraft fire from Gibraltar, the operations officer issued a special recognition code to the radio operators.

Wheels up for the first aircraft was scheduled for 0900. The Liberators were to take off in one minute intervals. Once in the air the group was to form into sets of three aircraft each for mutual protection. Their route would take them west over Gibraltar, then north over Portugal, and finally north by northeast to England. They were to avoid flying over Spanish territory and fly at four thousand feet to avoid detection while near the coast of France.

Hot Stuff lifted off of Tafaroui airbase at 0901. Once in the air the Liberator joined two others and proceeded toward Gibraltar.

Rondeau spoke into the intercom, "Well, guys how did you enjoy your ten day vacation in beautiful North Africa?"

"Seems like the big brass has trouble dealing with calendars," McQueen quipped. "They must think two and a half months consists of ten days."

"I counted each day since we left England," Craighead announced. "Looks like it's been about eighty days from when we went wheels up at Land's End on the anniversary of Pearl Harbor."

As they approached "the rock" Jeffers transmitted a Morse code message with the code for safe passage over the British antiaircraft guns at Gibraltar. Suddenly the air was filled with flak.

"What the hell is going on?" Shannon shouted. "Jeffers, did you send the code?"

"Yes, sir," the radioman replied. "I'll send it again."

Hot Stuff and the two accompanying Liberators continued to bounce through the friendly fire. Lentz held the controls in a death grip. "Jesus Christ, we've come all this way and now the Brits are trying to blow us out of the sky."

Frustrated, Shine ordered, "Goddamned it, Jeffers, try to contact Gibraltar by voice."

"Wilco," the radioman answered. After some quick frequency changes, Jeffers was able to establish voice communications with the British and Shannon spoke to the ground station.

After only a few minutes that seemed like a lifetime to Hot Stuff's crew, the antiaircraft fire ceased as quickly as it had begun. There was no apparent damage to the leading Liberators.

A voice with a purely American accent resonated over the net. "Sorry, guys. Appears you transmitted an outdated code. Fortunately I had been notified you'd be flying over Gibraltar at about this time and was able to shut down the antiaircraft fire."

Shannon took a deep breath and responded. "Glad someone got the word. Thanks."

McQueen complained over the intercom. "Son of a bitch, how many times do we have to fly over Gibraltar before they can figure out we're on their side."

"Aw, Paul, no need to snap your cap," Farley responded. "This is war. Shit happens."

"Yeah," Rondeau added. "George is right. Remember when three of our planes didn't get the word that our guys on the ground were in Tripoli and bombed the place? Luckily, the friendlies were at the edge of the city instead of in it. Nobody on our side got hurt."

"And lucky for us the Brits didn't get us this time either," McQueen said.

"Enough of that crap, fellas," Shannon said. "Let's concentrate on getting back to England in one piece. Keep a sharp eye out for enemy fighters as soon as we start heading north."

The flight from Gibraltar to England was uneventful. The late winter weather remained stable and no enemy fighters rose to challenge the Liberators.

Nearly eight hours after taking off from Tafaroui the sprawling airbase at Hardwick loomed in the distance. "Look at that!" exclaimed Lentz as he peered thorough Hot Stuff's windscreen. "There are three paved runways. They all look to be over five thousand feet in length."

As Hot Stuff touched down, the crew gazed wide-eyed at the expansive airbase. A jeep with a large "Follow Me" sign appeared to guide the aircraft to a parking apron. As soon as Shannon shut down the engines, a two and a half ton truck pulled up alongside to ferry the crew to their post-flight interrogation.

Before loading onto the truck, Rondeau gazed in all directions. "Hardwick looks like a small city. There must be a couple hundred buildings here."

"I'm looking forward to getting a real shower, clean sheets, and a lot of sack time," Eisel said.

As the truck carrying Hot Stuff's crew to the debriefing building drove down the tarmac, the airmen gasped at the array of concrete buildings. They stared at the surroundings as if they were aliens from another planet. Signs indicated there were fire stations, photo labs, maintenance shops, and Nissen huts for housing personnel. All structures were camouflaged in olive drab or brown.

Once the arrivals from North Africa were seated inside the large debriefing building the debriefing officers stared disbelievingly at the disheveled appearance of the "Desert Rats." The darkly tanned men of the 328th, 330th, and 409th squadrons sported beards, shaggy hair, filthy worn uniforms and an odd assortment of footwear. One of the officers in the debriefing room stood and spoke to the assembled arrivals. "Welcome to Hardwick Aerodrome. We know you're anxious to get cleaned up and get some chow so we'll make this debriefing as short as possible. "For security purposes the aircrews were instructed not to tell anyone where they had been. If asked they could only say they had been "South" as evidenced by their sun-darkened countenances.

Twenty minutes later the crews were shown to their quarters: Nissen huts dispersed in squadron groups and hidden among trees. At this time of year each sixteen by twenty four foot round-walled Nissen hut was heated by a small coke-burning stove which was fueled by a daily ration of one bucket of coal. The men were provided bunks made of angle iron which were covered with mattresses filled excelsior, fine curled wood shavings. Those who slept within six feet of the little stove luxuriated in the heat. Those further away had to huddle under multiple blankets.

Showers and toilet facilities were in separate buildings and there was no hot water.

Hot stuff's ravenous crew dropped their gear on the floor in what seemed like the coldest section of their assigned Nissen hut. "I'm starved," McQueen blurted. "Show me some food!"

BEFORE THE BELLE

At the debriefing they were informed there were four mess halls at Hardwick. One for combat officers, one for air crewmen, one for ground officers and one for ground enlisted personnel. Hot Stuff's enlisted men quickly washed up and jogged to the mess hall designated for air crewmen.

As they progressed through the waiting line, they filled their metal trays with mutton, Brussel sprouts, SOS (Shit on a Shingle, creamed dried beef on toast), spam, powdered eggs, bread and marmalade. They filled cups with recombined powder milk and coffee.

The mess sergeant stared at the bedraggled men in the filthy British battle dress uniforms and mismatched nonissue footwear caked with dried mud. He couldn't believe the amount of food the starved shaggy-haired and bearded airmen piled onto their trays. "How can you guys eat all that?"

Rondeau looked the NCO in the eye as he held out his tray for more, "If you had been down South like we were, you'd find it easy. Goddamned it, now load it up!"

The mess NCO got the message and spooned as much food onto the trays as the men wanted.

Farley sat and stared at the sliced meat on his tray. "This looks like beef, but it smells funny."

"That's because it mutton, you dope," Eisel responded. "It's like lamb roast. After a while you'll get used to it." He shoved a chunk of the meat into his mouth. "It tastes pretty good."

"My favorite is SOS," McQueen mumbled through a mouthful of the creamy chipped beef. "I could eat this for every meal. Best goddamned thing the army dishes out."

Forty-five minutes later, stuffed with army chow, Hot Stuff's sergeants strolled back to their Nissen hut. There they found the footlockers containing the uniforms and other clothes they had left at Alconbury two and a half months earlier. After long tepid showers, and having shaved off their scraggly beards, the exhausted men crawled into their clean beds.

"God, this feels good," Craighead moaned as he lay on the steel bunk's sheet-covered mattress. "And smell those clean blankets and sheets."

"Better yet, no bugs," McQueen commented.

Rondeau muttered, "Better than that, not a scorpion in sight."

Within minutes the only sound in the darkened Nissen hut was the soft snoring of its occupants.

CHAPTER 42

Renewal at Hardwick

Because there was no reveille at Hardwick, Hot Stuff's crew slept late on February 28. Only their growling stomachs pulled them out of their bunks. The men trudged to the shower building, reveled in being able to shave and shower again. The more they scrubbed the more their tans faded.

"I thought my tan was darker than this," Craighead observed as he watched the dark water swirl down the shower drain.

"Must be going so long without a shower the desert dirt was a part of our skin," Eisel responded.

McQueen was drying himself with a towel when his stomach growled. "Need to dress and get over to the chow hall."

Moments later, he opened his footlocker. "My underwear and socks should still be clean after all this time." As he rummaged through the clothing his hand felt a large flat round metal object. "Goddamned, almost forgot about this." He pulled out the movie reel he had brought from Gander and read the label. *Wuthering Heights*. "Hey, guys, let's see if we can find someone who can run this movie for us."

"What is it?" Craighead inquired.

"It's the movie! *Wuthering Heights*. You know the story about the guy who lived out in the boondocks and fell in love with a real Sheba. Then the damned dame dies on him."

Groans and moans filled the Nissen hut. "Not that gobbledygook!" Rondeau exclaimed. "You're not serious, are you? We saw that damned thing so many times in Gander I thought I knew that English guy personally. Count me out." The others agreed.

"Okay, I'll go it alone. I'm going to the movie theater later and find some guy to run it for me."

Jeffers looked at Farley. The uniform from the footlocker hung listlessly on George's thin frame. "Looks like you're wearing some other guy's uniform," he laughed as he pulled on the waist of his trousers. "Look at this. Even after all that chow last night, I really have to tighten up on my belt to keep my pants from falling around my ankles."

Farley buttoned his loose shirt collar as he gazed in a mirror. "Look at my scrawny neck. I'm starting to look like my grandfather."

Craighead pulled his trousers on and gazed around the hut. "I wonder how much weight we've lost since we left Alconbury?"

"Bet it's been a lot," Eisel said. "But after a couple of weeks in the chow line, we'll pack it back on for sure."

"Remember, when we get issued new uniforms tomorrow, you should leave room to expand back to your normal sizes," Rondeau added. "If you don't, you'll end up looking like a stuffed sausage before you know it. Oh, by the way don't forget the finance office will be open after breakfast and we have a formation on the tarmac at 1400."

"Food before pay!" McQueen shouted. "I'm hot footing it to the chow hall." He was first out the door headed for the mess hall closely followed by the other five crewmembers.

BEFORE THE BELLE

Shannon had donned the pinks and greens he had left behind at Alconbury. He looked in a mirror as he adjusted his tie. It felt good to be wearing the dress uniform again. As he reached for his crushed service cap, Lentz barged into the officers' Nissen hut. "Shine, the 'old man' wants to see you in his office, PDQ."

"Before breakfast?" Shine asked.

"Yeah. Better get going. Must be pretty goddamned important."

The pilot stood thinking since the boss wanted to see him pretty damn quick, it had to be something he had seriously screwed up.

On his way to Timberlake's office, Shine's stomach churned. "Must be something I did wrong or forgot to do. Has someone bitched about the way I commanded Hot Stuff? Son of a bitch I can't think of a thing."

A few minutes later, Shannon stood in front of the group commander's office door. "Well here goes nothing." He knocked.

"Enter!" boomed Timberlake's voice.

Shine looked around the room. Besides Timberlake there were over a dozen other officers present along with the group's adjutant. He walked up to the desk, stood at attention, saluted and reported.

Timberlake returned the salute as he stood and gestured toward the other pilots in the room. "Get in line with the others, Lieutenant." He looked over to his adjutant. "Major, read the orders."

Major Brannon nodded and then bellowed, "Attention to orders..." All those present stood at attention as the staff officer read the orders that promoted the young pilots present to the rank of captain. "Promoted to the rank of captain..." were the only words Shannon heard. As anxiety faded into relief, he exhaled.

After a few remarks by Timberlake, he and his adjutant pinned the captain's bars on the shoulders of the newly promoted officers and shook their hands.

A few moments later Shannon stepped into his Nissen hut. Lentz, Jacobson and Gott all stood. "Look at what we have here,"

Jake announced, "the man is wearing brand new 'railroad tracks' on his shoulders." He and the other two officers shook Shine's hand. "Congratulations, Captain," they all spoke simultaneously.

"Now we know who will be buying the drinks at the O Club tonight," Lentz laughed. "According to tradition, the promoted man pays for drinks equivalent to amount of his pay raise."

"Thanks, guys," Shine smirked. "I don't feel any different than when I was a lowly first lieutenant, but I know my wallet will feel the difference tonight. Enough of this chitchat let's go get some breakfast."

After breakfast Hot Stuff's six sergeants headed to the finance office to draw their back pay. As they strolled between the buildings, Rondeau saw Shannon and Lentz walking toward them.

Sunlight glistened off Shannon's new captain's bars. Rondeau popped to attention and they all saluted the newly promoted captain. "Congratulations, sir. We're proud to have served under you."

Shannon returned the salute, swallowed a lump rising in his throat. "Thanks. You're the best crew any bomber pilot could wish for. I look forward to continuing to have the honor."

The line leading to the finance office was long; however, the wait was worth it.

As McQueen stood at the pay window, he found himself flanked by Farley and Craighead. "Spread out," he said. "You're crowding me."

No sooner did McQueen draw his pay than two open palms greeted him. "Pay up, Paul," Craighead demanded.

"Pay up for what?" McQueen asked.

Farley looked at Craighead. "See, I told you he'd forget the Hardwick bet, didn't I?"

"Yeah," Craighead agreed. "You owe each of us two pounds, remember? You bet us Hardwick was another shit hole. Now pay up!"

"Oh that," McQueen said as he reluctantly counted four pounds out from his pay. "Here, use it to buy me a drink when we go on pass."

Rondeau stood waiting for the other five crewmembers to exit the finance office. "Now let's get some haircuts. The old man wants us to assemble at the debriefing building before noon."

At 11:30 the remnants of the three squadrons that had returned from North Africa were assembled awaiting the arrival of Timberlake. Upon his entrance, the operations officer called the group to attention and the commander strode to the small stage at the front of the large room.

"At ease, take seats," Timberlake ordered. After the men sat on the folding metal chairs and the room fell silent, he continued. "By now most of you should have cleaned up, had a good night's rest and drawn your back pay. To sweeten the pot, Eighth Air Force has granted all of us a week of leave. That starts the day after tomorrow, the second day of March."

The room erupted in loud chatter and laughter. "Settle down," the commanding officer shouted. When silence was restored, he continued. "For those who want to go to London, transportation will be available to take you to the train station.

"Ground personnel tell me the planes we took on our trek to North Africa look like they've aged five years and need a lot of work. So while you men are on leave your aircraft will be cleaned up, repaired, patched, and engines replaced. Although Eighth Air Force is growing, it needs every plane it can put in the air. HQ wants us to be ready for whatever missions they assign to us."

At 1400 the entire 93rd stood in ranks. Orders were read by the adjutant. Timberlake walked among the crewmembers and personally pinned Distinguished Flying Crosses, Purple Hearts, Air Medals, and other awards on the left chest pockets of the awardees.

Forty-five minutes later, the ceremony was concluded and the squadrons were dismissed.

Farley stood in the Nissen hut and looked at his watch. It was after 1700. Time to head to the mess hall. He looked around. Hot Stuff's chow hound, McQueen was missing. The waist gunner had disappeared shortly after the awards ceremony. "Hey, Joe, any idea where Paul went to?"

Craighead shook his head. "Nah. Haven't seen him since we were dismissed this afternoon."

"Can't remember when Paul wouldn't be first in line for chow. Where could he be?"

Farley sat on McQueen's bunk. His eyes fell on the open footlocker. "Jesus Christ. I know where he is. Want to go with me to get him?"

"Sure, as long as we don't miss chow," Craighead responded.

Ten minutes later, the two sergeants walked into the darkened movie theater. Sure enough there was Lawrence Olivier on the big screen calling for Cathy. There was only one seat occupied in the auditorium.

Farley moved down the row of seats where McQueen was wiping tears from his eyes with his uniform blouse sleeve. "Paul, have you been sitting here watching this gobbledygook for the past two hours?"

A disembodied voice from the back of the theater called out, "He gave me a carton of Lucky Strikes to run this flick."

Farley and Craighead grabbed the despondent airman by both arms and led him out of the theater. "You're going to miss chow, Paul."

"That's the most bad news story I ever knew," McQueen sniffed. "When we go on leave I'm going to have a few drinks in memory of Heathcliff. That poor son of a bitch."

CHAPTER 43

Return to London

The next day, Hot Stuff's sergeants were issued new uniforms, socks, underwear, and finally last but not least, new military issue shoes. The poor quality footwear they bought in Cairo was beginning to disintegrate and ended up in the trash.

With time on their hands and their pockets full of months of back pay many of the 93rd's crews turned to heavy gambling. Hot Stuff's enlisted men were no different. McQueen and Farley had been playing poker with other crews on and off for two days. "Paul, I barely broke even, but just like pennies from heaven you really raked in the lettuce. When we get to London you can treat us all to hooch at that underground pub. You know that place Eisel found in the dark last time we were there?"

"That's a keen idea, George," McQueen smiled as he counted the wad of British pounds lying on his bunk.

Hot Stuff's crew spent the evening preparing for the morning inspection before they were to depart for London.

Jeffers held his uniform blouse on a hangar and showed it to Rondeau. "Grant, is my air crewman's wings on straight over the ribbons?"

The flight engineer looked up from polishing his new shoes and nodded, "Yeah, your air medal and campaign ribbons look good to me. You'll have no trouble attracting a real Sheba when we get to that pub in London."

"Thanks," the radioman said as he pinned the freshly polished collar brass on his uniform.

The next morning after a hearty breakfast the crews of the 93rd formed up for inspection prior to boarding trucks that were to take them to the Norwich train station.

Before the men were to pile onto the trucks for the station, they stood in line at the post office with the mail and packages from the Brits at Gambut Main. It was the least they could do for the "Desert Rat" cheerleaders they left behind.

After a fifteen-minute ride, the men piled out of the two and a half ton trucks. The train for London was due in ten minutes; just enough time to buy their roundtrip tickets.

The train was crowded with uniformed personnel of Allied forces along with women and old men traveling with young children. Seats were at a premium and most of the military personnel stood leaning against the carriage walls allowing just enough space for passengers to get by. The air was thick with tobacco smoke. Conversations were held in varied languages seemingly all being spoken at one time.

Hot Stuff's four officers stood in the crammed passageway of the railway carriage near a partially open window. Jacobson offered an open Lucky Strike pack to the others. "Thanks, Jake," Shannon said as he pulled a slim silver flask from his uniform blouse and passed it among the other three officers. "Here, have a swig of this great Scotch. It'll make this train ride more bearable."

Lentz blew a smoke ring into the air and took a pull from the flask. "Shine, are you planning on seeing Helen when we get to London?"

"Yeah, sure am. And you should come with me. Remember I told you Helen's sister is a real Sheba. I think you two will get along swell."

"Sure. What's her name?"

"Eleanor. Unlike her sister she's a brunette. Reminds me of Gene Tierney. You might remember the actress who co-starred with Henry Fonda in the movie *Tobacco Road*."

As the conductor made his way through the crowded passageway where Hot Stuff's sergeants were standing, Eisel shouted above the din. "How long until we reach London?"

The train master looked at his pocket watch and responded in a thick cockney brogue. "Chap, if the Jerries haven't interrupted the rails, we should be there right before tea time."

Craighead leaning against the wall next to Eisel yelled, "What time did he say?"

"Around four or four thirty. Relax, have another smoke. We have another couple of hours before we get off this cattle car."

Hot Stuff's enlisted crew arrived at the Regent Palace Hotel well after tea time. The train was delayed while work crews repaired damaged rails outside of London. After checking in, the six-air crewmen made their way along the darkening streets in search of the pub Eisel had found three months earlier.

"I can hardly hear after almost four hours on that goddamned train," McQueen exclaimed. "Flak and the roar of Hot Stuff's engines can't compare to the screaming chatter of those two Dumb Doras standing next to me. Glad they got off before we got to London."

"If we could have at least gotten a drink on that train it would have made the ride almost bearable," Rondeau remarked.

"Speaking of hooch, where is that pub you found for us last time, George?"

"Follow me, I know just were that gin mill is located."

A few minutes later, the six American airmen stood disbelieving at what greeted them. What once had been the underground pub was now a pile of rubble.

"Are you sure this is the place?" Craighead asked.

"Yeah," Eisel responded. "This is it all right." He kicked at a pile of bricks and broken concrete. He pulled the familiar sign, now battered and charred from the rubble. It read:

During an air raid, lights will be extinguished.
No one will be permitted to enter or leave.
In event of a direct hit, this pub will close immediately.

Just then a London bobby strolled by. Eisel asked the police officer, "Excuse me, can you tell me what happened at this site?"

"I most certainly can," the police officer replied, his flaccid face grim. "It was on the seventeenth of January when the Jerries bombed us again. This building took a direct hit; not many survivors. I lost a few of my lifelong chums that night."

"What about the bar keep and the band members?" Eisel asked.

"They were buried in the rubble when the building collapsed. Funny thing, though, one of the survivors mentioned the band played right through the air raid until the bomb hit."

McQueen lamented. "Son of a bitch, this really pisses me off. We're going to make those Nazi bastards eat lead for this. Every time Annie and I shoot a Jerry out of the sky it'll be for those who were murdered here."

"I really need a drink," Eisel said. He turned to the bobby. "Could you tell us where another good pub is?"

The London policeman responded. "Come on, follow me. There's a nice place two blocks down."

Hot Stuff's officers checked into the Savoy, a luxury hotel located on the Strand in central London. Up to this time, the hotel staff had to cope with bomb damage, food rationing, and a shortage of personnel. After the Americans entered the war and began flowing into England, the hotel became a favorite for American officers, diplomats, and political leaders, and the hotel no longer had to struggle with shortages.

Gott and Jacobson had their own plans for their first night in London. Although the Savoy had two well-known restaurants, the Savoy Grill and the River Restaurant, Shannon and Lentz decided to skip having dinner, and instead went to the American Bar to have a drink before setting out for Helen's apartment. The bar was decorated in a warm art deco design and was one of the few establishments in London that served American-style cocktails. The two pilots managed to find two stools that had just become vacated in the mostly American crowd.

They ordered two whiskeys straight up. Unlike American drinks, ice was not served with liquor in the British Isles.

Shine took a sip of his drink and reached for his wallet. He pulled out a small slip of paper. "I've got the women's address right here. Last time we were in London Helen and Eleanor lived in the same apartment." He hefted his glass, "Drink up, let's get going. The Underground entrance is right around the corner."

Twenty minutes later, Shannon and Lentz emerged from the subway. Shine looked at the address again. "Yeah, their place is just two blocks down."

The skies over London were turning a dark gray as night approached. "I think it should be across the intersection right over there," Shine indicated.

"Are you sure?" Lentz asked. "The whole block is nothing but a pile of bricks and burnt wood."

Shannon stopped a passing man and asked, "Pardon me, do you live around here?"

The Londoner looked over Shine's uniform and smiled. "Quite so, Yank. I've lived here for nearly fifty years."

Shine showed the Englishman the address for the girls' apartment and pointed. "Are we in the right neighborhood?"

After the Brit glanced at the address, the smile faded from his middle-aged face. "You're in the right place, Chap." The man slowly shook his head. "But that apartment building was hit the night of January 17. No one in that place could have survived. But you know if they got to the shelter in time they could still be living anywhere in London."

"Is there any way I can find out what happened to my friends?"

"You might try the Red Cross or reunification centers. Everyone in London knows to go to those places to leave a forwarding address for relatives and friends. They've been doing a smashing job of getting people together after their homes have been lost."

The two officers found a friendly pub on their way back to the hotel. After getting settled in a booth, they ordered two pints of ale and fish and chips.

"John, I don't know how I feel right now," Shannon lamented. "It would take us weeks to find them if we went to all the centers the Brit mentioned. We don't have that kind of time."

Lentz took a sip of his ale. "Bet those girls are okay. It's just a question of how to find them. Did you meet any of their friends last time you were here?"

Shine toyed with his dinner. "Yeah, but I only remember a couple of first names like Mary or Barbara. I never heard any last names. It could take weeks to find out what happened to them."

"Do you remember exactly where you met Helen?"

"Of course, John, why didn't I think of that? When we finish here, we'll go to the pub where Helen and I first met." He hesitated then continued. "With any luck it's still there."

It was almost 2100 when the two pilots pulled the blackout curtains aside to the entranceway of the Tilted Crown tavern. The place was packed. The air was thick with tobacco smoke and the stale odor of spilled beer.

Lentz looked through the haze. "I don't think I could find my own mother in this mob."

The two officers shoved their way through a wide variety of American and Allied uniforms and locals. Lentz caught the bar keeper's eye and shouted for two pints of ale.

Shannon left Lentz at the bar and started moving through the swarm of humanity standing shoulder to shoulder as all of the tables were occupied. His eyes roamed across the expanse of the tavern. Suddenly he spotted a redhead sitting at a table among a crowd of American servicemen. He couldn't see her face, but it had to be Helen. Shine elbowed his way through the crush of revelers until he worked his way to the table.

"Helen," Shine shouted. The woman looked up at the sound of his voice. The smile faded from Shannon's lips. The disappointment was apparent on his face; the woman was a complete stranger.

Dejected, he turned toward the bar. Suddenly, a woman's hand touched his shoulder. "Robert? Is that you?"

Shine looked up and his sun-tanned face broke into a broad grin. There she was alive and well. His finding Helen like this in the place where they first met was a miracle. "I went to your apartment building and it was gone. I was so worried. I thought I'd never find you."

"I've been thinking about you ever since we parted at the train station."

"Let's get out of here so we can talk," Shine shouted.

"But I can't leave Eleanor alone here," Helen exclaimed.

"She won't be alone," he gestured toward the bar. "See that tall handsome guy at the bar? He's my copilot. Let's make some introductions."

Six days later, Shannon and Lentz stood in the crowded coach headed back to Norwich station. Shannon lit up a cigarette and leaned toward Lentz in the noisy, smoky surroundings. "I saw you and Eleanor saying a long good-bye at the station. It's obvious to me that you two were tight."

"Did you know Eleanor was engaged to marry an RAF pilot?" Lentz revealed.

"Oh, sorry, I didn't know."

"Well, the guy's bomber went down during a mission over Germany four months ago."

"What was your understanding when you left her at the station?"

"Eleanor and I will be exchanging letters. We'll see how it goes. It appears you're really stuck on Helen, aren't you?"

Shannon was silent for a moment, took a puff from his Chesterfield, and leaned over toward Lentz so he could be heard over the din. "I want you to be the first to know Helen and I are officially engaged. I bought her a ring yesterday. We haven't set a date."

"I knew you were serious about Helen when you were so concerned about finding her." With a lit Lucky Strike dangling from his lips, Lentz shook Shine's hand. "Congratulations. This calls for a drink." He pulled out a silver hip flask he had purchased in London. "Here, take a swig of Scotland's finest."

A minute passed in silence while the liquor burned through their guts. Shine stared at the flask in his hand. "I don't know what I'm going to say to my high school girl back in Iowa. It never was what I would consider a real romance. More like a teenage crush."

Lentz took the flask from Shine and took a swig. "If I were you I'd keep it short and to the point. Just say it and end it."

"Good advice. I'll write to her in the next few days."

"Our week in London didn't go like I thought it would," McQueen lamented. "Our finding the pub bombed out like we did and all those keen Brits gone really rattled my cage."

Hot Stuff's sergeants were once more standing in an overcrowded train headed back to Norwich.

Craighead sighed. "Of all the buildings in London, why did the Nazis murder our pub?"

"Even the dame I met with the classy chassis couldn't help me tune out my thinking of the sight of all that rubble," Farley added.

"I'll never forget what happened," Rondeau stated. "I can't wait to get those Nazi bastards in my sights again. I'm going to blow the shit out of them."

Hot Stuff's six enlisted crewmen were lost in their own thoughts as they puffed on Camels taken from a crushed pack they passed among themselves. They barely spoke a word for the remainder of the train ride back.

Due to repairs on the railway, the train carrying Hot Stuff's crew from London was an hour late arriving at the Norwich station. It was raining when they detrained. The officers and sergeants hastily pulled raincoats from their tote bags and trudged to the waiting trucks.

It was dark when the trucks carrying the leave-weary airmen pulled into Hardwick. Famished, the officers and enlisted men separated and immediately headed for their respective mess halls.

Shannon and his officers settled down at a table with their trays brimming with hot chow. "How was your leave, Captain?" Gott asked Shine.

Before Shannon could respond, Lentz spoke up, "Let me be the first to inform you our command pilot is officially engaged."

Both Gott and Jacobson exclaimed "congratulations" simultaneously.

"Bet it's that fifth avenue redhead we saw you with in December," Jacobson commented.

Shine smiled. "She's the one."

"You're a lucky guy, Shine," Gott said. "When's the big day?"

Shannon hesitated. "We've haven't set a date yet. Look, guys, I just got engaged. We need some time to make plans."

For several minutes, not a word was spoken as Hot Stuff's sergeants settled down at the long table in the mess hall. Their appetites demanded their full attention since they had not eaten since breakfast.

The silence was finally broken as McQueen took the last bite of his fruit cobbler. "After a week of fish and chips, this tasted as good as my grandma's Thanksgiving dinner back home."

Farley belched through a mouthful of the dessert. "If I never see another helping of fish again it would be too soon. I'll never complain about army chow."

Craighead drained his cup of coffee. "This is the best cup of Java I've had in a week." The belly gunner rose from the bench. "I'm going to get another cup."

"Joe, you've had nothing to drink but hooch and tea for a week," Rondeau commented.

Craighead gestured with his empty cup. "Maybe that's why this coffee tastes so goddamned good."

CHAPTER 44

A Little Larceny

On March 12, after a hearty breakfast Shannon and Lentz, joined by a ground maintenance officer, strolled to the parking apron to take a look at the work that had been done on Hot Stuff while the officers were on leave. The previous day's rain had moved on and the morning sky was partly cloudy and the sun warmed the late winter air.

The maintenance officer glanced at a clipboard and patted the aluminum skin of the Liberator as he led Shannon and Lentz around the plane. "We've been working on her for over a week now and just finished up yesterday." He proudly announced the holes in the fuselage had been repaired correctly unlike the field fixes that had to be made while Hot Stuff was in North Africa. His hand lovingly swept across the fuselage. "Feel how smooth and aerodynamic the repaired surfaces are."

Shannon and Lentz admired the craftsmanship of the ground crews. "She looks almost like new, Captain," Lentz observed. "Looks like your guys did a great job."

The maintenance officer nodded, looked at his clipboard and pointed up at the wings. "Best of all the engines have been replaced. I guarantee they purr like a kitten. Come on let's take a look at the flight deck."

Once inside Hot Stuff Shannon and Lentz were surprised at how clean and fresh-smelling the interior was. The maintenance officer gestured with his clipboard, "Cleaning out the desert sand and dust was a real bitch, but as you can see my guys did a great job. Even the Norden bombsight has been reconditioned."

Shannon took a deep breath, "Smells almost like when she was new last August back at Grenier."

"Hot Stuff has been declared mission worthy; unfortunately others in the 93rd not so," the maintenance officer said. He scanned his clipboard. "Ball of Fire was in such bad shape it's being converted to a hospital ship. The turrets, bombsight and armament will be removed and used on other B-24s. Two more of the Liberators from North Africa are in such poor condition they can't be brought up to standards. Not sure what we're going to do with them yet."

"What about the crews?" Lentz asked.

"They'll just have to wait for new Liberators when they arrive from the States."

Shannon thought about his friend Joe Tate, command pilot of grounded Ball of Fire. He addressed the maintenance officer, "How soon will the replacement B-24s arrive?"

"Looks like that may be a while because there aren't sufficient trained crews or ferry pilots available to bring them over. Only the guys in requisitions would know."

An idea was forming in the back of Shine's mind.

After they deplaned, Shannon thanked the maintenance officer and looked up at Hot Stuff. "I'd like to take her up for a test flight."

"I'll see when I can schedule it with operations," the maintenance officer replied. "With ongoing operations that'll probably be sometime after tomorrow."

That evening in the officers' club, Shannon and Lentz sought out Joe Tate. They found the grounded pilot sitting in a corner alone nursing a mug of beer. "Mind if we join you, Joe?" Shine asked as he pulled up a chair.

"Go ahead, take a seat. I'm in a shitty mood right now," Tate lamented. "Guess you heard what they're going to do to Ball of Fire."

Shannon took a sip of his scotch on ice, "Yeah, we heard. Sorry to hear it'll no longer fly combat missions." He and Lentz raised their glasses in a salute. "Here's to Ball of Fire and her crew."

Tate hesitated then raised his half empty mug. "Thanks, guys."

Shannon took a sip of his drink. "We know how much you and your crew want to get back into action." He leaned close to Tate so as not to be overheard. "John and I have been thinking about your situation and we think we know how to make things right."

Two days later, the morning of Hot Stuff's test flight, Shannon, Lentz and Tate ambled into the logistics office. Shannon leaned over the master sergeant's cluttered desk. "What's the latest on when we're going to be receiving replacement B-24s?"

The NCO looked up at the three officers. "Sorry, sirs. You'll have to wait; they're on requisition." He pointed to a pile of completed forms. "These are the requisitions for new B-24s." He hesitated and thought for a moment. "Understand there's one or two up at Prestwick undergoing modification. Once completed they'll be flown down here in the next couple of weeks."

The three officers looked at each other and smiled. Tate reached over the desk and snatched one of the requisitions. "Sir, you can't..." Before the supply NCO could finish his admonishment, Shannon, Lentz, and Tate were out of the office, leaving the bewildered soldier staring at the empty doorway.

Hot Stuff's crew enplaned for the maintenance test flight. They were joined by Tate and his copilot. The two passengers wore their headsets over their crushed service caps. Shannon had informed the crew that since they would be flying below twenty thousand feet, high-altitude gear would not be necessary. The entire crew wore heavy pants, boots, leather flight jackets, and an assortment of headgear.

McQueen stared at their two passengers. "Hey, Farley, any idea why Captain Tate and his copilot are aboard?"

"Aw, they're probably just coming along for the ride. Heard their plane Ball of Fire is no longer fit for combat and will be converted to a hospital ship."

"That's tough," McQueen said.

Farley gazed at the near-pristine interior and inhaled deeply. The smell of old upchuck was gone. He glared at McQueen, "Paul, if you have to upchuck, lean out *your* window or use the bucket. Don't even think about puking on me or the floor."

"Aw, that was a long time ago," McQueen blurted. "I don't upchuck like a kid on a carnival ride anymore."

Craighead stared up at McQueen. "Sure. Remember, I'm down here in the belly. I don't need any of your puke splattering on me."

After all crewmembers and passengers were settled in, Shannon started the new engines. They roared to life and ran smoothly just like the maintenance officer had boasted. After warming up, Shannon taxied the Liberator to the end of the runway. Lentz radioed the tower for clearance to takeoff.

The command pilot pushed the throttles forward and released the brakes. He was elated with the power the new engines generated. Hot Stuff almost leaped forward down the runway. "God, she feels like the first day we flew her at Grenier."

Lentz chuckled as the B-24 accelerated and pressed him deeper into his seat. "I sure can feel the difference." He looked at the fuel gauges. "We have more than enough fuel to make the round trip."

Shannon smiled as he pulled back on the controls and Hot Stuff took to the sky. "If necessary we'll get more when we get there."

The planned flight route took Hot Stuff north into Scotland, away from hostile areas. The gunners broke out the old plywood board. McQueen pulled a deck of cards from his jacket pocket as he sat on the floor. "Ante up, guys. Two pence to play five card stud."

Farley, Eisel, and Craighead joined the waist gunner on the floor and sat cross-legged. McQueen shuffled the deck and began dealing. "I'm feeling lucky today."

An hour and a half later, Hot Stuff began her descent into Prestwick. As the plane touched down and rolled down the runway, Lentz pointed to the right, "There's your prize, Joe."

Tate gazed out the small window above Jeffers' radio. "Goddamned, she's a beauty."

Shannon parked Hot Stuff on the apron near the new B-24. "Okay, Joe. Hop out. We'll keep the engines running."

Shannon and Lentz watched as Tate and his copilot ran across the runway toward the control tower. After a very few minutes the Ball of Fire pilots ran toward the new B-24 and waved at Shannon and Lentz as they climbed in. Within a moment the four Pratt & Whitney engines roared to life. Instead of waiting for the engines to warm up, Tate pushed the throttles forward and taxied his purloined acquisition to the end of the runway. Within minutes the new Liberator was airborne, headed south with Hot Stuff flying along its portside.

Over the command net Shannon radioed Tate. "Congratulations, glad you're back in the war. How did it go at the tower?"

Tate's disembodied voice responded, "I have no idea. I dropped the requisition on the desk and ran like hell. Didn't wait around for any embarrassing questions."

Hot Stuff's sergeants had gazed wide-eyed at what had transpired at Prestwick. Once their B-24 was flying alongside the newly acquired Liberator, McQueen looked at his fellow sergeants. "Son of a bitch, I think we just saw one of the keenest robberies since Bonnie and Clyde pulled their last bank job."

The sergeants broke into raucous laughter as they were surprised to see how far the officers would go to keep the 93rd in the fight; even so far as to risk their careers.

Just over an hour and a half later the two B-24s landed at Hardwick. Shannon, guided by the jeep with the "Follow Me" sign parked Hot Stuff on the apron. Another similar vehicle guided Tate and his newly acquired Liberator onto another apron.

That night after dinner Shannon, Lentz and Tate cornered the group's logistics officer at the O Club bar. After an hour of hushed conversation over drinks, Ball of Fire *Junior* found a new home. The 93rd's inventory of aircraft miraculously had a new addition.

The next day, Col. Timberlake was delighted to hear the group had received a new B-24. He was impressed with the initiative shown by a couple of his pilots which helped alleviate the 93rd's critical shortage of bombers. However, he could not openly condone such outright bending of regulations so he chose to not to look a "gift horse in the mouth." Nothing more was ever mentioned about how Ball of Fire *Junior* came to join the 93rd.

Within days the words Ball of Fire *Junior* were emblazoned on the fuselage of the bold daylight requisition. Shannon and Tate stood gazing at the newly painted flaming eight ball under the pilot's window. "What do you think, Shine?"

"Looks fifth avenue, Joe," he chuckled. "Your new plane is a sorely needed addition to the 93rd."

Tate took Shannon's outstretched hand. "Thanks, Shine. Your brainchild worked out just swell. It's going to be keen having the crew flying together again."

CHAPTER 45

March 17, 1943
Twenty-Eighth Combat
Mission: Diversion

Hot Stuff did not participate in diversionary missions conducted on March 12, 13, and 15. The purpose of those missions was to fly over the coast of France and the Low Countries to lure Luftwaffe fighters to intercept the 93rd's B-24s, thereby allowing B-17s from other bomber groups to conduct bombing missions deeper into enemy territory with minimal interference from enemy fighters.

On March 17 Hot Stuff was to participate in the 93rd's fourth diversionary mission. After a predawn breakfast, Shannon and his crew along with eleven other crews assembled in the briefing room where they took notes on the flight paths, altitudes and takeoff times. On diversionary missions, the only armament the Liberators carried was the Browning .50 caliber machine guns; no bombs would be onboard. New to Shannon was the configuration of the formation; three diamonds of four B-24s each. Recent experience by the 93rd found the new formation provided far greater mutual protection than the previous vee formation.

A number of the 93rd's men had been shuffled around among various Liberators to fill out vacant positions. None of the crewmen liked the idea, but it was necessary to keep the Liberators in the air. Fortunately, Hot Stuff's crew and a few others had not sustained casualties and so remained together.

Immediately following the briefing, Shannon went back to his quarters. He opened his foot locker and rummaged through the contents. "Here it is!"

Before takeoff Hot Stuff's gunners double checked their weapons and made sure the ground crews had loaded full belts of ammo. McQueen patted his machine gun just above where the name "Annie" was painted. "You and me are going to have a real busy day today, baby."

A tinge of purple light cast through the cloudy sky as the twelve Liberators took off. After reaching twenty thousand feet they formed into three diamonds and headed east.

"In case any of you hadn't noticed, today is St. Patrick's Day," Shannon announced in his best Irish brogue. "I feel lucky." He pulled a Kelly green scarf from his pocket, kissed it, and wrapped it around his neck, a good luck gift from this mother.

Lentz glanced at Shine's scarf and smiled. "Now if only we had St. Patrick's staff to swat those Nazi bastards out of the sky. It worked well on snakes over a thousand years ago, why not now?"

Less than fifty miles into enemy airspace, the ruse worked. The B-24s found themselves in a swarm of some thirty Me 109s and Fw 190s. With no ground target to bomb and no flak to contend with, the bombers' crews, particularly the gunners concentrated on the incoming enemy fighters.

Hot Stuff was positioned on the right side of one of the three diamond-shaped formations. Lentz looked to his right at the yellow-nosed Fw 190s. "Bogies at one o'clock high."

BEFORE THE BELLE

Jacobson and Rondeau swiveled their weapons toward the incoming fighters and began firing. Cannon fire from the pair of enemy aircraft pierced Hot Stuff's skin. The enemy planes skimmed over the fuselage of the Liberator.

As another attacking aircraft headed for the starboard side of the B-24, McQueen was ready and waiting. "Me 109 at three o'clock. He's all mine." The waist gunner squeezed the trigger. "This is for my pal Clive, the bar keep back in London you bastard."

Rondeau rotated his turret to interweave fire with McQueen's machine gun, but by then the enemy fighter began belching black smoke as it dove away from Hot Stuff.

Yet another Fw 190 made a pass at the formation. This time the enemy plane flew at Hot Stuff's twin stabilizers in hopes of bringing the bomber down. "Focke Wulf at five o'clock," Eisel shouted into the intercom. He swiveled the tail turret slightly to his left as the incoming enemy aircraft came into his sights. "I got him." He squeezed the triggers of the twin .50s. "That's for the band members in the pub."

The starboard waist gunner and turret gunner of the Liberator to the left rear of Hot Stuff added to Eisel's lethal fire. The diamond formation was beginning to pay off in improving the interweaving of protective fires.

One of the Nazi plane's wing sections shattered and the fighter began to spiral down. Eisel released the triggers and smiled as he took satisfaction in avenging those lost in the destruction of the London pub. He watched as the German pilot's parachute deployed.

A half dozen Fw 190s attacked the formation head-on, a new tactic used by the Luftwaffe fighters. "Bandits at eleven o'clock," Shannon shouted into the intercom. He and Lentz ducked as 20 mm cannon fire raked the flight deck's Plexiglas. Jacobson and Rondeau fired at the yellow noses of the incoming enemy aircraft. Their machine gun fire had little effect on the reduced cross-sectional area displayed by the oncoming Nazi fighters. Once the enemy aircraft passed Hot Stuff low on the portside Farley and Craighead engaged the Luftwaffe fighters. They both cursed the Nazi aircraft as they poured .50 caliber ammo at the fast moving targets.

The air battle lasted over a half an hour. Thanks to the integrated fire from the B-24s' diamond formations nine of the Luftwaffe's finest had either gone down or were sufficiently damaged as to leave the air battle and seek refuge. The twelve Liberators had done their job in drawing out the Nazi fighters and banked toward the west. As the B-24s headed out to sea, the surviving enemy aircraft turned away as they didn't have sufficient fuel or ammunition to pursue further.

"Everybody okay?" Shannon calmly spoke into the intercom. All crewmen reported they were once again unscathed.

"Damage report!"

A few seconds passed and one by one the crewmen reported several holes in the fuselage, but nothing major. Hot Stuff had the luck of the Irish on St. Patrick's Day.

Hot Stuff's gunners had been generous with feeding hot lead to the Fuhrer's Luftwaffe. Eisel examined the paltry amount of ammunition left in the tail guns' belt feeds. "Son of a bitch, I'm almost out of ammo, but it was worth every round. When I squeezed the trigger all I could think of was the guys in that pub's band who kept playing through the air raid three and a half months ago."

Rondeau felt the air rushing through two holes in the top turret's Plexiglas as he watched the German fighters fade into the east. "We made those bastards pay for those Brits who would never see the light of another day."

McQueen looked down at the empty shell casings lying around his feet. "Annie and I sure got our licks in. I just know a couple of those Heinies that went down felt our hot lead. We just wanted to make sure those goose-stepping bastards paid for what they did to our pub."

CHAPTER 46

After a Rough Mission

A far cry from North Africa, Hardwick was well equipped to handle crippled aircraft and wounded air crewmen. As Hot Stuff and the other eleven Liberators approached the airbase from the divisionary mission, Timberlake and his staff stood in the airbase's control tower, binoculars in hand anxiously searching the skies for the returning B-24s.

A wide assortment of emergency vehicles stood along the flight line. Crash cars, jeeps, fire trucks, ambulances and trucks along with trained personnel were ready to go into action should the need arise. The policy was for seriously damaged aircraft and those carrying wounded to have priority in landing.

A radio message was received in the tower that the 93rd's Liberators were inbound. Col. Timberlake searched the eastern sky with his binoculars. He began counting the aircraft as they broke through the cloud cover – twelve. The group commander breathed a sigh of relief.

Two of the Liberators trailed heavy black smoke from one of their engines and were given priority landing instructions. Three others had wounded personnel aboard and were next to land. The emergency vehicles that had been standing by leaped into action and sped onto the runway toward the still rolling B-24s.

Because Hot Stuff fared far better than others during the mission, it was one of the last to land. Shannon parked the B-24 on the apron and shut down the engines. He stared at the holes and cracks in the flight deck's Plexiglas. "Goddamned, that was like a meat grinder. I don't understand how we got back without any wounded or severe damage to Hot Stuff."

As the sergeants deplaned, they all lit up. The gunners motioned with their arms telling stories of how they peppered the enemy fighters with hot lead. While they described their encounters a two and a half ton truck rolled alongside Hot Stuff.

Hot Stuff's officers remained at their stations for several minutes after the gunners had left the aircraft.

Lentz patted his hip. "I never felt so helpless. I kept reaching for my .45 which wasn't there." The flight crews had been discouraged from carrying side arms on missions over enemy territory should they have to bailout. This was a precautionary measure if they were taken prisoner. "I could see the faces of those bastards flying straight at us. I really wanted to shoot back. Wish I had St. Patrick's staff to swat at them."

Shannon called down to his bombardier. "Jake, are you okay? I know you were the center of the bull's eye for those bastards."

Jacobson's face was ashen. The nose Plexiglas was riddled with holes. He couldn't believe he was still alive. The bombardier had never fired so furiously with his machine gun trying to ward off the enemy fighters.

After a moment, Jake sighed as he pulled his headset from his ears. "As far as I know I'm all right. I've just got a bad case of the heebie-jeebies. I need a long visit at the gin mill with a tall mug of hooch."

Gott felt nauseous. "Shine, I never felt so goddamned useless as I was on this mission. All I could do was sit there and sweat it out."

"After the debriefing I'm buying drinks at the O Club," Shine announced.

The still animated sergeants climbed aboard the truck followed by the more subdued officers.

At the debriefing, the crews informed Timberlake and his operations officer that for the most part the Germans were using new aerial tactics, namely attacking the formation head-on. However, the new diamond formation did provide much better protection for the Liberators.

The group commander declared he was going to lead the next mission in order to learn for himself about the Luftwaffe frontal attacks. That mission was scheduled for the next day, March 18. There would be no drinking at the O Club or at local pubs for those participating in the mission. Hot Stuff was designated to participate with eleven other Liberators. Any required repairs along with rearming and refueling would be completed before dawn.

Before Shannon and his crew headed for their respective mess halls, the command pilot emphasized there would be no consumption of alcoholic beverages that night. In addition, they would need a good night's sleep as they would be awakened early the next morning.

As Hot Stuff's sergeants made their way to their mess hall for the noon meal, there was general grousing among them. "Son of a bitch," Farley exclaimed. "Just when I could really use some hooch tonight, I have to settle for milk or coffee."

"Just wait until tomorrow night," McQueen said. "We'll get passes and go into town and get really ossified."

When Hot Stuff's officers got settled in their mess, there was very little small talk passed among them. Finally, Shine broke the strained muted conversation. "When the time is right, I'm still buying the drinks."

CHAPTER 47

March 18, 1943
Twenty-Ninth Mission: Vegesack

The duty NCO snapped on the overhead lights in Hot Stuff's officers' Nissen hut. "Gentlemen, time to rise and shine. It's another beautiful cloudy dark rainy day at Hardwick."

"My head just touched the pillow," Jacobson moaned. "What the hell time is it?"

The NCO glanced at his watch. "It's just after 0400. Time for you to prepare yourselves to make history." With that the NCO left the building to awaken other officers.

"My mouth feels like the bottom of a bird cage and I don't remember having a drink last night," Gott groused.

Shine sat up on his cot and pulled on his trousers over his shorts. "That's because you didn't have a drink last night, Jimmie. Now rise and shine, it's another beautiful morning at Hardwick." After slipping on his shoes he grabbed a towel and his shaving gear. The command pilot yawned and stretched as he walked toward the building's door. "Let's go guys. History awaits us."

The four officers shuffled through the cold early morning mist to the officers' shower building.

Hot Stuff's six sergeants waited in the chow line. Farley watched as McQueen began filling his tray. "Goddamned it, Paul, don't eat so much of that SOS. I swear if you upchuck on me today I'm going to beat the living shit out of you."

Craighead nodded. "You'll have to wait in line, George, because if Paul so much as belches he's a dead man."

McQueen guffawed. "You two act like a couple of Dumb Doras. You don't have anything to worry about."

"Yeah, sure," Farley said. "Just keep that goddamned bucket handy. It just may save your life."

Eisel commented. "Paul, just eat dry toast and coffee like me. It'll fill your belly and you won't upchuck."

Ignoring the comments of his crewmates McQueen filled his tray with SOS, powdered eggs, fried spam, toast and jam. "I'm still a growing boy. I gotta have a decent breakfast."

"Suit yourself," Eisel said. "I'm glad I won't be near you during the mission."

Forty five minutes later twelve Liberator crews crowded into the briefing building. Col. Timberlake began with announcing the day's target. "Today we're going hit the Vegesack U-boat and shipbuilding works on the northern outskirts of Bremen, Germany."

An excited buzz emanated from the seated crewmen. The 93rd was finally going to bomb Germany. After a moment the room fell silent and Timberlake continued.

"Our primary target will be the main power station. Without it the entire complex will grind to a halt. Teggie Ann will be the lead plane on this mission. Let's make it a mission to remember."

The operations officer then took over the briefing. He uncovered a map with strings denoting the ingress and egress flight paths. The Liberators were to fly east by northeast over the southern edge of the North Sea, then over the Netherlands and finally cross the German border to the targeted shipyard area. An overhead projector displayed an aerial photo of the German facilities where the power station was highlighted. In spite of the weather being overcast at Hardwick, clear conditions were expected over Vegesack.

Since the 93rd was to fly over Germany for the first time, flak was projected to be heavy. Luftwaffe fighters would pose a problem as they would be defending the "Vaterland." Therefore like on the diversionary missions, the group would form diamond formations for maximum protection.

When the Liberators reached a cruising altitude of twenty thousand feet, they formed into the planned diamond-shaped formations. All crews donned their high altitude gear: sheepskin-lined suits, boots and gloves. All men were on oxygen. The pilots, navigators, bombardiers, and radiomen wore crushed service or overseas caps under their headsets. The enlisted gunners optionally wore flak helmets or leather headgear and protective goggles. When the formation neared the target area, the planes were to climb to twenty-eight thousand feet where the temperature was minus fifty degrees Fahrenheit. Hot Stuff was positioned at the rear of their diamond formation.

An hour after takeoff the Dutch coast could be seen through the thinning clouds. Another 180 miles to Vegesack. As the three diamond formations of B-24s neared the German border, the air suddenly filled with heavy flak.

Hot Stuff bounced and shook from the antiaircraft bursts. "Son of bitch!" Lentz exclaimed as his gloved hands held the controls in a death grip. "This has got to be the shittiest flak we've ever flown through. It's so goddamned thick you can walk across it."

"How much further?" Shannon shouted into the intercom.

Gott replied, "Seventy more miles to the target."

Just then some fifty to sixty enemy fighters including Me 109s, Me 110s, Me 210s, Ju 88s, and Fw 190s rose up through the flak to meet the Liberators. The lead elements of the diamond formations took the brunt of the deadly head-on assault.

"Bandits at one o'clock," Shannon shouted into the intercom.

Rondeau rotated the upper turret to meet the onslaught of enemy fighters.

Fifteen minutes passed as Jacobson nervously fired his .50 from the nose of the B-24.

"It feels like they've been attacking us for hours; how far to the target now?" Shine shouted at the navigator.

"We're getting close to the target, Shine. Maybe ten minutes or so."

"Need someone to man my .50," the bombardier exclaimed.

"Jimmie, get on it!" Shannon shouted to the navigator.

"Right!" Gott left his seat at the small sloped chart table behind Jacobson and scrambled into the nose. He took the .50 caliber machine gun from the bombardier. He scanned the sky. "Jesus Christ, they're so many Jerries even I can't miss them." Immediately he began firing in all directions at the attacking Luftwaffe fighters.

Jacobson looked ahead. The huge power station was easily identified. As Hot Stuff drew closer, the bombardier began adjusting the bombsight. At the precise moment he opened the bomb bay doors and waited for the lead B-24 to drop its lethal cargo.

Shannon and Lentz watched as the cannon fire from an oncoming Me 110 shredded the nose of Hot Freight, the lead element of another diamond formation. Hot Stuff's pilots remained silent as the doomed Liberator began a steep descent through the flak. No parachutes were deployed. Another ten empty bunks.

Eisel saw a pair of Fw 190s diving for Hot Stuff's tail. "Two bogies at six o'clock high." He elevated the twin .50s and waited;

20 millimeter enemy cannon fire surrounded him. At the appropriate range to the target the tail gunner squeezed the triggers. The red spinner on the lead fighter blew off as Eisel's rounds tore into the engine. The Nazi aircraft exploded causing the trailing fighter to veer away. As the swarm of enemy fighters filled the sky, Eisel glanced around and muttered to himself, "This is a going to be one hell of a turkey shoot!"

McQueen engaged an Me 210 coming straight at him. "Bastard at three o'clock." The heavy fighter's cannon fire tore through Hot Stuff's skin. "That Nazi's cruisin' for a brusin'." He aimed and squeezed Annie's trigger. One of the enemy plane's twin engines began belching smoke as it dropped beneath the Liberator and retired from the fray.

A Fw 190 dove toward the center of Hot Stuff's diamond formation. "Bandit at ten o'clock high," Rondeau shouted into the intercom. As he began firing at the diving Luftwaffe fighter, Farley aimed his .50 high and began firing. They were joined by gunners from the three other defending Liberators in the formation. The withering fire literally tore the enemy plane to shreds.

As Hot Stuff approached the target area, Shannon gave control of the jolting bomber to his bombardier. Jacobson grabbed the small wheel and adjusted the bombsight. The power station for the shipbuilding complex came into focus. A few seconds after the lead bomber dropped its load, Jacobson's gloved hand flipped the bomb release switches. "Bombs away, Shine. Let's get the hell out of here!"

Shannon took control of Hot Stuff and maintained his position within the formation. The eleven Liberators, having done their job turned northwest out over the North Sea. The flak continued until the B-24s were beyond the German coast. However the enemy fighters were relentless as they continued to besiege the 93rd's eleven bombers.

"Conserve your ammo, guys," Shine warned. "It's not over yet."

The tortuous ordeal having lasted over an hour continued for another forty-five minutes as additional enemy fighters joined the fray.

Farley fired at a twin engine Me 110, its nose aimed right at him. "Paul, the bastard's coming right over us to your side."

McQueen shouted, "Got him!" He fired his .50 in anger at one the twin tails of the Luftwaffe heavy fighter. The tail of the Me 110 shattered and the crippled enemy aircraft peeled away toward the safety of the German coast.

Eisel spotted a Ju 88 diving toward the rear of the formation. He raised his pair of .50s and waited. He aimed at the portside engine of the German twin engine fighter. Pressing the triggers the engine of the enemy aircraft burst into flames. The rapidly descending plane just cleared the tail section of Hot Stuff.

Eisel's face behind the oxygen mask broke out into a cold sweat. "That was so goddamned close I could see the blue of that Nazi pilot's eyes."

Finally, after almost two hours it was all over. The Luftwaffe fighters retired from the fray. At that moment, the 93rd's formation reached the egress way point over the North Sea and turned southwest toward Hardwick. For several minutes Hot Stuff's crew was silent. The first to speak over the intercom was Shannon. "Anybody injured?"

Individually, the crewmen reported in. Unlike the other returning eleven Liberators which sustained casualties, miraculously none of Hot Stuff's crew had so much as a scratch. Their luck was holding.

With the good news on the condition of his crew, Shannon asked for a battle damage report.

Rondeau gazed through the perforated Plexiglas of the top turret. The outer starboard engine was leaking oil and streaming black smoke. The flight engineer recommended Shannon cut power to the damaged engine to prevent its catching fire. As the cold air blew through the holes in his turret he commented, "I don't know what the hell's keeping this turret together."

Eisel reported numerous holes in the tail section, but nothing serious.

McQueen, Farley and Craighead described the fuselage as being full of flak and cannon punctures; some large enough to put a gloved fist through. Otherwise the aircraft was sound.

The 93rd had downed nine Luftwaffe fighters with even more enemy aircraft badly damaged. The group had sustained one loss and every one of the remaining eleven B-24s had suffered moderate to heavy damage. A few of the Liberators limped back on two or three engines. Although the mission to Vegesack had been successful, it had been one of the most costly the 93rd had yet suffered.

CHAPTER 48

A Somber Return

The tower at Hardwick was alerted several of the returning Liberators were severely damaged and many of them had wounded aboard. The operations officer picked up the phone and ordered fire trucks, ambulances, jeeps and cargo trucks to standby. He raised his binoculars, scanned the skies to the northeast and searched for the inbound bombers.

Tense moments passed. One of the staff officers pointed at dots in the sky. "There they are!"

One by one the most bruised and battered aircraft were directed to land first. As each Liberator touched down and rolled to a stop, emergency vehicles raced to attend to the needs of the crews and their bombers.

Because Hot Stuff was deemed the most airworthy with no wounded, Shannon circled Hardwick for twenty minutes waiting for clearance to land. As the B-24 touched down, Hot Stuff's crew gazed out the windows at emergency vehicles attending to the wounded and damaged aircraft. As Hot Stuff rolled to a stop on the apron, a fire truck, a jeep and a cargo truck pulled alongside. Firemen doused the smoking engine with fire retardant as the crew deplaned.

Before boarding the truck to carry them to the debriefing room all the crewmen lit up. They looked at each other's tattered high altitude gear. "Son of a bitch, we're lucky that shrapnel and flying sheet metal didn't go through our leather," Rondeau exclaimed.

McQueen stared at his thick leather gloves. "Look, they're burnt from Annie's receiver. That's not supposed to happen."

Farley stared at Eisel's flak helmet. "George, you ought to see the dents and small holes in your helmet."

Eisel removed the headgear and whistled. "Well I'll be goddamned. It saved my ass."

"I'm hungry," McQueen blurted. "Let's find the Red Cross dames and get some doughnuts and hot java."

As the trucks ferried the battle-weary air crewmen to the debriefing building, ground maintenance crews immediately began inspection of the numerous cannon and flak holes in all the returning B-24s. Teggie Ann, Timberlake's Liberator which had led the raid sustained 358 punctures. The ground crew marveled that the group commander's B-24 had made it back to Hardwick. All the planes returning from the Vegesack mission would require major repairs.

Before entering the debriefing room, the crews paused at the mobile Red Cross canteen where the women in blue uniforms served fresh doughnuts and steaming cups of coffee. Once seated, Timberlake congratulated the crews on their ability to successfully conduct such a mission while under the most brutal of conditions. Aerial photos from the mission had been quickly processed and indicated most of the targeted power station had been destroyed and adjacent shipbuilding facilities were damaged. The results were exceptional. They had delivered a severe blow to the Nazi Kriegs Marine. After a pause, Timberlake declared he was now well versed in the viciousness of the new Luftwaffe tactic of using a frontal attack against the bomber formation. Guffaws broke out among those assembled. The "old man" now knew what it was like. The airmen that took part in the

Vegesack mission would be given three days off while the ground crews repaired damages to the Liberators.

A late winter wind blew off the North Sea as Hot Stuff's officers made their way toward the O Club. Lentz pulled the collar of his leather bomber jacket up around his neck. "Son of a bitch it's cold."

Jacobson jammed his hands deep into the pockets of his jacket. "We'll need a couple of drinks to thaw us out."

Once inside the oversized Nissen hut they forced their way through the crowd. As they approached the bar the four officers elbowed themselves a space in front of the bartender. Shannon ordered drinks for his copilot, navigator and bombardier. Hot Stuff's officers took their drinks and lit their Chesterfields and Lucky Strikes.

Shannon raised his glass and saluted Hot Stuff's crew. "Here's to the best goddamned B-24 crew any pilot ever had. We've come through a couple of very tough missions together and I'm proud to fly with you guys."

Jacobson sipped from his neat scotch, no ice. "After the diversionary mission yesterday, I had nightmares. I didn't think it could get any worse, but Vegesack was a real revelation."

"Today I felt like I was at the Kentucky state fair shooting at popup targets," Gott said. "The thing was this time the targets were shooting back at me." He took a gulp from his tankard of ale. "Christ, what a horror show. I can close my eyes and see the yellow noses of those bastards coming to get me."

Lentz drained his glass. "Shit. You think that's bad? All I could do was grip the controls and stare at the Nazi sons of bitches. Jim, at least you could shoot back."

Shine motioned to the bartender. "We'll have another round." He looked at Lentz. "We were more than lucky to make it through that flak. I thought it would never end. And then the Luftwaffe chased us through all that antiaircraft fire out over the North Sea.

God those crazy Nazi pilots were really determined to defend the fatherland."

"But you've got to admire those Nazi bastards," Lentz interjected. "They flew through the same shit we did for over an hour and a half. And then a bunch of them got bumped off in their fanatic attempts to knock us out of the sky."

"Bet Hermann Goering would have had them shot if they hadn't flown though that shit to get at us," Gott commented.

As another round of drinks was set on the bar, Shine lifted his scotch and soda. "Here's to the crew of Hot Freight," he shouted over the din. "May they always be a part of our victory over those Nazi creeps."

A round of cheers erupted throughout the expanse of the smoke-filled confines.

The calm of the cold clear night was shattered by the mournful wail of air raid sirens.

Hot Stuff's sergeants were rudely awakened by the all too familiar foreboding warning.

McQueen sat up on his bunk. He stared at the luminous dial on his army-issue wristwatch. After his eyes focused in the dark of the hut, he blurted, "It's just after midnight. Shit, I just closed my eyes and now those damned Nazi wise guys won't let me get any decent shuteye."

"Quit bitching and hurry!" Rondeau shouted. "Grab some threads and head for the shelter. No time to get dressed."

The atmosphere in the darkened bomb shelter was tense. The shivering men donned their jackets and trousers before lighting up. "Something's wrong with my feet," Craighead muttered.

Rondeau shined his flashlight at the belly gunner's shoes. He chuckled. "Joe you've got your shoes on the wrong feet." The whole interior of the shelter broke out in laughter.

"We really must have snapped those Nazi's caps today," Jeffers said. "They're all pissed off for what we did to them at Vegesack."

Farley took a drag on his Lucky Strike and exhaled. "Yeah. We must have really done a job on them for those Heinies to want to get at us all the way back here."

Minutes later flashes from British antiaircraft fire lighting up the night sky radiated through the bunker entranceway. Searchlights revealed the intruders to be Junkers 88s. The enemy medium bombers dropped a few dozen bombs that shook the earth near and far. Ten minutes later the "all clear" sirens wailed and the airmen emerged from their bunkers into the cold night air.

Hot Stuff's crewmen gazed around the darkened airbase. There were no fires on Hardwick itself, only some smoke and dust billowing in the moonlit air. Due to the poor accuracy of the Luftwaffe bombing there was no serious damage to the aerodrome. However on the horizon a few fires could be seen in the direction of the adjacent town of Norwich. Fire trucks and ambulances from Hardwick raced toward the neighboring English town to lend assistance in extinguishing the fires and attending to injured civilians.

As McQueen walked back to the Nissen hut with his fellow crewmen, he lit another Chesterfield. "After that I'm so wide awake now, I don't know if I can get back to sleep."

"That's a bunch of crap," Farley quipped. "You'll be out of it the minute you hit the sack. And I'll be the one who can't get to sleep because of your goddamned snoring."

CHAPTER 49

A Short Respite

Over the next three days, the 93rd's ground crews worked feverishly repairing the damage sustained by the eleven B-24s that returned from the Vegesack mission. Unlike North Africa, the maintenance personnel at Hardwick were far better equipped to repair damaged aircraft; hangars, support equipment and plentiful repair parts. They worked around the clock patching up holes, replacing engines, repairing Plexiglas, and replacing worn out .50 machine gun barrels.

While the ground crews readied the Liberators for the next mission, the air crews had three days of leisure. The days were spent sleeping late, gambling, writing letters, playing sports, going to the pubs in Norwich and attending movies.

On the way to evening chow, Rondeau stopped to read the movie schedule posted on the airbase bulletin board. "Say, there's a new movie playing tonight at the post theater."

"Who's in it?" Farley asked.

"Humphrey Bogart and Ingrid Bergman," the flight engineer replied. "That Ingrid Bergman is a real fifth avenue dame."

"Does it say what it's about?" Craighead asked.

Rondeau read from the posting. "Yeah. It's about this American guy who runs a gin mill in a town in Morocco; it's called 'Casablanca'."

"Morocco?" Jeffers exclaimed. "That's in North Africa. We've done Africa. Who the hell wants to see that again?"

"I don't care." Eisel rubbed his chin. "I'm bored with going to the pub in town. I've seen plenty of English gin mills. I want to see if this is different. After chow, I'm taking in this flick."

"I'm with you, George," Farley said.

McQueen shrugged, "Oh well, why not. Count me in."

Three hours later the theater lights came up and two hundred men of the 93rd rose from the steel folding chairs and began to exit the theater. Only McQueen and Farley remained seated.

Farley looked at McQueen's red teary-eyed face. "You all right Paul?"

"Son of bitch," McQueen exclaimed as he wiped his tears with his shirt sleeve. "I can't believe it! It's happened again. Just like in 'Wurthering Heights.' This poor bastard Rick reminds me of Heathcliff, loses the dame and ends up alone."

"Jesus Christ, Paul. It's only a story. Look at it like this, Rick rubs out the Nazi creep and that French police big cheese sides with him. With guys like that we're going to win this war."

McQueen sniffled as he looked around the empty theater. "Who knows? Maybe after the war Rick and Elsa will get together again in Paris."

Farley and McQueen stepped out into darkened windswept night. "Hurry up, Paul," Farley encouraged. "It's colder than a well digger's ass out here."

As McQueen caught up with Farley, he commented, "Did you notice all the new guys in the chow hall?"

"Yeah. Those are the replacements for the guys we lost since we left the US six months ago. Getting harder to find any of the guys we came over with."

On March 21, Major Willard Babcock, the group's maintenance officer reported to Col. Timberlake on the status of the 93rd's aircraft. "Sir, as a result of my inspection, only fourteen of our B-24s are mission worthy."

"Thanks, Will," the group commander replied. "You and your guys did a great job." Timberlake stood and gazed at the status chart on the office wall. "Well, for tomorrow's mission, we'll go with the best twelve of the lot. That'll be all, Will."

The maintenance officer saluted and left the office.

Timberlake turned to his operations officer, Major Keith Compton. "Let's take a look at tomorrow's target, Keith."

The operations officer glanced at his clipboard and put his finger on the March 22 target. "Wilhemshaven."

"What're we going after, Mike?" Timberlake asked his intelligence officer.

Lieutenant Phipps unrolled an enlarged aerial photo of Wilhelmshaven and laid it on Timberlake's desk. He pointed to a number of images. "Sir, the specific targets are the port facilities and the adjacent industrial complex."

CHAPTER 50

March 22, 1943
Thirtieth Combat Mission: Wilhemshaven

That evening before chow Shannon and his crew were notified they would be flying along with eleven other Liberators on the next day's mission. As per standard operating procedure, the target would not be revealed until the early morning briefing. No consumption of alcohol that night.

As Hot Stuff's sergeants walked to the mess hall they speculated about the next day's mission. "Maybe we're going to bomb Berlin," Craighead guessed.

"Nah, not this time." Jeffers responded. "That's too far. My money's on someplace near our last target."

"If you're right I just hope we don't have to fly through that shit again like we did over Vegesack," McQueen lamented. "Thought the flak would never end. And the goddamned Heinies were all over the place."

"One of the armorers told me they changed out all our barrels on the .50s," Rondeau commented. "Seems like we've been doing so much shooting lately the barrels were all worn out."

Eisel nodded. "That's good to hear. I thought my aim was getting bad."

"Well, at least we're still flying together on Hot Stuff," Craighead said. "I hear a lot of the guys bitching about their crews being split up to fill in for wounded guys on other Libs."

Rondeau agreed. "Glad that hasn't happened to us except that one time in North Africa when George here filled in on Ambrose." He slapped Eisel on the back. "You were damned lucky to come out of that crash landing with only a limp and a few bruises."

The next morning Hot Stuff's officers and sergeants were rousted from their bunks at 0330. After a hearty breakfast they assembled in the briefing room with eleven other of the 93rd's Liberator crews.

After Timberlake entered the briefing room he told the men to take seats. He uncovered the large map. "Today's target will be Wilhelmshaven." With a long wooden pointer, he tapped the location on the map. "To orient you, Wilhelmshaven is about forty miles west of Vegesack."

A loud groan erupted from the seated crews. Lentz leaned over to Shine and whispered, "Don't forget to bring your lucky green scarf."

Timberlake turned the briefing over to Lieutenant Phipps who presented intelligence information on the target. He pointed to a large photo of the Wilhelmshaven area. "Your specific targets are the port and industrial facilities here, here and here." He continued with target specifics for the crews to note. He added, "Flak will be heavy and expect the Luftwaffe to rise up to meet you in large numbers. Conserve your ammo."

Next Major Compton briefed on the flight routes indicated by ribbons on the large map. The ingress and egress paths looked remarkably like those for the Vegesack mission. Gott leaned over to Jacobson, "I won't have to change my flying chart much. This'll be like watching a bad movie you've seen before."

The takeoff time for the first Liberator was 0600 and the remaining eleven were to follow at thirty-second intervals. Like with the Vegesack raid, the B-24s were to assemble in diamond formations at the cruising altitude of twenty thousand feet. Thirty minutes from the target area they were to climb to twenty-eight thousand feet. As with any high altitude mission the crews would be wearing high altitude gear.

The eastern sky was a deep purple when Shine started Hot Stuff's engines. After a several minute warmup and instrument checkout period, he taxied the Liberator into the queue. At 0600 a green flare arced toward the predawn clouds and the lead B-24 began to roll.

When Hot Stuff reached cruising altitude and slipped into the diamond formation, Shannon reached into his leather flight jacket and pulled out the green scarf. "John, take over for a minute."

Lentz grasped the controls. He watched as the command pilot wrapped the bright green knit scarf around his neck. "Shine, thought you may have forgotten our lucky charm. Think we're going to need it."

Shannon smiled as his gloves grasped the controls. "The luck of the Irish flies with Hot Stuff today."

An hour and a half after lifting off from Hardwick the nightmare began. The twelve Liberators were once again surrounded by heavy flak. The early morning sky was thick with red flashes and black smoke. As Hot Stuff was severely jostled by the antiaircraft fire Gott reported they were fifteen minutes from the target. As expected over thirty Luftwaffe fighters rose to intercept the formation. A mixed bag of Me 109s, Me 110s, and Ju 88s swarmed to attack.

Hot Stuff's gunners waited until the enemy aircraft were within lethal range of their .50s. To conserve ammunition they fired sporadically at specific targets. The crew called each target so that other gunners would know when and where to engage.

When Gott called out ten minutes to Wilhelmshaven, Jacobson began adjusting the bomb sight. Jeffers crawled into the nose and grabbed the .50, chose a target and fired.

Attempting to maintain a tight formation Shannon and Lentz gripped the controls of the violently shaking Liberator. In the distance streams of light gray smoke from smoke generators blew over the target area.

"Goddamn it, Shine, the smoke's so thick I can't see the target." Jacobson's voice fluttered in synch with Hot Stuff's vibrations. "I sure as hell hate to think we have to make another pass through all this crap."

The formation pressed on toward Wilhelmshaven. "Looks like we'll have to make a go around again before cancelling the mission," Shannon spoke over the intercom.

"Jesus Christ," Lentz remarked as his gloved hands held the controls in a death grip. "I sure as hell don't look forward to going through this meat grinder again."

"Wait! Wait!" Jacobson yelled. "The wind is shifting. I can see the target." As the formation closed in, the prevailing winds shifted and dissipated the smoke unmasking the port and industrial facilities.

The lead bomber reported the target was in sight. Shannon relinquished the controls to Hot Stuff's bombardier. "It's all yours, Jake."

The Luftwaffe fighters persisted in attacking the twelve B-24s as the bombers began delivering their deadly payloads. Jacobson released the bombs and observed the detonations on the port and industrial facilities seconds later. "Right in the pickle barrel again. Let's go home."

Shannon took control of the violently shaking Liberator. The aerial combat was not over. Hot Stuff's crew continued to call out incoming enemy fighters as the formation turned northwest toward the North Sea. The 93rd's gunners made the attackers pay a heavy price. Seven of the Luftwaffe's best went down before they broke off the attack. Although flak and cannon-fire ridden, none of the twelve Liberators was lost.

As Hot Stuff approached Hardwick's runway, Lentz leaned to his left. "Bring that lucky scarf of yours on every mission." He looked back at a large hole in the fuselage near Gott's head. "I firmly believe it keeps us flying and in good health."

"My Mom always said the luck of the Irish will keep me safe," Shannon responded. "That's why she knitted it for me."

Timberlake stood in the Hardwick control tower and watched as all twelve Liberators returned. Many had sustained flak and cannon-fire damage; however, they maintained formation and landed without incident. Miraculously only one of the 93rd's crewmen was wounded.

At the debriefing aerial photos confirmed Jacobson's analysis. Timberlake congratulated the crews on their highly successful mission.

Hot Stuff was not selected to participate in missions flown by the 93rd on March 25 and 28. During this period the crewmen enjoyed the usual leisure activities while ground crews repaired their damaged B-24.

On the night of March 30, Shannon was notified he and his crew would be included in the next morning's mission.

CHAPTER 51

March 31, 1943
Thirty-First and Last Combat Mission: Rotterdam

At 0500 Hot Stuff's crew along with eleven other crews were awakened for the March 31 mission. At breakfast, Shannon observed the decreasing number of officers seated in the mess. "At the rate we're losing crewmen without adequate replacements, the 93rd won't last through the end of the war."

Lentz forked a piece of canned sausage into his mouth. "You're right, Shine. I'm seeing fewer and fewer of the guys we came over with."

"If we don't get new planes soon and replacements, I don't know what's going to happen," Shine remarked.

"When I walk down the apron, a lot of our Libs have so many holes you can almost see through them," Jacobson commented.

"I heard from Major Babcock a number of the planes are in such bad shape they'll be deleted from the mission-ready roster," Gott added. "Luckily, Hot Stuff's not among them."

"After all we've been through I sure as hell don't want her to end up on the scrap heap," Shannon said. He sipped his coffee and continued. "You know, if all goes well today we'll have completed thirty-one combat missions."

Lentz spoke through a mouthful of powdered eggs and gestured with his fork. "Yeah. And we really haven't had anyone injured on any mission with Hot Stuff either. That's really something."

Forty-five minutes later the twelve crews sat in the briefing room. Timberlake unveiled the large map on the stage. He pointed at a spot on the coast of the Netherlands. "Today's mission is the engineering works at the Rotterdam shipyards."

Lieutenant Phipps briefed on the details of the target using a blown-up aerial photo. He adjusted his glasses and continued. "Flak is expected to be light. Nothing like what was experienced at Vegesack or Wilhelmshaven. If any, only a few enemy fighters may be encountered."

The room buzzed over the relative ease of having to deal with antiaircraft fire and the Luftwaffe.

Major Compton provided information on the ingress and egress routes. The estimated flying time to the target was relatively short; just over an hour. The first B-24 was to have wheels up at 0700 and as per past missions the remaining eleven aircraft were to depart in thirty second intervals. Since the flight time was of short duration the formation was to form up at twenty thousand feet and maintain that altitude to attack the target.

For this mission Hot Stuff had been designated as lead bomber. Twenty minutes following the mission briefing Shannon taxied the Liberator into the head of the queue. At 0700, the green flare shot into the air and Hot Stuff's pilot shoved the throttles forward. Seconds later the B-24 was airborne headed for the group's rendezvous point.

The formation of Liberators had been in the air forty-five minutes when the entire sky erupted into red flashes and clouds of black smoke. Hot Stuff shook violently. Surprised, Shannon and Lentz struggled to keep the aircraft from colliding with the other three B-24s in the lead diamond formation.

"Son of a bitch," Lentz grimaced. "Wait till I get my hands around Phipps' neck. I'm going to strangle that little four-eyed framer. I feel like he set us up for a bruising."

Shannon responded as he fought to control the Liberator. "John, give the little shit a break. He's the fall guy for Eighth Air Force. If their intel is screwed up so is Phipps."

Farley lost his balance and was thrown against McQueen. After the two of them regained their footing McQueen groused, "Jesus Christ, George, what's the matter with you? Can't you stand on your own two feet?"

"This goddamned flak is as bad as Vegesack. I thought Lieutenant Phipps said we had it made in the shade. Where did he get his intel from, Hermann Goering?"

"Oh, shit," Rondeau exclaimed from the top turret. "Here they come. Six Me 109s at two o'clock." He swiveled his .50s to meet the threat.

McQueen pulled back on the receiver. "What about that son of a bitch Phipps telling us that there wouldn't be any Nazi fighters around Rotterdam?" He aimed and began firing.

"I've got two Me 110s coming at our tail," Eisel shouted into the intercom.

Craighead peered down towards a Ju 88 rising toward Hot Stuff's belly. "Aw shit, a Heine at seven o'clock low. The bastards are all over the place."

All of Hot Stuff's gunners began firing at the swarm of Luftwaffe fighters that attacked the formation.

As Jacobson fired his .50 at a passing Me 109, he yelled at the navigator, "Jimmie, how soon to the target?"

"We're about ten minutes out," Gott shouted.

"Then get someone down here so I can get to work," Jake bellowed.

"Jimmie, take over for Jake," Shannon ordered.

A minute later, with the navigator on the nose gun, the bombardier adjusted the Norden bomb sight. "The clouds are pretty damned thick, but I can see the shipyards."

"We're going on in," Shannon said. "There'll be no scrubbing this mission while we're lead bomber."

Jacobson opened the bomb bay doors and waited.

During the next five minutes the gunners on the twelve Liberators continued to engage the enemy fighters with interweaving fire. Two Me 109s broke apart in a burst of flames during the melee.

"I've got the target in my sight," Jake announced.

"You have the plane," Shine relayed as his gloved hands released the controls.

In spite of the jostling caused by the heavy flak, Jacobson managed to keep Hot Stuff steady. At the moment the crosshairs intersected with the shipyard structures, his gloved fingers toggled the bomb release switches. "Bombs away! Take us out of here, Shine!"

The remaining eleven bombers dropped their ordnance and followed the lead bomber. Hot Stuff led the formation out over the North Sea. The 93rd left the target area in smoke and flames. The persistent enemy fighters angrily followed the group of B-24s as they headed west.

Eisel furiously rotated his rear turret to fire at incoming Nazi fighters that appeared intent on destroying the tail section. "The bastards keep coming at us." He had fired at so many Luftwaffe planes he was concerned about running out of ammo. He shouted to Rondeau. "Grant, can you fire on those two Me 109s at five o'clock high?"

"Coming around," the flight engineer replied as he rotated the upper turret toward the rear and began firing. Between the two gunners one of the Me 109s began belching smoke and spiraled toward the cold North Sea. The second enemy fighter fired its cannons briefly and broke off.

Fifteen minutes after bomb release, it was all over. The flak had ceased and the remaining thirty odd German interceptors gave up their pursuit and returned to their bases.

Lead aircraft pilot Shannon spoke over the command net to the formation for status. All aircraft had sustained minor to moderate damage, one with two engines inoperative. The twelve B-24s were able to continue on to Hardwick. Several crewmen had been wounded, some severely. Again, remarkably no one on Hot Stuff received as much as a scratch.

Nervously Timberlake gripped the railing on the control tower and searched the thick overcast sky for the first Liberator. Compton raised his binoculars and pointed. "There they are!" He counted the aircraft as they began circling to land in priority order as directed by the control tower. "One, two, three… twelve." He smiled at Timberlake. "Sir, they're all back."

The first B-24 approaching the runway had two engines out of commission and was trailing smoke. As soon as its wheels touched down, fire trucks and ambulances raced toward the rolling plane. As soon as the crippled Liberator came to a complete stop, fire retardant was sprayed on the smoldering engines. Wounded personnel were taken by medics and loaded onto ambulances. As the uninjured crewman deplaned they didn't hesitate to light up.

The remaining B-24s from the Rotterdam mission landed in priority of severity of damage and critical condition of wounded onboard. Hot Stuff was the last Liberator to land.

Thirty minutes later with doughnuts and coffee in hand the airmen filed into the debriefing room. As Phipps approached the front of the room he was greeted with some low boos and grumbling. Timberlake ordered the crews to settle down. "I understand our intel was a bit off." The men broke into laughter. "Rest assured Eighth Air Force is going to get an earful from me." A few men applauded at the remark.

Timberlake looked directly at Shannon. "On the bright side, I want to congratulate you on a highly successful mission. On examination of aerial photos just processed, we find the direct hits on the engineering works and shipyards are going to set the Nazi navy back for quite a while; maybe forever in the Netherlands."

CHAPTER 52

Twenty-Five Combat Missions for Rotation

As April 1943 began, Hot Stuff underwent extensive maintenance and repairs. With the anticipated influx of replacements, Shannon and his crew along with several other veteran crews were selected to begin preparation for training. During the first week of the month those crewmen enjoyed leisure time.

Hot Stuff and its crew sat out the 93rd's April 5 mission over Antwerp. Shannon, always eager to learn results of combat missions, sat in on the debriefing. The bombing of the aero repair depot was a success. One Luftwaffe fighter was shot down and another damaged. All twelve Liberators returned to Hardwick.

Although the "instructor crews" were ready, few replacements had arrived for training.

On the morning of April 10, Timberlake issued an order for all of the 93rd's crews to assemble in a hangar at noon. No one had any idea what the purpose of the meeting was. Speculation ran rampant among the men. Was the 93rd getting new Liberators? Were replacement crews finally on the way? Were the crews to receive extended leave?

The four depleted squadrons stood in formation in front of a hastily erected stage with a microphone and loudspeakers. Timberlake nervously looked at his watch as a C-47 touched down and taxied toward the hangar. He and his staff walked briskly onto the tarmac where the military cargo plane was parked. As the port hatch opened, a ground crewman placed a small aluminum ladder against the doorway. High ranking army air force brass then began filing down onto the tarmac.

Timberlake saluted and shook hands with General 'Hap' Arnold, the commander of the USAAF, fresh from the Pentagon. The four-star general was followed by a string of officers, among them Lt. Gen. Frank Andrews, now commander of all American forces in Europe. Introductions were made all around. Andrews, already familiar with the 93rd smiled as he shook Timberlake's hand.

Moments later the assembled crewmen were called to attention and given the order to hand salute as Timberlake escorted Arnold and the other officers to the stage. Once the visitors were seated on steel folding chairs Timberlake introduced Arnold to the assembled crews. The four star general rose and told the crews to stand at ease.

After some congratulatory comments on the 93rd's highly successful achievements, Arnold got to the point of his visit. "We have determined that upon completion of twenty-five combat missions, aircrewmen will have completed a tour of duty. By that, qualified crewmen will be entitled to a month of rest and recuperation in the States before reassignment."

Up to this point the airmen had believed they would be flying missions for the duration of the war; that is if they survived. Upon the surprise announcement by Arnold, the assembled four squadrons broke into cheers and laughter.

By definition, credit for a combat mission was dependent on the crewmen actually being engaged by the enemy either from the air or the ground. A good number of the crewmen had already exceeded the magic number.

After a few more words by Arnold, the four squadrons were called to attention. The brass stepped off the stage and was escorted by Timberlake to the officers' mess. After Arnold and the visiting officers exited the hangar, the 93rd's executive officer dismissed the crews.

On the way to the aircrew mess McQueen slapped Farley on the back. "Son of bitch. All of us on Hot Stuff have more than twenty-five combat missions. Won't be long before we'll be heading back to the good old USA."

Eisel overheard McQueen's remarks. "Don't be a pushover, Paul. I heard what the general said. But what he didn't say was nobody goes anywhere until we get trained replacements."

"George is right," Rondeau added. "It's going to be sometime before we get a sufficient number of people through the pipeline."

"Aw shit," McQueen groused. "I should have known it sounded too good to be true. By the time we get our replacements trained I could be an old man and they'd have to retire me."

Jeffers consoled the waist gunner. "I heard the way they're putting out new crews we could be out of here before the fourth of July."

"I'm going to do my damnedest to make sure the new guys I'll be training will be combat qualified PDQ," Craighead remarked. "I sure as hell don't want to mess up my chance of rotating back home."

On April 16 Shannon sat in on the Brest mission debriefing even though Hot Stuff didn't participate. Although the results of the bombing of the port facilities were marginal, the 93rd paid a heavy price. Three planes went down during the mission. Night Raider, Ball of Fire, Junior, and Liberty Lad were lost and the crews were declared missing in action. One plane, Yard Bird, was severely damaged and crash landed at an RAF airfield, no casualties. However, thirty men would not return to Hardwick or enjoy a month's leave.

When Hot Stuff's sergeants learned of the Brest raid, they were stunned. So many more of their buddies were now dead, wounded or taken prisoner. Morale of the 93rd plummeted.

On April 25, sunrise services were held on Easter Sunday at 0630. The attendees at the nondenominational service sang "My Country Tis of Thee" and repeated the pledge of allegiance. Col. Timberlake made a few comments about the 93rd's achievements and reminded the assemblage the group was formed one year ago.

CHAPTER 53

The Chosen Crew

On April 27, 1943 Shannon was summoned to Timberlake's office. Shine looked at Lentz. "What the hell did I do now? All we've been doing is preparing to train new guys whenever they show up."

"Maybe we're the first in line for rotation," the copilot replied.

"I doubt it. Anyway, whatever it is, I'll find out soon enough," the command pilot sighed as he donned his crushed service cap.

A few minutes later Shannon knocked on Timberlake's door. "Enter!" the disembodied voice resonated from behind the closed door.

Shannon stood before the group commander's desk and saluted. "Sit down, Shine. I've got some good news for you."

Hot Stuff's pilot sat on the hard metal folding chair as he exhaled.

"What I am about to tell you is classified secret," Timberlake disclosed. "I've just received orders through channels that one of our B-24s is to be prepared for a long flight. Six seats are to be fitted in the bomb bay.

"I want you to know you and your crew have been chosen to make this flight. You're to fly to Bovington on May 1. Once there you will receive further instructions."

"Why has Hot Stuff's crew been singled out?"

"Heavy bomber crews completing ten or fifteen missions are considered very fortunate. You and your crew have proven to have a mix of luck and skill. You've stood up against Luftwaffe fighters and enemy antiaircraft fire during thirty-one combat missions. You stayed alive and out of enemy hands. As a result you and your crew have been chosen to be the first in the Eighth Air Force to rotate back to the United States. Congratulations. As I see it, Hot Stuff is perhaps the first battle-hardened heavy bomber crew from any theater of operations to achieve that goal."

"Sir, I don't know what to say," Shine replied.

"As we speak, Hot Stuff is being readied for the long flight. While your aircraft is being serviced, the interior will be scrubbed down and plywood sheets will cover the bomb bay for passenger seating."

"Who will be our passengers?"

"That information is not available at this time. You'll find out once you land at Bovington."

"What do I say to my crew as this is a classified mission?"

"Tell them about the rotation, but nothing else."

Timberlake rose from his desk and offered his hand. "You and your crew earned the right to rotate first in the Eighth Air Force. I only wish I were in you place right now. You and your crew are the heroes of the 93rd and the whole goddamned Army Air Force."

"Thank you, sir. I'm proud to have served with the 93rd."

Within fifteen minutes Shine had assembled Hot Stuff's crew in front of the sergeants' Nissen hut. Upon announcement of the early rotation, a jubilant roar rose from Hot Stuff's crew.

"Paul, when you named our B-24 Hot Stuff back at Grenier, that was our lucky day," Farley shouted as he slapped his fellow waist gunner on the back.

"I feel like a kid opening his presents on Christmas morning." McQueen chortled.

"This calls for a celebration in town tonight," Eisel remarked. "Can you get us passes, Captain?"

"I'll take care of it. Just don't get ossified on me."

Jeffers was grinning so widely his jaws hurt. He looked at Shannon. "You're not shitting us, are you sir?"

"I never kid about something this important," Shine replied. "One thing though, don't any of you mention this to anyone in town."

The sergeants all nodded as they returned to the hut to change into clean uniforms.

"Come on," Shine said to the other three officers. "The drinks are on me."

After Shannon made arrangements for his sergeants' passes he met Lentz, Jacobson and Gott at the O Club. He raised his glass to his fellow officers, "It's been a long hard year for all of us. During that time we've become a cohesive team that beat whatever the Nazis threw at us. So, here's to having a ball back home."

After the evening meal, Shannon and Lentz decided to walk over to the hangar where Hot Stuff was parked. As they entered the cavernous round-walled structure, they could see ground crewmen scrambling all over the B-24's fuselage. Major Willard, the group engineer officer and Rondeau stood looking up at one of the engines. "Is there a problem with the engine, Major?" Shannon asked.

"Not now. We couldn't get the replacement to run smoothly so we changed it out. Something was out of balance."

"Rondeau, you happy with it?" Lentz asked.

"It purrs like a kitten now, Lieutenant. I was a little worried it would crap out on us."

Willard walked Shannon and Lentz around Hot Stuff for a visual inspection. The skin was blemish free; no discernable dents or holes. Lentz ran his hand along the fuselage. Although the paint was worn, the exterior of Hot Stuff was clean and free of oil and exhaust stains. "Looks like your guys did a spiffy job, Major."

"Wait'll you see the interior," Willard smiled. "Let's take a look."

Once inside the flight deck Shannon took a deep breath. "Goddamn, Major, it smells so clean; almost like it did back at Grenier." The Plexiglas was new and the controls and instruments were clean and polished.

"Let me show you where your passengers will be riding," Willard said.

As the three officers moved further into the interior, the group engineer officer pointed out the thick plywood flooring that covered the bomb bay. "Sitting on the wood floor is not very comfortable, but with some blankets for padding your passengers should be able to make the trek."

"Where are the six seats that are to be fitted in the bomb bay?" Shannon asked.

"What you see is the best we could do on short notice," Willard replied.

"Crewmembers have sat on the floor before." Lentz said. "Our passengers can do the same."

Shannon observed the interior was as pristine as the day Harry Byron and Florene Watson delivered the Liberator at Grenier nine months earlier. "Well, Major, once we're all gassed up, we'll be mission ready for our passengers. We're to fly to Bovington in two days."

As the three officers climbed out of Hot Stuff, a sergeant from Timberlake's office was waiting. He saluted. "Captain Shannon, Colonel Timberlake wants to see you PDQ."

Shine glanced at Lentz. "Wonder what this is all about?" He then followed the sergeant to the jeep.

A few minutes later, Shannon was standing in front of Timberlake's desk.

"Sit down, Shine," Timberlake said. "I just received a change in the orders for your crew. It seems like you'll be carrying a few more passengers and a lot of baggage when you fly out of Bovington. Because of this new development, your bombardier and two of your gunners will not be flying with you on this mission. Based on these guidelines it's up to you to select the men who will be flying with you."

Later that afternoon, Shannon took Jacobson to the O Club. Over a couple of beers Shine turned serious. "Jake, I don't know how to tell you this, but you won't be flying with us when we go to Bovington."

"Why, Shine?"

"My orders are quite clear. I just found out there will be additional passengers and luggage. There isn't enough room in Hot Stuff. I was directed to leave you and two of our gunners at Hardwick. I gave Craighead and Farley the bad news this afternoon."

"When will we be rotated?"

"I have no idea, Jake. All I know about is this specific flight."

Jacobson took a sip from his glass. "After all this time, I'm sorry they're going to break up our crew."

"I don't like this any more than you do, Jake."

After Shannon notified the three crewmembers they were not flying on the Bovington mission, the entire crew was dejected.

As he packed his duffle bag for the long flight McQueen looked at his crewmates. "We came all this way together and now they're breaking us up? It just doesn't seem right."

"I agree," Farley said. "But I just know Joe and me will be close behind you."

"I know this has happened to other crews, but somehow I never thought they'd break up our crew," Craighead lamented.

"I heard from the grapevine that you guys will be rotating back to the States real soon." Hot Stuff's sergeants all turned to see Bill Gros walk into the Nissen hut carrying a small cardboard box.

Jeffers smiled. "Hi, Bill. Yeah, four of us will be rotating." He gestured toward Craighead and Farley. "But, Joe and George will stay here at Hardwick."

"Son of a bitch," Eager Beaver's radioman exclaimed. "They're breaking up your crew too?"

"Yeah," Jeffers replied. "Seems like they're going to stuff Hot Stuff with bigwig passengers. As a result our bombardier Lieutenant Jacobson along with Joe and George have been bumped."

"But Ken, you're still rotating, right?"

"Far as I know," Hot Stuff's radioman replied.

"Well, in that case, can you do me a favor?"

"Sure. What is it?"

"Can you get this box of photos back to my family? The address is on the top."

"Sure thing," Jeffers replied.

CHAPTER 54

General Andrews and His Entourage

On midmorning of May 1, Hot Stuff's wheels touched down at Bovington Aerodrome north of London. Shannon complied with the large "FOLLOW ME" sign on the rear of a jeep and taxied the B-24 onto an empty concrete apron. The first leg of the odyssey had been completed.

An Eighth Air Force staff officer greeted Shannon, Lentz and Gott as they deplaned. "The three of you are to report to Col. Cleveland at headquarters. You'll receive further instructions then."

Once in Cleveland's office, the Eighth Air Force staff officer stood and shook each man's hand. "As a reward for completion of the most combat missions in the Eighth Air Force, you have been chosen by Lieutenant General Andrews to fly him and his staff on a secret mission. Lieutenant Lentz will remain behind as Gen. Andrews will have the copilot's seat." Cleveland looked at a typed sheet in his hand. "In addition, Master Sergeant Lloyd Weir, a highly experienced crew chief and flight engineer will replace your flight engineer who also will remain here at Bovington."

Shannon looked at Lentz and then at Cleveland. "Sir, Lieutenant Lentz has been my copilot since the beginning. I really don't feel right about leaving him behind. In bad weather there's no one better at instrument flying."

"Let me remind you, *Captain*, General Andrews is combat pilot rated for the B-24. He's been awarded the DFC for flying under difficult conditions, including inclement weather. He *will* be your copilot, Captain."

After the dressing down, Shannon decided it best to keep his own counsel.

Cleveland walked over to a large wall map. His index finger outlined what would be Hot Stuff's flight path. "You'll fly north to Prestwick where you'll refuel and then fly on to Iceland.

"As commander of US Forces in the European Theater of Operations, Iceland falls under Gen. Andrews' command. It would appear he is going to make an inspection of American troops stationed there." Cleveland paused. "Now here's why this mission is so highly classified. He is to continue on to Washington to meet with General Marshall. My guess is General Andrews is going to receive his fourth star or to participate in the upcoming Trident Conference in Washington. Any other reasons are highly speculative.

"Now when you get back to the States, you'll be welcomed as heroes. Your job will be morale boosting and selling war bonds. You'll be in parades, making speeches to various organizations and visiting factory production lines."

After the meeting with Cleveland, Shannon, Lentz, and Gott slowly ambled toward the Bovington O Club in silence. Gott broke the strained atmosphere. "My gut tells me there's something wrong with this whole plan, John. I know from what Cleveland said Andrews is an experienced pilot but it gives me the heebie-jeebies to think you won't be in the copilot's seat."

"I just can't imagine not flying with you guys," Lentz commented. "I feel like my family's going away and leaving me behind." He turned to Shannon. "You sure stuck your neck out for me, Shine. I thought Cleveland was going to have you court martialed for insubordination."

"Well, I wanted Cleveland to know how I felt," Shannon said.

Lentz thought for a moment. "Shine, I heard the Air Transport Command runs regular flights across the Atlantic via Iceland on new C-54 Skymasters. I understand they are really plush with upholstered seating, heating and sound proofing. I can't believe Andrews is going to make the other passengers sit on blankets on plywood flooring in Hot Stuff's bomb bay. The cold, wind and noise alone would be next to unbearable for them."

"Now that I think about it, Hot Stuff was chosen to take him back to the states for a reason," replied Shannon. "He knows we have a damned good crew. We made it through thirty-one combat missions and shot down a shit load of enemy planes without losing a man. He probably wants the protection of a bomber in the event the Germans find out about the mission and try to intercept us on our way to Iceland.

"And what better bomber and crew for the mission than that of Hot Stuff! No matter, John, I wish you were going to be in the right seat."

Unknown to Shannon, General Andrews had been delayed at Prestwick in the past. Since he was on a tight schedule, he was not going to endure that hindrance again. He had one of his aides, Captain Johnson, meet with Colonel Burrows of the Air Transportation Command to arrange for a direct flight from Bovington to Iceland. Since it was against regulations to bypass Prestwick, ATC would not be responsible for this flight. Furthermore, due to shortages of personnel, no one from Prestwick would be made available to conduct a briefing at Bovington. Authorization for the flight would not be forthcoming until Burrows had the proper clearances from Prestwick.

On May 2, the necessary paperwork finally arrived at Bovington. This included maps covering the flight path, landing charts, radio frequencies, the North Atlantic air route manual, and briefing material. Shortly after the arrival of the paperwork, Shannon and Gott were given a two-hour briefing for the flight.

That night, Shannon went to get the weather forecast for the flight to Iceland. He approached the Bovington meteorologist on duty. "I'm Captain Shannon. I have orders to fly out of here tomorrow morning for Iceland. Can you provide me with the latest weather forecast?"

The young lieutenant looked up from his desk, removed his glasses and shook his head. "Captain, the only forecast I can provide is the leg from Bovington to Prestwick." He shuffled through a pile of papers on his desk and handed Shine the weather forecast to the aerodrome in Scotland.

An hour later, Shannon requested the forecast to Iceland from an RAF weather station. It was then Shine was informed that the weather was not fit for flying on to Iceland, but he was to refer back to Prestwick before continuing on from Scotland to Iceland.

At 0715 on May 3, Shannon taxied *Hot Stuff* to a position on Bovington's runway to pick up the passengers. He sent Gott to the tower to get clearances for the direct flight to Iceland. The navigator was informed that the flight was not cleared to fly directly to Iceland because they did not have the necessary weather forecast information.

Hearing Gott explain the situation, Shannon shut down the engines and made his way up to Bovington's tower. Once inside the building he confronted the flight operations officer. "I'm Captain Shannon. I have orders to fly General Andrews to Reykjavik, Iceland, this morning."

The operations officer refused permission. "Either you wait here at Bovington or call Prestwick for permission to proceed to Iceland."

General Andrews, upon hearing of the delay, was quite angry. He gave the Bovington operations officer hell because the clearances should have been taken care of. However, he did agree to land in Scotland pending weather clearance for the leg to Iceland.

As General Andrews entered the flight deck he greeted Shine, a smile on his face. He offered his hand. "Good to see you again, Captain Shannon. It's been a while since we last saw each other in North Africa."

"Yes, sir," Shine responded as he shook the general's outstretched hand."

"You don't know how much I'm looking forward to flying back to Washington with you in Hot Stuff. May I offer my congratulations to you and your crew for being first in the Eighth Air Force to successfully complete twenty five combat missions. That in itself is quite an achievement. It's an honor for me to be part of your crew if just for one day."

Shannon replied, "Thank you, sir. I had a great crew."

Andrews sat in the copilot's seat while eight passengers began boarding Hot Stuff. The entourage included the following:

1. Brigadier General Charles Barth, ETO Chief of Staff
2. Bishop Adna Leonard, Chairman of the General Commission of Army and Navy Chaplains and special envoy of President Roosevelt traveling around the world visiting military installations as a representative of thirty million American Protestants
3. Colonel Frank Miller, Army Chaplain and Plans and Training Officer in the Chief of Chaplains Office
4. Colonel Morrow Krum, ETO Public Relations Officer
5. Lt. Colonel Fred Chapman, Senior Aide to General Andrews

6. Major Robert Humphry, Army Chaplain and Aide to Bishop Leonard
7. Major Theodore Totman, Personal Secretary to General Andrews
8. Captain Joseph Johnson, Junior Aide to General Andrews

Jeffers, McQueen, and Eisel assisted in stowing the passengers' luggage.

CHAPTER 55

Bound for Iceland

With all the delays, Hot Stuff's takeoff time was now pushed back to 0922.

Once in the air their flight path took them northwest to Worcester, Rhyl, the Isle of Man, and Monrieth. The weather was inclement until they crossed into Scotland. The further north they flew the more the weather cleared. Andrews turned to Shannon and smiled, "Looks like we're going to have good weather all the way to Iceland."

Since Shannon had not received a forecast for the leg to Iceland, he was dubious. "We'll check the forecast once we get to Prestwick."

All communications to and from Hot Stuff were encoded and sent in Morse code by Jeffers. When he finally contacted Prestwick, he was informed he had the wrong call sign. It took some time to identify Hot Stuff and its position.

Finally, Jeffers was able to send a request to Prestwick for Reykjavik, Iceland weather. The response received was the weather was socked in and Hot Stuff was ordered to land at Prestwick. Moments later Jeffers lost all contact with Prestwick due to a complete power failure at the airbase.

Shannon then requested a weather report on Reykajavik from Stornoway RAF on the Isle of Lewis on the west coast of Scotland. He learned the ceiling was a thousand feet and visibility was two miles. Minutes later Shannon requested another forecast for Iceland from Stornoway, which was misunderstood as a request for the RAF aerodrome on Lewis. The report indicated the weather was good.

Rather than proceed to Iceland, Shannon was sure that landing at Stornoway would be the correct decision until they received a more precise weather report for Iceland.

Andrews, satisfied with the Stornoway forecast, leaned over his shoulder and asked Gott and Weir if they were able to make Reykajavik without a stop at Prestwick or Stornoway. A moment after checking fuel levels and navigation charts, both replied it was possible.

At that moment, Andrews made the decision to press on to Iceland. Obviously the general was in a hurry. Shannon looked over at his copilot. Although Shine was the commander of Hot Stuff, he once again decided to keep his own counsel; he had been admonished two days earlier by Col. Cleveland at Bovington. He didn't want to make things worse by irritating the commander of US Forces in the European Theater of Operations as well.

As they proceeded northwest, Shannon wondered what made this General Andrews tick?

CHAPTER 56

Man in a Hurry

In January 1943 at the Casablanca Conference in French Morocco, General Marshall, the US Army Chief of Staff, informed Lieutenant General Andrews he was to assume command of all US Forces in Europe. In Marshall's opinion Andrews was the right man at the right time for the job. Why? Over his career which spanned nearly thirty-seven years, Andrews had proven himself to be a strong leader. He was endowed with a keen knack for organizing and planning military operations. If there was one key attribute Marshall was looking for it was Andrews' ability to persuade others to do what was best for eventual victory. This was crucial when it came to dealing with the narrow mindedness of the various Allies, each concerned with their own particular agenda. Andrews possessed the conviction and vision necessary for combining the various ground, air, and naval forces to destroy the Axis powers.

In his new position, Andrews was a man in a hurry.

What brought him to this moment in history?

Frank Andrews, a Tennessee native, graduated from the United States Military Academy at West Point, NY in 1906. He was commissioned a second lieutenant in the cavalry. He served in that capacity for eleven years in the Philippines and Hawaii. When the United

BEFORE THE BELLE

States entered WWI Andrews looked for opportunities to garner valuable combat experience. He felt the cavalry was outmoded for modern warfare and made a transfer to the aviation branch of the signal corps.

In 1918 he earned his aviator wings; however, he never left the United States. Instead Andrews commanded various air fields around the country. Following a stint in that position, Andrews served in the war plans division of the Army General Staff. When WWI ended, he replaced Brig. Gen. Billy Mitchell as the air officer for the Army of Occupation in Germany.

When Andrews returned to the United States he became commandant of the first flying school at Kelly Field, Texas. By 1928 he attended the Air Corps Tactical School at Langley Field, Virginia. A year later he attended the Army Command and General Staff School at Ft. Leavenworth, Kansas. By now he had become well rounded in military ground and air operations.

When promoted to lieutenant colonel, Andrews served as chief of the Army Air Corps Air Training and Operations Division.

In 1933, he graduated from the Army War College and returned as the first aviation officer to be on the army general staff.

In 1935, the Army Chief of Staff, General Douglas MacArthur was convinced by Andrews that all of the United States air forces should be consolidated and a new long range bomber should be brought on line in order for the air force to conduct independent missions. MacArthur gave Andrews command of the new General Headquarters of Air Forces. Andrews was promoted to Brig. General and commanded all the Army Air Corps tactical units. A year later he was promoted to the temporary rank of Major General. Under his command he created the American air arm that eventually became known as the US Army Air Force.

In the late 1930s Andrews was a vocal proponent of acquiring large numbers of heavy, long-range four engine B-17 bombers as the mainstay of the American bomber force. He was opposed by the general staff who thought it better to purchase less expensive light twin engine medium bombers. However, Andrews prevailed enough for the army to purchase sufficient numbers of B-17s to keep the heavy bomber program alive. This was later to prove fortuitous for the United States as WWII loomed on the horizon.

In 1941, General Marshall, the Army Chief of Staff assigned Andrews as commander of the Caribbean Defense Command. With his assignment, Andrews was promoted to Lieutenant General. This command was primarily a defense organization that protected the southern approaches to the United States and the defense of the strategic Panama Canal. The area extended from the Canal Zone to Trinidad, Brazil and Ecuador. One of Andrews' most noteworthy accomplishments was to coordinate the activities of Army, Navy and Air Corps to include Latin American forces. He organized the air forces of the Caribbean Defense Command into bomber, interceptor and service commands. A key element of this organization was establishing an effective antisubmarine defense program from the air. One of the units that temporarily fell under Andrews' command was the 93rd Bombardment Group while it conducted antisubmarine operations in the summer of 1942 out of Ft. Myers, Florida.

It was just after the 93rd deployed to England when General Douglas MacArthur, the Supreme Allied Commander in the Pacific, requested Andrews be made his chief of air forces in the Pacific. Marshall denied the request because he felt this would be a demotion for Andrews. Being taken from command of a theater and placed under another theater commander was out of order. Instead Marshall had other plans for the talented Andrews.

By late summer of 1942, Marshall, with President Roosevelt's approval, sent Andrews to North Africa to take command of all United States Forces in the Middle East. There he established his headquarters in Cairo where he became highly knowledgeable of air and ground combat operations and developed a knack for dealing with the diverse objectives of Allied leaders.

Under his command the American Ninth Air Force carried out with great success the bombing of enemy held ports and destruction of enemy fighter aircraft in North Africa, Sicily and Italy. It was during this time the 93rd Bombardment Group was temporarily assigned to the Ninth and Andrews had a second opportunity to have the 93rd fall under his command. While on his way to attend the Casablanca Conference in French Morocco in January 1943, he conducted an informal inspection of the group while it was stationed at Gambut Main. It was becoming apparent Andrews had a growing affinity for the 93rd and its daring risk-taking airmen. Prominent among them were Shannon and Hot Stuff's crew. Three months later they would be chosen to fly the general on a secret mission to the United States.

Following his visit to Gambut Main Andrews attended the Casablanca Conference held from January 14 through 24, 1943. The meeting was headed by US President Franklin Roosevelt and British Prime Minister Winston Churchill. Included in the meeting were high ranking American and British officers. Among them was the American Army's Chief of Staff General Marshall. The purpose of the meeting was to finalize the Allied strategic plan against the Axis Powers. It was decided to establish a European Theater of Operations with headquarters in England as a precursor to the invasion of Europe. A highlight of the meeting was to begin concentration of Allied forces in England in preparation for eventual landings in Northern France. Towards this end the United States and Great Britain were first to focus efforts in the Mediterranean Theater of Operations with the end game being to knock Italy out of the war. Another highlight agreed upon was for the United States and Great Britain to strengthen strategic bombing against Germany. On the last day of the Conference Roosevelt and Churchill agreed in order to preserve post-war peace the unconditional surrender of Germany was paramount.

Until this conference, both Archibald Sinclair, the British Secretary of State for Air and Air Chief Marshal Charles Portal, Chief of the Royal Air Force's Air Staff and several other senior RAF officers strongly advised Churchill to try to switch the USAAF to night bombing until the Americans had gotten sufficient forces to try their long held concept of daylight bombing. His air staff believed the best way to conduct a bombing campaign against Germany at this time was through nighttime bombing.

General Arnold learned that Churchill might broach the subject of changing the USAAF to night bombing. During a lull in the conference at Casablanca General Arnold requested a meeting with Churchill. Arnold quickly summoned Major General Eaker, the Eighth Air Force commander in England to brief Churchill. Andrews was at the meeting to lend support to Eaker along with General Spaatz the overall commander of the USAAF in the European Theater of Operations. Andrews agreed with Eaker that day and night bombing would keep Germany off balance. He also knew a great deal of money and time had been spent training American bomber crews to conduct daylight bombing.

Eaker gave Churchill a very convincing briefing and concluded by saying, "We can bomb the devils around-the-clock." The prime minister backed off his earlier position and the senior RAF officials then agreed the Americans proceed with daylight bombing. Daylight bombing was to be carried out by American heavy bombers, namely B-17s and B-24s.

The persuasive talents Marshall had seen in Andrews were just what were needed to deal with the various independent thinking of the Allies. After General Billy Mitchell, Andrews was considered the leading airmen by most in the USAAF. He had not only proven his brilliant leadership qualities at the highest levels, but he had demonstrated exceptional piloting skills.

With Operation Torch and the Allied landings in North Africa in November 1942, Lieutenant General Eisenhower had been appointed commander of all US forces in the Mediterranean. With Eisenhower's appointment there was no further need for Andrews to be commander of American Forces in the Middle East. At first it seemed Andrews would be without a job, but General Marshall had other plans for Andrews' talents. It was at the Casablanca Conference where Marshall, with President Roosevelt's blessing, informed Andrews he was now the commander of all United States Forces in the European Theater of Operations, his third theater command. In this new position, as Marshall had predicted, Andrews would demonstrate his leadership and organizational attributes in dealing with the Allies in initial planning for the eventual invasion of France. At this point, Andrews, now fifty-nine, and a grandfather, was on the ascendency for greatness.

With Andrews' assumption of command of all US Forces in Europe the 93rd Bombardment Group, part of the Eighth Air Force stationed in England, was once again a part of his command. In late April, after Hot Stuff and her crew had been selected to be the first to rotate back home, Andrews arrived at Hardwick for an inspection of the 93rd. After the inspection, Andrews informed his friend Col. Ted Timberlake, commander of the 93rd BG he wanted Capt. Robert "Shine" Shannon to fly with him and his staff back to Washington, D.C. in Hot Stuff.

CHAPTER 57

The Final Flight

It was seven hours since Hot Stuff had wheels up at Bovington. Shannon purposely flew between five and seven thousand feet for the comfort of the passengers. Even at this lower altitude, the air temperature within the confines of the Liberator was frigid and the noise level close to unbearable. Each passenger had his own thermos of hot coffee and a box of C rations for the long flight. Since they were not afforded a stopover at Prestwick where a hot meal and a leg-stretching period would have been welcomed, they endured the uncomfortable conditions sitting on the plywood flooring wrapped in wool army blankets.

By this time, the C rations had been consumed and the thermos bottles were nearly empty. McQueen chewed on a D ration as he shared the contents of his thermos with the chaplains. Weir also tried his best to make the passengers more comfortable.

At this point Hot Stuff didn't have sufficient fuel to fly to Gander; it was necessary to refuel in Iceland before proceeding to the United States via Newfoundland. Unknown to Shannon and Andrews the weather forecast for Iceland was grim. The meteorologist in northern Scotland was not happy with the report. It was obvious the weather was not fit for flying.

Before leaving the northern coast of Scotland, Hot Stuff had received a report from Stornoway on the Isle of Lewis that the weather was clear for landing. Unfortunately, this report was only for the Isle of Lewis and was misunderstood by Hot Stuff's crew as the weather report for Iceland. Armed with this erroneous information Shannon and Andrews decided they would press on for Reykjavik.

On the leg from Scotland to Iceland, Andrews was at Hot Stuff's controls. To Eisel in the tail gunner's turret it was apparent Shannon was not flying the aircraft. It was not until Hot Stuff approached the coast of Iceland that he sensed Shannon was once again at the controls.

"What's our position, Jimmie?" Shine asked Gott over the intercom.

After a moment the navigator responded, "Shine, we're about fifty miles southeast of the coast of Iceland. By my calculations we should be able to see it in less than a half hour."

"Captain Gott, you've done an excellent job of navigating," Andrews said. "I'm sure our passengers will be more than glad to put their feet on terra firma."

"Thanks, sir."

After another half hour of flying, the shrouded coast of Iceland came into view. "There it is!" Shannon exclaimed. He banked the bomber west and north along the coast of Iceland's Reykjanes Peninsula at about sixty feet above the sea. "Jeffers, contact the airbase at Reykjavik."

"Wilco, Captain."

Jeffers tried several times but he was unable to establish contact with Reykjavik or any other station in Iceland. Because Hot Stuff had not landed at Prestwick for an updated briefing, Jeffers had no way of knowing he had incorrect radio frequencies for Iceland.

The ceiling was extremely low and it was now apparent to Shannon a landing at Reykjavik was questionable. From briefings he had received at Bovington he knew the runways there were short and were surrounded by built-up areas. As a result he didn't want to endanger the local populace. As Hot Stuff circled the western coast of Iceland, RAF Kaldedarnes airfield was briefly spotted though the clouds. In an attempt to signal the aerodrome of their intention to land, Shannon banked the Liberator over the field and dropped signal flares.

Because of the extremely heavy cloud cover the British didn't see the flares but heard the B-24 as it circled the field and sent up green flares signaling it was clear to land. However, Hot Stuff was back in the clouds in driving rain and snow and the crew never saw the signal.

"Let's see if we can land at Meeks Field," Shannon spoke over the intercom.

The new American airfield in Keflavik was less than thrity miles away so Shannon turned west flying along the coast at about sixty feet above the water and within sight of land. Within minutes they reached the west end of the Reykjanes Peninsula and turned north. Reykjanes bout du monde, a large granite rock protruding out of the water suddenly appeared directly in front of the B-24.

"Pull up!" Shannon shouted into the intercom. He and Andrews strained at the controls to pull the nose of the Liberator up and turn away from the jagged rock formation. The bomber was close to stall speed as it nosed up and banked sharply to the right. The left wing just cleared the top of the jagged rock.

McQueen stared wide-eyed out the gunner's window as the left wing grazed a short shrub on the stone outcrop. "Holy shit that was close!" He looked down at Bishop Leonard who was staring up at him. "Sorry, Bishop."

Leonard looked up at the waist gunner. "My sentiments exactly, Son."

Hot Stuff was in the clouds once again. Shannon dropped altitude to forty feet above the water. Flying below the cloud cover, Shine circled the aircraft attempting to get a visual sighting of Meeks. The airfield had become obscured in the heavy fog and driving rain and snow.

After considering his options, Shannon decided to turn back, retrace their original flight path and attempt a landing at Kaldedarnes. Visibility began to improve and they were flying at an altitude of 850 feet, just below the clouds following the coastline. As the Liberator turned north just west of Grindavik they abruptly ran into heavy cloud cover. Before Shine had time to turn east toward the sea, the clouds parted to reveal an ominous dark mountain directly ahead.

"Jesus Christ! Pull up! Pull up!" Shannon shouted to Andrews as he advanced the throttles. He and Andrews strained as they pulled back on the controls. The four 1,200 horsepower Pratt & Whitney engines screamed as the propellers bit into the heavy cloud-shrouded air. The thunderous boom of the Liberator colliding with the stone surface echoed for miles. All contact with the aircraft was lost at about 1530 hours. The debris of the Liberator was scattered over a vast area just below the crest of the Kast Ridge on the southwest side of Mount Fagradalsfjall.

All aboard perished except Eisel. The impact would have thrown him forward of the rear turret had his leg not gotten caught in the collapsing tail section. Unable to free his leg, he remained semiconscious as gasoline seeped from the damaged fuel tanks onto his body. The plane caught fire and machine gun ammunition began to go off. Eisel could only watch as the flames slowly moved toward the broken tail section and exploding ammunition began flying in all directions. The intense heat of the fire singed his face and eyebrows. He thought for sure he was going to die. For some unknown reason, the fuel on his clothing did not ignite. He let out a scream as a fragment of an exploding .50 caliber shell went through his left hand. Because of the pain and stress he was hardly aware that it had begun to rain. The sudden cloudburst drenched the entire area and quickly extinguished the flames. Lady Luck had smiled on George Eisel. He had survived his second crash.

All became quite and the silence became deafening. "Can anybody hear me?" he yelled several times. There was no response. He soon realized he was the sole survivor.

The rain turned into a wet snow and Eisel felt the cold as a light wind made it very uncomfortable. Hours went by as he shivered in his half frozen clothes and realized he might die of exposure before anyone would find him.

Eisel was to endure this perilous situation for twenty-seven hours before search teams could find the site of the wreckage. During those hours he suffered from exposure, dehydration and shock.

CHAPTER 58

A Search for Answers

The weather in Iceland on the morning of May 4 was clear. All available planes were put into the air to search for Hot Stuff. Shortly after noon one of the search aircraft reported sighting widely scattered debris from what appeared to be the results of a horrendous air accident. The pilot reported no one could have survived the crash.

Eisel had remained trapped after the sun had dropped below the horizon on May 3. The tail gunner thought rescue teams would immediately begin searching for Hot Stuff. When dawn broke, the skies cleared and Eisel waited. He wasn't quite sure what time it was. Although his watch was still working, he hadn't set it to Iceland time. He estimated it was mid-day when he first heard the sounds of aircraft. One flew directly overhead. As a natural reaction he waved his arm and shouted, "Help! I'm here, over here!"

His ankle was hurting badly and his hand was throbbing. He tried everything he could to free his leg but every time he moved it, the pain caused him to cry out and he almost lost consciousness. His situation was hopeless. He was freezing, hungry, extremely thirsty and in severe pain. Then suddenly he heard another airplane approaching. He could barely see it through the broken clouds as it flashed by. Based on the profile of the single-engine aircraft, he surmised it was a British Spitfire. Although the plane flew beyond his field of vision, Eisel could hear it circle around. Then he clearly saw it as it dropped below the clouds. It circled low several times just above the remnants of Hot Stuff. Even though he was very weak, Eisel knew the wreck had been spotted and he would soon be rescued. He let out a yell. No sooner had the words left this mouth the fighter disappeared into the distant clouds.

Time dragged on. One, two, three hours went by and no rescue team. What he wouldn't have given for a drink of water and a dry blanket. It began clouding up again and a steady mist began to fall. Eisel felt he might not make it if they didn't get to him soon. It was getting to be late afternoon and the temperature was dropping when he thought he heard voices off in the distance. He yelled for help but there was no answer. It became silent again. A few minutes later he just knew he heard voices. He screamed as loud as he could for help and he heard someone yell back "We're coming!"

Eisel yelled "I'm here by the tail turret. My leg is caught and I can't move." A moment later a face appeared just above the tail gunner's precarious position. "You're the most beautiful site I've ever seen!" Eisel exclaimed. "Get me out of here!" It took more than an hour to free the gunner from the wreckage.

When the search teams finally reached the isolated crash site, there were only three identifiable parts of the Liberator. The severe impact of the B-24 hitting the mountain had caused the aircraft to be completely destroyed hurling debris over a wide area. Only the wings and the burnt tail section were recognizable. An uncharred olive drab sheet of metal with the white number 41-23728 stenciled on it identified the remains of Hot Stuff. Miraculously an undamaged .50 caliber Browning machine gun was found on the rock-strewn mountainside, the name "Annie" in white letters seemed to glow in the misty Icelandic afternoon. Any documents, records and flight logs were consumed by fire. The searchers had found the B-24's clock had stopped at about 1530.

After cutting Eisel out of the metal enclosure, he was transported to a local military hospital near Reykjavik where he was treated for his injuries. He would remain hospitalized there for several weeks. Eisel was then evacuated to the United States where he underwent extensive rehabilitation. He was honorably discharged a year later. While a crewmember of Hot Stuff, he was the only one to receive the Purple Heart. In addition, he was awarded the Distinguished Flying Cross and the Air Medal. Eisel without a doubt was the 93rd's best gunner having achieved eight unofficial kills to his credit along with countless untold kills and damage to enemy fighters.

There was a complete news blackout about the crash for twenty-four hours. On May 5, the US War Department finally released the news of the crash. The cover story was since Andrews was the commander of all US forces in Europe he was traveling to Iceland to inspect American troops stationed there when the disastrous accident occurred.

As a precursor to an article in Time magazine on Andrews becoming the Allied Commander of the European Theater of Operations, artwork of him overlaid on a map of Europe had been completed. Upon receiving notification of Andrews' death, the article and artwork were silently suppressed in the interest of security and American morale.

A thorough investigation of the accident concluded there was no blame put on Shannon or Andrews. It was determined they had lost visual contact with the ground and had collided with a mountain in full flight.

The search team removed the fourteen bodies from the crash site and moved them to the airbase at Reykjavik. Three days later funeral services were held at the Lutheran and Catholic cathedrals in the city. Andrews and those who perished with him were buried with full military honors at the US military plot in Fossvogur Cemetery in Reykjavik on May 8. There the bodies remained along with those of 212 other Americans who perished in Iceland during WWII. In 1947, the bodies were exhumed and transported to the United States for final disposition.

General Andrews' body was interred at Arlington National Cemetery. The airbase in Maryland outside of Washington, DC, an airbase in Essex, England, and the main airport in the Dominican Republic were named in his honor.

Having been grounded at Bovington just outside London, Lentz was given leave to go to the big city. The next day, he paced outside the American Embassy wondering if his fellow crewmen had made it safely back to the States. After a few cigarettes he glanced at his watch and decided Hot Stuff should have arrived back home by now. After inquiring about the flight he was informed about the tragedy. Without a word he turned and trudged away. He had to give Helen the bad news; like many servicemen Shine would not be coming back.

Lentz was remorseful of the fact he had been bumped as copilot for General Andrews. After all, he and Shannon had flown together successfully as a team through thirty-one combat missions. He should have been at Shine's right side.

When word of the crash reached the men of the 93rd, there was no doubt they believed had Lentz been copilot of the ill-fated flight, the tragedy might have been averted.

Shine was by far the better overall pilot; however, on numerous occasions Lentz's strong arms and legs proved invaluable in getting Hot Stuff through tight situations. In addition, Lentz was regarded as a better pilot for flying in poor visibility. These factors haunted Lentz as he felt if he had been in Hot Stuff's copilot seat the tragedy may not have occurred.

Because Lentz had accrued thirty-one combat missions like the other Hot Stuff crewmembers, well over the required twenty-five for rotation, he was granted an extended leave in the United States. However, before he was able to take advantage of that leave he spent the next six months training replacement personnel in England before rotating back to the States in December 1943. Shortly thereafter he was promoted to captain and was transferred to the Air Transport Command. There he piloted aircraft ferrying personnel and cargo throughout the United States.

On March 24, 1944, while piloting a B-24 from Romulus Field, Michigan to Tuscaloosa, Alabama one of the engines caught fire and he was not able to maintain altitude. He ordered his copilot and flight engineer to bail out. Lentz, concerned that the aircraft could crash into a populated area decided to land in a sparsely populated region. When the plane hit the ground, it plowed a one-hundred-yard furrow into a hill near Birmingham. Lentz was pulled from the wreckage by two local farmers. He suffered major injuries and was hospitalized in Tuscaloosa for fifteen months. As copilot of Hot Stuff he had earned an Air Medal with five oak leaf clusters and the Distinguished Flying Cross.

Jacobson returned to the United States on June 14, 1943, and enjoyed a month-long leave. While on leave, he journeyed to Washington, Iowa, to visit Shannon's family and return the pilot's personal effects. Among them was the forgotten green scarf Shine had worn for good luck on combat missions. Jake shook his head believing had Shine worn the scarf perhaps he'd still be alive. He also visited his best friend Jimmy Gott's family in Berea, Kentucky.

When his leave was over he was reassigned as a bombardier instructor where he received a master bombardier rating. A year later, Jacobson received orders to train as a bombardier for B-29s. From November 1944 until the end of the war he served in the Pacific where he flew on fourteen combat missions out of Isley Field, on the island of Saipan. His last combat mission was over Osaka on August 14, 1945, the day Japan surrendered. Jacobson received the Air Medal with oak leaf cluster and the Distinguished Flying Cross.

Rondeau was shocked when he first learned of the tragic accident where four of his fellow crewmen were killed. He couldn't believe what fate had dealt those men. They survived thirty-one combat missions and perished in a totally inconceivable way. Personally, Rondeau felt fortunate not to have been on that fateful flight. He was happy to hear Eisel had survived yet another Liberator crash.

Having reached the magic number of twenty-five combat missions, Rondeau remained at Hardwick to train replacement crews until he was relieved from further combat duty on June 14, 1943. He was awarded the Distinguished Flying Cross and the Air Medal with three oak leaf clusters.

Rondeau returned to the United States aboard the Queen Mary in October 1943 and spent the duration of the war as an instructor training gunners and combat flight engineers. He was discharged from the army on August 28, 1945.

As of this writing, little information could be found on Craighead and Farley following the crash. However, Bill Gros mentioned seeing Farley at Davis Monthan airfield outside of Tucson, Arizona in early 1944.

CHAPTER 59

What Might Have Been

History cannot be changed; however, one may consider what might have been. Had the events not played out tragically as they did, perhaps history would have told a different story. The mystique of Hot Stuff and her heroic crew remains forever as a spellbinding footnote of World War II. One may ponder on two possible outcomes.

The first being General Andrews and his entourage returning to the United States on a C-54 military transport instead of on Hot Stuff. If this had occurred, Hot Stuff's crew most likely would not have been broken up and would have returned to the States to receive the accolades they so richly deserved as having completed over twenty-five combat missions; parades, speeches, visiting families and friends, selling war bonds and boosting the morale of the American people.

The second being Hot Stuff flying from Bovington with Andrews and his entourage and laying over at Prestwick or Stornoway. In this case, the weather would have cleared overnight before proceeding on to Iceland. Most likely General Andrews and all aboard Hot Stuff could have arrived safely in Washington, DC.

It is not clearly documented why Andrews was summoned to meet with General Marshall in Washington. He may have been sent for to participate in the upcoming Trident Conference between Prime Minister Churchill and President Roosevelt and their military staffs. It was to be a strategy meeting to outline plans for the Italian Campaign, air attacks on Nazi Germany, the Pacific Campaign and setting a date for the invasion of Europe. In any event, Andrews was up for promotion and would most likely have received his fourth star. One may speculate that he could have been selected to be Chief of the Army Air Force to replace General Hap Arnold who had recently suffered a heart attack. However a stronger case may be made for Andrews's fourth star as his being commander of all American forces in the European Theater. By promoting him in that position, Andrews would have equal rank to the only other four star general commanding a theater of operations at that time, General Douglas MacArthur.

Given the latter case, Gen. Andrews, having already initiated plans for the invasion of Europe, combined with his keen attributes of leadership, planning and persuasiveness would most likely have been appointed Supreme Allied Commander of the European Theater of Operations; not Dwight Eisenhower who at that time was commander of all US Forces in the Mediterranean. This premise is reinforced by correspondence to Jim Lux by retired Brig. General Charles P. Cabell Jr. USAF. Cabell stated in the letter that his father, then a general on General Hap Arnold's advisory council at the Pentagon, was informed that General Ira Eaker, then commander of the Eighth Air Force had been ordered by General Marshall to carry a message to Andrews on May 3, 1943. The message stipulated Andrews was selected to command all Allied forces that would participate in the invasion of Europe.

Had this occurred it may be speculated Eisenhower may have been subordinated to Andrews on his staff. Such a high level appointment would necessitate the approval of President Roosevelt, the possible main reason for the urgency of Andrews' return to Washington.

A point in taking was Roosevelt had become personally acquainted with Andrews at the Casablanca Conference in January 1943 when Andrews was given command of all American forces in Europe. Andrews persuading Churchill of the advantages of Americans to conduct daylight bombing while the British bombed at night was a key consideration; the ability to firmly deal with Allied leaders.

If Andrews had returned to England as Supreme Allied Commander would there have been any differences in the conduct of the war in Europe? This is highly probable. Beginning with the planning and preparation for the invasion, he would most likely not have been influenced by various Allied agendas as was Eisenhower. Andrews' views were well known concerning the use of air power. Therefore it is logical he would have used heavy bombers to soften up the German coastal defenses at Normandy prior to the invasion of France. He was a strong advocate of air power to be used in a tactical role.

Eisenhower and his staff were reluctant to use heavy bombers for two main reasons; maintenance of strict secrecy of where and when the Allied landings would take place and not wanting excessive collateral damage on French soil. One could argue Eisenhower was correct. However, had the Eighth Air Force been used to attack a number of coastal areas for several days from Pas de Calais all the way through Normandy prior to the Allied invasion, the German high command would have no iron clad information as to the location of the invasion. By bombing the Pas de Calais area, it would appear to the Germans this was the more likely place for the invasion since it was closest to the English coast.

Given this speculation, it is possible the landings would have suffered fewer losses and Allied forces would have been able to move further inland in a shorter period of time. This brings to mind the landings would have been more effective and the thrust toward Germany would have accelerated if Andrews as Supreme Allied Commander had appointed General Patton to lead the American invasion forces rather than Omar Bradley. After all, Patton had successful combat experience from WWI, North Africa and Sicily. According to some American intelligence reports the Germans considered Patton to be the best ground commander the Allies could field.

On the other hand if Andrews had chosen someone else to command the American invasion forces and Patton had been given command of the Third Army as per history Andrews may have supported Patton more than Eisenhower and Bradley had.

Andrews, as cited earlier, would have advocated the use of heavy and medium bombers in support of tactical ground operations much like the carpet bombing used at St. Lo in July 1944 for Patton's Third Army to break through the German lines. Had carpet bombing been used more in support of Allied advances, forces like Patton's Third Army could have run through France at will sooner in the thrust toward Germany.

In August 1944, the German Seventh Army had been partially encircled by Patton's Third Army and Montgomery's British forces near Falaise, France. In this case Andrews letting Patton have his way instead of being denied closing the gap by Bradley, the Third Army would have completed encirclement of the German Seventh Army taking them out of the war. Had this been done, those German forces would never have escaped to fight another day at the Battle of the Bulge.

Another point in taking is that although Andrews was a risk taker, he would most likely not have gone along politically to support British General Montgomery's scheme known as Operation Market Garden to capture the critical bridge across the Rhine at Arnhem, Netherlands. The assets used to support this unsuccessful venture would have been better used to fuel and arm Patton's Third Army to rapidly advance through the Siegfried Line into Germany. It is highly likely Andrews would have listened to the American army's best ground commander, George Patton far more than Eisenhower or Bradley who appeared at times to be more concerned with the Allies' political agendas.

Another thought is Andrews, being an airman, might have made more use of Allied airborne forces to support ground force advances that would have a higher chance of success. One such example would be to support Patton's Third Army in its drive toward Germany.

Andrews rather than Eisenhower would have received his fifth star sometime during the European campaign. With the inevitable victory in Europe and the conquering of more territory toward Eastern Europe, the Soviet Union would not have been able to take control of so much of Eastern Europe as Andrews would have been able to persuade Allied leaders, Roosevelt and later Truman along with Churchill not to cede so much territory to the Soviets.

In the end it is highly likely with the victory in Europe, Andrews could have been elected the thirty-fourth president of the United States rather than Eisenhower.

Epilogue

In some small way, we have chronicled the history of a B-24 named Hot Stuff that never attained the notoriety it so richly deserved. It came to life when it was delivered to an untried ten-man crew at Grenier, New Hampshire, in August, 1942. From that time on, the aircraft and its crew served with distinction through the Liberator's nine-month existence as a combat aircraft. It survived combat missions flown from the cold, damp environment of England and from the hot dry desert of North Africa. It completed thirty-one perilous journeys through the hostile skies of the North Atlantic, France, North Africa, Italy, Sicily, Germany, and the Netherlands. In doing so, Hot Stuff completed twenty-five combat missions ahead of all other heavy bombers in the Eighth Air Force. Although on numerous occasions the Liberator sustained damage, it was miraculous the crew remained unscathed through not just twenty-five but all thirty-one combat missions.

From New Hampshire to its tragic demise on a frigid Icelandic mountainside, Hot Stuff and its crew were the epitome of what gallant men and their bonding with an American war machine were capable of achieving. Hot Stuff's combat missions contributed to the reduction of the U-boat threat in the Atlantic, driving the Axis forces out of North Africa, the fall of Italy, and destruction of the Nazi war machine. This was done at a time when an Eighth Air Force bomber and its crew completing ten or fifteen combat missions without being lost was something beyond comprehension.

This historical narrative is a tribute to all the service men and women who served. The untold sacrifices made during World War II are unimaginable in the minds of many today. The Eighth Air Force continued to grow into the "Mighty Eighth" for two years following Hot Stuff's demise and suffered more than its fair share of losses. To give the reader an idea of how perilous it was to be flying as an air crewman, particularly in the Eighth Air Force during World War II, we compare the number of US Marines killed in action at that time with those of the Eighth; the Marines lost almost twenty thousand whereas the Eighth Air Force alone lost over twenty-six thousand.

In a letter written by Bill Gross to General Mark A. Welsh, Chief of Staff of the United States Air Force on June 9, 2013, he wrote:

> *Dear Sir:*
>
> *My name is William L. Gross. I served as radio operator on the Eager Beaver, a B-24 Liberator in the 328th Squadron of the 93rd Bomb Group. Like the crew of B-24 Hot Stuff, we were one of the original crews and entered combat on October 9, 1942. The reason for this letter is to bring justice to the Hot Stuff crew. Their radio operator, Kenneth Jeffers was a close friend of mine.*
>
> *I met Ken at Scott Field in the fall of 1941. Although we both lived in small towns only forty miles apart, we first met while attending Air Force Radio School. While we were not classmates, we maintained a close friendship. Fortunately, we were both assigned to the 93rd Bomb Group,*

although in different squadrons. We were able to retain our friendship until Ken's untimely death in Iceland. On his final flight he carried many photos I had taken in the UK. He wrote my mother that he was coming home and he would hand deliver them to her. They knew they were coming home and that General Andrews was riding with them. They were going to refuel in Iceland, a common place at that time, especially for westbound across the Atlantic flight.

After the crash Hot Stuff's record as the first crew in the Eighth Air Force to complete twenty-five missions was hushed up. A few weeks later on the 19th of May, the crew of the B-17 named Memphis Belle *was heralded as the first crew to complete twenty-five missions. I personally had flown thirty-one missions before April 17 and Hot Stuff's crew reached twenty-five before we did. I am now ninety years old and would really love to see the Hot Stuff crew to get credit for their record.*

They earned it!

Sincerely,
William L. Gros

Although Hot Stuff and its crew have passed into history, they nonetheless were the first in the Eighth Air Force to reach twenty-five combat missions. Given the facts presented in this narrative, there is no doubt Hot Stuff and its crew most certainly deserve a prominent place in World War II history.

Primary References

1. Bowman, Martin W. *B-24 Combat Missions.* New York, Metro Books.
2. Cabell, Charles P. Jr., Brig. Gen. USAF (Ret). *Letter to Jim Lux on Gen. Andrews.* March 31, 2013.
3. *Certified Bombing Missions, 1st Lt. Robert T. Jacobson.* 330th Squadron, 93rd Bombardment Group (H) AAF.
4. *Combat Chronology, US Army Air Forces, Mediterranean, 1943, Part 1.*
5. Dorr, Robert F. *B-24 Liberator Units of the Eighth Air Force,* Long Island City, NY. Osprey Publishing.
6. Eydal, Fridthor. "Flight Accidents," in the book *World War to the Defense Agreement, the Keflavik Base 1942–1951.*
7. *Fact Sheet – Lt. Gen. Frank M. Andrews.* National Museum of the US Air Force.
8. Graf, Cory. *Flying Warbirds,* Minneapolis, MN. Quarto Publishing.
9. Gros, William L. *Oral narratives on personal experiences in the 93rd Bombardment Group.*
10. Hanson, David. "The Death of General Andrews," from the November 2004 issue of *After the Battle.*
11. Hildreth, Tom. *Manchester, New Hampshire Airport (Grenier Army Air Field) in WWII.*

12. Ingles, H. O., Maj. Gen., US Army, Deputy Theater Commander. *Letter to General George C. Marshall dated 6 May 1943.*
13. Malone, Dr. Henry O. *Paving the Way: Remembering Frank Andrews.* dcmilitary.com.
14. *Radio Interview of John Lentz.* Northington General Hospital Open House. Tuscaloosa, AL, 5 August 1944.
15. Stewart, Carroll. *Ted's Travelling Circus, 93rd Bombardment Group, USAAF 1942–45.* Lincoln, NE. Nebraska Printing Center.
16. *The Casablanca Conference, 1943.* Office of the Historian, US Department of State.
17. *The Entire History of the 93rd Bombardment Group.* Internet Home Page.

You can help remember these American heroes with a tax deductible donation for a memorial monument that will be located near the crash site. For information on how to make a donation through PayPal or by check, use the Hot Stuff/Gen. Andrews website: www.b24hotstuff.wikispaces.com

About the Authors

Cassius Mullen is a graduate of the U.S. Military Academy at West Point. Early in his military career he married Betty Byron, a graduate of Miami University of Ohio. Cassius spent twenty-one years on active duty in the United States with overseas assignments in Korea, Vietnam and Germany. He earned a Master of Science degree from the Georgia Institute of Technology. During and after his military career Cassius and Betty traveled extensively around the world. They co-authored Within the Walls of Santo Tomas and The Iris Covenant. They reside in Texas.

CPSIA information can be obtained
at www.ICGtesting.com
Printed in the USA
LVHW041049140419
614129LV00001B/226

9 781682 136218